THE MATT SCUDDER MYSTERIES

ALSO BY LAWRENCE BLOCK

THE MATT SCUDDER MYSTERIES

THE SINS OF THE FATHERS

TIME TO MURDER AND CREATE

IN THE MIDST OF DEATH

Lawrence Block

ORION

Copyright

The Sins of the Fathers © 1976 by Lawrence Block
Time to Murder and Create © 1976 by Lawrence Block
In the Midst of Death © 1976 by Lawrence Block

The right of Lawrence Block to be identified as the author of this work has been asserted by him in accordance with the Copyright, Designs and Patents Act 1988

This edition first published in Great Britain in 1997 by
Orion
An imprint of Orion Books Ltd
Orion House, 5 Upper St Martin's Lane, London WC2H 9EA

Second impression 1997

A CIP catalogue record for this book is available from the British Library

ISBN 0 75280 492 8 (cased)
ISBN 0 75280 536 3 (trade paperback)

Typeset by Deltatype Limited, Birkenhead, Merseyside

Printed in Great Britain by Clays Ltd, St Ives plc

CONTENTS

THE SINS
OF THE FATHERS

FOR ZANE

Who was present at the creation,
and in memory of LENNIE SHECTER
who introduced me to Scudder

ONE

He was a big man, about my height with a little more flesh on his heavy frame. His eyebrows, arched and prominent, were still black. The hair on his head was iron gray, combed straight back, giving his massive head a leonine appearance. He had been wearing glasses but had placed them on the oak table between us. His dark brown eyes kept searching my face for secret messages. If he found any, his eyes didn't reflect them. His features were sharply chiseled – a hawk-bill nose, a full mouth, a craggy jawline – but the full effect of his face was as a blank stone tablet waiting for someone to scratch commandments on it.

He said, 'I don't know very much about you, Scudder.'

I knew a little about him. His name was Cale Hanniford. He was around fifty-five years old. He lived upstate in Utica where he had a wholesale drug business and some real estate holdings. He had last year's Cadillac parked outside at the curb. He had a wife waiting for him in his room at the Carlyle.

He had a daughter in a cold steel drawer at the city mortuary.

'There's not much to know,' I said. 'I used to be a cop.'

'An excellent one, according to Lieutenant Koehler.'

I shrugged.

'And now you're a private detective.'

'No.'

'I thought –'

'Private detectives are licensed. They tap telephones and follow people. They fill out forms, they keep records, all of that. I don't do those things. Sometimes I do favors for people. They give me gifts.'

'I see.'

I took a sip of coffee. I was drinking coffee spiked with bourbon. Hanniford had a Dewar's and water in front of him but wasn't taking much interest in it. We were in Armstrong's, a good sound saloon with dark wood walls and a stamped tin

3

ceiling. It was two in the afternoon on the second Tuesday in January, and we had the place pretty much to ourselves. A couple of nurses from Roosevelt Hospital were nursing beers at the far end of the bar, and a kid with a tentative beard was eating a hamburger at one of the window tables.

He said, 'It's difficult for me to explain what I want you to do for me, Scudder.'

'I'm not sure that there's anything I *can* do for you. Your daughter is dead. I can't change that. The boy who killed her was picked up on the spot. From what I read in the papers, it couldn't be more open-and-shut if they had the homicide on film.' His face darkened; he was seeing that film now, the knife slashing. I went on quickly. 'They picked him up and booked him and slapped him in the Tombs. That was Thursday?' He nodded. 'And Saturday morning they found him hanging in his cell. Case closed.'

'Is that your view? That the case is closed?'

'From a law enforcement standpoint.'

'That's not what I meant. Of course the police have to see it that way. They apprehended the killer, and he's beyond punishment.' He leaned forward. 'But there are things I have to know.'

'Like what?'

'I want to know why she was killed. I want to know who she was. I've had no real contact with Wendy in the past three years. Christ, I didn't even know for certain that she was living in New York.' His eyes slipped away from mine. 'They say she didn't have a job. No apparent source of income. I saw the building she lived in. I wanted to go up to her apartment, but I couldn't. Her rent was almost four hundred dollars a month. What does that suggest to you?'

'That some man was paying her rent.'

'She shared that apartment with the Vanderpoel boy. The boy who killed her. He worked for an antiques importer. He earned something in the neighborhood of a hundred and twenty-five dollars a week. If a man were keeping her as his mistress, he wouldn't let her have Vanderpoel as a roommate, would he?' He drew a breath. 'I guess it must be fairly obvious that she was a prostitute. The police didn't tell me that in so many words. They were tactful. The newspapers were somewhat less tactful.'

They usually are. And the case was the kind the newspapers like to play with. The girl was attractive, the murder took place in the Village, and there was a nice core of sex to it. And they had picked up Richard Vanderpoel running in the streets with her blood all over him. No city editor worth a damn would let that one slide past him.

He said, 'Scudder? Do you see why the case isn't closed for me?'

'I guess I do.' I made myself look deep into his dark eyes. 'The murder was a door starting to open for you. Now you have to know what's inside the room.'

'Then you do understand.'

I did, and wished I didn't. I had not wanted the job. I work as infrequently as I can. I had no present need to work. I don't need much money. My room rent is cheap, my day-to-day expenses low enough. Besides, I had no reason to dislike this man. I have always felt more comfortable taking money from men I dislike.

'Lieutenant Koehler didn't understand what I wanted. I'm sure he only gave me your name as a polite way of getting rid of me.' That wasn't all there was to it, but I let it pass. 'But I really need to know these things. Who was she? Who did Wendy turn into? And why would anyone want to kill her?'

Why did anyone want to kill anybody? The act of murder is performed four or five times a day in New York. One hot week last summer the count ran to fifty-three. People kill their friends, their relatives, their lovers. A man on Long Island demonstrated karate to his older children by chopping his two-year-old daughter to death. Why did people do these things?

Cain said he wasn't Abel's keeper. Are those the only choices, keeper or killer?

'Will you work for me, Scudder?' He managed a small smile. 'I'll rephrase that. Will you do me a favor? And it would be a favor.'

'I wonder if that's true.'

'How do you mean?'

'That open door. There might be things in that room you won't want to look at.'

'I know that.'

'And that's why you have to.'

'That's right.'

I finished my coffee. I put the cup down and took a deep breath. 'Yeah,' I said, 'I'll give it a shot.'

He settled into his chair, took out a pack of cigarettes and lit one. It was his first since he'd walked in. Some people reach for a cigarette when they're tense, others when the tension passes. He was looser now, and looked as though he felt he had accomplished something.

I had a new cup of coffee in front of me and a couple of pages filled in my notebook. Hanniford was still working on the same drink. He had told me a lot of things I would never need to know about his daughter. But any of the things he said might turn out to matter, and there was no way to guess which it might be. I had learned long ago to listen to everything a man had to say.

So I learned that Wendy was an only child, that she had done well in high school, that she had been popular with her classmates but had not dated much. I was getting a picture of a girl, not sharply defined, but a picture that would eventually have to find a way of blending with one of a slashed-up whore in a Village apartment.

The picture started to blur when she went away to college in Indiana. That was evidently when they began to lose her. She majored in English, minored in government. A couple of months before she was due to graduate she packed a suitcase and disappeared.

'The school got in touch with us. I was very worried, she had never done anything like this before. I didn't know what to do. Then we had a postcard. She was in New York, she had a job, there were some things she had to work out. We had another card several months after that from Miami. I didn't know whether she had moved there or was vacationing.'

And then nothing until the telephone rang and they learned she was dead. She was seventeen when she finished high school, twenty-one when she dropped out of college, twenty-four when Richard Vanderpoel cut her up. That was as old as she was ever going to get.

He began telling me things I would learn over again in more detail from Koehler. Names, addresses, dates, times. I let him talk. Something bothered me, and I let it sort itself out in my mind.

He said, 'The boy who killed her. Richard Vanderpoel. He was younger than she was. He was only twenty.' He frowned at a memory. 'When I heard what happened, what he had done, I wanted to kill that boy. I wanted to put him to death with my hands.' His hands tightened into fists at the recollection, then opened slowly. 'But after he committed suicide, I don't know,

6

something changed inside me. It struck me that he was a victim, too. His father is a minister.'

'Yes, I know.'

'A church in Brooklyn somewhere. I had an impulse. I wanted to talk to the man. I don't know what I thought I might want to say to him. Whatever it was, after a moment's reflection I realized I could never have that conversation. And yet –'

'You want to know the boy. In order to know your daughter.'

He nodded.

I said, 'Do you know what an Identikit portrait is, Mr Hanniford? You've probably seen them in newspaper stories. When the police have an eye-witness, they use this kit of transparent overlays to piece together a composite picture of a suspect. "Is this nose like this? Or is this one more like it? Bigger? Wider? How about the ears? Which set of ears comes the closest?" And so on until the features add up to a face.'

'Yes, I've seen how that works.'

'Then you've probably also seen actual photographs of the suspect side by side with the Identikit portraits. They never seem to resemble one another, especially to the untrained eye. But there is a *factual* resemblance, and a trained officer can often make very good use of it. Do you see what I'm getting at? You want photographs of your daughter and the boy who killed her. I'm not equipped to offer you that. No one is. I can dig up enough facts and impressions to make composite Identikit portraits for you, but the result may not be all that close to what you really want.'

'I understand.'

'You want me to go ahead?'

'Yes. Definitely.'

'I'm probably more expensive than one of the big agencies. They'd work for you either per diem or on an hourly basis. Plus expenses. I take a certain amount of money and pay my own expenses out of it. I don't like keeping records. I also don't like writing reports, or checking in periodically when there's nothing to say for the sake of keeping a client contented.'

'How much money do you want?'

I never know how to set prices. How do you put a value on your time when its only value is personal? And when your life has been deliberately restructured to minimize involvement in the lives of others, how much do you charge the man who forces you to involve yourself?

7

'I want two thousand dollars from you now. I don't know how long this will take or when you'll decide you've seen enough of the dark room. I may ask you for more money somewhere along the way, or after it's over. Of course you always have the option of not paying me.'

He smiled suddenly. 'You're a very unorthodox businessman.'

'I suppose so.'

'I've never had occasion to hire a detective, so I don't really know how this is usually done. Do you mind a check?'

I told him a check was fine, and while he was writing it out, I figured out what had been bothering me earlier. I said, 'You never hired detectives after Wendy disappeared from college?'

'No.' He looked up. 'It wasn't that long before we received the first of the two postcards. I'd considered hiring detectives, of course, but once we knew she was all right I dropped the idea.'

'But you still didn't know where she was, or how she was living.'

'No.' He lowered his eyes. 'That's part of it, of course. Why I'm busy now, locking up the empty stable.' His eyes returned to mine, and there was something in them that I wanted to turn` from, and couldn't. 'I have to know how much to blame myself.'

Did he really think he would ever have the answer to that one? Oh, he might find himself an answer, but it would not be the right answer. There is never a right answer to that inescapable question.

He finished writing the check and passed it to me. He had left space blank where my name belonged. He told me he thought I might like it made out to *Cash*. I said payable to me was fine, and he uncapped his pen again and wrote *Matthew Scudder* on the right line. I folded it and put it in my wallet.

I said, 'Mr Hanniford, there's something you left out. You don't think it's important, but it might be, and you think it might be.'

'How do you know that?'

'Instinct, I suppose. I spent a lot of years watching people decide how close they cared to come to the truth. There's nothing you *have* to tell me, but –'

'Oh, it's extraneous, Scudder. I left it out because I didn't think it would fit in, but – Oh, the hell with it. Wendy's not my biological daughter.'

'She was adopted?'

'I adopted her. My wife is Wendy's mother. Wendy's father was killed before Wendy was born, he was a Marine, he died in the

8

landing at Inchon.' He looked away again. 'I married Wendy's mother three years after that. From the beginning I loved her as much as any real father could have. When I found out that I was ... unable to father children myself, I was even more grateful for her existence. Well? Is it important?'

'I don't know,' I said. 'Probably not.' But of course it was important to me. It told me something more about Hanniford's load of guilt.

'Scudder? You're not married, are you?'

'Divorced.'

'Any children?'

I nodded. He started to say something, and didn't. I began wanting him to leave.

He said, 'You must have been a very good policeman.'

'I wasn't bad. I had cop instincts, and I learned the moves. That's at least ninety percent of it.'

'How long were you on the force?'

'Fifteen years. Almost sixteen.'

'Isn't there a pension or something if you stay twenty?'

'That's right.'

He didn't ask the question, and that was strangely more annoying than if he had.

I said, 'I lost the faith.'

'Like a priest?'

'Something like that. Not exactly, because it's not rare for a cop to lose the faith and go on being a cop. He may never have had it in the first place. What it amounted to was that I found out I didn't want to be a cop anymore.' Or a husband, or a father. Or a productive member of society.

'All the corruption in the department? That sort of thing?'

'No, no.' The corruption had never bothered me. I would have found it hard to support a family without it. 'No, it was something else.'

'I see.'

'You do? Hell, it's not a secret. I was off duty one night in the summer. I was in a bar in Washington Heights where cops didn't have to pay for their drinks. Two kids held up the place. On their way out they shot the bartender in the heart. I chased them into the street. I shot one of them dead and caught the other in the thigh. He's never going to walk right again.'

'I see.'

'No, I don't think you do. That wasn't the first time I ever

9

killed anyone. I was glad the one died and sorry the other recovered.'

'Then —'

'One shot went wide and ricocheted. It hit a seven-year-old girl in the eye. The ricochet took most of the steam off the bullet. An inch higher and it probably would have glanced off her forehead. Would have left a nasty scar but nothing much worse than that. This way, though, nothing but soft tissue, and it went right on into her brain. They tell me she died instantly.' I looked at my hands. The tremor was barely visible. I picked up my cup and drained it. I said, 'There was no question of culpability. As a matter of fact, I got a departmental commendation. Then I resigned. I just didn't want to be a cop anymore.'

I sat there for a few minutes after he left. Then I caught Trina's eye and she brought over another cup of laced coffee. 'Your friend's not much of a drinker,' she said.

I agreed that he wasn't. Something in my tone must have alerted her because she sat down in Hanniford's chair and put her hand on top of mine for a moment.

'Troubles, Matt?'

'Not really. Things to do, and I'd rather not do them.'

'You'd rather just sit here and get drunk.'

I grinned at her. 'When did you ever see me drunk?'

'Never. And I never saw you when you weren't drinking.'

'It's a nice middle ground.'

'Can't be good for you, can it?'

I wished she would touch my hand again. Her fingers were long and slender, her touch very cool. 'Nothing's much good for anybody,' I said.

'Coffee and booze. It's a very weird combination.'

'Is it?'

'Booze to get you drunk, and coffee to keep you sober.'

I shook my head. 'Coffee never sobered anybody. It just keeps you awake. Give a drunk plenty of coffee and you've got a wide-awake drunk on your hands.'

'That what you are, baby? A wide-awake drunk?'

'I'm neither,' I told her. 'That's what keeps me drinking.'

I got to my savings bank a little after four. I stuck five hundred in my account and took the rest of Hanniford's money in cash. It was my first visit since the first of the year, so they entered some interest in my passbook. A machine figured it all out in the wink of an eye. The sum involved was hardly large enough to warrant wasting the machine's time on it.

I walked back on Fifty-seventh Street to Ninth, then headed uptown past Armstrong's and the hospital to St Paul's. Mass was just winding up, and I waited outside while a couple dozen people straggled out of the church. They were mostly middle-aged women. Then I went inside and slipped four fifty-dollar bills into the poor box.

I tithe. I don't know why. It's become a habit, as indeed it has become my habit to visit churches. I began doing this shortly after I moved into my hotel room.

I like churches. I like to sit in them when I have things to think about. I sat around the middle of this one on the aisle. I suppose I was there for twenty minutes, maybe a little longer.

Two thousand dollars from Cale Hanniford to me, two hundred dollars from me to St Paul's poor box. I don't know what they do with the money. Maybe it buys food and clothing for poor families. Maybe it buys Lincolns for the clergy. I don't really care what they do with it.

The Catholics get more of my money than anybody else. Not because I'm partial to them, but because they put in longer hours. Most of the Protestants close up shop during the week.

One big plus for the Catholics, though. You get to light candles. I lit three on the way out. For Wendy Hanniford, who would never get to be twenty-five, and for Richard Vanderpoel, who would never get to be twenty-one. And, of course, for Estrellita Rivera, who would never get to be eight.

TWO

The Sixth Precinct is on West Tenth Street. Eddie Koehler was in his office reading reports when I got there. He didn't look surprised to see me. He pushed some papers to one side, nodded at the chair alongside his desk. I settled into it and reached over to shake hands with him. Two tens and a five passed smoothly from my hand to his.

'You look like you need a new hat,' I told him.

'I do indeed. One thing I can always use is another hat. How'd you like Hanniford?'

'Poor bastard.'

'Yeah, that's about it. It all happened so quick he's left standing there with his jaw hanging. That's what did it for him, you know. The time element. If it takes us a week or a month to make a collar, say. Or if there's a trial, and it drags on for a year or so. That way things keep going on for him, it gives him a chance to get used to what happened while it's all still in process. But this way, bam, one thing after another, we got the killer in a cell before he even hears his daughter's dead, and by the time he gets his ass in gear the kid hangs himself, and Hanniford can't get used to it because he's had no time.' He eyed me speculatively. 'So I figured an old buddy could make a couple of bills out of it.'

'Why not?'

He took a cold cigar out of the ashtray and relit it. He could have afforded a fresh one. The Sixth is a hot precinct, and his desk was a good one. He could also have afforded to send Hanniford home instead of referring him to me so that I could knock back twenty-five to him. Old habits die hard.

'Get yourself a clipboard, bounce around the neighborhood, ask some questions. Run yourself a week's work out of it without wasting more'n a couple of hours. Hit him up for a hundred a day plus expenses. That's close to a K for you, for Christ's sake.'

I said, 'I'd like a look at your file on the thing.'

'Why go through the motions? You're not gonna find anything there, Matt. It was closed before it was opened. We had cuffs on the fucking kid before we even knew what he did.'

'Just for form.'

His eyes narrowed just a little. We were about the same age, but I had joined the force earlier and was just getting into plainclothes when he was going through the Academy. Koehler looked a lot older now, droopy in the jowls, and his desk job was spreading him in the seat. There was something about his eyes I didn't care for.

'Waste of time, Matt. Why take the trouble?'

'Let's say it's the way I work.'

'Files aren't open to unauthorized personnel. You know that.'

I said, 'Let's say another hat for a look at what you've got. And I'll want to talk to the arresting officer.'

'I could set that up, arrange an introduction. Whether he wants to talk to you is up to him.'

'Sure.'

Twenty minutes later I was alone in the office. I had twenty-five dollars less in my wallet and a manila folder on the desk in front of me. It didn't look like good value for the money, didn't tell me much I didn't already know.

Patrolman Lewis Pankow, the arresting officer, led off with his report. I hadn't read one of those in a while, and it took me back, from 'While proceeding in a westerly direction on routine foot patrol duty' all the way through to 'at which time the alleged perpetrator was delivered for incarceration to the Men's House of Detention.' The Coptic jargon is a special one.

I read Pankow's report a couple of times through and took some notes. What it amounted to, in English, was a clear enough statement of facts. At eighteen minutes after four he'd been walking west on Bank Street. He heard sounds of a commotion and shortly encountered some people who told him there was a lunatic on Bethune Street, dancing around with blood all over him. Pankow ran around the block to Bethune Street where he found 'the alleged miscreant, subsequently identified as Richard Vanderpoel of 194 Bethune Street, his clothes in disarray and covered with what appeared to be blood, uttering obscene language at high volume and exposing his private parts to passersby.'

Pankow sensibly cuffed him and managed to determine where

13

he lived. He led the suspect up two flights of stairs and into the apartment Vanderpoel and Wendy Hanniford had occupied, where he found Wendy Hanniford 'apparently deceased, unclothed, and disfigured by slashes apparently inflicted by a sharp weapon.'

Pankow then phoned in, and the usual machinery went into action. The medical examiner's man had come around to confirm what Pankow had figured out – that Wendy was, in fact, dead. The photo crew took their pictures, several of the blood-spattered apartment, a great many of Wendy's corpse.

There was no telling what she might have looked like alive. She had died from loss of blood, and Lady Macbeth was right about that; no one would guess how much blood a body can lose in the process of dying. You can put an ice pick in a man's heart and barely a drop of blood will show on his shirtfront, but Vanderpoel had cut her breasts and thighs and belly and throat, and the whole bed was an ocean of blood.

After they'd photographed the body, they removed it for autopsy. A Dr Jainchill of the medical examiner's office had done the full postmortem. He stated that the victim was a Caucasian female in her twenties, that she had had recent sexual inter- course, both oral and genital, that she had been slashed twenty- three times with a sharp instrument, most probably a razor, that there were no stab wounds (which might have been why he was opting for the razor), that various veins and arteries, which he conscientiously named, had been wholly or partially severed in the course of this mistreatment, that death had occurred at approximately four o'clock that afternoon, give or take twenty minutes, and that there was in his opinion no possibility whatsoever that the wounds had been self-inflicted.

I was proud of him for taking such a firm stand on the last point.

The rest of the folder consisted of bits of information which would ultimately be supplemented by copies of formal reports filed by other branches of the machine. There was a note to the effect that the prisoner had been brought before a magistrate and formally charged with homicide the day after his arrest. Another memo gave the name of the court-appointed attorney. Another noted that Richard Vanderpoel had been found dead in his cell shortly before six Saturday morning.

The folder would grow fatter in time to come. The case was closed, but the Sixth's file would go on growing like a corpse's hair and fingernails. The guard who looked in and saw Richard Vanderpoel hanging from the steam pipe would write up his findings. So would the physician who pronounced him dead and the physician who established beyond a shadow of a doubt that it was the strips of bedclothing tied together and knotted around his neck that had done him in. Ultimately a coroner's inquest would conclude that Wendy Hanniford had been murdered by Richard Vanderpoel and that Richard Vanderpoel had in turn taken his own life. The Sixth Precinct, and everyone else connected with the case, had already reached this conclusion. They had reached the first part of it well before Vanderpoel had been booked. The case was closed.

I went back and read through some of the material again. I studied the photos in turn. The apartment itself didn't look to be greatly disturbed, which suggested the killer had been someone known to her. I went back to the autopsy. No skin under Wendy's fingernails, no obvious signs of a struggle. Facial contusions? Yes, so she could have been unconscious while he cut her up.

She had probably been awhile dying. If he'd cut the throat first, and got the jugular right, she would have gone fast. But she had lost a lot of blood from the wounds on the torso.

I picked out one print and tucked it inside my shirt. I wasn't sure why I wanted it but knew it would never be missed. I knew a desk cop in the Cobble Hill section of Brooklyn who used to take home a copy of every grisly picture he could get his hands on. I never asked why.

I had everything back in order and returned to the file folder by the time Koehler came back. He had a fresh cigar going. I got out from behind his desk. He asked me if I was satisfied.

'I'd still like to talk to Pankow.'

'I already set it up. I figured you're too fucking stubborn to change your mind. You find a single damn thing in that mess?'

'How do I know? I don't even know what I'm looking for. I understand she was hooking. Any evidence of that?'

'Nothing hard. There would be if we looked. Good wardrobe, couple hundred in her handbag, no visible means of support. What's that add up to?'

'Why was she living with Vanderpoel?'

'He had a twelve-inch tongue.'

'Seriously. Was he pimping for her?'

'Probably.'

'You didn't have a sheet on either of them, though.'

'No. No arrest. They didn't exist officially for us until he decided to cut her up.'

I closed my eyes for a minute. Koehler said my name. I looked up. I said, 'Just a thought. Something you said before about time putting Hanniford on the spot. It's true in a way besides the one you mentioned. If she was killed by person or persons unknown, you'd have put the past two years of her life on slides and run them through a microscope. But it was over before it started, and it's not your job to do that now.'

'Right. So it's your job instead.'

'Uh-huh. What did he kill her with?'

'Doc says a razor.' He shrugged. 'Good a guess as any.'

'What happened to the murder weapon?'

'Yeah, I figured you wouldn't miss that. We didn't turn it up. You can't make much out of that. There was a window open, he could have pitched it out.'

'What's outside of the window?'

'Airshaft.'

'You checked it?'

'Uh-huh. Anybody coulda picked it up, any kid passing through.'

'Check for blood spots in the airshaft?'

'Are you kidding? An airshaft in the Village? People piss out windows, they throw Tampax out, garbage, everything. Nine out of ten airshafts you'll find blood spots. Would you have checked? With the killer already wrapped up?'

'No.'

'Anyway, forget the airshaft. He bolts out of the apartment with the knife in his hand. Or the razor, whatever the fuck it was. He drops it on the staircase. He runs out in the street and drops it on the sidewalk. He puts it in an open garbage can. He drops it down a sewer. Matt, we don't have an eyewitness who saw him come out of the building. We woulda turned one up if we needed one, but the son of a bitch was dead thirty-six hours after he cooled the girl.'

It kept coming back to that. I was doing a job the police would have done if they had had to do it. But Richard Vanderpoel had saved them the trouble.

'So we don't know when he hit the street,' Koehler was saying. 'Two minutes before Pankow got to him? Ten minutes? He coulda chewed up the knife and ate it in that amount of time. Christ knows he was crazy enough.'

'Was there a razor in the apartment?'

'You mean a straight razor? No.'

'I mean a man's razor.'

'Yeah, he had an electric. Why the hell don't you forget about the razor? You know what those fucking autopsies are like. I had one a couple years ago, the asshole in the medical examiner's office said the victim had been killed with a hatchet. We already caught the bastard on the premises with a croquet mallet in his hand. Anybody who could mistake the damage done by splitting someone's skull with a hatchet and beating it in with a mallet couldn't tell a razor slash from a cunt.'

I nodded. I said, 'I wonder why he did it.'

'Because he was out of his fucking mind, that's why he did it. He ran up and down the street covered with her blood, screaming his head off and waving his cock at the world. Ask him why he did it and he wouldn't know himself.'

'What a world.'

'Jesus, don't let me get started on that. This neighborhood gets worse and worse. Don't get me started.' He gave me a nod, and we walked together out of his office and out through the squad room. Men in plainclothes and men in uniforms sat at type-writers, laboriously pounding out stories about presumed miscreants and alleged perpetrators. A woman was making a report in Spanish to a uniformed officer, pausing intermittently to weep. I wonder what she had done or what had been done to her.

I didn't see anybody in the squad room that I recognized.

Koehler said, 'You hear about Barney Segal? They made it permanent. He's head of the Seventeenth.'

'Well, he's a good man.'

'One of the best. How long you been off the force, Matt?'

'Couple of years, I guess,'

'Yeah. How're Anita and the boys? Doing okay?'

'They're fine.'

'You keep in touch, then.'

'From time to time.'

As we neared the front desk he stopped, cleared his throat. 'You ever think about putting the badge back on, Matt?'

'No way, Eddie,'

'That's a goddam shame, you know that?'

'You do what you have to do.'

'Yeah.' He drew himself up and got back to business. 'I set it with Pankow so he'll be looking for you around nine tonight. He'll be at a bar called Johnny Joyce's. It's on Second Avenue, I forget the cross street.'

'I know the place.'

'They know him there, so just ask the bartender to point him out to you. He's on his own time tonight, so I told him you'd make it worth his while.'

And told him to make sure a piece of it came back to the lieutenant, no doubt.

'Matt?' I turned. 'What the hell are you gonna ask him, anyway?'

'I want to know what obscene language Vanderpoel was using.'

'Seriously?' I nodded. 'I think you're as crazy as Vanderpoel,' he told me. 'For the price of a hat you can hear all the dirty words in the world.'

THREE

Bethune Street runs west from Hudson toward the river. It is narrow and residential. Some trees had been recently planted. Their bases were guarded by little picket fences hung with signs imploring dog owners to thwart their pets' natural instincts. WE LOVE OUR TREE/PLEASE CURB YOUR DOG. Number 194 was a renovated brownstone with a front door the color of Astroturf. There were five apartments, one to a floor. A sixth bell in the vestibule was marked SUPERINTENDENT. I rang it and waited.

The woman who opened the door was around thirty-five. She wore a man's white shirt with the top two buttons open and a pair of stained and faded jeans. She was built like a fireplug. Her hair was short and seemed to have been hacked at randomly with a pair of dull shears. The effect was not displeasing, though. She stood in the doorway and looked up at me and decided within five seconds that I was a cop. I gave her my name and learned that hers was Elizabeth Antonelli. I told her I wanted to talk to her.

'What about?'

'Your third-floor tenants.'

'Shit. I thought that was over and done with. I'm still waiting for you guys to unlock the door and clear their stuff out. The landlord wants me to show the apartment, and I can't even get into it.'

'It's still padlocked?'

'Don't you guys talk to each other?'

'I'm not on the force. This is private.'

Her eyes did a number. She liked me better now that I wasn't a cop, but now she had to know what angle I was working. Also if I wasn't on official business, that meant she didn't have to feel compelled to waste her time on me.

She said, 'Listen, I'm in the middle of something. I'm an artist, I got work to do.'

'It'll take you less time to answer my questions than it will to get rid of me.'

She thought this over, then turned abruptly and walked into the building. 'It's freezing out there,' she said. 'C'mon downstairs, we'll talk, but don't figure on taking up too much of my time, huh?'

I followed her down a flight of stairs to the basement. She had a single large room with kitchen appliances in one corner and an army cot on the west wall. There were exposed pipes and electrical cables overhead. Her art was sculpture, and there were several examples of her work in evidence. I never saw the piece she was currently working on. A wet cloth was draped over it. The other pieces were abstract, and there was a massive quality to them, a ponderousness suggestive of sea monsters.

'I'm not going to be able to tell you much,' she said. 'I'm the super because I get a deal on the rent that way. I'm handy, I can fix most things that go wrong, and I'm mean enough to yell at people when they're late with the rent. Most of the time I keep to myself. I don't pay much attention to what goes on in the building.'

'You knew Vanderpoel and Miss Hanniford?'

'By sight.'

'When did they move in?'

'She was here before I moved in, and I've been here two years in April. He moved in with her I guess a little over a year ago. I think just before Christmas if I remember right.'

'They didn't move in together?'

'No. She was living with someone else before that.'

'A man?'

'A woman.'

She didn't have any records, didn't know the name of Wendy's former roommate. She gave me the landlord's name and address. I asked her what she remembered about Wendy.

'Not a hell of a lot. I only notice people if they make trouble. She never had loud parties or played the stereo too loud. I was in the apartment a few times. The valve was shot on the bedroom radiator, and they were getting too much heat, they couldn't regulate it. I put a new valve in. That was just a couple of months ago.'

'They kept the apartment neat?'

'Very neat. Very attractive. They had the trim painted, and the place was furnished nice.' She thought for a moment. 'I think maybe that was his doing. I was in the place before he moved in, and I think I remember it wasn't as nice then. He was sort of artsy.'

'Did you know she was a prostitute?'

'I still don't know it. I read lots of lies in the papers.'

'You don't think she was?'

'I don't have an opinion either way. I never had any complaints about her. Then again, she could have had ten men a day up there, and I wouldn't have known about it.'

'Did she have visitors?'

'I just told you. I wouldn't know about it. People don't have to get past me to get upstairs.'

I asked her who else lived in the building. There were five floor-through apartments, and she gave me the names of the tenants in each. I could talk to them if they were willing to talk to me, she said. But not the couple on the top floor – they were in Florida and wouldn't be back until the middle of March.

'You got enough?' she said. 'I want to get back to what I was doing.' She flexed her fingers, indicating an impatience to return them to the clay.

I told her she had been very helpful.

'I don't see that I told you anything much.'

'There's something more you could tell me.'

'What?'

'You didn't know them, either of them, and I realize you don't take much interest in the people in the building. But everybody invariably forms an impression of people they see frequently over an extended period of time. You must have had some sort of image of the two of them, some feeling that extended beyond your hard factual knowledge of them. That's probably been shifted out of position by what's happened in the past week, what you've learned about them, but I'd like to know what your impression of them was.'

'What good would that do you?'

'It would tell me what they looked like to human eyes. And you're an artist, you've got sensibilities.'

She gnawed at a fingernail. 'Yeah, I see what you mean,' she said after a moment. 'I just can't find where to pick up on it.'

'You were surprised when he killed her.'

'Anybody'd be surprised.'

'Because it changed how you saw them. How did you see them?'

'Just as tenants, just ordinary – wait a minute. All right, you jarred something loose. I never even put words to the tune before, but you know how I thought of them? As brother and sister.'

'Brother and sister?'

'Right.'

'Why?'

She closed her eyes, frowned. 'I can't say exactly,' she said. 'Maybe the way they acted when they were together. Not anything they did. Just the vibrations they gave off, the sense you got of them when they were walking along. The sense of how they related to each other.'

I waited.

'Another thing. I didn't dwell on this, I mean I didn't give it any thought to speak of, but I sort of took it for granted that he was gay.'

'Why?'

She had been sitting. She got up now and walked to one of her creations, a gunmetal-colored mound of convex planes taller and wider than herself. She faced away from me, tracing a curved surface with her stubby fingers.

'Physical type, I suppose. Mannerisms. He was tall and slender, he had a way of speaking. You'd think I would know better than to think in those terms. With my figure and short hair, and working with my hands, and being good with electrical and mechanical things. People generally assume I'm a lesbian.' She turned around, and her eyes challenged me. 'I'm not,' she said.

'Was Wendy Hanniford?'

'How would I know?'

'You guessed Vanderpoel might be gay. Did you make the same guess about her?'

'Oh. I thought – No, I'm sure she wasn't. I generally know if a woman is gay by the way she relates to me. No, I assumed she was straight.'

'And you assumed he wasn't.'

'Right.' She looked up at me. 'You want to know something? I *still* think he was a faggot.'

FOUR

I had some dinner in an Italian place on Greenwich Avenue, then hit a couple of bars before I took a cab over to Johnny Joyce's. I told the bartender I was looking for Lewis Pankow, and he pointed me toward a booth in the back.

I could have found him without help. He was tall and rangy and towheaded, with an open face and a recent shave. He stood up when I approached him. He was in civilian clothes, a gray glen-plaid suit that couldn't have cost him much, a pale blue shirt, a striped tie. I said I was Scudder, and he said he was Pankow, and he put out his hand, so I shook it. I sat down opposite him and ordered a double bourbon when the waiter came around. Pankow still had half a beer left in front of him.

He said, 'The lieutenant said you wanted to see me. I guess it's about the Hanniford murder?'

I nodded. 'Hell of a good collar for you.'

'I was lucky. The right place at the right time.'

'It'll look good on your record.'

He flushed.

'Probably get a commendation out of it, too.'

The flush deepened. I wondered how old he was. Say twenty-two at the outside. I thought about his report and decided he'd make detective third in a year or so.

I said, 'I read your report. There was a lot of detail, but there were some things that you didn't have room for. When you got to the scene, Vanderpoel was standing about two doors from the building where the murder took place. Now what was he doing exactly? Dancing around? Running?'

'More or less standing in one place. But moving around wildly. Like he had a lot of energy he had to work off. Like when you drink too much coffee and your hands get shaky, but his whole body was like that.'

'You said his clothing was disarrayed. How?'

23

'His shirttail was out of his pants. His belt was fastened, but his pants were unbuttoned and unzipped and his thing was hanging out.'

'His penis?'

'Right, his penis.'

'Was he exposing himself deliberately?'

'Well, it was hanging right out. He must of known about it.'

'But he wasn't handling himself or thrusting out with his hips or anything like that?'

'No.'

'Did he have an erection?'

'I didn't notice.'

'You saw his cock and didn't notice if he had a hard-on or not?'

He flushed again. 'He didn't have one.'

The waiter brought my drink. I picked it up and looked into the glass. I said, 'You put down that he was uttering obscenities.'

'Shouting them. I heard him shouting before I even turned the corner.'

'What was he saying?'

'You know.'

He embarrassed easy, this one. I kept myself from snapping at him. 'The words he used,' I said.

'I don't like to use them.'

'Force yourself.'

He asked if it was important, and I said it might be. He leaned forward and pitched his voice low. 'Motherfucker,' he said.

'He just kept yelling motherfucker?'

'Not exactly.'

'I want the words he used.'

'Yeah, okay. What he said was, he kept yelling, "I'm a motherfucker, I'm a motherfucker, I fucked my mother." He kept shouting this over and over.'

'He said he was a motherfucker and he fucked his mother.'

'Right, that's what he said.'

'What did you think?'

'I thought he was crazy.'

'Did you think he killed someone?'

'Oh. No, the first thing I thought was he was hurt. He had blood all over him.'

'His hands?'

'Everywhere. His hands, his shirt, his pants, his face, he was all covered with blood. I thought he was cut, but then I saw he was all right and the blood must of come from somebody else.'

'How could you tell?'

'I just knew. He was all right, it wasn't his blood, so it was somebody else's.' He hoisted his glass and drained it. I motioned for the waiter and ordered another beer for Pankow and a cup of coffee for myself. We sat there looking at the table until the waiter brought the order. Pankow was remembering things he'd spent the past few days trying to forget, and he wasn't enjoying it much.

I said, 'So you expected to find a body in the apartment.'

'I knew I would, yeah.'

'Who did you think it would be?'

'Hell, I thought it would be his mother. From what he was saying, motherfucker, I fucked my mother, I thought he went nuts or something and killed his mother. I even thought that's who it was when I went in there, you know, on account of you couldn't tell age or anything at first, just this naked woman with blood everywhere, the sheets soaked, the blanket, all this very dark blood –'

His face was white tinged with green. I said, 'Easy, Lew.'

'I'm all right.'

'I know you are. Put your head down between your knees. C'mon, swing out from behind the table and put your head down. You're all right.'

'I know.'

I thought he might faint, but he got hold of himself. He kept his head lowered for a minute or two, then sat up straight again. He had some color in his face now. He took a couple of deep breaths and a long swig of beer.

He said, 'Jesus Christ.'

'You're okay now.'

'Yeah, right. I took one look at her lying there and I had to puke. I seen dead people before. My old man, he had a heart attack in his sleep, and I was the one walked in and found him. And since I joined the force, you know. But I never seen one like this and I hadda puke and I'm handcuffed to this asshole and he's still got his dick hanging out. I dragged the stupid bastard over to the corner and I just puked in the corner of the room, just like that, and what I did next, I had a fit of the giggles. I just couldn't help it, I stood there giggling like an idiot, and this guy cuffed to me, so help me God, he stops all this yelling of his and he asks me, "What's so funny?" Can you believe it? Like he wants me to explain the joke to him so he can laugh, too. "What's so funny?"'

I poured the rest of my bourbon into my coffee and stirred it with a spoon. I was getting bits and pieces of Richard Vanderpoel. So far they didn't begin to fit together, but they were fragments of what might ultimately be a full picture. Or they might never add up to anything real. Sometimes the whole is a lot less than the sum of its parts.

I spent another twenty minutes or so with Pankow, going back and forth over places we'd already been without getting anything much from him. He talked a little about his reactions to the murder scene, the nausea, the hysteria. He wanted to know if you ever got used to that sort of thing. I thought of the photograph I had taken from the file. I hadn't felt much looking at it. But if I had walked into that bedroom as Pankow had done, I might have reacted in very much the same way.

'You get used to some of it,' I told him, 'but every once in a while something new comes along and knocks you on your ass.'

When I had all I was going to get, I put a five on the table for the drinks and passed him twenty-five dollars. He didn't want to take it.

'C'mon,' I said. 'You did me a favor.'

'Well, that's all it was, was a favor. I feel funny taking money for it.'

'You're being stupid.'

'Huh?' The blue eyes were very wide.

'Stupid. This isn't graft. It's clean money. You did somebody a favor and made a couple of bucks for it.' I pushed the bills across the table at him. 'Listen to me,' I said. 'You just made a good collar. You wrote a decent report, and you handle yourself well, and pretty soon you'll be in line to get off the beat and into a prowl car. But nobody's going to want you in a car with him if you've got the wrong kind of reputation.'

'I don't get you.'

'Think about it. If you don't take money when somebody puts it in your hand, you're going to make a lot of people very nervous. You don't have to be a crook. Certain kinds of money you can turn down. And you don't have to walk the streets with your hand out. But you've got to play the game with the cards they give you. Take the money.'

'Jesus.'

'Didn't Koehler tell you there would be something in it for you?'

'Sure. But that's not why I came here. Hell, I generally drop in for a couple of beers when my shift ends. I usually meet my girl here around ten thirty. It's not like –'

'Koehler's going to expect a five-dollar bill for steering twenty-five your way. You want to pay him out of your own pocket?'

'Jesus. What do I do, just walk into his office and hand him five dollars?'

'That's the idea. You can say something like, "Here's that five you loaned me." Something like that.'

'I guess I got a lot to learn,' he said. He didn't sound delighted at the prospect.

'You don't have to worry about it,' I said. 'You've got plenty to learn, but they make it easy for you. The system takes you through it a step at a time. That's what makes it such a good system.'

He insisted on buying me a drink out of his new-found wealth. I sat there and drank it while he told me what it meant to him to be a police officer. I nodded at the right times without paying very much attention to what he was saying. I couldn't keep my mind on his words.

I got out of there and walked crosstown on Fifty-seventh to my hotel. The early edition of the *Times* was just in at the newsstand on Eighth Avenue. I bought it and took it home with me.

There were no messages for me at the desk. I went up to my room and took my shoes off and stretched out on the bed with the paper. It turned out to be about as gripping as Lewis Pankow's conversation.

I got undressed. When I took off my shirt, the photo of Wendy Hanniford's dead body fell onto the floor. I picked it up and looked at it and imagined myself as Lewis Pankow, walking in on a scene like that with the killer manacled to my wrist, then hauling him across the room so that I could vomit in the corner, then giggling hysterically until Richard Vanderpoel quite reasonably asked the cause of my mirth.

'What's so funny?'

I took a shower and put my clothes back on again. It had been snowing hesitantly earlier, and now it was beginning to accumulate. I walked around the corner to Armstrong's and took a stool at the bar.

He lived with her like brother and sister. He killed her and shrieked that he had fucked his mother. He rushed out into the street covered with her blood.

I knew too few facts, and the ones I did know did not seem to fit together.

I drank a few drinks and sidestepped a few conversations. I looked around for Trina, but she had left when her shift ended. I let the bartender tell me what was the matter with the Knicks this year. I don't remember what he said, just that he felt very strongly about it.

FIVE

Gordon Kalish had an old-fashioned pendulum clock on his wall, the kind that used to hang in railway stations. He kept glancing at it and checking the time against his wristwatch. At first I thought he was trying to tell me something. Later I realized it was a habit. Early in life someone must have told him his time was valuable. He had never forgotten, but he still couldn't entirely make himself believe it.

He was a partner in Bowdoin Realty Management. I had arrived at the company's offices in the Flatiron Building a few minutes after ten and waited for about twenty minutes until Kalish could give me a chunk of his time. Now he had papers and ledgers spread out on his desk and was apologetic that he couldn't be more helpful.

'We rented the apartment to Miss Hanniford herself,' he said. 'She may have had a roommate from the beginning. If so, she didn't tell us about it. She was the tenant of record. She could have had anyone living with her, man or woman, and we wouldn't have known about it. Or cared.'

'She had a female roommate when Miss Antonelli moved in as superintendent. I'd like to contact that woman.'

'I have no way of knowing who she was. Or when she moved in or out. As long as Miss Hanniford came up with the rent the first of every month, and as long as she didn't create a nuisance, we had no reason to take any further interest.' He scratched his head. 'If there was another woman and she moved out, wouldn't the post office have a forwarding address?'

'I'd need her name to get it.'

'Oh, of course.' His eyes went to the clock, then to his watch, then again to me. 'It was a very different matter when my father first got into the business. He ran things on a much more personal basis. He was a plumber originally. He saved his money and bought property, a building at a time. Did all his own repair

29

work, put the profits from one building into the acquisition of another. And he knew his tenants. He went around to collect the rent in person. The first of the month, or once a week in some of the buildings. He would carry certain tenants for months if they were going through hard times. Others he had out on the street if they were five days late. He said you had to be a good judge of people.'

'He must have been quite a man.'

'He still is. He's retired now, of course. He's been living down in Florida for five or six years now. Picks oranges off his own trees. And still pays his dues in the plumbers union every year.' He clasped his hands together. 'It's a different business now. We've sold off most of the buildings he bought. Ownership is too much of a headache. It's a lot less grief to manage property for somebody else. The building where Miss Hanniford lived, 194 Bethune, the owner is a housewife in a suburb of Chicago who inherited the property from an uncle. She's never seen it, just gets her check from us four times a year.'

I said, 'Miss Hanniford was a model tenant, then?'

'In that she never did anything to draw our attention. The papers say she was a prostitute. Could be, I suppose. We never had any complaints.'

'You never met her?'

'No.'

'She was always on time with the rent?'

'She was a week late now and then, just like everybody. No more than that.'

'She paid by check?'

'Yes.'

'When did she sign the lease?'

'What did I do with the lease? Here it is. Let's see, now. October 23, 1970. Standard two-year lease, renewing automatically.'

'And the monthly rent was four hundred dollars?'

'It's three eighty-five now. It was lower then, there've been some allowable increases since then. It was three forty-two fifty when she signed it.'

'You wouldn't rent to someone with no visible means of support.'

'Of course not.'

'Then she must have claimed to be working. She must have provided references.'

30

'I should have thought of that,' he said. He shuffled more papers and came up with the application she had filled out. I looked at it. She had claimed to be employed as an industrial systems analyst at a salary of seventeen thousand dollars a year. Her employer was one J. J. Cottrell, Inc. There was a telephone number listed, and I copied it down.

I asked if the references had been checked.

'They must have been,' Kalish said. 'But it doesn't amount to anything. It's simple enough to fake. All she needs is someone at that number to back up her story. We make the calls automatically, but I sometimes wonder if it's worth the trouble.'

'Then someone must have called this number. And someone answered the phone and swore to her lies.'

'Evidently.'

I thanked him for his time. In the lobby downstairs I put a dime in a pay phone and dialed the number Wendy had given. A recording informed me that the number I had dialed was no longer in service.

I put my dime back in the phone and called the Carlyle. I asked the desk for Cale Hanniford's room. A woman answered the phone on the second ring. I gave my name and asked to speak to Mr Hanniford. He asked me if I was making any progress.

'I don't know,' I said. 'Those postcards you received from Wendy. Do you still have them?'

'It's possible. Is it important?'

'It would help me get the chronology in order. She signed the lease on her apartment three years ago in October. You said she dropped out of college in the spring.'

'I believe it was in March.'

'When did you get the first postcard?'

'Within two or three months, as I remember it. Let me ask my wife.' He was back a moment later. 'My wife says the first card arrived in June. I would have said late May. The second card, the one from Florida, was a few months after that. I'm sorry I can't make it more specific than that. My wife says she thinks she remembers where she put the cards. We'll be returning to Utica tomorrow morning. I gather you want to know whether Wendy went to Florida before or after she took the apartment.'

That was close enough, so I said yes. I told him I'd call him in a day or two. I already had his office number in Utica, and he gave me his home number as well. 'But please try to call me at the office,' he said.

*

31

Burghash Antiques Imports was on University Place between Eleventh and Twelfth. I stood in one aisle surrounded by the residue of half the attics in Western Europe. I was looking at a clock just like the one I had seen on Gordon Kalish's wall. It was priced at $225.

'Are you interested in clocks? That's a good one.'

'Does it keep time?'

'Oh, those pendulum clocks are indestructible. And they're extraordinarily accurate. You just raise or lower the weight to make them run faster or slower. The case of the one you're looking at is in particularly good condition. It's not a rare model, of course, but they're hard to find in such nice shape. The price might be somewhat negotiable if you're really interested.'

I turned to take a good look at him. He was in his middle or late twenties, a trim young man wearing flannel slacks and a powder-blue turtleneck sweater. His hair had been expensively styled. His sideburns were even with the bottoms of his earlobes. He had a very precise moustache.

I said, 'Actually, I'm not interested in clocks. I wanted to talk to someone about a boy who used to work here.'

'Oh, you must mean Richie! You're a policeman? Wasn't it the most unbelievable thing?'

'Did you know him well?'

'I hardly knew him at all. I've only been here since just before Thanksgiving. I used to work at the auction gallery down the block, but it was terribly hectic.'

'How long had Richie worked here?'

'I don't honestly know. Mr Burghash could tell you. He's in back in the office. It has been pure hell for all of us since that happened. I still can't believe it.'

'Were you working here the day it happened?'

He nodded. 'I saw him that morning. Thursday morning. Then I was on a delivery all afternoon, a load of perfectly hideous French country furniture for an equally hideous split-level chateau in Syosset. That's on Long Island.'

'I know.'

'Well, *I* didn't. I lived all these many years in blissful ignorance that there even *was* a place known as Syosset.' He remembered the gravity of what we were talking about, and his face turned serious again. 'I got back here at five, just in time to help close up shop. Richie had left early. Of course by then it had all happened, hadn't it?'

'The murder took place around four.'

'While I was fighting traffic on the Long Island Expressway.' He shivered theatrically. 'I had no idea until I caught the eleven o'clock news that night. And I couldn't believe it was our Richard Vanderpoel, but they mentioned the name of the firm and –' He sighed and let his hands drop to his sides. 'One never knows,' he said.

'What was he like?'

'I hardly had time to know him. He was pleasant, he was courteous, he was anxious to please. He didn't have a great *knowledge* of antiques, but he had a good *sense* of them if you know what I mean.'

'Did you know he was living with a girl?'

'How would I have known that?'

'He might have mentioned it.'

'Well, he didn't. Why?'

'Does it surprise you that he was living with a girl?'

'I'm sure I never thought about it one way or the other.'

'Was he homosexual?'

'How on earth would *I* know?'

I stepped closer to him. He backed away without moving his feet. I said, 'Why don't you cut the shit.'

'Pardon me?'

'Was Richie gay?'

'I certainly had no interest in him myself. And I never saw him with another man, and he never seemed to be cruising anyone.'

'Did you think he was gay?'

'Well, I always assumed it, for heaven's sake. He certainly *seemed* gay.'

I found Burghash in the office. He was a little man with a furrowed brow that went almost to the top of his head. He had a ragged moustache and two days' worth of beard. He told me he'd had cops and newspapermen coming out of his ears and he had a business to run. I told him I wouldn't take much of his time.

'I have a few questions,' I said. 'Let's go back to Thursday, the day of the murder. Did Richie behave differently than usual?'

'Not really.'

'He wasn't agitated or anything like that?'

'No.'

'He went home early.'

'That's right. He didn't feel well when he came back from

33

lunch. He had some curry at the Indian place around the corner, and it didn't agree with him. I was always telling him to stay with bland food, ordinary American food. He had a sensitive digestive system, and he was always trying exotic foods that didn't agree with him.'

'What time did he leave here?'

'I don't keep track. He came back from lunch feeling lousy. I told him right away to take the rest of the day off. You can't work with your guts on fire. He wanted to tough it out, though. He was an ambitious kid, a hard worker. Sometimes he'd have indigestion like that, and then an hour later he'd be all right again, but this time it got worse instead of better, and I finally told him to get the hell out and go home. He must have left here, oh, I don't know. Three? Three thirty? Something like that.'

'How long had he been working for you?'

'Just about a year and a half. He went to work for me a year ago last July.'

'He moved in with Wendy Hanniford the following December. Did you have a previous address for him?'

'The YMCA on Twenty-third Street. That's where he was living when he came to work for me. Then he moved a few times. I don't have the addresses, and then I guess it was in December when he moved to Bethune Street.'

'Did you know anything about Wendy Hanniford?'

He shook his head. 'Never met her. Never knew her name.'

'You knew he was rooming with a girl?'

'I knew he said he was.'

'Oh?'

Burghash shrugged. 'I figured he was rooming with somebody, and if he wanted me to think it was a girl, I was willing to go along with it.'

'You thought he was homosexual.'

'Uh-huh. It's not exactly unheard of in this business. I don't care if my employees go to bed with orangutans. What they do on their own time is their own business.'

'Did he have any friends that you knew of?'

'Not that I knew of, no. He kept to himself most of the time.'

'And he was a good worker.'

'Very good. Very conscientious, and he had a feeling for the business.' He fixed his eyes on the ceiling. 'I sensed that he had personal problems. He never talked about them, but he was, oh, how shall I put it? High-strung.'

34

'Nervous? Touchy?'

'No, not that, exactly. High-strung is the best adjective I can think of to describe him. You sensed that he had things weighing him down, keying him up. But you know, that was more noticeable when he first started here. For the past year he seemed more settled, as if he had managed to come to terms with himself.'

'The past year. Since be moved in with the Hanniford girl, in other words.'

'I hadn't thought of it that way, but I guess that's right.'

'You were surprised when he killed her.'

'I was astonished. I simply could not believe it. And I'm still astonished. You see someone five days a week for a year and a half, and you think you know them. Then you find out you don't know them at all.'

On my way out the young man in the turtleneck stopped me. He asked me if I had learned anything useful. I told him I didn't know.

'But it's all over,' he said. 'Isn't it? They're both dead.'

'Yes.'

'So what's the point in poking around in corners?'

'I have no idea,' I said. 'Why do you suppose he was living with her?'

'Why does anybody live with anybody else?'

'Let's assume he was gay. Why would he live with a woman?'

'Maybe he got tired of dusting and cleaning. Sick of doing his own laundry.'

'I don't know that she was that domestic. It seems likely that she was a prostitute.'

'So I understand.'

'Why would a homosexual live with a prostitute?'

'Gawd, *I* don't know. Maybe she let him take care of her overflow. Maybe he was a closet heterosexual. For my own part, I'd never live with anyone, male *or* female. I have trouble enough living with myself.'

I couldn't argue with that. I started toward the door, then turned around again. There were too many things that didn't fit together, and they were scraping against each other like chalk on a black-board. 'I just want to make sense out of this,' I said, to myself as much as to him. 'Why in hell would he kill her? He raped her and he killed her. Why?'

'Well, he was a minister's son.'

35

'So?'

'They're all crazy,' he said. 'Aren't they?'

SIX

The Reverend Martin Vanderpoel didn't want to see me. 'I have spoken with enough reporters,' he told me. 'I can spare no time for you, Mr Scudder. I have my responsibilities to my congregation. What time remains, I feel the need to devote to prayer and meditation.'

I knew the feeling. I explained that I wasn't a reporter, that I was representing Cale Hanniford, the father of the murdered girl.

'I see,' he said.

'I wouldn't need much of your time, Reverend Vanderpoel. Mr Hanniford has suffered a loss, even as you have. In a sense, he lost his daughter before she was killed. Now he wants to learn more about her.'

'I'd be a poor source of information, I'm afraid.'

'He told me he wanted to see you himself, sir.'

There was a long pause. I thought for a moment that the phone had gone dead. Then he said, 'It is a difficult request to refuse. I will be occupied with church affairs this afternoon, I'm afraid. Perhaps this evening?'

'This evening would be fine.'

'You have the address of the church? The rectory is adjacent to it. I will be waiting for you at – shall we say eight o'clock?'

I said eight would be fine. I found another dime and looked up another number and made a call, and the man I spoke to was a good deal less reticent to talk about Richard Vanderpoel. In fact he seemed relieved that I'd called him and told me to come right on up.

His name was George Topakian, and he and his brother constituted Topakian and Topakian, Attorneys-at-Law. His office was on Madison Avenue in the low Forties. Framed diplomas on the wall testified that he had graduated from City College twenty-two years ago and had then gone on to Fordham Law.

37

He was a small man, trimly built, dark complected. He seated me in a red leather tub chair and asked me if I wanted coffee. I said coffee would be fine. He buzzed his secretary on the intercom and had her bring a cup for each of us. While she was doing this, he told me he and his brother had a general practice with an emphasis on estate work. The only criminal cases he'd handled, aside from minor work for regular clients, had come as a result of court assignments. Most of these had involved minor offenses – purse snatching, low-level assault, possession of narcotics – until the court had appointed him as counsel to Richard Vanderpoel.

'I expected to be relieved,' he said. 'His father was a clergyman and would almost certainly have arranged my replacement by a criminal lawyer. But I did see Vanderpoel.'

'When did you see him?'

'Late Friday afternoon.' He scratched the side of his nose with his index finger. 'I could have gotten to him earlier, I guess.'

'But you didn't.'

'No. I stalled.' He looked at me levelly. 'I was anticipating being replaced,' he said. 'And if replacement was imminent, I thought I could save myself the time I'd spend seeing him. And my time wasn't the half of it.'

'How do you mean?'

'I didn't want to see the son of a bitch.'

He got up from behind his desk and walked over to the window. He toyed with the cord of the venetian blinds, raising and lowering them a few inches. I waited him out. He sighed and turned to face me.

'Here was a guy who committed a horrible murder, slashed a young woman to death. I didn't want to set eyes on him. Do you find that hard to understand?'

'Not at all.'

'It bothered me. I'm an attorney, I'm supposed to represent people without regard to what they have or haven't done. I should have thrown myself right into it, finding the best defense for him. I certainly shouldn't have presumed my own client guilty as charged without even talking to him.' He came back to his desk and sat down again. 'But of course I did. The police picked him up right on the scene of the crime. I might have challenged their case if I saw it all the way into court, but in my own mind I had already tried the bastard and found him guilty as

38

charged. And since I had every expectation that I would be taken off the case, I found ways to avoid seeing Vanderpoel.'

'But you eventually went that Friday afternoon.'

'Uh-huh. He was in his cell in the Tombs.'

'You saw him in his cell, then.'

'Yes. I didn't pay much attention to the surroundings. They've finally torn down the Women's House of Detention. I used to walk past it all the time years ago when my wife and I lived in the Village. A horrible place.'

'I know.'

'I wish they'd do the same for the Tombs.' He touched the side of his nose again. 'I suppose I saw the very steam pipe that poor bastard hanged himself from. And the bedsheet he used to do the job. He sat on his bed while we talked. He let me have the chair.'

'How long were you with him?'

'I don't think it was more than half an hour. It seemed considerably longer.'

'Did he talk?'

'Not at first. He was off somewhere with his own thoughts. I tried to get through to him but didn't have very much luck. He had a look in his eyes as if he was having some intense wordless dialogue with himself. I tried to open him up, and at the same time I began planning the defense I would use if I had the chance. I didn't expect to have the chance, understand. It was a hypothetical exercise as far as I was concerned. But I had more or less decided to try for an insanity plea.'

'Everyone seems to agree he was crazy.'

'There's a difference between that and legal insanity. It becomes a battle of experts – you line up your witnesses, and the prosecution lines up theirs. Well, I went on talking to him, just trying to get him to open up a little, and then he turned to me and looked at me as if wondering where I had come from, as if he hadn't known I was in the room before. He asked me who I was, and I went over everything I had said to him the first time around.'

'Did he seem rational?'

Topakian considered the question. 'I don't know that he seemed to *be* rational,' he said. 'He seemed to be *acting* rationally at that moment.'

'What did he say?'

'I wish I could remember it exactly. I asked him if he had killed the Hanniford girl. He said, now let me think, he said, "She couldn't have done it herself."'

'"She couldn't have done it herself."'

'I think that's the way he put it. I asked if he remembered killing her. He claimed that he didn't. He said his stomach ached, and at first I thought he meant he had a stomachache at the time of our conversation, but I gathered that he had had a stomach-ache on the day of the murder.'

'He left work early because of indigestion.'

'Well, he remembered the stomachache. He said his stomach ached and he went to the apartment. Then he kept talking about blood. "She was in the bathtub and there was blood all over." I understand they found her in bed.'

'Yes.'

'She hadn't been in the tub or anything?'

'She was killed in bed, according to police reports.'

He shook his head. 'He was a very confused young man. He said that she had been in the tub with blood everywhere. I asked him if he had killed her, I asked him several times, and he never really gave me an answer. Sometimes he said that he didn't remember killing her. Other times he said that he must have killed her because she couldn't have done it herself.'

'He said that more than once, then.'

'Quite a few times.'

'That's interesting.'

'Is it?' Topakian shrugged. 'I don't think he ever lied to me. I mean, I don't believe he remembered killing the girl. Because he admitted something, oh, worse.'

'What?'

'Having sex with her.'

'That's worse than killing her?'

'Having sex with her afterward.'

'Oh.'

'He didn't make any attempt to conceal it. He said he found her lying in her blood and he had sex with her.'

'What words did he use?'

'I don't know exactly. You mean for the sex act? He said he fucked her.'

'After she was dead.'

'Evidently.'

'And he had no trouble remembering that?'

'None. I don't know whether he had sex with her before or

after the murder. Did the autopsy indicate anything one way or the other?'

'If it did, it wasn't in the report. I'm not sure they can tell if the two acts are close together in time. Why?'

'I don't know. He kept saying, "I fucked her and she's dead." As if his having had sex with her was the chief cause of her death.'

'But he never remembered killing her. I suppose he could have blocked it out easily enough. I wonder why he didn't block out the whole thing. The sex act. Let me go over this once more. He said he walked in and found her like that?'

'I can't remember everything all that clearly myself, Scudder. He walked in and she was dead in the tub, that's what he said. He didn't even say specifically that she was dead, just that she was in a tub full of blood.'

'Did you ask him about the murder weapon?'

'I asked him what he did with it.'

'And?'

'He didn't know.'

'Did you ask him what the murder weapon was?'

'No. I didn't have to. He said, "I don't know what happened to the razor."'

'He knew it was a razor?'

'Evidently. Why wouldn't he know?'

'Well, if he didn't remember having it in his hand, why should he remember what it was?'

'Maybe he heard someone talk about the murder weapon and speak of it as a razor.'

'Maybe,' I said.

I walked for a while, heading generally south and west. I stopped for a drink on Sixth Avenue around Thirty-seventh Street. A man a couple of stools down was telling the bartender that he was sick of working his ass off to buy Cadillacs for niggers on welfare. The bartender said, 'You? Chrissake, you're in here eight hours a day. The taxes you pay, they don't get more'n a hubcap out of you.'

A little farther south and west I went into a church and sat for a while. St John's, I think it was. I sat near the front and watched people go in and out of the confessional. They didn't look any different coming out than they had going in. I thought how nice it might be to be able to leave your sins in a little curtained booth.

41

Richie Vanderpoel and Wendy Hanniford, and I kept picking at threads and trying to find a pattern to them. There was a conclusion I kept feeling myself drawn toward, and I didn't want to take hold of it. It was wrong, it had to be wrong, and as long as it reached out, tantalizing me, it kept me from doing the job I had signed on for.

I knew what had to come next. I had been ducking it, but it kept waving at me and I couldn't duck it forever. And now was the best time of day for it. Much better than trying it in the middle of the night.

I hung around long enough to light a couple of candles and stuff a few bills in the offerings slot. Then I caught a cab in front of Penn Station and told the driver how to get to Bethune Street.

The first-floor tenants were out. A Mrs Hacker on the second floor said she had had very little contact with Wendy and Richard. She remembered that Wendy's former roommate had had dark hair. Sometimes, she said, they had played their radio or stereo loud at night, but it had never been bad enough to complain about. She liked music, she said. She liked all kinds of music, classical, semiclassical, popular – all kinds of music.

The door to the third-floor apartment had a padlock on it. It would have been easy enough to crack it but impossible to do so unobtrusively.

There was nobody home on the fourth floor. I was very glad of that. I went on up to the fifth floor. Elizabeth Antonelli had said the tenants wouldn't be back until March. I rang their bell and listened carefully for sounds within the apartment. I didn't hear any.

There were four locks on the door, including a Taylor that is as close as you can come to pickproof. I knocked off the other three with a celluloid strip, an old oil-company credit card that is otherwise useless since I no longer own a car. Then I kicked the Taylor in. I had to kick it twice before the door flew inward.

I locked the other three locks after me. The tenants would have a lot of fun trying to figure out what had happened to the Taylor, but that was their problem, and it wouldn't come up until sometime in March. I poked until I found the window that fed onto the fire escape, opened it, and climbed down two stories to the HannifordVanderpoel apartment.

The window wasn't locked. I opened it, let myself in, closed it after me.

An hour later I went out the window and back up the fire

escape. There were lights on in the fourth-floor apartment by now, but the shade was drawn on the window I had to pass. I reentered the fifth-floor apartment, let myself out into the hallway, locked the door behind me, and went downstairs and out of the building. I had enough time to grab a sandwich before I kept my appointment with Martin Vanderpoel.

SEVEN

I got off the BMT at Sixty-second Street and New Utrecht and walked a couple of blocks through a part of Brooklyn where Bay Ridge and Bensonhurst rub shoulders with one another. A powdery rain was melting some of yesterday's snow. The weather bureau expected it to freeze sometime during the night. I was a little early and stopped at a drugstore lunch counter for a cup of coffee. Toward the rear of the counter a kid was demonstrating a gravity knife to a couple of his friends. He took a quick look at me and made the knife disappear, reminding me once again that I haven't stopped looking like a cop.

I drank half my coffee and walked the rest of the way to the church. It was a massive edifice of white stone toned all shades of gray by the years. A cornerstone announced that the present structure had been erected in 1886 by a congregation established 220 years before that date. An illuminated bulletin board identified the church as the First Reformed Church of Bay Ridge, Reverend Martin T. Vanderpoel, Pastor. Services were held Sundays at nine thirty; this coming Sunday Reverend Vanderpoel was slated to speak on 'The Road to Hell Is Paved with Good Intentions.'

I turned the corner and found the rectory immediately adjacent to the church. It was three stories tall and built of the same distinctive stone. I rang the bell and stood on the front step in the rain for a few minutes. Then a small gray-haired woman opened the door and peered up at me. I gave my name.

'Yes,' she said. 'He said he was expecting you.' She led me into a parlor and pointed me to an armchair. I sat down across from a fireplace with an electric fire glowing in it. The wall on either side of the fireplace was lined with bookshelves. An Oriental rug with a muted pattern covered most of the parquet floor. The room's furniture was all dark and massive. I sat there waiting for

44

him and decided I should have stopped for a drink instead of a cup of coffee. I wasn't likely to get a drink in this cheerless house.

He let me sit there for five minutes. Then I heard his step on the stairs. I got to my feet as he entered the room. He said, 'Mr Scudder? I'm sorry to keep you waiting. I was on the telephone. But please have a seat, won't you?'

He was very tall and rail-thin. He wore a plain black suit, a clerical collar, and a pair of black leather bedroom slippers. His hair was white with yellow highlights here and there. It would have been considered long a few years ago, but now the abundant curls were conservative enough. His horn-rimmed glasses had thick lenses that made it difficult for me to see his eyes.

'Coffee, Mr Scudder?'

'No, thank you.'

'And none for me, either. If I have more than one cup with my dinner, I'm up half the night.' He sat down in a chair that was a mate to mine. He leaned toward me and placed his hands on his knees. 'Well, now,' he said. 'I don't see how I can possibly help you, but please tell me if I can.'

I explained a little more fully the errand I was running for Cale Hanniford. When I had finished he touched his chin with his thumb and forefinger and nodded thoughtfully.

'Mr Hanniford has lost a daughter,' he said. 'And I have lost a son.'

'Yes.'

'It's so difficult to father children in today's world, Mr Scudder. Perhaps it was always thus, but it seems to me that the times conspire against us. Oh, I can sympathize fully with Mr Hanniford, more fully than ever since I have suffered a similar loss.' He turned to gaze at the fire. 'But I fear I have no sympathy for the girl.'

I didn't say anything.

'It's a failing on my part, and I recognize it as such. Man is an imperfect creature. Sometimes it seems to me that religion has no higher function than to sharpen his awareness of the extent of his imperfection. God alone is perfect. Even Man, His greatest handiwork, is hopelessly flawed. A paradox, Mr Scudder, don't you think?'

'Yes.'

'Not the least of my own flaws is an inability to grieve for Wendy Hanniford. You see, her father no doubt holds my son

45

responsible for the loss of his daughter. And I, in turn, hold his daughter responsible for the loss of my son.'

He got to his feet and approached the fireplace. He stood there for a moment, his back perfectly straight, warming his hands. He turned toward me and seemed on the point of saying something. Instead, he walked slowly to his chair and sat down again, this time crossing one leg over the other.

He said, 'Are you a Christian, Mr Scudder?'

'No.'

'A Jew?'

'I have no religion.'

'How sad for you,' he said. 'I asked your religion because the nature of your own beliefs might facilitate your understanding my feelings toward the Hanniford girl. But perhaps I can approach the matter in another way. Do you believe in good and evil, Mr Scudder?'

'Yes, I do.'

'Do you believe that there is such a thing as evil extant in the world?'

'I know there is.'

He nodded, satisfied. 'So do I,' he said. 'It would be difficult to believe otherwise, whatever one's religious outlook. A glance at a daily newspaper provides evidence enough of the existence of evil.' He paused, and I thought he was waiting for me to say something. Then he said, '*She* was evil.'

'Wendy Hanniford?'

'Yes. An evil, Devil-ridden woman. She took my son away from me, away from his religion, away from God. She led him away from good paths and unto the paths of evil.' His voice was picking up a timbre, and I could imagine his forcefulness in front of a congregation. 'It was my son who killed her. But it was she who killed something within him, who made it possible for him to kill.' His voice dropped in pitch, and he held his hands palms down at his sides. 'And so I cannot mourn Wendy Hanniford. I can regret that her death came at Richard's hands, I can profoundly regret that he then took his own life, but I cannot mourn your client's daughter.'

He let his hands drop, lowered his head. I couldn't see his eyes, but his face was troubled, wrapped up in chains of good and evil. I thought of the sermon he would preach on Sunday, thought of all the different roads to Hell and all the paving stones therein. I

46

pictured Martin Vanderpoel as a long, lean Sisyphus arduously rolling the boulders into place.

I said, 'Your son was in Manhattan a year and a half ago. That was when he went to work for Burghash Antiques.' He nodded. 'So he left here some six months before he began sharing Wendy Hanniford's apartment.'

'That is correct.'

'But you feel she led him astray.'

'Yes.' He took a deep breath and let it out slowly. 'My son left my home shortly after his high school graduation. I did not approve, but neither did I object violently. I would have wanted Richard to go to college. He was an intelligent boy and would have done well in college. I had hopes, naturally enough, that he might follow me into the ministry. I did not force him in this direction, however. One must determine for oneself whether one has a vocation. I am not fanatical on the subject, Mr Scudder. I would prefer to see a son of mine as a contented and productive doctor or lawyer or businessman than as a discontented minister of the gospel.

'I realized that Richard had to find himself. That's a fashionable term with the young these days, is it not? He had to find himself. I understood this. I expected that this process of self-discovery would ultimately lead him to enter college after a year or two. I hoped this would occur, but in any event I saw no cause for alarm. Richard had an honest job, he was living in a decent Christian residence, and I felt that his feet were on a good path. Not perhaps the path he would ultimately pursue, but one that was correct for him at that point in his life.

'Then he met Wendy Hanniford. He lived in sin with her. He became corrupted by her. And, ultimately –'

I remembered a bit of men's-room graffiti: *Happiness is when your son marries a boy of his own faith.* Evidently Richie Vanderpoel had functioned as some variety of homosexual without his father ever suspecting anything. Then he moved in with a girl, and his father was shattered.

I said, 'Reverend Vanderpoel, a great many young people live together nowadays without being married.'

'I recognize this, Mr Scudder. I do not condone it, but I could hardly fail to recognize it.'

'But your feeling in this case was more than a matter of not condoning it.'

'Yes.'

47

'Why?'

'Because Wendy Hanniford was evil.'

I was getting the first twinges of a headache. I rubbed the center of my forehead with the tips of my fingers. I said, 'What I want more than anything else is to be able to give her father a picture of her. You say she was evil. In what way was she evil?'

'She was an older woman who enticed an innocent young man into an unnatural relationship.'

'She was only three or four years older than Richard.'

'Yes, I know. In chronological terms. In terms of worldliness she was ages his senior. She was promiscuous. She was amoral. She was a creature of perversion.'

'Did you ever actually meet her?'

'Yes,' he said. He breathed in and out. 'I met her once. Once was enough.'

'When did that take place?'

'It's hard for me to remember. I believe it was during the spring. April or May, I would say.'

'Did he bring her here?'

'No. No, Richard surely knew better than to bring that woman into my house. I went to the apartment where they were living. I went specifically to meet with her, to talk to her. I picked a time when Richard would be working at his job.'

'And you met Wendy.'

'I did.'

'What did you hope to accomplish?'

'I wanted her to end her relationship with my son.'

'And she refused.'

'Oh, yes, Mr Scudder. She refused.' He leaned back in his chair, closed his eyes. 'She was foulmouthed and abusive. She taunted me. She – I don't want to go into this further, Mr Scudder. She made it quite clear that she had no intention of giving Richard up. It suited her to have him living with her. The entire interview was one of the most unpleasant experiences of my life.'

'And you never saw her again.'

'I did not. I saw Richard on several occasions, but not in that apartment. I tried to talk to him about that woman. I made no progress whatsoever. He was utterly infatuated with her. Sex – evil, unscrupulous sex – gives certain women an extraordinary hold upon susceptible men. Man is a weakling, Mr Scudder, and he is so often powerless to cope with the awful force of an evil woman's sexuality.' He sighed heavily. 'And in the end she was destroyed by means of her own evil nature. The sexual spell she cast upon my son was the instrument of her own undoing.'

'You make her sound like a witch.'

He smiled slightly. 'A witch? Indeed I do. A less enlightened generation than our own would have seen her burned at the stake for witchcraft. Nowadays we speak of neuroses, of psychological complications, of compulsion. Previously we spoke of witchcraft, of demonic possession. I wonder sometimes if we're as enlightened now as we prefer to think. Or if our enlightenment does us much good.'

'Does anything?'

'Pardon?'

'I was wondering if anything did us much good.'

'Ah,' he said. He took off his glasses and perched them on his knee. I hadn't seen the color of his eyes before. They were a light blue flecked with gold. He said, 'You have no faith, Mr Scudder. Perhaps that accounts for your cynicism.'

'Perhaps.'

'I would say that God's love does us a great deal of good. In the next world if not in this one.'

I decided I would rather deal with one world at a time. I asked if Richie had had faith.

'He was in a period of doubt. He was too preoccupied with his attempt at self-realization to have room for the realization of the Lord.'

'I see.'

'And then he fell under the spell of the Hanniford woman. I use the word advisedly. He literally fell under her spell.'

'What was he like before that?'

'A good boy. An aware, interested, involved young man.'

'You never had any problems with him?'

'No problems.' He put his glasses back on. 'I cannot avoid blaming myself, Mr Scudder.'

'For what?'

'For everything. What is it that they say? 'The cobbler's children always go barefoot.' Perhaps that maxim applies in this case. Perhaps I devoted too much attention to my congregation and too little attention to my son. I had to raise him by myself, you see. That did not seem a difficult chore at the time. It may have been more difficult than I ever realized.'

'Richard's mother –'

He closed his eyes. 'I lost my wife almost fifteen years ago,' he said.

'I didn't know that.'

'It was hard for both of us. For Richard and for myself. In retrospect I think that I should have married again. I never ... never entertained the idea. I was able to have a housekeeper, and my own duties facilitated my spending more time with him than the average father might have been able to manage. I thought that was sufficient.'

'And now you don't think so?'

'I don't know. I occasionally think there is very little we can do to change our destiny. Our lives play themselves out according to a master plan.' He smiled briefly. 'That is either a very comforting thing to believe or quite the opposite, Mr Scudder.'

'I can see how it could be.'

'Other times I think there ought to have been something I could have done. Richard was drawn very much into himself. He was shy, reticent, very much a private person.'

'Did he have much of a social life? I mean during high school, while he was living here.'

'He had friends.'

'Did he date?'

'He wasn't interested in girls at that time. He was never interested in girls until he came into that woman's clutches.'

'Did it bother you that he wasn't interested in girls?'

That was as close as I cared to come to intimating that Richie was interested in boys instead. If it registered at all, Vanderpoel didn't show it. 'I was not concerned,' he said. 'I took it for granted that Richard would ultimately develop a fine and healthy loving relationship with the girl who would eventually become his wife and bear his children. That he was not involved in social dating in the meantime did not upset me. If you were in a position to see what I see, Mr Scudder, you would realize that a great deal of trouble stems from too much involvement of one sex with the other sex. I have seen girls pregnant in their early teens. I have seen young men forced into marriage at a very tender age. I have seen young people afflicted with unmentionable diseases. No, I was if anything delighted that Richard was a late bloomer in this area.'

He shook his head. 'And yet,' he said, 'perhaps if he had been more experienced, perhaps if he had been less innocent, he would not have been so easy a victim for Miss Hanniford.'

We sat for a few moments in silence. I asked him a few more things without getting anything significant in reply. He asked again if I wanted a cup of coffee. I declined and said it was time I was getting on my way. He didn't try to persuade me to stay.

I got my coat from the vestibule closet where the housekeeper had stashed it. As I was putting it on I said, 'I understand you saw your son once after the killing.'

'Yes.'

'In his cell.'

'That is correct.' He winced almost imperceptibly at the recollection. 'We didn't speak at length. I tried only to do what little I could to put his mind at rest. Evidently I failed. He ... he elected to mete out his own punishment for what he had done.'

'I talked to the lawyer his case was assigned to. A Mr Topakian.'

'I didn't meet the man myself. After Richard ... took his own life ... well, I saw no point in seeing the lawyer. And I couldn't bring myself to do it.'

'I understand.' I finished buttoning my coat. 'Topakian said Richard had no memory of the actual murder.'

'Oh?'

'Did your son say anything to you about it?'

He hesitated for a moment, and I didn't think he was going to answer. Then he gave his head an impatient shake. 'There's no harm in saying it now, is there? Perhaps he was speaking truthfully to the lawyer, perhaps his memory was clouded at the time.' He sighed again. 'Richard told me he had killed her. He said he did not know what had come over him.'

'Did he give any explanation?'

'Explanation? I don't know if you would call it an explanation, Mr Scudder. It explained certain things to me, however.'

'What did he say?'

He looked off over my shoulder, searching his mind for the right words. Finally he said, 'He told me that there was a sudden moment of awful clarity when he saw her face. He said it was as if he had been given a glimpse of the Devil and knew only that he must destroy, destroy.'

'I see.'

'Without absolving my son, Mr Scudder, I nevertheless hold Miss Hanniford responsible for the loss of her own life. She snared him, she blinded him to her real self, and then for a moment the veil slipped aside, the blindfold was loosed from around his eyes, and he saw her plain. And saw, I feel certain, what she had done to him, to his life.'

'You almost sound as though you feel it was right for him to kill her.'

He stared at me, eyes briefly wide in shock. 'Oh, no,' he said. 'Never that. One does not play God. It is God's province to punish and reward, to give and to take away. It is not Man's.'

I reached for the doorknob, hesitated. 'What did you say to Richard?'

'I scarcely remember. There was little to be said, and I'm afraid I was in too deep a state of personal shock to be very communicative. My son asked my forgiveness. I gave him my blessing. I told him he should look to the Lord for forgiveness.' At close range his blue eyes were magnified by the thick lenses. There were tears in their corners. 'I only hope he did,' he said. 'I only hope he did.'

EIGHT

I got out of bed while the sky was still dark. I still had the same headache I'd gone to bed with. I went into the bathroom, swallowed a couple of aspirins, then forced myself to put in some time under a hot shower. By the time I was dry and dressed, the headache was mostly gone and the sky was starting to brighten up.

My head was full of fragments of conversation from the night before. I'd returned from Brooklyn with a headache and a thirst, and I'd treated the second more thoroughly than the first. I remember a sketchy conversation with Anita on Long Island – the boys were fine, they were sleeping now, they'd like to come in to New York and see me, maybe stay overnight if it was convenient. I'd said that would be great, but I was working on a case right now. 'The cobbler's children always go barefoot,' I told her. I don't think she knew what I was talking about.

I got to Armstrong's just as Trina was going off duty. I bought her a couple of stingers and told her a little about the case I was working on. 'His mother died when he was six or seven years old,' I said. 'I hadn't known that.'

'Does it make a difference, Matt?'

'I don't know.'

After she left I sat by myself and had a few more drinks. I was going to have a hamburger toward the end, but they had already closed the kitchen. I don't know what time I got back to my room. I didn't notice, or didn't remember.

I had breakfast and a lot of coffee next door at the Red Flame. I thought about calling Hanniford at his office. I decided it could wait.

The clerk in the branch post office on Christopher Street informed me that forwarding addresses were only kept active for a year. I suggested that he could check the back files, and he said it wasn't his job and it could be very time-consuming and he was overworked as it was. That would have made him the first overworked postal employee since Benjamin Franklin. I took a hint and palmed him a ten-dollar bill. He seemed surprised, either at the amount or at being given anything at all besides an argument. He went off into a back room and returned a few minutes later with an address for Marcia Maisel on East Eighty-fourth near York Avenue.

The building was a high-rise with underground parking and a lobby that would have served a small airport. There was a little waterfall with pebbles and plastic plants. I couldn't find a Maisel in the directory of tenants. The doorman had never heard of her. I managed to find the super, and he recognized the name. He said she'd gotten married a few months ago and moved out. Her married name was Mrs Gerald Thal. He had an address for her in Mamaroneck.

I got her number from Westchester Information and dialed it. It was busy the first three times. The fourth time around it rang twice and a woman answered.

I said, 'Mrs Thal?'

'Yes?'

'My name is Matthew Scudder. I'd like to talk to you about Wendy Hanniford.'

There was a long silence, and I wondered if I had the right person after all. I'd found a stack of old magazines in a closet of Wendy's apartment with Marcia Maisel's name and the Bethune Street address on them. It was possible that there had been a false connection somewhere along the way – the postal clerk could have pulled the wrong Maisel, the superintendent could have picked the wrong card out of his file.

Then she said, 'What do you want from me?'

'I want to ask you a few questions.'

'Why me?'

'You lived in the Bethune Street apartment with her.'

'That was a long time ago.' Long ago, and in another country. And besides, the wench is dead. 'I haven't seen Wendy in years. I don't even know if I would recognize her. Would *have* recognized her.'

'But you did know her at one time.'

'So what? Would you hold on? I have to get a cigarette.' I held on. She returned after a moment and said, 'I read about it in the

54

newspapers, of course. The boy who did it killed himself, didn't he?'

'Yes.'

'Then why drag me into it?'

The fact that she didn't want to be dragged into it was almost reason enough in itself. But I explained the nature of my particular mission, Cale Hanniford's need to know about the recent past of his daughter now that she had no future. When I had finished she told me that she guessed she could answer some questions.

'You moved from Bethune Street to East Eighty-fourth Street a year ago last June.'

'How do you know so much about me? Never mind, go on.'

'I wondered why you moved.'

'I wanted a place of my own.'

'I see.'

'Plus it was nearer my work. I had a job on the East Side, and it was a hassle getting there from the Village.'

'How did you happen to room with Wendy in the first place?'

'She had an apartment that was too big for her, and I needed a place to stay. It seemed like a good idea at the time.'

'But it didn't turn out to be a good idea?'

'Well, the location, and also I like my privacy.'

She was going to give me whatever answers would get rid of me most efficiently. I wished I were talking to her face-to-face instead of over the telephone. At the same time I hoped I wouldn't have to kill a day driving out to Mamaroneck.

'How did you happen to share the apartment?'

'I just told you, she had a place –'

'Did you answer an ad?'

'Oh, I see what you mean. No, I ran into her on the street, as a matter of fact.'

'You had known her previously?'

'Oh, I thought you realized. I knew her at college. I didn't know her well, we were never close, see, but it was a small college and everybody more or less knew everybody; and I ran into her on the street and we got to talking.'

'You knew her at college.'

'Yeah, I thought you realized. You seem to know so many facts about me, I'm surprised you didn't know that.'

'I'd like to come out and talk with you, Mrs Thal.'

'Oh, I don't think so.'

55

'I realize it's an imposition on your time, but –'

'I just don't want to get involved,' she said. 'Can't you understand that? Jesus Christ, Wendy's dead, right? So what can it help her? Right?'

'Mrs Thal –'

'I'm hanging up now,' she said. And did.

I bought a newspaper, went to a lunch counter and had a cup of coffee. I gave her a full half hour to wonder whether or not I was all that easy to get rid of. Then I dialed her number again.

Something I learned long ago. It is not necessary to know what a person is afraid of. It is enough to know the person is afraid.

She answered in the middle of the second ring. She held the phone to her ear for a moment without saying anything. Then she said, 'Hello?'

'This is Scudder.'

'Listen, I don't –'

'Shut up a minute, you foolish bitch. I intend to talk to you. I'll either talk to you in front of your husband or I'll talk to you alone.'

Silence.

'Now you just think about it. I can pick up a car and be in Mamaroneck in an hour. An hour after that I'll be back in my car and out of your life. That's the easy way. If you want it the hard way I can oblige you but I don't see that it makes much sense for either of us.'

'Oh, God.'

I let her think about it. The hook was set now, and there was no way she was going to shake it loose.

She said, 'Today's impossible. Some friends are coming over for coffee, they'll be here any minute.'

'Tonight?'

'No. Gerry'll be home. Tomorrow?'

'Morning or afternoon?'

'I have a doctor's appointment at ten. I'm free after that.'

'I'll be at your place at noon.'

'No. Wait a minute. I don't want you coming to the house.'

'Pick a place and I'll meet you.'

'Just give me a minute. Christ. I don't even know this area, we just moved here a few months ago. Let me think. There's a restaurant and cocktail lounge on Schuyler Boulevard. It's called the Carioca. I could stop there for lunch after I get out of the doctor's.'

'Noon?'

'All right. I don't know the address.'

'I'll find it. The Carioca on Schuyler Boulevard.'

'Yes. I don't remember your name.'

'Scudder. Matthew Scudder.'

'How will I recognize you?'

I thought, I'll be the man who looks out of place. I said, 'I'll be drinking coffee at the bar.'

'All right. I guess we'll find each other.'

'I'm sure we will.'

My illegal entry the night before had yielded little hard data beyond Marcia Maisel's name. The search of the premises had been complicated by my not knowing precisely what I was searching for. When you toss a place, it helps if you have something specific in mind. It also helps if you don't care whether or not you leave traces of your visit. You can search a few shelves of books far more eminently, for example, if you feel free to flip through them and then toss them in a heap on the rug. A twenty-minute job stretches out over a couple of hours when you have to put each volume neatly back in place.

There were few enough books in Wendy's apartment, and I hadn't bothered with them, anyway. I wasn't looking for something which had been deliberately concealed. I didn't know what I was looking for, and now, after the fact, I wasn't at all sure what I had found.

I had spent most of my hour wandering through those rooms, sitting on chairs, leaning against walls, trying to rub up against the essence of the two people who had lived here. I looked at the bed Wendy had died on, a double box spring and mattress on a Hollywood frame. They had not yet stripped off the blood-soaked sheets, though there would be little point in doing so; the mattress was deeply soaked with her blood, and the whole bed would have to be scrapped. At one point I stood holding a clot of rusty blood in my hand, and my mind reeled with images of a priest offering Communion. I found the bathroom and gagged without bringing anything up.

While I was there, I pushed the shower curtain aside and examined the tub. There was a ring around it from the last bath taken in it, and some hair matted at the drain, but there was nothing to suggest that anyone had been killed in it. I had not suspected that there would be. Richie Vanderpoel's recapitulation had not been a model of concise linear thought.

The medicine cabinet told me that Wendy had taken birth-control pills. They came in a little card with a dial indicating the days of the week so that you could tell whether you were up-to-date or not. Thursday's pill was gone, so I knew one thing she had done the day she died. She had taken her pill.

Along with the birth-control pills I found enough bottles of organic vitamins to suggest that either or both of the apartment's occupants had been a believer. A small vial with a prescription label indicated that Richie had suffered from hay fever. There was quite a bit in the way of cosmetics, two different brands of deodorant, a small electric razor for shaving legs and underarms, a large electric razor for shaving faces. I found some other prescription drugs – Seconal and Darvon (his), Dexedrine span-sules labeled *For Weight Control* (hers), and an unlabeled bottle containing what looked like Librium. I was surprised the drugs were still around. Cops are apt to pocket them, and men who would not take loose cash from the dead have trouble resisting the little pills that pick you up or settle you down.

I took the Seconal and the Dex along with me.

A closet and a dresser in the bedroom filled with her clothes. Not a large wardrobe, but several dresses had labels from Bloomingdale's and Lord & Taylor. His clothes were in the living room. One of the closets there was his, and he kept shirts and socks and underwear in the drawers of a Spanish-style kneehole desk.

The living-room couch was a convertible. I opened it up and found it made up with sheets and blankets. The sheets had been slept on since their last laundering. I closed the couch and sat on it.

A well-equipped kitchen, copper-bottomed frying pans, a set of burnt-orange enameled cast-iron pots and pans, a teak rack with thirty-two jars of herbs and spices. The refrigerator held a couple of TV dinners in the freezer compartment, but the rest of it was abundantly stocked with real food. So were the cupboards. The kitchen was a large one by Manhattan standards, and there was a round oak table in it. There were two captain's chairs at the table. I sat at one of them and pictured cozy domestic scenes, one of them whipping up a gourmet meal, the two of them sitting at this table and eating it.

I had left the apartment without finding the helpful things one hopes to find. No address books, no checkbooks, no bank statements. No revealing stacks of canceled checks. Whatever their financial arrangements, they had evidently conducted them on a cash basis.

Now, a day later, I thought of my impressions of that apartment and tried to match them up with Martin Vanderpoel's portrait of Wendy as evil incarnate. If she had trapped him with sex, why did he sleep on a folding bed in the living room? And why did the whole apartment have such an air of placid domesticity to it, a comfortable domesticity that all the blood in the bedroom could not entirely drown?

NINE

When I got back to my hotel there was a phone message at the desk. Cale Hanniford had called at a quarter after eleven. I was to call him. He had left a number, and it was one he had already given me. His office number.

I called him from my room. He was at lunch. His secretary said he would call me back. I said no, I'd try him again in an hour or so.

The call reminded me of J. J. Cottrell, Inc., Wendy's employment reference on her lease application. I found the number in my notebook and tried it again on the chance I'd misdialed it first time around. I got the same recording. I checked the telephone directory for J. J. Cottrell and didn't come up with anything. I tried Information, and they didn't have anything, either.

I thought for a few minutes, then dialed a special number. When a woman picked up, I said, 'Patrolman Lewis Pankow, Sixth Precinct. I have a listing that's temporarily out of service, and I have to know in what name it's listed.'

She asked the number. I gave it to her. She asked me to please hold the line. I sat there with the phone against my ear for almost ten minutes before she came back on the line.

'That's not a temporary disconnect,' she said. 'That's a permanent disconnect.'

'Can you tell me who the number was assigned to last?'

'I'm afraid I can't, officer.'

'Don't you keep that information on file?'

'We must have it somewhere, but I don't have access to it. I have recent disconnects, but that was disconnected over a year ago, so I wouldn't have it. I'm surprised it hasn't been reassigned by now.

'So all you know is that it's been out of service for more than a year.'

That was all she knew. I thanked her and rang off. I poured

60

myself a drink, and by the time it was gone I decided that Hanniford ought to be back in his office. I was right.

He told me he had managed to find the postcards. The first one, postmarked New York, had been mailed on June 4. The second had been mailed in Miami on September 16.

'Does that tell you anything, Scudder?'

It told me she had been in New York in early June if not before then. It told me she had taken the Miami trip prior to signing the lease on her apartment. Beyond that, it didn't tell me a tremendous amount.

'Another piece of the puzzle,' I said. 'Do you have the cards with you now?'

'Yes, they're right in front of me.'

'Could you read me the messages?'

'They don't say very much.' I waited, and he said, 'Well, there's no reason not to read them. This is the first card. 'Dear Mom and Dad. Hope you haven't been worrying about me. Everything is fine. Am in New York and like the big city very much. School got to be too much of a hassle. Will explain everything when I see you.' 'His voice cracked a little on that line, but he coughed and went on. '"Please don't worry. Love, Wendy."'

'And the other card?'

'Hardly anything on it. "Dear Mom and Dad. Not bad, huh? I always thought Florida was strictly for wintertime, but it's great this time of year. See you soon. Love, Wendy."'

He asked me how things were going. I didn't really know how to answer the question. I said I had been very busy and was putting a lot of bits and pieces together but that I didn't know when I would have something to show him. 'Wendy was sharing her apartment with another girl for several months before Vanderpoel came on the scene.'

'Was the other girl a prostitute?'

'I don't know. I rather doubt it, but I'm not sure. I'm seeing her tomorrow. Evidently she was someone Wendy knew at college. Did she ever mention a friend named Marcia Maisel?'

'Maisel? I don't think so.'

'Do you know the names of any of her friends from college?'

'I don't believe I do. Let me think. I seem to recall that she would refer to them by first names, and they didn't stick in my mind.'

'It's probably unimportant. Does the name Cottrell mean anything to you?'

'Cottrell?' I spelled it, and he said it aloud again. 'No, it doesn't mean anything to me. Should it?'

'Wendy used a firm by that name as a job reference when she signed her apartment lease. The firm doesn't seem to exist.'

'Why did you think I would have heard of it?'

'Just a shot in the dark. I've been taking a lot of them lately, Mr Hanniford. Was Wendy a good cook?'

'Wendy? Not as far as I know. Of course she may have developed an interest in cooking at college. I wouldn't know about that. When she was living at home, I don't think she ever made anything more ambitious than a peanut-butter-and-jelly sandwich. Why?'

'No reason.'

His other phone rang, and he asked if there was anything else. I started to say that there wasn't and then thought of what I should have thought of at the beginning. 'The postcards,' I said.

'What about them?'

'What's on the other side?'

'The other side?'

'They're picture postcards, aren't they? Turn them over. I want to know what's on the other side.'

'I'll see. Grant's Tomb. Is that an important piece of the puzzle, Scudder?'

I ignored the sarcasm. 'That's New York,' I said. 'I'm more interested in the Miami one.'

'It's a hotel.'

'What hotel?'

'Oh, for Christ's sake. I didn't even think of it that way. It could mean something, couldn't it?'

'What hotel, Mr Hanniford?'

'The Eden Roc. Does that give you an important lead?'

It didn't.

I got the manager at the Eden Roc and told him I was a New York City police officer investigating a fraud case. I had him dig out his registration cards for the month of September 1970. I was on the phone for half an hour while he located the cards and went through them, looking for a registration in the name of either Hanniford or Cottrell. He came up empty.

I wasn't too surprised. Cottrell didn't have to be the man who took her to Miami. Even if he was, that didn't mean he would necessarily sign his real name on a registration card. It would have made life simpler if he had, but nothing about Wendy Hanniford's life and death had been simple so far, and I couldn't expect a sudden rush of simplicity now.

I poured another drink and decided to let the rest of the day spin itself out. I was trying to do too much, trying to sift all the sand in the desert. Pointless, because I was looking for answers to questions my client hadn't even asked. It didn't much matter who Richie Vanderpoel was, or why he had drawn red lines on Wendy. All Hanniford wanted was a hint of the life that lately she led. Mrs Gerald Thal, the former Miss Marcia Maisel, would provide as much tomorrow.

So until then I could take it easy. Look at the paper, drink my drink, wander over to Armstrong's when the walls of my room moved too close to one another.

Except that I couldn't. I made the drink last almost half an hour, then rinsed out the glass and put my coat on and caught the A train downtown.

When you hit a gay bar in the middle of a weekday afternoon you wonder why they don't call it something else. In the evenings, with a good crowd drinking and cruising, there is a very real gaiety in the air. It may seem forced, and you may sense an undercurrent of insufficiently quiet desperation, but gay then is about as good a word as any. But not around three or four on a Thursday afternoon, when the place is down to a handful of serious drinkers with no place else to go and a bartender whose face says he knows how bad things are and that he's stopped waiting for them to get better.

I made the rounds. A basement club on Bank Street where a man with long white hair and a waxed moustache played the bowling machine all by himself while his beer went flat. A big room on West Tenth, its ambience pitched for the old college athlete crowd, sawdust on the floor and Greek-letter pennants on the exposed brick walls. In all, half a dozen gay bars within a four-block radius of 194 Bethune Street.

I got stared at a lot. Was I a cop? Or a potential sexual partner? Or both?

I had the newspaper photo of Richie, and I showed it around a lot to whoever was willing to look at it. Almost everyone recognized the photo because they had seen it in the paper. The murder was recent, and it had happened right in the neighborhood, and heterosexuals have no monopoly on morbid curiosity.

So most of them recognized the picture, and quite a few had seen him in the neighborhood, or said they had, but nobody recalled seeing him around the bars.

'Of course I don't come here all that often,' I heard more than once. 'Just drop in now and then for a beer when the throat gets scratchy.'

In a place called Sinthia's the bartender recognized me and did an elaborate double take. 'Do my eyes deceive me? Or is it really the one and only Matthew Scudder?'

'Hello, Ken.'

'Now don't tell me you've finally converted, Matt. It was enough of a shock when I heard you left the pigpen. If Matthew Scudder's come around to the belief that Gay is Good, why, I'd be properly devastated.'

He still looked twenty-eight, and he must have been almost twice that. The blond hair was his own, even if the color came out of a bottle. When you got up close you could see the face-lift lines, but from a couple of yards away he didn't look a day older than when I'd booked him fifteen years ago for contributing to the delinquency of a minor. I hadn't taken much pride in the collar; the minor had been seventeen, and had already been more delinquent than Ken had ever hoped to be, but the minor had a father and the father filed a complaint and I had had to pick Kenny up. He got himself a decent lawyer, and the charges were dropped.

'You're looking good,' I told him.

'Booze and tobacco and lots of sex. It keeps a lad young.'

'Ever see this young lad?' I dropped the news photo on top of the bar. He looked at it, then gave it back.

'Interesting.'

'You recognize him?'

'It's the young chap who was so nasty last week, isn't it? Ghastly story.'

'Yes.'

'Where do you come in?'

'It's hard to say. Ever see him in here, Kenny?'

He planted his elbows on the bar and made a V of his hands, then tucked his chin between them. 'The reason I said it was interesting,' he said, 'is that I thought I recognized that picture when the *Post* ran it. I have an extraordinary memory for faces. Among other anatomical areas.'

'You've seen him before.'

'I *thought* so, and now I find myself certain of it. Why don't you buy us each a drink while I comb my memory?'

I put a bill on the bar. He poured bourbon for me and mixed something orange for himself. He said, 'I'm not stalling, Matthew. I am trying to recall what went with the face. I know I haven't seen it in a long time.'

'How long?'

'At least a year.' He sipped at his drink, straightened up, clasped his hands behind his neck, closed his eyes. 'A year at the very least. I remember him now. Very attractive. And *very* young. I asked him for ID the first time he came in, and he didn't seem surprised, as if he always got asked for proof of age.'

'He was only nineteen then.'

'Well, he could have passed for a ripe sixteen. There was a period of a couple of weeks when he was in here almost every night. Then I never saw him again.'

'I gather he was gay.'

'Well, he wouldn't have come here to pick up girls, would he?'

'He could have been window shopping.'

'Too true. We do get our fair share of those, don't we? Not Richie, though. He wasn't much of a drinker, you know. He'd order a vodka Collins and make it last until all the ice had melted.'

'Not a very profitable customer.'

'Oh, when they're young and gorgeous you don't care whether they spend much. They're window dressing, you know. They bring others in. From window shopping to window dressing, and no, our lad was not just looking, thank you. I don't think there was a night he came here that he didn't let someone take him home.'

He moved to the other end of the bar to replenish someone's drink. When he returned I asked him if he had ever taken Vanderpoel home himself.

'Matthew, honey, if I had, I wouldn't have had that much trouble remembering him, would I now?'

'You might.'

'*Bitch*! No, I was going through a very monogamous period at the time. Don't raise your brows so skeptically, luv. It doesn't become you. I suppose I might have been tempted, but cute as he was, he was not my type.'

'I would have thought he'd be just your type.'

'Oh, you don't know me as well as you think you do, do you,

Matthew? I like a bit of chicken now and then, I'll admit it. God knows it's not the world's best-kept secret in the first place. But it's not just youth that does it for me, you know. It's corrupt youth.'

'Oh?'

'That luscious air of immature decadence. Young fruit rotting on the vines.'

'You have a lovely way of putting things.'

'Don't I? But Richard was not like that at all. He had this untouchable innocence. You could be his eighth trick of the night, and you would still feel that you were seducing a virgin. And that, dear boy, is not my scene at all, as the children say.'

He made himself a fresh drink and collected for it out of my change. I still had enough bourbon left. I said, 'You said something about the eighth trick of the night. Was he selling himself?'

'No way. He didn't get the chance to pay for his own drinks, but if he had one drink a night, it was a lot. He wasn't hustling a buck.'

'Was he running the numbers?'

'No, one partner a night was all he seemed to want. As far as I could tell.'

'And then he stopped coming in here. I wonder why.'

'Maybe he got allergic to the decor.'

'Was there anyone in particular he tended to go home with?'

Ken shook his head. 'Never the same friend twice. I would guess that he came around over a period of three weeks, and maybe he paid us fifteen or eighteen visits in all, and I never saw him repeat. That's not terribly unusual, you know. A lot of people are hung up on variety. Especially the young ones.'

'He started living with Wendy Hanniford around the time he stopped coming here.'

'I gathered he was living with her. I wouldn't know about the time element.'

'Why would he live with a woman, Ken?'

'I didn't really know him, Matt. And I'm not a psychiatrist. I *had* a psychiatrist, but that wasn't one of the topics we got around to discussing.'

'Why would any homosexual live with a woman?'

'God knows.'

'Seriously, Kenny.'

He drummed the bar with his fingers. 'Seriously? All right. He

66

could be bisexual, you know. It's not exactly unheard of, especially in this day and age. Everybody's doing it, I understand. Straight types are trying the gay scene on for size. Gay types are making tentative experiments with heterosexuality.' He yawned elaborately. 'I'm afraid I'm a hopelessly reactionary old thing myself. One sex is complicated enough for me. Two would be disastrous.'

'Any other ideas?'

'Not really. If I'd *known* him, Matt. But he was just another pretty face to me.'

'Who knew him?'

'Does anyone know anyone? I suppose whoever took him to bed came closest to knowing him.'

'Who took him to bed?'

'I'm not a scorekeeper, darling. And we've had quite the turnover here these past few months. Most of the old crowd has gone off in search of greener pastures. We're getting a lot of smarmy little leather boys lately.' He frowned at the thought, then remembered that frowning gives you lines and willed his face to return to its normal expression. 'I don't much adore the crew we've been attracting lately. Motorcycle boys, S-and-M types. I don't really want anyone killed in my bar, you know. Most especially my estimable self.'

'Why not do something about it?'

'To be horribly candid, they scare me.'

I finished my drink. 'There's an easy way for you to handle it.'

'Do tell.'

'Go over to the Sixth Precinct and talk to Lieutenant Edward Koehler. Tell him your problem and ask him to raid you a few times.'

'You've got to be kidding.'

'Think about it. Slip Koehler a couple of bucks. Fifty should do it. He'll arrange to raid you a few times and give your leather crowd a hard time. There won't be any charges against you, so it won't screw you up with the SLA. Your liquor license won't be in jeopardy. The motorcycle boys are like everybody else. They can't afford hassles. They'll find some other house to haunt. Of course your business will fall off for a couple of weeks.'

'It's off, anyway. The little cunts are all beer drinkers, and they don't leave tips.'

'So you won't be losing much. Then in a month or so you'll start getting the kind of clientele you want.'

67

'What a devious mind you have, Matthew. I think it might work, at that.'

'It should. And don't give me too much credit. It's done all the time.'

'You say fifty dollars should do it?'

'It ought to. It would have when I was on the force, but everything's been going up lately, even bribery. If Koehler wants more, he'll let you know about it.'

'I don't doubt it. Well, it's not as if I never gave money to New York's Finest. They come around every Friday to collect, and you wouldn't believe what Christmas cost me.'

'Yes, I would.'

'But I never gave them money in the hope of anything beyond being allowed to remain in business. I didn't realize you could ask favors in return.'

'It's a free-enterprise system.'

'So it seems. I just might try it, and I'll buy you a drink on the strength of it.'

He poured a generous shot into my glass. I picked it up and eyed him over the top of it. 'There's something else you could do for me,' I said.

'Oh?'

'Ask around a little about Richie Vanderpoel. I know you don't want to give me any names. That's reasonable. But see if you can find out what he was like. I'd appreciate it.'

'Don't expect much.'

'I won't.'

He ran his fingers through his beautiful blond hair. 'Do you really *care* what he was like, Matt?'

'Yes,' I said. 'Evidently I do.'

Maybe it was a reaction to too many visits to bars that were gay in name alone. I'm not sure, but on my way to the subway I stopped at an outdoor phone booth and looked up a number in my notebook. I dropped in a dime and dialed it, and when she answered I said, 'Elaine? Matt Scudder.'

'Oh, hi, Matt. How's it going?'

'Not too bad. I was wondering if you felt like company.'

'I'd love to see you. Give me a half hour? I was just getting into the shower.'

'Sure.'

I had coffee and a roll and read the *Post*. The new mayor was having trouble appointing a deputy mayor. His investigative board kept discovering that his prospective appointees were corrupt in any of several uninteresting ways. There was an obvious answer, and he would probably hit on it sooner or later. He was going to have to get rid of the investigative board.

Some more citizens had killed each other since yesterday's edition went to press. Two off-duty patrolmen had had a few drinks in a bar in Woodside and shot each other with their service revolvers. One was dead, the other in critical condition. A man and woman who had served ninety days each for child abuse had sued successfully to regain custody of the child from the foster parents who had had the kid for three and a half years. The nude torso of an adolescent boy had been discovered on a tenement roof on East Fifth Street. Someone had carved an X into the chest, presumably the same person who had removed the arms and legs and head.

I left the newspaper on the table and got a cab.

She lived in a good building on Fifty-first between First and Second. The doorman confirmed that I was expected and nodded me toward the elevator. She was waiting at the door for me, wearing royal-blue hip-huggers and a lime-green blouse. She had gold hoop earrings in her ears and she smelled of a rich, musky perfume.

I draped my coat over an Eames chair while she closed the door and fastened the bolt. She came into my arms for an open-mouthed kiss and rubbed her little body against me. 'Mmmm,' she said. 'That's nice.'

'You're looking good, Elaine.'

'Let me look at you. You don't look so bad yourself, in a rugged, rough-hewn sort of a way. How've you been?'

'Pretty good.'

'Keeping busy?'

'Uh-huh.'

There was chamber music stacked on her stereo. The last record was just ending, and I sat on the couch and watched as she walked to the turntable and inverted the stack of records. I wondered whether the hip wiggle was for my benefit or if it came naturally to her. I had always wondered that.

I liked the room. White wall-to-wall shag carpet, stark modern furniture more comfortable than it looked, a lot of primary colors and chrome. A couple of abstract oils on the walls. I couldn't have lived in a room like that, but I enjoyed spending occasional time in it.

'Drink?'

'Not just now.'

She sat on the couch next to me and talked about books she had read and movies she had seen. She was very good at small talk. I suppose she had to be.

We kissed a few times, and I touched her breasts and put a hand on her round bottom. She made a purring sound.

'Want to come to bed, Matt?'

'Sure.'

The bedroom was small, with a more subdued color scheme. She turned on a small stained-glass lamp and killed the overhead light. We got undressed and lay down on the queen-size bed.

She was warm and young and eager, with soft, perfumed skin and a tautly muscled body. Her hands and mouth were clever. But it was not working, and after a few minutes I moved away from her and patted her gently on the shoulder.

'Relax, honey.'

'No, it's not going to work,' I said.

'Something I should be doing?'

I shook my head.

'Too much to drink?'

It wasn't that. I was far too completely locked into my own head. 'Maybe,' I said.

'It happens.'

'Or maybe it's the wrong time of the month for me.'

She laughed. 'Right, you got your period.'

'Must be.'

We put our clothes on. I got three tens from my wallet and put them on the dresser. As usual, she pretended not to notice.

'Want that drink now?'

'Uh-huh, I guess. Bourbon, if you have it.'

She didn't. She had Scotch, and I settled for that. She poured herself a glass of milk, and we sat on the couch together and listened to the music without saying anything for a while. I felt as relaxed as if we had made love.

'Working these days, Matt?'

'Uh-huh.'

'Well, everybody has to work.'

'Uh-huh.'

She shook a cigarette out of her pack, and I lit it for her. 'You got things on your mind,' she said. 'That's what's the matter.'

'You're probably right.'

'I know I'm right. Want to talk about anything?'

'Not really.'

'Okay.'

The telephone rang, and she answered it in the bedroom. When she came back I asked her if she had ever lived with a man.

'You mean like a pimp? Never have and never will.'

'I meant like a boyfriend.'

'Never. It's a funny thing about boyfriends in this business. They always turn out to be pimps.'

'Really?'

'Uh-huh. I've known so many girls. 'Oh, he's not a pimp, he's my boyfriend.' But it always turns out that he's between jobs, and that he makes a life's work out of being between jobs, and she pays for everything. But he's not a pimp, just a boyfriend. They're very good at kidding themselves, those girls. I'm lousy at kidding myself. So I don't even try.'

'Good for you.'

'I can't afford boyfriends. Busy saving for my old age.'

'Real estate, right?'

'Uh-huh. Apartment houses in Queens. You can keep the stock market. I want something I can reach out and touch.'

'You're a landlady. That's funny.'

'Oh, I never see tenants or anything. There's a company manages it for me.'

I wondered if it was Bowdoin Management but didn't bother asking. She asked if I wanted to try the bedroom again. I said I didn't.

'Not to rush you, but I'm expecting a friend in about forty minutes.'

'Sure.'

'Have another drink if you want.'

'No, it's time I was on my way.' She walked me to the door and held my coat for me. I kissed her goodbye.

'Don't be so long between visits next time.'

'Take care, Elaine.'

'Oh, I will.'

TEN

Friday morning came clear and crisp. I picked up an Olin rental car on Broadway and took the East Side Drive out of town. The car was a Chevrolet Malibu, a skittish little thing that had to be pampered on curves. I suppose it was economical to run.

I caught the New England Expressway up through Pelham and Larchmont and into Mamaroneck. At an Exxon station the kid who topped up the tank didn't know where Schuyler Boulevard was. He went inside and asked the boss, who came out and gave me directions. The boss also knew the Carioca, and I had the Malibu parked in the restaurant's lot at twenty-five minutes of twelve. I went into the cocktail lounge and sat on a vinyl stool at the front end of a black Formica bar. I ordered a cup of black coffee with a shot of bourbon in it. The coffee was bitter, left over from the night before.

The cup was still half full when I looked over and saw her standing hesitantly in the archway between the dining room and the cocktail lounge. If I hadn't known she was Wendy Hanniford's age, I would have guessed high by three or four years. Dark, shoulder-length hair framed an oval face. She wore dark plaid slacks and a pearl-gray sweater beneath which her large breasts were aggressively prominent. She had a large brown leather handbag over her shoulder and a cigarette in her right hand. She did not look happy to see me.

I let her come to me, and after a moment's hesitation she did. I turned slowly to her.

'Mr Scudder?'

'Mrs Thal? Should we take a table?'

'I suppose so.'

The dining room was uncrowded, and the head waitress showed us to a table in back and out of the way. It was an overdecorated room, a room that tried too hard, done in someone's idea of a flamenco motif. The color scheme involved a lot of red and black and ice blue. I had left my bitter coffee at the bar and now ordered bourbon with water back. I asked Marcia Thal if she wanted a drink.

'No, thank you. Wait a minute. Yes, I think I will have something. Why shouldn't I?'

'No reason that I know of.'

She looked past me at the waitress and ordered a whiskey sour on the rocks. Her eyes met mine, glanced away, came back again.

'I can't say I'm happy to be here,' she said.

'Neither am I.'

'It was your idea. And you had me over a barrel, didn't you? You must get a kick out of making people do what you want them to do.'

'I used to pull wings off flies.'

'I wouldn't be surprised.' She tried to glare, and then she lost the handle of it and grinned in spite of herself. 'Oh, shit,' she said.

'You're not going to be dragged into anything, Mrs Thal.'

'I hope not.'

'You won't be. I'm interested in learning something about Wendy Hanniford's life. I'm not interested in turning your life upside down.'

Our drinks arrived. She picked hers up and studied it as if she had never seen anything quite like it before. It seemed an ordinary enough whiskey sour. She took a sip, set it down, fished out the maraschino cherry and ate it. I swallowed a little bourbon and waited for her.

'You can order something to eat if you want. I'm not hungry.'

'Neither am I.'

'I don't know where to start. I really don't.'

I wasn't sure myself. I said, 'Wendy doesn't seem to have had a job. Was she working when you first moved in with her?'

'No. But I didn't know that.'

'She told you she had a job?'

She nodded. 'But she was always very vague about it. I didn't pay too much attention, to tell you the truth. I was mainly interested in Wendy to the extent that she had an apartment I could share for a hundred dollars a month.'

'That's all she charged you?'

'Yes. At the time she told me the apartment was two hundred a month and we were splitting it down the middle. I never saw the lease or anything, and I sort of assumed that I was paying a little

73

more than half. That was all right with me. It was her furniture and everything, and it was such a bargain for me. Before that I was at the Evangeline House. Do you know what that is?'

'On West Thirteenth?'

'That's right. Somebody recommended it to me, it's a residence for proper young ladies on their own in the big city.' She made a face. 'They had curfews and things like that. It was really pretty ridiculous, and I was sharing a small room with a girl, she was some kind of a Southern Baptist and she was praying all the time, and you couldn't have male visitors, and it was all pretty lame. And it cost me almost as much as it cost to share the apartment with Wendy. So if she was making a little money on me, that was fine. It wasn't until quite a bit later that I found out the apartment was renting for a lot more than two hundred a month.'

'And she wasn't working.'

'No.'

'Did you wonder where her money came from?'

'Not for a while. I gradually managed to realize that she never seemed to have to go to the office, and when I said something, she admitted she was between jobs at the moment. She said she had enough money so that she didn't care if she didn't find anything for a month or two. What I didn't realize was that she wasn't even looking for work. I would come home from my own job, and she would say something about employment agencies and job interviews, and I would have no way of knowing that she hadn't even been looking.'

'Was she a prostitute at the time?'

'I don't know if you would call it that.'

'How do you mean?'

'She was taking money from men. I guess she had been doing that for as long as she was in the apartment. But I don't know if she was exactly a prostitute.'

'How did you first figure out what was going on?'

She picked up her drink and took another sip of it. She put the glass down and worried her forehead with her fingertips. 'It was gradual,' she said.

I waited.

'She was dating a lot. Older men, but that didn't surprise me. And usually, uh, well, she and her date would go to bed.' She lowered her eyes. 'I wasn't snooping, but it was impossible not to notice this. The apartment, she had the bedroom and I had the living room, there was a convertible sofa in the living room –'

'I've seen the apartment.'

'Then you know the layout. You have to go through the living room to get into the bedroom, so if I was home, she would bring her date through my room and into the bedroom, and they would be in there for half an hour or an hour, and then either Wendy would walk him to the door or he would go out by himself.'

'Did this bother you?'

'That she was having sex with them? No, it didn't bother me. Why would it bother me?'

'I don't know.'

'One of the reasons I moved out of Evangeline House was to live like an adult. I wasn't a virgin myself. And the fact that Wendy brought men to the apartment meant I could feel free to bring men home myself if I wanted to.'

'Did you?'

She colored. 'I wasn't seeing anyone special at the time.'

'So you knew Wendy was promiscuous, but you didn't know she was taking money.'

'Not at the time, no.'

'She was seeing a great many different men?'

'I don't know. I saw the same men over again on several occasions, especially at first. A lot of the time I didn't meet the men she was with. I spent a lot of the time away from the apartment. Or I would come home when she was already in the bedroom with someone, and I might go out for a drink or something and come back after he had left.'

I studied her, and she averted her eyes. I said, 'You suspected something almost from the beginning, didn't you?'

'I don't know what you mean.'

'There was something about the men.'

'I suppose so.'

'What was it? What were the men like?'

'Older, of course, but that didn't surprise me. Also, they were all well dressed. They looked like, oh, I don't know. Businessmen, lawyers, professional men. And I just had the feeling that most of them were married. I couldn't tell you why I thought so, but I did. It's hard to explain.'

I ordered another round of drinks, and she started to loosen up. The picture began to fill in and take form. There were telephone calls which she answered when Wendy was out of the apartment, cryptic messages she had to relay. There was the drunk who showed up one night when Wendy wasn't home who told Marcia that she would do just fine and made a clumsy pass at her. She had managed to get rid of him, but still didn't realize that Wendy's male friends constituted a source of income to her.

'I thought she was a tramp,' she said. 'I'm not a moralist, Mr Scudder. During that time I was probably going overboard in the opposite direction. Not in terms of how I behaved, but how I felt about things. All those uptight virgins at Evangeline House, and the result was that I had sort of mixed feelings about Wendy.'

'How?'

'I thought what she was doing was probably a bad idea. That it would be bad for her emotionally. You know, ego damage, that kind of thing. Because down underneath she was always so innocent.'

'Innocent?'

She gnawed a fingernail. 'I don't know how to explain this. There was this little girl quality to her. I had the feeling that whatever kind of sex life she led she would still be a little girl underneath it all.' She thought for a moment, then shrugged. 'Anyway, I thought her behavior was basically self-destructive. I thought she was going to get hurt.'

'You don't mean physically injured.'

'No, I mean emotionally. And at the same time I have to say I envied her.'

'Because she was free?'

'Yes. She didn't seem to have any hang-ups. She was completely free of guilt as far as I could see. She did whatever she wanted to do. I envied that because I believed in that kind of freedom, or thought I did, and yet my own life didn't reflect it.' She grinned suddenly. 'I also envied her life because it was so much more exciting than mine. I had some dates but nothing very interesting, and the boys I went out with were around my own age and didn't have much money. Wendy was going out for dinners at places like Barbetta's and the Forum, and I was seeing the inside of a lot of Orange Julius's. So I couldn't help envying her a little.'

She excused herself and went to the ladies room. While she was gone I asked the waitress if there was any fresh coffee. She said there was, and I asked her to bring a couple of cups. I sat there waiting for Marcia Thal and wondering why Wendy had wanted a roommate in the first place, especially one who was ignorant of how she earned her keep. The hundred dollars a month seemed insufficient motive, and the inconvenience of functioning as a prostitute under the conditions Marcia had described would have greatly outweighed the small source of income Marcia represented.

She returned to the table just as the waitress was bringing the coffee. 'Thanks,' she said. 'I was just starting to feel those drinks. I can use this.'

'So can I. I've got a long drive back.'

She took a cigarette. I picked up a pack of matches and lit it for her. I asked how she had found out that Wendy was taking money for her favors.

'She told me.'

'Why?'

'Hell,' she said. She blew out smoke in a long, thin column. 'She just told me, okay? Let's leave it at that.'

'It's a lot easier if you just tell me everything, Marcia.'

'What makes you think there's anything more to tell?'

'What did she do, pass on one of her dates to you?'

Her eyes flared. She closed them briefly, drew on her cigarette. 'It was almost like that,' she said. 'Not quite, but that's pretty close. She told me a friend of hers had a business associate in from out of town and asked if I'd like to date the guy, to double with her and her friend. I said I didn't think so, and she talked about how we would see a good show and have a good dinner and everything. And then she said, "Be sensible, Marcia. You'll have a good time, and you'll make a few dollars out of it."'

'How did you react?'

'Well, I wasn't shocked. So I must have suspected all along that she was getting money. I asked her what she meant, which was a pretty stupid question at that point, and she said that the men she dated all had plenty of money, and they realized it was tough for a young woman to earn a decent living, and at the end of the evening they would generally give you something. I said something about wasn't that prostitution, and she said she never asked men for money, nothing like that, but they always gave her something. I wanted to ask how much but I didn't and then she told me anyway. She said they always gave at least twenty dollars and sometimes a man would give her as much as a hundred. The man she was going to be seeing always gave her fifty dollars, she said, so if I went along it would mean that his friend would be almost certain to give me fifty dollars, and she asked if I didn't think that was a good return on an evening that involved nothing but eating a great dinner and seeing a good show and then

77

spending a half hour or so in bed with a nice, dignified gentleman. That was her phrase. "A nice, dignified gentleman."'

'How did the date go?'

'What makes you so sure I went?'

'You did, didn't you?'

'I was earning eighty dollars a week. Nobody was taking me to great dinners or Broadway shows. And I hadn't even met anyone I wanted to sleep with.'

'Did you enjoy the evening?'

'No. All I could think about was that I was going to have to sleep with this man. And he was *old.*'

'How old?'

'I don't know. Fifty-five, sixty. I'm never good at guessing how old people are. He was too old for me, that's all I knew.'

'But you went along with it.'

'Yes. I had agreed to go, and I didn't want to spoil the party. Dinner was good, and my date was charming enough. I didn't pay much attention to the show. I couldn't. I was too anxious about the rest of the evening.' She paused, focused her eyes over my shoulder. 'Yes, I slept with him. And yes, he gave me fifty dollars. And yes, I took it.'

I drank some coffee.

'Aren't you going to ask me why I took the money?'

'Should I?'

'I wanted the damned money. And I wanted to know how it felt. Being a whore.'

'Did you feel that you were a whore?'

'Well, that's what I was, isn't it? I let a man fuck me, and I took money for it.'

I didn't say anything. After a few moments she said, 'Oh, the hell with it. I took a few more dates. Maybe one a week on the average. I don't know why. It wasn't the money. Not exactly. It was, I don't know. Call it an experiment. I wanted to know how I felt about it. I wanted to … learn certain things about myself.'

'What did you learn?'

'That I'm a little squarer than I thought. That I didn't care for the things I kept finding hiding in corners of my mind. That I wanted, oh, a cleaner life. That I wanted to fall in love with somebody. Get married, make babies, that whole trip. It turned out to be what I wanted. When I realized that, I knew I had to move out on my own. I couldn't go on rooming with Wendy.'

'How did she react?'

'She was very upset.' Her eyes widened at the recollection. 'I hadn't expected that. We weren't terribly close. At least I never thought we were terribly close. I never showed her the inside of my head, and she never showed me what was going on inside hers. We were together a lot, especially once I started taking dates, and we talked a great deal, but it was always about superficial things. I didn't think my presence was especially important to her. I told her I had to move out, and I told her why, and she was really shook. She actually begged me to stay.'

'That's interesting.'

'She told me she'd pay a larger share of the rent. That was when I found out she'd actually been paying twice as much as I was all along. I think she would have let me stay there rent-free if I wanted. And of course she insisted I didn't have to take any dates, that she wouldn't want me to do it if it was putting me uptight. She even suggested that she would limit her activities to times when I was at work – actually a lot of her dates were during the afternoon, businessmen who couldn't get away from their wives during the evening, which was one reason why it took me as long as it did to realize how she was making her living. She said evening dates would have to take her to a hotel or something, that the place would be just for us when I was around. But that wasn't it, I had to get away from the life entirely. Because it was too much of a temptation for me, see. I was making eighty dollars a week and working hard for it, and there was an enormous temptation to quit work, which is something I never did, but I recognized the temptation for what it was. And it scared me.'

'So you moved out.'

'Yes. Wendy cried when I packed my stuff and left. She kept saying she didn't know what she would do without me. I told her she could get another roommate without any trouble, someone who would fit in with her life better. She said she didn't want anyone who fit in too well because she was more than one kind of person. I didn't know what she meant at the time.'

'Do you know now?'

'I think so. I think she wanted someone who was a little straighter than she was, someone who was not a part of the sexual scene she was involved in. I think now that she was a little disappointed when I took that first double date with her. She did her best to talk me into it, but she was disappointed that she was successful. Do you know what I mean?'

'I think so. It fits in with some other things.' There was something she had said earlier that had been bothering me, and I poked around in my memory, looking for it. 'You said you weren't surprised that she was seeing older men.'

'No, that didn't surprise me.'

'Why not?'

'Well, because of what happened at school.'

'What happened at school?'

She frowned. She didn't say anything, and I repeated the question.

'I don't want to get anybody in trouble.'

'She was involved with someone at school? An older man?'

'You have to remember I didn't know her very well. I knew who she was to say hello to, and maybe I was in a class or two with her at one time or another, but I barely knew her.'

'Was it tied in with her leaving school just a few months shy of graduation?'

'I don't really know that much about it.'

I said, 'Marcia, look at me. Anything you tell me about what happened at college will be something I would otherwise find out, anyway. You'll just save me a great deal of time and travel. I'd rather not have to make a trip out to Indiana to ask a lot of people some embarrassing questions. I –'

'Oh, don't do that!'

'I'd rather not. But it's up to you.'

She told it in bits and pieces, largely because she didn't know too much of it. There had been a scandal shortly before Wendy's departure from campus. It seemed that she had been having an affair with a professor of art history, a middle-aged man with children Wendy's age or older. The man had wanted to leave his wife and marry Wendy, the wife had swallowed a handful of sleeping pills, was rushed to the hospital, had her stomach pumped, and survived. In the course of the ensuing debacle, Wendy packed a suitcase and disappeared.

And according to campus gossip this was not the first time she had been involved with an older man. Her name had been linked with several professors, all of them considerably older than she was.

'I'm sure a lot of it was just talk,' Marcia Thal told me. 'I don't think she could have had affairs with that many men without more people knowing about it, but when the whole thing blew

80

up, people were really talking about her. I guess some of it must have been true.'

'Then you knew when you first roomed with her that she was unconventional.'

'I told you. I didn't care about her morals. I didn't see anything wrong with sleeping with a lot of men. Not if that was what she wanted to do.' She considered this for a moment. 'I guess I've changed since then.'

'This professor, the art historian. What was his name?'

'I'm not going to tell you his name. It's not important. Maybe you can find out yourself. I'm sure you can, but *I'm* not going to tell you.'

'Was it Cottrell?'

'No. Why?'

'Did she know anyone named Cottrell? In New York?'

'I don't think so. The name doesn't ring a bell or anything.'

'Was there anyone she was seeing regularly? More than the others?'

'Not really. Of course she could have had someone who came over a lot during the afternoons and I wouldn't have known it.'

'How much money do you suppose she was making?'

'I don't know. That wasn't really something we talked about. I suppose her average price was thirty dollars. On the average. No more than that. A lot of men gave twenty. She talked about men who would give her a hundred, but I think they were pretty rare.'

'How many tricks a week do you think she turned?'

'I honestly don't know. Maybe she had someone over three nights a week, maybe four nights a week. But she was also seeing people in the daytime. She wasn't trying to make a fortune, just enough to live the way she wanted to live. A lot of the time she would turn down dates. She never saw more than one person a night. It wasn't always a full date with dinner and everything. Sometimes a man would just come over, and she would go straight to bed with him. But she turned down a lot of dates, and if she went with a man and she didn't like him she wouldn't see him again. Also, when she was seeing someone she had never met before, if she didn't like him she wouldn't go to bed with him, and then of course he wouldn't give her any money. There would be men who would get her number from other men, see, and she would go out with them, but if they weren't her type or something, well, she'd say she had a headache and go home. She wasn't trying to make a million dollars.'

'So she must have earned a couple hundred dollars a week.'

'That sounds about right. It was a fortune compared to what I was earning, but in the long run it wasn't a tremendous amount of money. I don't think she did it for the money, if you know what I mean.'

'I'm not sure I do.'

'I think she was, you know, a happy hooker?' She flushed as she said the phrase. 'I think she enjoyed what she was doing. I really do. The life and the men and everything, I think she got a kick out of it.'

I had obtained more from Marcia Thal than I'd expected. Maybe it was as much as I needed.

You have to know when to stop. You can never find out everything, but you can almost always find out more than you already know, and there is a point at which the additional data you discover is irrelevant and time you spend on it wasted.

I could fly out to Indiana. I would learn more, certainly. But when I was done I didn't think I would necessarily know more than I did now. I could fill in names and dates. I could talk to people who had memories of their own of Wendy Hanniford. But what would I get for my client?

I signaled for the check. While the waitress was adding things up, I thought of Cale Hanniford and asked Marcia Thal if Wendy had spoken often of her parents.

'Sometimes she talked about her father.'

'What did she say about him?'

'Oh, wondering what he was like.'

'She felt she didn't know him?'

'Well, of course not. I mean, I gather he died before she was born, or just about. How could she have known him?'

'I meant her stepfather.'

'Oh. No, she never talked about him that I remember, except to say vaguely that she ought to write them and let them know everything was all right. She said that several times, so I got the impression it was something she kept not getting around to.'

I nodded. 'What did she say about her father?'

'I don't remember, except I guess she idolized him a lot. One time I remember we were talking about Vietnam, and she said something about how whether the war was bad or not, the men who were fighting it were still good men, and she talked about how her father was killed in Korea. And one time she said, 'If he had lived, I guess everything would be different.'

'Different how?'

'She didn't say.'

ELEVEN

I gave the car back to the Olin people a little after two. I stopped for a sandwich and a piece of pie and went through my notebook, trying to find a way that everything would connect with everything else.

Wendy Hanniford. She had a thing for older men, and if you wanted to you could run a trace on it all the way back to unresolved feelings for the father she never saw. At college she realized her own power and had affairs with professors. Then one of them fell too hard for her and a wheel came off, and by the time it was over she was out of school and on her own in New York.

There were plenty of older men in New York. One of them took her to Miami Beach. The same one, or another, provided her with a job reference when she rented her apartment. And all along the line there must have been plenty of older men to take her to dinner, to slip her twenty dollars for taxi fare, to leave twenty or thirty or fifty dollars on the bureau.

She had never needed a roommate. She had subsidized Marcia Maisel, asking considerably less than half the rent. It was likely she had subsidized Richie Vanderpoel as well, and it was just as likely she had taken him as a roommate for the same reason she'd taken Marcia in, the same reason she had wanted Marcia to stick around.

Because it was a lonely world, and she had always lived alone in it with only her father's ghost for company. The men she got, the men she was drawn to, were men who belonged to other women and who went home to them when they were through with her. She wanted someone in that Bethune Street apartment who didn't want to take her to bed. Someone who would just be good company. First Marcia – and hadn't Wendy perhaps been a little disappointed when Marcia agreed to go along on dates with her? I guessed that she had, because at the same time that she

84

gained a companion on dates she lost a companion who had been not of that brittle world but of a piece with the innocence Marcia had sensed in Wendy herself.

Then Richie, who had probably made an even better companion. Richie, a timid and reticent homosexual, who had improved the decor and cooked the gourmet meals and made a home for her while he kept his clothes in the living room and spent his nights on the convertible couch. And she in turn had provided Richie with a home. She'd given him a woman's companionship without posing the sexual challenge another woman might have constituted. He moved in with her and out of the gay bars.

I paid the check and left, heading down Broadway and back to the hotel. A panhandler, red-eyed and ragged, blocked my path. He wanted to know if I had any spare change. I shook my head and kept walking at him, and he scuttled out of the way. He looked as though he wanted to tell me to fuck myself if only he had the nerve.

How much deeper did I want to go with it? I could fly to Indiana and make a nuisance of myself on the campus where Wendy had learned to define her role in life. I could easily enough learn the name of the professor whose affair with her had had such dramatic results. I could find that professor, whether he was still at that school or not. He would talk to me. I could make him talk to me. I could track down other professors who had slept with her, other students who had known her.

But what could they tell me that I didn't know? I was not writing her biography. I was trying to capture enough of the essence of her so that I could go to Cale Hanniford and tell him who she was and how she got that way. I probably had enough to do a fair job of that already. I wouldn't find out much more in Indiana.

There was only one problem. In a very real sense, my arrangement with Hanniford was more than a dodge around the detective licensing laws and the income tax. The money he gave me was a gift, just as the money I'd give Koehler and Pankow and the postal clerk had been. And in return I was doing him a favor, just as they had done me favors. I was not working for him.

So I couldn't call it quits just because I had the answers to Cale Hanniford's questions. I had a question or two of my own, and I didn't have all the answers nailed down yet. I had most of it, or thought I did, but there were still a few blank spaces and I wanted to fill them in.

*

Vincent was at the desk when I walked in. He had given me a hard time awhile back, and he still wasn't sure how I felt about him. I'd just given him a ten for Christmas, which should have clued him in that I harbored no ill feelings, but he still had a tendency to cringe when I approached. He cringed a little now, then handed me my room key and a slip of paper that informed me Kenny had called. There was a number where I could reach him.

I called it from my room. 'Ah, Matthew,' he said. 'How nice of you to call.'

'What's the problem?'

'There is no problem. I'm just busy enjoying a day off. It was that or go to jail, and I'm none too fond of jails. I'm sure they would bring back unpleasant memories.'

'I don't follow you.'

'Am I being terribly oblique? I talked to the good Lieutenant Koehler, just as you suggested. Sinthia's is scheduled to be raided sometime this evening. Forewarned is forearmed, to coin a phrase, so I took the precaution of engaging one of my bartenders to mind the store this afternoon and evening.'

'Does he know what's coming?'

'I'm not diabolical, Matthew. He knows he'll be locked up. He also knows that he'll be bailed out in nothing flat and charges will be dropped in short order. And he knows he'll be fifty dollars richer for the experience. Personally, I wouldn't suffer the indignity of an arrest for ten times that sum, but different strokes for different folks, to coin another phrase. Your Lieutenant Koehler was most cooperative, I might add, except he wanted a hundred dollars instead of the fifty you suggested. I don't suppose I ought to have tried bargaining with him?'

'Probably not.'

'That's what I thought. Well, if it works out, the price is a pittance. I hope you don't mind that I mentioned your name?'

'Not at all.'

'It seemed to afford me a certain degree of entrée. But it leaves me owing you a favor, and I'm delighted to be able to discharge my obligation forthwith.'

'You got a line on Richie Vanderpoel?'

'I did indeed. I devoted quite a few hours to asking pertinent questions at an after-hours place. The one on Houston Street?'

'I don't know it.'

'Quite my favorite blind pig. I'll take you there some night if you'd like.'

'We'll see. What did you find out?'

'Ah, let me see. What *did* I find out? I talked to three gentlemen who were willing to remember taking our bright-eyed boy home for milk and cookies. I also talked to a few others who I would happily swear did the same, but their memories were clouded, sad to say. It seems I was quite right in thinking that he hadn't been hustling a buck. He never asked anyone for money, and one chap said he'd tried to press a few bob on Richie for cabfare home and the lad wouldn't take it. Sterling character, wouldn't you say?'

'I would.'

'And all too rare in this day and age. That's it in the hard-fact department. The rest is impressions, but I gather that's what you're most interested in.'

'Yes.'

'Well, it seems Richard wasn't terribly sexy.'

'Huh?'

He sighed. 'The dear boy didn't like it much and wasn't terribly good at it. I gather it wasn't just a matter of nerves, although he does seem to have been a nervous and apprehensive sort. It was more a matter of being uncomfortable with the whole thing and getting blessed little pleasure out of sex itself. And he retreated from intimacy. He'd perform the dirty deed willingly enough, but he didn't want to have his hand held or his shoulder stroked. That's not unheard of, you know. There's a species of faggot that craves the sex but can't stand the closeness. All their friends are doomed to stay strangers. But he didn't seem to enjoy the sex all that much, either.'

'Interesting.'

'I thought you'd say so. Also, once it was over, Richie was ever so anxious to be on his way. Not the sort to stay the night. Didn't even care to linger for coffee and brandy. Just wham-bam-thank-you-sir. And no interest in a repeat performance at a later date. One chap really wanted to see the boy again, not because the sex was good, as it wasn't, but because he was intrigued. Thought he might pierce that grim exterior given another opportunity. Richie would have none of it. Didn't even want to speak to anyone once he'd shared a pillow with him.'

'These three men –'

'No names, Matthew. I has me code of ethics, I does.'

'I'm not interested in their names. I just wondered if they ran to type.'

'In what way?'

'Age. Are they all about the same age?'

'More or less.'

'All fifty or more?'

'How did you know?'

'Just a guess.'

'Well, it's a good one. I'd place them all between fifty or sixty. And they look their years, poor devils, unlike those of us who have bathed in the fountain of youth.'

'It all fits.'

'How?'

'Too complicated to explain.'

'Meaning bugger off? *I* don't mind. The mere satisfaction of knowing I've been helpful, Matthew, is reward enough for me. It's not as though I'd want a story to tell my grandchildren in my old age.'

TWELVE

Eddie Koehler was away from his desk. I left a message for him to call me back, then went downstairs and picked up a paper at the newsstand in the lobby. I had worked my way through to Dear Abby when the phone rang.

He thanked me for sending Kenny to him, his voice wary as he did so. I wasn't on the force, and he shouldn't have to kick any of it back to me.

I set his mind at rest. 'You could do me a little favor in return. You can find someone to make a few phone calls or look in the right books. I could probably do it myself, but it would take me three times as long.'

I spelled it out for him. It was an easy way for him to balance the books with me, and he was glad to grab it. He said he'd get back to me, and I told him I'd hang around and wait for his call.

It came almost exactly an hour later. J. J. Cottrell, Inc., had had offices in the Kleinhans Building at William and Pine. The firm had published a Wall Street tip sheet for about a dozen years, going out of business at the time of the proprietor's death. The proprietor had been one Arnold P. Leverett, and he'd died two and a half years ago. There had been no one named Cottrell connected with the firm.

I thanked him and rang off. That rounded things out neatly enough. I hadn't been able to find a Cottrell because there had never been one in the first place. It was reasonable to assume that Leverett had played some sort of role in Wendy Hanniford's life, but whether it had been a large or a small role was now no longer material. The man couldn't be reached for comment without the services of a medium.

For the hell of it I put through a call to the Eden Roc and got the manager again. He remembered me. I asked him if he could check the same register for Leverett, and it didn't take him as long this time because he knew right away where to find the records. Not too surprisingly, his records indicated that Mr and Mrs Arnold P. Leverett had been guests of the Eden Roc from the fourteenth to the twentieth of September.

So I had the name of one of the men in her life. If Leverett had left a widow, I could go and annoy her, but it would be hard to think up a less purposeful act. What I'd really accomplished was more negative than positive. I could now forget about tracing the man who had taken her to Florida, and I could quit wondering who in hell J. J. Cottrell was. He wasn't a person, he was a corporation, and he was out of business.

I went around the corner to Armstrong's and sat at the bar. It had already been a long day, and the drive to Mamaroneck and back had tired me more than I realized. I figured on spending the rest of the night on that barstool, balancing coffee and bourbon until it was late enough to go back to my room and go to sleep.

It didn't work out that way. After two drinks I thought of something to do and couldn't talk myself out of doing it. It looked to be a waste of time, but everything was a waste of time, one way or another, and evidently something in me demanded that I waste my time in this particular fashion.

And it wasn't such a waste after all.

I caught a cab on Ninth and listened to the driver bitch about the price of gasoline. It was all a conspiracy, he said, and he explained just how it was structured. The big oil companies were all owned by Zionists and by cutting off the oil they would turn public opinion in favor of the United States teaming up with Israel to seize the oil-rich Arab territory. He even found a way to tie it all in with the assassination of Kennedy. I forget which Kennedy.

'It's my own theory,' he said. 'Whaddaya think of it?'

'It's a theory.'

'Makes sense, doesn't it?'

'I don't know that much about the subject.'

'Yeah, sure. That's the American public for you. Nobody knows from nothing. Nobody cares. Take a poll on a subject, any subject, and half the people got no opinion. No opinion! That's why the country's going to hell.'

'I figured there was a reason.'

He let me out in front of the library at Forty-second and Fifth. I walked between the stone lions and up the stairs to the Microfilm Room. I checked my notebook for the date of Arnold

P. Leverett's death and filled out a slip. A sad-eyed girl in jeans and a plaid blouse brought me the appropriate spool of film.

I threaded it into the scanner and started going through it. It's almost impossible to go through old issues of the *Times* on microfilm without getting sidetracked. Other stories catch your eye and waste your time. But I forced myself to locate the proper obituary page and read the article on Arnold Philip Leverett.

He didn't warrant much space. Four paragraphs, and nothing tremendously exciting in any of them. He had died of a heart attack at his home in Port Washington. He had left a wife and three children. He had gone to various schools and worked for various stockbrokers before leaving in 1959 to start his own Wall Street newsletter, *Cottrell's Weekly Analyzer*. He had been fifty-eight years old at the time of his death. The last fact was the only one that could possibly be considered pertinent, and it only confirmed what I had already taken pretty much for granted.

I wonder what makes people think of things. Maybe some other story caught the corner of my eye and jogged something loose in my mind. I don't know what did it, and I wasn't even aware of it until I had already left the Microfilm Room and gone halfway down the stairs. Then I turned around and went back where I'd come from and got the *Times Index* for 1959.

That was the year Leverett started his tip sheet, so maybe that was what had triggered it. I looked through the *Index* and established that it was also the year in which Mrs Martin Vanderpoel died.

I hadn't really expected to find an obituary. She had been a clergyman's wife, but he wasn't all that prominent, a minister with a small congregation out in the wilds of Brooklyn. I'd been looking for nothing more than a death notice, but there was a regular *Times* obit, and when I had the right spool in the scanner and ran down the page with her obituary on it, I knew why they'd thought she was worth the space.

Mrs Martin Vanderpoel, the former Miss Frances Elizabeth Hegermann, had committed suicide. She had done so in the bathroom of the rectory of the First Reformed Church of Bay Ridge. She had slashed her wrists, and she had been discovered dead in the bathtub by her young son, Richard.

I went back to Armstrong's, but it was the wrong place for the mood I was in. I headed uptown on Ninth and kept going after it turned into Columbus Avenue. I hit a lot of bars, stopping for a quick drink whenever I got tired of walking. There are plenty of bars on Columbus Avenue.

I was looking for something but I didn't know what it was until I found it. I should have been able to tell in advance. I had had nights like this before, walking through bad streets, waiting for an opportunity to blow off some of the things that had been building up inside me.

I got the chance on Columbus somewhere in the high Eighties. I had left a bar with an Irish name and Spanish-speaking customers, and I was letting myself walk with the rolling gait that is the special property of drunks and sailors. I saw movement in a doorway ten or twelve yards ahead of me, but I kept right on walking, and when he came out of the doorway with a knife in his hand, I knew I'd been looking for him for hours.

He said, 'Come on, come on, gimme your money.'

He wasn't a junkie. Everybody thinks they're all junkies, but they're not. Junkies break into apartments when nobody's home and take television sets and typewriters, small things they can turn into quick cash. Not more than one mugger out of five has a real jones. The other four do it because it beats working.

And it lets them know how tough they are.

He made sure I could see the knife blade. We were in the shadows, but the blade still caught a little light and flashed wickedly at me. It was a kitchen knife, wooden handle, six or seven inches of blade.

I said, 'Just take it easy.'

'Let's see that fucking money.'

'Sure,' I said. 'Just take it easy with the knife. Knives make me nervous.'

I suppose he was about nineteen or twenty. He'd had a fierce case of acne not too many years ago, and his cheeks and chin were pitted. I moved toward my inside breast pocket, and in an easy, rolling motion I dropped one shoulder, pivoted on my right heel, and kicked his wrist with my left foot. The knife sailed out of his hand.

He went for it and that was a mistake because it landed behind him and he had to scramble for it. He should have done one of two things. He should have come straight at me or he should have turned around and run away but instead he went for the knife and that was the wrong thing to do.

He never got within ten feet of it. He was off balance and scrambling, and I got a hand on his shoulder and spun him like a top. I threw a right, my hand open, and I caught him with the heel of my hand right under his nose. He yelped and put both hands to his face, and I hit him three or four times in the belly. When he folded up I cupped my hands on the back of his head and brought my knee up while I was bringing his head down.

The impact was good and solid. I let go of him, and he stood in a dazed crouch, his legs bent at right angles at the knees. His body didn't know whether to straighten up or fall down. I took his chin in my hand and shoved, and that made the decision for him. He went up and over and sprawled on his back and stayed that way.

I found a thick roll of bills in the right-hand pocket of his jeans. He wasn't looking to buy milk for his hungry brothers and sisters, not this one. He'd been carrying just under two hundred dollars on his hip. I tucked a single back in his pocket for the subway and added the rest to my wallet. He lay there without moving and watched the whole operation. I don't think he believed it was really happening.

I got down on one knee. I picked up his right hand in my left hand and put my face close to his. His eyes were wide and he was frightened, and I was glad because I wanted him to be frightened. I wanted him to know just what fear was and just how it felt.

I said, 'Listen to me. These are hard, tough streets, and you are not hard enough or tough enough. You better get a straight job because you can't make it out here, you're too soft for it. You think it's easy out here, but it's harder than you ever knew, and now's your chance to learn it.'

I bent the fingers of his right hand back one at a time until they broke. Just the four fingers. I left his thumb alone. He didn't scream or anything. I suppose the terror blocked the pain.

I took his knife along with me and dropped it in the first sewer I came to. Then I walked the two blocks to Broadway and caught a cab home.

THIRTEEN

I don't think I actually slept at all.

I got out of my clothes and into bed. I closed my eyes and slipped into the kind of dream you can have without being entirely asleep, aware that it was a dream, my consciousness standing off to one side and watching the dream like a jaded critic at the theater. Then a batch of things came together, and I knew I wouldn't be able to sleep and didn't want to, anyway.

So I ran the shower as hot as it gets and stood by the side of the tub with the bathroom door closed to create an improvised steam bath. I sweated exhaustion and alcohol out of my system for half an hour or so. Then I lowered the temperature of the shower enough to make it bearable and stood under it. I finished with a minute under an ice-cold spray. I don't know if it's really good for you. I think it's just Spartan.

I dried off and put on a clean suit. I sat on the bed and picked up the telephone. Allegheny turned out to have the flight I wanted. It was leaving LaGuardia at five forty-five and would get me where I was going a little after seven. I booked a round-trip ticket, return open.

The Childs' at Fifty-eighth and Eighth stays open all night. I had corned beef hash and eggs and a lot of black coffee.

It was very close to five o'clock when I got into the back of a Checker cab and told the driver to take me to the airport.

The flight had a stop in Albany. That's what took it so long. It touched down there on schedule. A few people got off, and a few other people got on, and the pilot put us into the air again. We never had time to level off on the second lap; we began our descent as soon as we stopped climbing. He bounced us around a little on the Utica runway, but it was nothing to complain about.

'Have a good day,' the stewardess said. 'Take care now.'

Take care.

It seems to me that people have only been saying that phrase on parting for the past few years or so. All of a sudden everyone started to say it, as if the whole country abruptly recognized that ours is a world which demands caution.

I intended to take care. I wasn't too sure about having a good day.

By the time I got from the airport into Utica itself, it was around seven thirty. A few minutes of twelve I called Cale Hanniford at his office. No one answered.

I tried his home and his wife answered. I gave my name and she told me hers. 'Mr Scudder,' she said tentatively. 'Are you, uh, making any progress?'

'Things are coming along,' I said.

'I'll get Cale for you.'

When he came on the line I told him I wanted to see him.

'I see. Something you don't want to go into over the telephone?'

'Something like that.'

'Well, can you come to Utica? It would be inconvenient for me to come to New York unless it's absolutely necessary, but you could fly up this afternoon or possibly tomorrow. It's not a long flight.'

'I know. I'm in Utica right now.'

'Oh?'

'I'm in a Rexall drugstore at the corner of Jefferson and Mohawk. You could pick me up and we could go over to your office.'

'Certainly. Fifteen minutes?'

'Fine.'

I recognized his Lincoln and was crossing the sidewalk to it as he pulled up in front of the drugstore. I opened the door and got in next to him. Either he wore a suit around the house as a matter of course or he had taken the trouble to put one on for the occasion. The suit was dark blue with an unobtrusive stripe.

'You should have let me know you were coming,' he said. 'I could have picked you up at the airport.'

'This way I had a chance to see something of your city.'

'It's not a bad place. Probably very quiet by New York standards. Though that's not necessarily a bad thing.'

'No, it's not.'

'Ever been here before?'

'Once, and that was years ago. The local police had picked up someone we wanted, so I came up to take him back to New York with me. I took the train that trip.'

'How was your flight today?'

'All right.'

He was dying to ask me why I had dropped in on him like this, but he had manners. You didn't discuss business at lunch until the coffee was poured, and we wouldn't discuss our business until we were in his office. The Hanniford Drugs warehouse was on the western edge of town, and he had picked me up right in the heart of the downtown area. We managed small talk on the ride out. He pointed out things he thought might interest me, and I put on a show of being mildly interested. Then we were at the warehouse. They worked a five-day week and there were no other cars around, just a couple of idle trucks. He pulled the Lincoln to a stop next to a loading dock and led me up a ramp and inside. We walked down a hallway to his office. He turned on the overhead lights, pointed me to a chair, and seated himself behind his desk.

'Well,' he said.

I didn't feel tired. It occurred to me that I ought to, no sleep, a lot of booze the night before. But I didn't feel tired. Not eager, either, but not tired.

I said, 'I came to report. I know as much about your daughter as I'll ever know, and it's as much as you need to know. I could spend more of my time and your money, but I don't see the point.'

'It didn't take you very long.'

His tone was neutral, and I wondered how he meant it. Was he admiring my efficiency or annoyed that his two thousand dollars had only purchased five days of my time?

I said, 'It took long enough. I don't know that it would have taken any less time if you had given me everything in the beginning. Probably not. It would have made things a little easier for me, though.'

'I don't understand.'

'I can understand why you didn't. You felt I had all I needed to know. If I had just been looking for facts you might have been right, but I was looking for facts that would make up a picture, and I'd have done better knowing everything in front.' He was puzzled, and the heavy dark eyebrows were elevated above the top rims of his glasses. I said, 'The reason I didn't let you know I was coming was that I had some things to do in Utica. I caught a dawn flight up here, Mr Hanniford. I spent about five hours learning things you could have told me five days ago.'

'What sort of things?'

'I went to a few places. The Bureau of Vital Statistics in City Hall. The *Times-Sentinel* offices. The police station.'

'I didn't hire you to ask questions here in Utica.'

'You didn't hire me at all, Mr Hanniford. You married your wife on – well, I don't have to tell you the date. It was a first marriage for both of you.'

He didn't say anything. He took his glasses off and put them on the desk in front of him.

'You might have told me Wendy was illegitimate.'

'Why? She didn't know it herself.'

'Are you sure of that?'

'Yes.'

'I'm not.' I drew a breath. 'There were two U.S. Marines from the Utica area killed in the Inchon landing. One of them was black, so I ruled him out. The other was named Robert Blohr. He was married. Was he also Wendy's father?'

'Yes.'

'I'm not trying to pick scabs, Mr Hanniford. I think Wendy knew she was illegitimate. And it's possible that it doesn't matter whether she did or not.'

He stood up and walked to the window. I sat there wondering whether Wendy had known about her father and decided it was ten-to-one that she had. He was the chief character in her personal mythology, and she had spent all her life looking for an incarnation of him. The ambivalence of her feelings about the man seemed to derive from some knowledge over and above what she had been told by Hanniford and her mother.

He stayed at the window for a time. Then he turned and looked thoughtfully at me. 'Perhaps I should have told you,' he said finally. 'I didn't conceal it on purpose. That is, I gave little thought at the time to Wendy's ... illegitimacy. That's been a completely closed chapter for so many years that it never occurred to me to mention it.'

'I can understand that.'

'You said you had a report to make,' he said. He returned to his chair and sat down. 'Go ahead, Scudder.'

I started all the way back in Indiana. Wendy at college, not interested in boys her own age, interested always in older men. She had had affairs with her professors, most of them probably casual liaisons, one at least other than casual, at least on the man's part. He had wanted to leave his wife. The wife had taken pills, perhaps in a genuine suicide attempt, perhaps as a grandstand play to save her marriage. And perhaps she herself hadn't known which.

'At any rate, there was a scandal of sorts. The whole campus was aware of it, whether or not it became officially a matter of record. That explains why Wendy dropped out of school a couple of months short of graduation. There was really no way she could stay there.'

'Of course not.'

'It also explains why the school wasn't desperately concerned that she had disappeared. I'd wondered about that. From what you said, their attitude was fairly casual. Evidently they wanted to let you know she was gone but weren't prepared to tell you why she had left, but they knew she had good reasons to leave and weren't concerned about her physical well-being.'

'I see.'

'She went to New York, as you know. She became involved with older men almost immediately. One of them took her to Miami. I could give you his name, but it doesn't matter. He died a couple of years ago. It's hard to tell now just how big a role he played in Wendy's life, but in addition to taking her to Miami he let her use his name when she applied for her apartment. She put his firm down as her employer, and he backed her up when the rental agent called.'

'Did he pay her rent?'

'It's possible. Whether he paid all or part of her support at the time is something only he could tell you, and there's no way to ask him. If you want my guess, her involvement with him was not an exclusive one.'

'There were other men in her life at the same time?'

'I think so. This particular man was married and lived in the suburbs with his family. I doubt that he could have spent all that much time with her even if either of them wanted it that way. And I have a feeling she was leery of getting too involved with one man. It must have shaken her a great deal when the professor's wife took the pills. If he was sufficiently infatuated with her to leave his wife for her, she was probably committed to him herself, or at least thought she was. After that fell apart she was careful not to invest too much of herself in any one man.'

'So she saw a lot of men.'

'Yes.'

'And took money from them.'

'Yes.'

'You know that for a fact? Or is it conjecture?'

'It's fact.' I told him a little about Marcia Maisel and how she had gradually become aware of the manner in which Wendy was supporting herself. I didn't add that Marcia had tried the profession on for size.

He lowered his head, and a little of the starch went out of his shoulders. 'So the newspapers were accurate,' he said. 'She was a prostitute.'

'A kind of prostitute.'

'What does that mean? It's like pregnancy, isn't it? Either you are or you aren't.'

'I think it's more like honesty.'

'Oh?'

Some people are more honest than others.'

'I always thought honesty was unequivocal, too.'

'Maybe it is. I think there are different levels.'

'And there are different levels of prostitution?'

'I'd say so. Wendy wasn't walking the streets. She wasn't turning one trick after another, wasn't handing her money over to a pimp.'

'Isn't that what the Vanderpoel boy was?'

'No. I'll get to him.' I closed my eyes for a moment. I opened them and said, 'There's no way to know this for certain, but I doubt that Wendy set out to be a prostitute. She probably took money from quite a few men before she could pin that label on herself.'

'I don't follow you.'

'Let's say a man took her out to dinner, brought her home, wound up going to bed with her. On his way out the door he might hand her a twenty-dollar bill. He'd say something like, "I'd like to send you a big bouquet of flowers or buy you a present, but why not take the money and pick out something you like?" Maybe she tried not to take the money the first few times this happened. Later on she'd learn to expect it.'

'I see.'

'It wouldn't be long before she would start getting telephone calls from men she hadn't met. A lot of men like to pass girls' phone numbers around. Sometimes it's an act of charity. Other times they think they enhance their own image this way. "She's a great kid, she's not exactly a hooker, but slip her a few bucks afterward because she doesn't have a job, you know, and it's tough for a girl to make it in the big city." So you wake up one morning and realize that you're a prostitute, at least according to the dictionary definition of the term, but by then you're used to the way you're living and it doesn't seem unnatural to you. As far as I can determine, she never asked for money. She never saw more than one man during an evening. She turned down dates if she didn't like the man involved. She would even plead a fake headache if she met a man for dinner and decided she didn't want to sleep with him. So she earned her money that way, but she wasn't in it for the money.'

'You mean she enjoyed it.'

'She certainly found it tolerable. She wasn't kidnapped by white slavers. She could have found a job if she wanted one. She could have come home to Utica, or called up and asked for money. Are you asking if she was a nymphomaniac? I don't know the answer to that, but I'd be inclined to doubt it. I think she was compelled.'

'How?'

I stood up and moved closer to his desk. It was dark mahogany and looked at least fifty years old. Its top was orderly. There was a blotter in a tooled leather holder, a two-tiered in-and-out box, a spindle, a pair of framed photographs. He watched me pick up both photographs and look at them. One showed a woman about forty, her eyes out of focus, an uncertain smile on her face. I sensed that the expression was not uncharacteristic. The other photo was of Wendy, her hair medium in length, her eyes bright, and her teeth shiny enough to sell toothpaste.

'When was this taken?'

'High school graduation.'

'And this is your wife?'

'Yes. I don't know when that was taken. Six or seven years ago, I would guess.'

'I don't see a resemblance.'

'No. Wendy favored her father.'

'Blohr.'

'Yes. I never met him. I'm told she resembled him. I couldn't say one way or the other, on the basis of my own knowledge, but I'm told she does. Did.'

I returned Mrs Hanniford's photo to its place on his desk. I looked into Wendy's eyes. We had become too intimate these past few days, she and I. I probably knew more about her than she might have wanted me to know.

'You said you thought she was compelled.'

I nodded.

'By what?'

I put the photo back where it belonged. I watched Hanniford try not to meet Wendy's eyes. He didn't manage it. He looked into them and winced.

I said, 'I'm not a psychologist, a psychiatrist, any of those things. I'm just a man who used to be a cop.'

'I know that.'

'I can make guesses. I'd guess she could never stop looking for Daddy. She wanted to be somebody's daughter, and they kept wanting to fuck her. And that was all right with her because that was what Daddy was, he was a man who took Mommy to bed and got her pregnant and then went away to Korea and was never heard from again. He was somebody who was married to somebody else, and that was all right, because the men she was attracted to were always married to somebody else. It could get very hairy looking for Daddy because if you weren't careful he might like you too much and Mommy might take a lot of pills and it would be time for you to go away. That's why it was safer all around if Daddy gave you money. Then it was all on a cash-and-carry basis and Daddy wouldn't flip out over you and Mommy wouldn't take pills and you could stay where you were, you wouldn't have to leave. I'm not a psychiatrist and I don't know if this is the way it works in textbooks or not. I never read the textbooks and I never met Wendy. I didn't get inside of her life until her life was over. I kept trying to get into her life and I kept getting into her death instead. Do you have anything to drink?'

'Pardon me?'

'Do you have anything to drink? Like bourbon.'

'Oh. I think there's a bottle of something or other.'

How could you not know whether or not you had any liquor around?

'Get it.'

His face went through some interesting changes. He started off

IOI

wondering who the hell I thought I was to order him around, and then he realized that it was immaterial, and then he got up and went over to a cabinet and opened a door.

'It's Canadian Club,' he announced.

'Fine.'

'I don't believe I have anything to mix it with.'

'Good. Just bring the bottle and a glass.' And if you don't have a glass, that's all right, sir.

He brought the bottle and a water tumbler and watched with clinical interest as I poured whiskey until the glass was two-thirds full. I drank off about half of it and put the glass down on top of his desk. Then I picked it up quickly because it might have left a ring otherwise, and I made hesitant motions and he decoded them and handed me a couple of memo slips that could serve as a coaster.

'Scudder?'

'What?'

'Do you suppose a psychiatrist could have helped her?'

'I don't know. Maybe she went to one. I couldn't find anything in her apartment to suggest that she did, but it's possible. I think she was helping herself.'

'By living the way she did?'

'Uh-huh. Her life was a fairly stable one. It may not look like it from the outside, but I think it was. That's why she carried the Maisel girl as a roommate. It's also why she hooked up with Vanderpoel. Her apartment had a very settled feel to it. Well-chosen furniture. A place to live in. I think the men in her life represented a stage she was working her way through, and I would guess that she consciously saw it that way. The men represented physical and emotional survival for the time being, and I think she anticipated reaching a point where she wouldn't need them anymore.'

I drank some more whiskey. It was a little sweet for my taste, and a little too smooth, but it went down well enough.

I said, 'In some ways I learned more about Richie Vanderpoel than I did about Wendy. One of the people I talked to said all ministers' sons are crazy. I don't know that that's true, but I think most of them must have a hard time of it. Richie's father is a very uptight type. Stern, cold. I doubt that he ever showed the boy much in the way of warmth. Richie's mother killed herself when he was six years old. No brothers or sisters, just the kid and his father and a dried-up housekeeper in a rectory that could double as a mausoleum. He grew up with mixed-up feelings about both of his parents. His feelings in that area complemented Wendy's pretty closely. That's why they were so good for each other.'

'Good for each other!'

'Yes.'

'For God's sake, he killed her!'

'They were good for each other. She was a woman he wasn't afraid of, and he was a man she couldn't mistake for her father. They were able to have a domestic life together that gave them both a measure of security they hadn't had before. And there was no sexual relationship to complicate things.'

'They didn't sleep together?'

I shook my head. 'Richie was homosexual. At least he'd been functioning as a homosexual before he moved in with your daughter. He didn't like it much, wasn't comfortable about it. Wendy gave him a chance to get away from that life. He could live with a woman without having to prove his manhood because she didn't want him as a lover. After he met her he stopped making the rounds of the gay bars. And I think she stopped seeing men in the evenings. I couldn't prove it, but earlier she had been getting taken out for dinner several nights a week. The kitchen in her apartment was fully stocked when I saw it. I think Richie cooked dinner for the two of them just about every night. I told you a few minutes ago that I thought Wendy was working things out. I think both of them were working things out together. Maybe they would have started sleeping together eventually. Maybe Wendy would have stopped seeing men professionally and gone out and taken a job. I'm just guessing, that's all any of this is, but I'd take the guess a little further. I think they would have gotten married eventually, and they might even have made it work.'

'That's very hypothetical.'

'I know.'

'You make it sound as though they were in love.'

'I don't know that they were in love. I don't think there's any doubt that they loved each other.'

He picked up his glasses, put them on, took them off again. I poured more whiskey in my glass and took a small sip of it. He sat for a long while, looking at his hands. Every now and then he looked up at the two photographs on top of his desk.

Finally he said, 'Then why did he kill her?'

'No way to answer that. He didn't have any memory of the act, and the whole scene got mixed up with memories of his mother's death. Anyway, that's not your question.'

'It's not?'

'Of course not. What you want to know is how much of it was your fault.'

He didn't say anything.

'Something happened the last time you saw your daughter. Do you want to tell me about it?'

He didn't want to, not a whole hell of a lot, and it took him a few minutes to get warmed up. He talked vaguely about the sort of child she had been, very bright and warm and affectionate, and about how much he had loved her.

Then he said, 'When she was, it's hard to remember, but I think she must have been eight years old. Eight or nine. She would always sit on my lap and give me hugs and ... hugs and kisses, and she would squirm around a little, and –'

He had to stop for a minute. I didn't say anything.

'One day, I don't know why it happened, but one day she was on my lap, and I – oh, Christ.'

'Take your time.'

'I got excited. Physically excited.'

'It happens.'

'Does it?' His face looked like something from a stained-glass window. 'I couldn't ... couldn't even think about it. I was so disgusted with myself. I loved her the way you love a daughter, at least I had always thought that was what I felt for her, and to find myself responding to her sexually –'

'I'm no expert, Mr Hanniford, but I think it's a very natural thing. Just a physical response. Some people get erections from riding on trains.'

'This was more than that.'

'Maybe.'

'It was, Scudder. I was terrified of what I saw in myself. Terrified of what it could lead to, the harm it could have for Wendy. And so I made a conscious decision that day. I stopped being so close to her.' He lowered his eyes. 'I withdrew. I made myself limit my affection for her, the affection I expressed, that is. Maybe the affection I felt as well. There was less hugging and kissing and cuddling. I was determined not to let that one occasion repeat itself.'

He sighed, fixed his eyes on mine. 'How much of this did you guess at, Scudder?'

'A little of it. I thought it might even have gone farther than that.'

'I'm not an animal.'

'People do things you wouldn't believe. And they aren't always animals. What happened the last time you saw Wendy?'

'I've never told anyone about this. Why do I have to tell you?'

'You don't. But you want to.'

'Do I?' He sighed again. 'She was home from college. Everything was the way it had always been, but there was something about her that was different. I suppose she had already established a pattern of getting involved with older men.'

'Yes.'

'She came home late one night. She'd gone out alone. Perhaps she let someone pick her up, I don't know.' He closed his eyes and looked back at that evening. 'I was awake when she came home. I wasn't purposely waiting up for her. My wife had gone to sleep early, and I had a book I wanted to read. Wendy came home around one or two in the morning. She'd been drinking. She wasn't reeling, but she was at least slightly drunk.

'I saw a side of her I had never seen before. She ... she propositioned me.'

'Just like that?'

'She asked me if I wanted to fuck. She said ... obscene things. Described acts she wanted to perform with me. She tried to grab me.'

'What did you do?'

'I slapped her.'

'I see.'

'I told her she was drunk. I told her to go upstairs and get to bed. I don't know if the slap sobered her, but a shadow passed over her face and she turned away without a word and climbed the stairs. I didn't know what to do. I thought perhaps I ought to go to her and tell her it was all right, that we would just forget about it. In the end I did nothing. I sat up for another hour or so, then went to bed myself.' He looked up. 'And in the morning we both pretended nothing had happened. Neither of us ever referred to the incident again.'

I drank what was in my glass. It all meshed now, every bit of it.

'The reason I didn't go to her ... I was sickened by the way she acted. Disgusted. But something in me was ... excited.'

I nodded.

'I'm not sure I trusted myself to go to her room that night, Scudder.'

'Nothing would have happened.'

'How do you know that?'

'Everybody has mean little places inside himself. It's the ones who aren't aware of them who fly off the handle. You were able to see what was happening. That made you capable of keeping a lid on it.'

'Maybe.'

After a while I said, 'I don't think you have much to blame yourself for. It seems to me that everything was already set in motion before you were in a position to do anything about it. It wasn't a one-sided thing when you responded physically to Wendy squirming around on your lap. She was behaving seductively, although I'm sure she didn't realize it at the time. It all fits together – competing with her mother, trying to find Daddy hiding inside every older man she found attractive. Lots of girls try to seduce professors, you know, and most professors learn to be very good at discouraging that sort of thing. Wendy had a pretty high success ratio. She was evidently very good at it.'

'It's funny.'

'What is?'

'Earlier you made her sound like a victim. Now she sounds like a villain.'

'Everybody's both.'

Neither of us had very much to say on the way out to the airport. He seemed more relaxed than before, but I had no way of knowing how much of that was just on the surface. If I'd done him any good, I'd done so less by what I had found out for him than by what I'd made him tell me. There were priests and psychiatrists who would have listened to him, and they probably would have done him more good than I did, but I'd been elected instead.

At one point I said, 'Whatever blame you decide to assign yourself, keep one thing in mind. Wendy was in the process of turning out all right. I don't know how long it would have taken her to find a cleaner way of making a living, but I doubt it would have been much more than a year.'

'You can't be certain of that.'

'I certainly can't prove it.'

'That makes it worse, doesn't it? It makes it more tragic.'

'It makes it more tragic. I don't know if that's better or worse.'

'What? Oh, I see. That's an interesting distinction.'

I went to the Allegheny desk. There was a flight to New York within the hour, and I checked in for it. When I turned around, Hanniford was standing next to me with a check in his hand. I asked him what it was for. He said I hadn't mentioned more money and he didn't know what constituted a fair payment, but he was pleased with the job I had done for him and he wanted to give me a bonus.

I didn't know what was fair payment, either. But I remembered what I had told Lewis Pankow. When somebody hands you money, you take it. I took it.

I didn't get around to unfolding it until I was on the plane. It was for a thousand dollars. I'm still not sure why he gave it to me.

FOURTEEN

In my hotel room I opened a paperback dictionary of saints and flipped through it. I found myself reading about St. Mary Goretti, who was born in Italy in 1890. When she was twelve a young man began making overtures to her. Eventually he attempted to ravish her and threatened to kill her if she resisted. She did, and he did, stabbing her over and over again with his knife. She died within twenty-four hours.

After eight years of unrepentant imprisonment her murderer had a change of heart, I learned. At the end of twenty-seven years he was released, and on Christmas Day, 1937, he contrived to receive Communion side by side with Mary's widowed mother. He has since been cited as an example by those who advocate the abolition of capital punishment.

I always find something interesting in that book.

I went next door for dinner but didn't have much appetite. The waiter offered to put my leftover steak in a doggie bag. I told him not to bother.

So I went around the corner to Armstrong's and wound up at the corner table in back where it had all started just a few days ago. Cale Hanniford walked into my life on Tuesday, and now it was Saturday. It seemed as though it had been a lot longer than that.

It had started on Tuesday as far as I was concerned, but it had in fact started a lot earlier than that, and I sipped bourbon and coffee and wondered how far you could trace it back. At some point or other it had probably become inevitable, but I didn't know just when that point was. There was a day when Richie Vanderpoel and Wendy Hanniford met each other, and that had to be a turning point of one sort or another, but maybe their separate ends had been charted far in advance of that date and their meeting only arranged that they would happen to one another. Maybe it went a lot further back, to Robert Blohr dying in Korea and Margaret Vanderpoel opening her veins in her bathtub.

Maybe it was Eve's fault, messing around with apples. Dangerous thing, giving humanity the knowledge of good and evil. And the capacity to make the wrong choice more often than not.

'Buy a lady a drink?'

I looked up. It was Trina, dressed in civilian clothes and wearing a smile that faded as she studied my face. 'Hey,' she said. 'Where *were* you?'

'Chasing private thoughts.'

'Want to be alone?'

'That's the last thing I want. Did you say something about buying you a drink?'

'It was an idea I had, yes.'

I flagged the waiter and ordered a stinger for her and another of the same for myself. She talked about a couple of strange customers she'd had the night before. We coasted through a few rounds on small talk, and then she reached out a hand and touched the tip of my chin with her finger.

'Hey.'

'Hey?'

'Hey, you're in a bad way. Troubles?'

'I had a rotten day. I flew upstate and had a conversation that wasn't much fun.'

'The business you were telling me about the other night?'

'Was I talking about it with you? Yes, I guess I was.'

'Feel like talking about it now?'

'Maybe a little later.'

'Sure.'

We sat for a while, not saying much. The place was quiet as it often is on Saturdays. At one point two kids came in and walked over to the bar. I didn't recognize them.

'Matt, is something wrong?'

I didn't answer her. The bartender sold them a couple of six-packs and they left. I let out a breath I hadn't known I was holding.

'Matt?'

'Just a reflex. I thought the place was about to be held up. Put it down to nerves.'

'Sure.' Her hand covered mine. 'Getting late,' she said.

'Is it?'

'Kind of. Would you walk me home? It's just a couple of blocks.'

She lived on the tenth floor of a new building on Fifty-sixth between Ninth and Tenth. The doorman roused himself enough to flash her a smile. 'There's some booze,' she told me, 'and I can make better coffee than Jimmie can. Want to come up?'

'I'd like to.'

Her apartment was a studio, one large room with an alcove that held a narrow bed. She showed me where to hang my coat and put on a stack of records. She said she'd put on some coffee, and I told her to forget about the coffee. She made drinks for both of us. She curled up on a red plush sofa and I sat in a frayed gray armchair.

'Nice place,' I said.

'It's getting there. I want pictures for the walls and some of the furniture will have to be replaced eventually, but in the meantime it suits me.'

'How long have you been here?'

'Since October. I lived uptown, and I hated taking cabs to and from work.'

'Were you ever married, Trina?'

'For three years, almost. I've been divorced for four.'

'Ever see your ex?'

'I don't even know what state he lives in. I think he's out on the Coast, but I'm not sure. Why?'

'No reason. You didn't have any kids?'

'No. He didn't want to. Then when things fell apart I was glad we didn't. You?'

'Two boys.'

'That must be rough.'

'I don't know. Sometimes, I guess.'

'Matt? What would you have done if there was a holdup tonight?'

I thought it over. 'Nothing, probably. Nothing I could do, really. Why?'

'You didn't see yourself when it was going on. You looked like a cat getting ready to spring.'

'Reflexes.'

'All those years being a cop.'

'Something like that.'

She lit a cigarette. I got the bottle and freshened our drinks. Then I was sitting on the couch next to her and telling her about Wendy and Richard, telling her just about all of it. I don't know whether it was her or the booze or a combination of the two, but it was suddenly very easy to talk about it, very important that I talk about it.

And I said, 'The impossible thing was knowing how much to tell the man. He was afraid of what he might have done to her, either by limiting his affection for her or by behaving seductively toward her without knowing it himself. I can't find those answers any better than he can. But other things. The murder, the way his daughter died. How much of that was I supposed to tell him?'

'Well, he already knew all that, didn't he, Matt?'

'I guess he knew what he had to know.'

'I don't follow you.'

I started to say something, then let it go. I poured more booze in both our glasses. She looked at me. 'Trying to get me drunk?'

'Trying to get us both drunk.'

'Well, I think it's working. Matt –'

I said, 'It's hard to know just how much a person has any right to do. I suppose I was on the force too long. Maybe I never should have left. Do you know about that?'

She averted her eyes. 'Somebody said something once.'

'Well, if that hadn't happened, would I have left anyway sooner or later? I always wonder about that. There was a great security in being a cop. I don't mean the job security, I mean the emotional security. There weren't as many questions, and the ones that came up were likely to have obvious answers, or at least they seemed obvious at the time.

'Let me tell you a story. This happened maybe ten years ago. Maybe twelve. It also happened in the Village and it involved a girl in her twenties. She was raped and murdered in her own apartment. Nylon stocking wrapped around her neck.' Trina shuddered. 'Now this one wasn't open-and-shut, there was nobody running around the streets with her blood on him. It was one of those cases where you just keep digging, you check out everybody who ever said boo to the girl, everybody in the building, everybody who knew her at work, every man who played any role whatsoever in her life. Christ, we must have talked to a couple of hundred people.

'Well, there was one guy I liked for it from the start. Big

brawny son of a bitch, he was the super in the building she lived in. Ex-Navy man, got out on a bad-conduct discharge. We had a sheet on him. Two arrests for assault, both dropped when the complainants refused to press charges. Complainants in both cases were women.

'All that is enough reason to check him out down to the ground. Which we did. And the more I talked to him the more I knew the son of a bitch did it. Sometimes you just plain know.

'But he had himself covered. We had the time of death pinpointed to within an hour, and his wife was prepared to swear on a stack of bibles that he'd spent the entire day never out of her sight. And we had nothing on the other side of it, not one scrap of anything to place him in the girl's apartment at the time of the murder. Nothing at all. Not even a lousy fingerprint, and even if we did, it meant nothing because he was the super and he could have put his prints there fixing the plumbing or something. We had nothing, not a smell of anything, and the only reason we knew he did it was we simply knew, and no district attorney would dream of trying to run that by a grand jury.

'So we checked out everybody else who was vaguely possible. And of course we didn't get anywhere because there was nowhere to get, and the case wound up in the open file, which meant we knew it was never going to be closed out, which meant to all intents and purposes it was closed already because nobody would bother to look at it anymore.'

I got to my feet, walked across the room. I said, 'But we knew he did it, see, and it was driving us crazy. I don't know how many people get away with murder every year. A lot more than anyone realizes. This Ruddle, though, we *knew* he was our boy, and we still couldn't do anything about it. That was his name, Jacob Ruddle.

'So after the case was marked open, my partner and I, we couldn't get it out of our heads. Just couldn't get it out of our heads, there wasn't a day one of us didn't bring it up. So eventually we went to this Ruddle and asked him if he'd take a polygraph test. You know what that is?'

'A lie detector?'

'A lie detector. We were completely straight with him, we told him he could refuse to take the test, and we also told him it couldn't be entered in evidence against him, which it can't. I'm not sure that's a good idea, incidentally, but that's the law.

'He agreed to take the test. Don't ask me why. Maybe he

thought it would look suspicious of him to refuse, although he must have known we damn well knew he killed her and nothing was going to make him stop looking suspicious to us. Or maybe he honestly thought he could beat the machine. Well, he took the test, and I made sure we had the best operator available to administer the test, and the results were just what we expected.'

'He was guilty?'

'No question about it. It nailed him to the wall, but there was nothing we could do with it. I told him the machine said he was lying. 'Well, those machines must make a few mistakes now and then,' he said, 'because it made one right now.' And he looked me right in the eye, and he knew I didn't believe him, and he knew there was nothing on earth I could do about it.'

'God.'

I went over and sat down next to her again. I sipped some of my drink and closed my eyes for a moment, remembering the look in that bastard's eyes.

'What did you do?'

'My partner and I tossed it back and forth. My partner wanted to put him in the river.'

'You mean kill him?'

'Kill him and set him in cement and drop him somewhere in the Hudson.'

'You wouldn't do a thing like that.'

'I don't know. I might have gone along with it. See, he did it, he killed that girl, and he was an odds-on candidate to do it again sooner or later. Oh, hell, that wasn't all of it. Knowing he did it, knowing he knew we knew he did it, and sending the bastard home. Putting him in the river started sounding like a hell of a good idea, and I might have done it if I hadn't thought of something better.'

'What?'

'I had this friend on the narcotics squad. I told him I needed some heroin, a lot of it, and I told him he would be getting every bit of it back. Then one afternoon when Ruddle and his wife were both out of the apartment I let myself in, and I flaked that place as well as it's ever been done. I stuffed smack inside the towel bar, I stuck a can of it in the ball float of his toilet, I put the shit in every really obvious hiding place I could find.

'Then I got back to my friend in narcotics, and I told him I knew where he could make himself a hell of a haul. And he did it right, with a warrant and everything, and Ruddle was upstate in

Dannemora before he knew what hit him.' I smiled suddenly. 'I went to see him between the trial and the sentencing date. His whole defense was that he had no idea how that heroin got there, and not too surprisingly the jury didn't sit up all night worrying about that one. I went to see him and I said, 'You know, Ruddle, it's a shame you couldn't take a lie-detector test. It might make people believe you didn't know where that smack came from.' And he just looked at me because he knew just how it had been done to him and for a change there was nothing *he* could do about it.'

'God.'

'He drew ten-to-twenty for possession with intent to sell. About three years into his sentence he got in a grudge fight with another inmate and got stabbed to death.'

'God.'

'The thing is, you wonder just how far you have a right to turn things around like that. Did we have a right to set him up? I couldn't see letting him walk around free, and what other way was there to nail him? But if we couldn't do that, did we have a right to put him in the river? That's a harder one for me to answer. I have a lot of trouble with that one. There must be a line there somewhere, and it's hard to know just where to draw it.'

A little while later she said it was getting to be her bedtime.

'I'll go,' I said.

'Unless you'd rather stay.'

We turned out to be good for each other. For a stitch of time all the hard questions went away and hid in dark places.

Afterward she said that I should stay. 'I'll make us breakfast in the morning.'

'Okay.'

And, sleepily, 'Matt? That story you were telling before. About Ruddle?'

'Uh-huh.'

'What made you think of it?'

I sort of wanted to tell her, probably for the same reason I'd told her the story in the first place. But part of what I had to do was not tell her, just as I had avoided telling Cale Hanniford.

'Just the similarities in the cases,' I said. 'Just that it was another case of a girl raped and murdered in the Village, and the one case put me in mind of the other.'

She murmured something I couldn't catch. When I was sure

she was sleeping soundly, I slipped out of bed and got into my clothes. I walked the couple of blocks to my hotel and went to my room.

I thought I would have trouble sleeping, but it came easier than I expected.

FIFTEEN

The service had just gotten under way when I arrived. I slipped into a rear pew, took a small black book from the rack, and found the place. I'd missed the invocation and the first hymn, but I was in time for the reading of the Law.

He seemed taller than I remembered. Perhaps the pulpit added an impression of height. His voice was rich and commanding, and he spoke the Law with absolute certainty.

'God spake all these words, saying, I am the Lord thy God, which have brought thee out of the land of Egypt, out of the house of bondage.

'Thou shalt have no other gods before Me.

'Thou shalt not make unto thee any graven image, or any likeness of any thing that is in heaven above, or that is in the earth beneath, or that is in the water under the earth; thou shalt not·bow down thyself to them, nor serve them, for I the Lord thy God am a jealous God, visiting the iniquity of the fathers upon the third and fourth generation of them that hate Me; and showing mercy unto thousands of them that love Me, and keep My commandments ...'

The room was not crowded. There were perhaps eighty persons present, most of them my age or older, with only a few family groups with children. The church could have accommodated four or five times the number in attendance. I guessed most of the congregation had made the pilgrimage to the suburbs in the past twenty years, their places taken by Irish and Italians whose former neighborhoods were now black and Puerto Rican.

'Honor thy father and thy mother, that thy days may be long upon the land which the Lord thy God giveth thee.'

Were there more people in attendance today than normally? Their minister had experienced great personal tragedy. He had not conducted the service the preceding Sunday. This would be their first official glimpse of him since the murder and suicide.

Would curiosity bring more of them out? Or would restraint and embarrassment – and the cold air of morning – keep many at home?

'Thou shalt not kill.'

Unequivocal statements, these commandments. They brooked no argument. Not *Thou shalt not kill except in special circumstances.*

'Thou shalt not commit adultery ... Thou shalt not bear false witness against thy neighbour ...'

I rubbed at a pulse point in my temple. Could he see me? I remembered his thick glasses and decided he could not. And I was far in the back, and off to the side.

'Hear also what our Lord Jesus Christ saith: Thou shalt love the Lord thy God with all thy heart and with all thy soul and with all thy might. This is the first and greatest commandment. And the second is like unto it. Thou shalt love thy neighbor as thyself. On these two commandments hang all the law and the prophets.'

We stood up and sang a psalm.

The service took a little over an hour. The Old Testament reading was from Isaiah, the New Testament reading from Mark. There was another hymn, a prayer, still another hymn. The offering was taken and consecrated. I put a five on the plate.

The sermon, as promised, dealt with the proposition that the road to Hell was paved with good intentions. It was not enough for us to act with the best and most righteous goals in mind, Martin Vanderpoel told us, because the highest purpose could be betrayed if it were advanced by actions which were not good and righteous in and of themselves.

I didn't pay too much attention to how he elaborated on this because my mind got caught up in the central thesis of the argument and played with it. I wondered whether it was worse for men to do the wrong things for the right reason or the right things for the wrong reason. It wasn't the first time I wondered, or the last.

Then we were standing, and his arms were spread, his robes draping like the wings of an enormous bird, his voice vibrant and resonant.

'The peace of God, which passeth all understanding, keep your hearts and minds in the knowledge and love of God, and of His Son Jesus Christ our Lord; and the blessing of God Almighty, the

Father, and the Son, and the Holy Spirit, be amongst you, and remain with you always. Amen.'

Amen.

A few people slipped out of the church without stopping for a few words with Reverend Vanderpoel. The rest lined up for a handshake. I managed to be at the end of the line. When it was finally my turn Vanderpoel blinked at me. He knew my face was familiar, but he couldn't figure out why.

Then he said, 'Why, it's Mr Scudder! I certainly never expected to see you at our services.'

'It was enjoyable.'

'I'm pleased to hear you say that. I hardly anticipated seeing you again, and I didn't dream of hoping that our incidental meeting might lead you to search for the presence of God.' He looked past my shoulder, a half-smile on his lips. 'He does work in mysterious ways, does He not?'

'So it seems.'

'That a particular tragedy could have this effect upon a person like yourself. I imagine I might find myself using that as a theme for a sermon at some later date.'

'I'd like to talk to you, Reverend Vanderpoel. In private, I think.'

'Oh, dear,' he said. 'I'm quite pressed for time today, I'm afraid. I'm sure you have a great many questons about religion, one is always filled with questions that seem to have a great need for immediate answers, but –'

'I don't want to talk about religion, sir.'

'Oh?'

'It's about your son and Wendy Hanniford.'

'I already told you all that I know.'

'I'm afraid I have to tell *you* some things, sir. And we'd better have that conversation now, and it really will have to be private.'

'Oh?' He looked at me intently, and I watched the play of emotions on his face. 'Very well,' he said. 'I do have a few tasks that need to be attended to. I'll just be a moment.'

I waited, and he wasn't more than ten minutes. Then he took me companionably by the arm and led me through the back of the church and through a door into the rectory. We wound up in the room we had been in before. The electric fire glowed on the hearth, and again he stood in front of it and warmed his long-fingered hands.

'I like a cup of coffee after morning services,' he said. 'You'll join me?'

'No, thank you.'

He left the room and came back with coffee. 'Well, Mr Scudder? What's so urgent?' His tone was deliberately light, but there was tension underneath it.

'I enjoyed the services this morning,' I said.

'Yes, so you said, and I'm pleased to hear it. However –'

'I was hoping for a different Old Testament text.'

'Isaiah is difficult to grasp, I agree. A poet and a man of vision. There are some interesting commentaries on today's reading if you're interested.'

'I was hoping the reading might be from Genesis.'

'Oh, we don't start over until Whitsunday, you know. But why Genesis?'

'A particular portion of Genesis, actually.'

'Oh?'

'The Twenty-second Chapter.'

He closed his eyes for a moment and frowned in concentration. He opened them and shrugged apologetically. 'I used to have a fair memory for chapter and verse. It's been one of the casualties of the ageing process, I'm afraid. Shall I look it up?'

I said, '"*And it came to pass after these things, that God did tempt Abraham, and said unto him, Abraham; and he said, Behold, here I am. And he said, Take now thy son, thine only son Isaac, whom thou lovest, and get thee into the land of Moriah; and offer him there for a burnt offering upon one of the mountains which I will tell thee of.*"'

'The temptation of Abraham. "*God will provide himself a lamb for a burnt offering.*" A very beautiful passage.' His eyes fixed on me. 'It's unusual that you can quote Scripture, Mr Scudder.'

'I had reason to read that passage the other day. It stayed with me.'

'Oh?'

'I thought you might care to explain the chapter to me.'

'At some other time, certainly, but I scarcely see the urgency of –'

'*Don't you!*'

He looked at me. I got to my feet and took a step toward him. I said, 'I think you do. I think you could explain to me the interesting parallels between Abraham and yourself. You could tell me what happens when God doesn't oblige by providing a lamb for the burnt offering. You could tell me more about how the road to Hell is paved with good intentions.'

'Mr Scudder –'

'You could tell me why you were able to murder Wendy Hanniford. And why you let Richie die in your place.'

SIXTEEN

'I don't know what you're talking about.'

'I think you do, sir.'

'My son committed a horrible murder. I'm sure he did not know what he was doing at the moment of his act. I forgive him for what he did, I pray God forgives him –'

'I'm not a congregation, sir. I'm a man who knows all the things you thought no one would ever be able to figure out. Your son never killed anybody until he killed himself.'

He sat there for a long moment, taking it all in. He bowed his head a little. His pose was an attitude of prayer, but I don't think he was praying. When he spoke his tone was not defensive so much as it was curious, the words very nearly an admission of guilt.

'What makes you ... believe this, Mr Scudder?'

'A lot of things I learned. And the way they all fit together.'

'Tell me.'

I nodded. I wanted to tell him because I had been feeling the need to tell someone all along. I hadn't told Cale Hanniford. I had come close to telling Trina, had begun hinting at it, but in the end I had not told her, either.

Vanderpoel was the only person I could tell.

I said, 'The case was open-and-shut. That's how the police saw it, and it was the only way to see it. But I didn't start out looking for a murderer. I started out trying to learn something about Wendy and your son, and the more I learned, the harder it was for me to buy the idea that he had killed her.

'What nailed him was turning up on the sidewalk covered with blood and behaving hysterically. But if you began to dismiss that from your mind, the whole idea of him being the killer began to break down. He left his job suddenly in the middle of the afternoon. He hadn't planned on leaving. That could have been staged. But instead he came down with a case of indigestion and his employer finally managed to talk him into leaving.

'Then he got home with barely enough time to rape her and kill her and run out into the street. He hadn't been acting oddly during the day. The only thing evidently wrong with him was a stomachache. Theoretically he walked in on her and something about her provoked him into flipping out completely.

'But what was it? A rush of sexual desire? He lived with the girl, and it was a reasonable assumption that he could make love to her any time he wanted to. And the more I learned about him, the more certain I became that he never made love to her. They lived together, but they didn't sleep together.'

'What makes you say that?'

'Your son was homosexual.'

'That is not true.'

'I'm afraid it is.'

'Relations between men are an abomination in the eyes of God.'

'That may be. I'm no authority. Richie was homosexual. He wasn't comfortable with it. I gather it was impossible for him to be comfortable with any kind of sexuality. He had very mixed-up feelings about you, about his mother, and they made any real sexual relationship impossible.'

I walked over to the fake fire. I wondered if the fireplace was fake, too. I turned and looked at Martin Vanderpoel. He had not changed position. He was still sitting in his chair with his hands on his knees, his eyes on the patch of rug between his feet.

I said, 'Richie seems to have been stabilized by his relationship with Wendy Hanniford. He was able to regulate his life, and I'd guess he was relatively happy. Then he came home one afternoon, and something set him reeling. Now what would do that?'

He didn't say anything.

'He might have walked in and found her with another man. But that didn't add up because why would it upset him that much? He must have known how she supported herself, that she saw other men during the afternoons while he was at work. Besides, there would have to be some trace of that other man. He wouldn't just run off when Richie started slicing with a razor.

'And where would Richie get a razor? He used an electric. Nobody twenty years old shaves with a straight razor anymore. Some kids carry razors the way other kids carry knives, but Richie wasn't that kind of kid.

'And what did he do with the razor afterward? The cops decided he flipped it out the window or dropped it somewhere and somebody picked it up and walked off with it.'

'Isn't that plausible, Mr Scudder?'

'Uh-huh. If he had a razor in the first place. And it was also possible he'd used a knife instead of a razor. There were plenty of knives in the kitchen. But I was in that kitchen, and all the cupboards and drawers were neatly closed, and you don't grab up a knife to slaughter someone in a fit of passion and remember to close the drawer carefully behind you. No, there was only one way it made sense to me. Richie came home and found Wendy already dead or dying, and that knocked him for a loop. He couldn't handle it.'

My headache was coming back again. I rubbed at my temple with a knuckle. It didn't do much good.

'You told me Richie's mother died when he was quite young.'

'Yes.'

'You didn't tell me she killed herself.'

'How did you learn that?'

'When something's a matter of record, sir, anyone can find out about it if he takes the trouble to look for it. I didn't have to dig for that information. All I had to do was think of looking for it. Your wife killed herself in the bathtub by slashing her wrists. Did she use a razor?'

He looked at me.

'Your razor, sir?'

'I don't see that it matters.'

'Don't you?' I shrugged. 'Richie walked in and found his mother dead in a pool of blood. Then, fourteen years later, he walked into an apartment on Bethune Street and found the woman he was living with dead in her bed. Also slashed with a razor, and also lying in a pool of blood.

'I suppose Wendy Hanniford was a mother to him in certain ways. They must have played a lot of different surrogate roles in each other's lives. But all of a sudden Wendy became his dead mother, and Richie couldn't handle it, and he wound up doing something I guess he'd never been able to do before.'

'What?'

'He had intercourse with her. It was a pure, uncontrollable reaction. He didn't even take time to take his clothes off. He fell on her and he had intercourse with her, and when it was over he ran out into the streets and started screaming his lungs out because his head was full of the fact that he had had intercourse with his mother and now she was dead. You can see what he thought, sir. He thought he fucked her to death.'

'God,' he said.

I wondered if he'd ever pronounced it quite that way before.

My headache was getting worse. I asked him if I could have some aspirins. He told me how to find the first-floor lavatory. There were aspirin tablets in the medicine cabinet. I took two and drank half a glass of water.

When I went back into the living room he hadn't changed position. I sat down in my chair and looked at him. There was a lot more and we would get to it, but I wanted to wait for him to pick it up.

He said, 'This is extraordinary, Mr Scudder.'

'Yes.'

'I never even considered the possibility that Richard was innocent. I just assumed he had done it. If what you think is true –'

'It's true.'

'Then he died for nothing.'

'He died for you, sir. He was the lamb for the burnt offering.'

'You can't seriously believe I killed that girl.'

'I know you did, sir,'

'How can you possibly know that?'

'You met Wendy in the spring.'

'Yes. I believe I told you that the last time you were here.'

'You picked a time when you knew Richie would be at work. You wanted to meet this girl because you were bothered at the idea of Richie living in sin with her.'

'I already told you as much.'

'Yes, you did.' I took a breath. 'Wendy Hanniford was very strongly drawn to older men, men who functioned as father figures for her. She was aggressive in situations involving a man who attracted her. She managed to seduce several of her professors at college.

'She met you, and she was attracted to you. It's not hard to imagine why. You're a very commanding figure of a man. Very stern and forbidding. And on top of everything you were Richie's actual father, and she and Richie were living like brother and sister.

'So she made a play for you. I gather she was very good at

getting her point across. And you were very vulnerable. You'd been a widower for a good many years. Your housekeeper may have been very efficient at her appointed tasks, but you certainly couldn't have picked her as a potential sexual outlet. The last time you were here you told me you felt in retrospect that you should have remarried for Richie's sake. I think you were really saying that you should have remarried for your own sake, so that you wouldn't have been vulnerable to Wendy Hanniford.'

'This is all guesswork on your part, Mr Scudder.'

'You went to bed with her. Maybe that was the first time you went to bed with anybody since your wife died. I wouldn't know, and it doesn't much matter. But you went to bed with her and I guess you liked it because you kept going back. You thought it was a sin, but that didn't change things much because you went right on sinning.

'You certainly hated her. Even after she was dead you made it a point to tell me how evil she was. I thought at the time you were justifying your son's act. I didn't believe then that he did it, but I believed *you* thought so.

'Then you told me he admitted his guilt.'

He didn't say anything. I watched him wipe perspiration from his forehead, then wipe his hand on his robe.

'That didn't have to mean anything. You might have been talking yourself into the belief that Richie died penitent. Or he could well have admitted it to you because he could have become sufficiently confused after the fact. Everything was jumbled up for him. He told his lawyer he found Wendy dead in the bathtub. A little more reflection and he must have decided that he had killed her even if he couldn't remember it.

'But the more I found out about Wendy, the harder it was to picture her as evil. I don't doubt she had an evil effect on the lives of certain other people. But why would she *seem* evil to you? There was really only one explanation for that, sir. She made you want to do something you were ashamed of. And that made you do something more shameful. You killed her.

'You planned it. You took your razor along. And you had sex with her one final time before you murdered her.'

'That's a lie.'

'It's not. I can even tell you what you did. The autopsy showed that she had had both oral and vaginal intercourse shortly before death. Richie would have had genital intercourse with her, so what you did, sir, was take off all your clothes and let her perform fellatio upon you, and then you whipped out your razor and slashed her to death, and then you went home and let your son hang himself for it.'

I stood up and planted my feet in front of his chair. 'I'll tell you what I think. I think you're a son of a bitch. You knew Richie would be home from work in another couple of hours. You knew he'd discover the body. You didn't necessarily know he'd go nuts, but you knew the cops would grab him and lean on him hard. You set him up for it.'

'*No!*'

'No?'

'I was going to ... to call the police. I was going to report the crime anonymously. They would have found the body while he was still at work. They would have known he had nothing to do with it, they would have blamed it on some anonymous sex partner of hers. They never would have thought –'

'Why didn't you follow through?'

He fought to catch his breath. He said, 'I left the apartment. My head was reeling, I was ... badly shaken by what I had done. And then I saw Richie on his way home. He didn't see me. I saw him mount the stairs, and I knew ... I knew it was too late. He was already on the scene.'

'So you let him go upstairs.'

'Yes.'

'And when you went to see him in jail?'

'I wanted to tell him. I wanted to ... to say something to him. I ... I couldn't.'

He leaned forward and put his head in his hands.

I let him sit like that for a while. He didn't sob, didn't make a sound, just sat there looking somewhere into the black parts of his soul. Finally I got up and took a half-pint flask of bourbon from my pocket. I uncapped it and offered it to him.

He wasn't having any. 'I don't use spirits, Mr Scudder.'

'Think of it as a special occasion.'

'I don't use spirits. I don't allow them in my house.'

I thought about that and decided he wasn't in a position to set rules. I took a long drink.

He said, 'You can't prove any of this.'

'Are you sure of that?'

'Some conjecture on your part. A great deal of it, as a matter of fact.'

'So far you haven't refuted any of it.'

'No, if anything I've confirmed it, haven't I? But I'll deny having said any such thing to you. You haven't the slightest bit of truth.'

'You're absolutely right.'

'Then I don't see what you're driving at.'

'I can't prove anything. The cops will be able to, though, when I go to them. They never had any reason to dig before. But they'll start digging, and they'll turn something up. They'll start by asking you to account for your movements on the day of the murder. You won't be able to. That's nothing in and of itself, but it's enough to encourage them to keep looking. They've still got that apartment sealed off. They never had a reason to dust it for prints. They'll have a reason now, and they'll find your prints somewhere. I'm sure you didn't run around wiping surfaces.

'They'll ask to see your razor. If you bought a new one since then, they'll wonder why. They'll go through all your wardrobe, looking for bloodstains. I guess you had your clothes off when you killed her, but you'll have gotten traces of blood on something or other and it won't all wash out.

'They'll put a case together a piece at a time, and they won't even need a full case because you'll crack under questioning in no time at all. You'll crack wide open.'

'I may be stronger than you seem to think, Mr Scudder.'

'You're not strong so much as you're rigid. You'll break. I couldn't tell you how many suspects I've questioned. It gives you a pretty good idea of who's going to crack easy. You'd be a cinch.'

He looked at me, then averted his eyes.

'But it doesn't matter whether you crack or not, and it doesn't matter whether they put a solid case together or not, because all they have to do is start looking and you've had it. Take a look at your life, Reverend Vanderpoel. Once they start, you're finished. You won't be up there on the pulpit Sunday mornings reading the Law to your congregation. You'll be disgraced.'

He sat for a few minutes in silence. I took out my flask and had another drink. Drinking was against his religion. Well, murder was against mine.

'What do you want, Mr Scudder? I have to tell you that I'm not a rich man.'

'Pardon me?'

'I suppose I could arrange regular payments. I couldn't afford very much, but I could –'

'I don't want money.'

'You're not trying to blackmail me?'

'No.'

He frowned at me, puzzled. 'Then I don't understand.'

I let him think about it.

'You haven't gone to the police?'

'No.'

'Do you intend to go to them?'

'I hope I won't have to.'

'I don't understand what you mean.'

I took another little drink. I capped the flask and put it back in my pocket. From another pocket I took a small vial of pills.

I said, 'I found these in the medicine cabinet at the Bethune Street apartment. They were Richie's. He had them prescribed fifteen months ago. They're Seconal, sleeping pills.

'I don't know if Richie had trouble sleeping or not, but he evidently didn't take any of these. The bottle's still full. There are thirty pills. I think he bought them with the intention of committing suicide. A lot of people make false starts like that. Sometimes they throw the pills away when they change their minds. Other times they keep them around in order to simplify things if they decide to kill themselves at a later date. And there are people who find some security in having the means of suicide close at hand. They say thoughts of self-destruction get people through a great many bad nights.'

I walked over to him and placed the vial on the little table beside his chair.

'There are enough there,' I said. 'If a person were to take them all and go to bed, he wouldn't wake up.'

He looked at me. 'You have everything all worked out.'

'Yes. I haven't been able to think of much else.'

'You expect me to end my life.'

'Your life is over, sir. It's just a question of how it finishes up.'

'And if I take these pills?'

'You leave a note. You're despondent over the death of your son, and you can't find it within yourself to go on living. It won't be that far from the truth, will it?'

'And if I refuse?'

'I go to the police Tuesday morning.'

He breathed deeply several times. Then he said, 'Do you honestly think it would be so bad to let me go on living my life,

Mr Scudder? I perform a valuable function, you know. I'm a good minister.'

'Perhaps you are.'

'I honestly think I do some good in this world. Not a great deal, but some. Is it illogical for me to want to go on doing good?'

'No.'

'And I am not a criminal, you know. I did kill ... that girl.'

'Wendy Hanniford.'

'I killed her. Oh, you're so quick to see it as a calculated, cold-blooded act, aren't you? Do you know how many times I swore not to see her again? Do you know how many nights I lay awake, wrestling with demons? Do you even know how many times I went to her apartment with my razor in my pocket, torn between the desire to slay her and the fear of committing such a monstrous sin? Do you know any of that?'

I didn't say anything.

'I killed her. Whatever happens, I will never kill anyone again. Can you honestly say I constitute a danger to society?'

'Yes.'

'How?'

'It's bad for society when murders remain unpunished.'

'But if I do as you suggest, no one will know I've taken my life for that reason. No one will know I was punished for murder.'

'I'll know.'

'You'd be judge and jury, then. Is that right?'

'No. You will, sir.'

He closed his eyes, leaned back in his chair. I wanted another drink, but I let the flask stay in my pocket. The headache was still there. The aspirin hadn't even touched it.

'I regard suicide as a sin, Mr Scudder.'

'So do I.'

'You do?'

'Absolutely. If I didn't I probably would have killed myself years ago. There are worse sins.'

'Murder.'

'That's one of them.'

He fixed his eyes on me. 'Do you think I am an evil man, Mr Scudder?'

'I'm not an expert on that. Good and evil. I have a lot of trouble figuring those things out.'

'Answer my question.'

'I think you've had good intentions. You were talking about that earlier.'

'And I've paved a road to Hell?'

'Well, I don't know where the road leads, but there are a lot of wrecks along the highway, aren't there? Your wife committed suicide. Your mistress got slashed to death. Your son went crazy and hanged himself for something he didn't do. Does that make you good or evil? You'll have to work that one out for yourself.'

'You intend to go to the police Tuesday morning.'

'If I have to.'

'And otherwise you'll keep your silence.'

'Yes.'

'Ah, and what about you, Mr Scudder? Are you a force for good or evil? I'm sure you've asked yourself the question.'

'Now and then.'

'How do you answer it?'

'Ambivalently.'

'And now, in this act? Forcing me to kill myself?'

'That's not what I'm doing.'

'Isn't it?'

'No. I'm allowing you to kill yourself. I think you're a damned fool if you don't, but I'm not forcing you to do anything.'

SEVENTEEN

I was awake early Monday morning. I got a *Times* at the corner and read it over bacon and eggs and coffee. A cabdriver had been murdered in East Harlem. Someone had stuck an icepick into him through one of the air holes in his partition. Now everyone who read the *Times* would know a new way to score off a cabdriver.

I walked over to the bank when it opened and deposited half of Cale Hanniford's thousand-dollar check. I took the rest in cash, then walked a few blocks to the post office and bought a money order for a few hundred dollars. I addressed an envelope in my hotel room, put a stamp on it, picked up the phone and called Anita.

I said, 'I'm sending you a couple of bucks.'

'You don't have to do that.'

'Well, to pick out something for the boys. How have they been?'

'Fine, Matt. They're in school now, of course. They'll be sorry they missed your call.'

'It's never much good over the phone, anyway. I was thinking, I could get tickets for the Mets game Friday night. If you could get them to the Coliseum I could send them home in a cab. If you think they'd like to go.'

'I know they would. I could drive them there with no trouble.'

'Well, I'll see if I can pick up tickets. They shouldn't be too hard to come by.'

'Should I tell them, or should I wait until you actually have the tickets? Or do you want to tell them yourself?'

'No, you tell them. In case they have something else lined up.

'They'd cancel anything to see the game with you.'

'Well, not if it's something important.'

'They could even go back to the city with you. You could rent them a room at your hotel and put them on the train the next day.'

'We'll see.'

'All right. How have you been, Matt?'

'Fine. You?'

'All right.'

'Things about the same with you and George?'

'Why?'

'Just wondered.'

'We're still seeing each other if that's what you mean.'

'He thinking about getting a divorce from Rosalie?'

'We don't talk about it. Matt, I've got to go, they're honking for me.'

'Sure.'

'And let me know about the tickets.'

'Sure.'

It wasn't in the early *Post*, but around two in the afternoon I had the radio on to one of the all-news stations and they had it. The Reverend Martin Vanderpoel, minister of the First Reformed Church of Bay Ridge, had been found dead in his bedroom by his housekeeper. The death had been tentatively attributed, pending autopsy, to the voluntary ingestion of an overdose of barbiturates. Reverend Vanderpoel was identified as the father of Richard Vanderpoel, who had recently hanged himself after having been arrested for the murder of Wendy Hanniford in the apartment the two had shared in Greenwich Village. Reverend Vanderpoel was reported to have been profoundly despondent over his son's death, and this despondency had evidently led him to take his own life.

I turned off the radio and sat around for half an hour or so. Then I walked around the block to St Paul's and put a hundred dollars in the poor box, a tenth of what I'd received as a bonus from Cale Hanniford.

I sat near the back for a while, thinking about a lot of things.

Before I left I lit four candles. One for Wendy, one for Richie, the usual one for Estrellita Rivera.

And one for Martin Vanderpoel, of course.

TIME TO MURDER
AND CREATE

*Therefore was a single man only first created
to teach thee that whosoever destroyeth a single
soul from the children of man, Scripture charges
him as though he had destroyed the whole world.*

THE TALMUD

ONE

For seven consecutive Fridays I got telephone calls from him. I wasn't always there to receive them. It didn't matter, because he and I had nothing to say to each other. If I was out when he called, there would be a message slip in my box when I got back to the hotel. I would glance at it and throw it away and forget about it.

Then, on the second Friday in April, he didn't call. I spent the evening around the corner at Armstrong's, drinking bourbon and coffee and watching a couple of interns fail to impress a couple of nurses. The place thinned out early for a Friday, and around two Trina went home and Billie locked the door to keep Ninth Avenue outside. We had a couple of drinks and talked about the Knicks and how it all depended on Willis Reed. At a quarter of three I took my coat off the peg and went home.

No messages.

It didn't have to mean anything. Our arrangement was that he would call every Friday to let me know he was alive. If I was there to catch his call, we would say hello to each other. Otherwise he'd leave a message: *Your laundry is ready*. But he could have forgotten or he could be drunk or almost anything.

I got undressed and into bed and lay on my side looking out the window. There's an office building ten or twelve blocks downtown where they leave the lights on at night. You can gauge the pollution level fairly accurately by how much the lights appear to flicker. They were not only flickering wildly that night, they even had a yellow cast to them.

I rolled over and closed my eyes and thought about the phone call that hadn't come. I decided he hadn't forgotten and he wasn't drunk.

The Spinner was dead.

They called him the Spinner because of a habit he had. He carried an old silver dollar as a good-luck charm, and he would haul it out of his pants pocket all the time, prop it up on a table top with his left forefinger, then cock his right middle finger and give the edge of the coin a flick. If he was talking to you, his eyes would stay on the spinning coin while he spoke, and he seemed to be directing his words as much to the dollar as to you.

I had last witnessed this performance on a weekday afternoon in early February. He found me at my usual corner table in Armstrong's. He was dressed Broadway sharp: a pearl-gray suit with a lot of flash, a dark-gray monogrammed shirt, a silk tie the same color as the shirt, a pearl tie tack. He was wearing a pair of those platform shoes that give you an extra inch and a half or so. They boosted his height to maybe five six, five seven. The coat over his arm was navy blue and looked like cashmere.

'Matthew Scudder,' he said. 'You look the same, and how long has it been?'

'A couple of years.'

'Too damn long.' He put his coat on an empty chair, settled a slim attaché case on top of it, and placed a narrow-brimmed gray hat on top of the attaché case. He seated himself across the table from me and dug his lucky charm out of his pocket. I watched him set it spinning. 'Too goddamned long, Matt,' he told the coin.

'You're looking good, Spinner.'

'Been havin' a nice run of luck.'

'That's always good.'

'Long as it keeps runnin'.'

Trina came over, and I ordered another cup of coffee and a shot of bourbon. Spinner turned to her and worked his narrow little face into a quizzical frown. 'Gee, I don't know,' he said. 'Do you suppose I could have a glass of milk?'

She said he could and went away to fetch it. 'I can't drink no more,' he said. 'It's this fuckin' ulcer.'

'They tell me it goes with success.'

'It goes with aggravation is what it goes with. Doc gave me a list of what I can't eat. Everything I like is on it. I got it aced, I can go to the best restaurants and then I can order myself a plate of fuckin' cottage cheese.'

He picked up the dollar and gave it a spin.

I had known him over the years while I was on the force. He'd been picked up maybe a dozen times, always on minor things, but he'd never done any time. He always managed to buy his way off the hook, with either money or information. He set me up for a good collar, a receiver of stolen goods, and another time he gave us a handle on a homicide case. In between he would peddle us information, trading something he'd overheard for a ten- or twenty-dollar bill. He was small and unimpressive and he knew the right moves and a lot of people were stupid enough to talk in his presence.

He said, 'Matt, I didn't just happen to walk in here off the street.'

'I had that feeling.'

'Yeah.' The dollar started to wobble, and he snatched it up. He had very quick hands. We always figured him for a sometime pickpocket, but I don't think anybody ever nailed him for it. 'The thing is, I got problems.'

'They go with ulcers, too.'

'You bet your ass they do.' Spin. 'What it is, I got something I want you to hold for me.'

'Oh?'

He took a sip of milk. He put the glass down and reached over to drum his fingers against the attaché case. 'I got an envelope in here. What I want is for you to hold on to it for me. Put it some place safe where nobody's gonna run across it, you know?'

'What's in the envelope?'

He gave his head an impatient little shake. 'Part of it is you don't have to know what's in the envelope.'

'How long do I have to hold it?'

'Well, that's the whole thing.' Spin. 'See, lots of things can happen to a person. I could walk out, step off the curb, get hit by the Ninth Avenue bus. All the things that can happen to a person, I mean, you just never know.'

'Is somebody trying for you, Spinner?'

The eyes came up to meet mine, then dropped quickly. 'It could be,' he said.

'You know who?'

'I don't even know if, never mind who.' Wobble, snatch. Spin. 'The envelope's your insurance.'

'Something like that.'

I sipped coffee. I said, 'I don't know if I'm right for this, Spinner. The usual thing, you take your envelope to a lawyer and work out a set of instructions. He tosses it into a safe and that's it.'

'I thought of that.'

'So?'

'No point to it. The kind of lawyers I know, the minute I walk out of their office they got the fuckin' envelope open. A straight lawyer, he's gonna run his eyes over me and go out and wash his hands.'

'Not necessarily.'

'There's something else. Say I get hit by a bus, then the lawyer would only have to get the envelope to you. This way we cut out the middleman, right?'

'Why do I have to wind up with the envelope?'

'You'll find out when you open it. *If* you open it.'

'Everything's very roundabout, isn't it?'

'Everything's very tricky lately, Matt. Ulcers and aggravation.'

'And better clothes than I ever saw you wear in your life.'

'Yeah, they can fuckin' bury me in 'em.' Spin. 'Look, all you gotta do is take the envelope, you stick it in a safe-deposit box, something, somewhere, that's up to you.'

'Suppose *I* get hit by a bus?'

He thought it over and we worked it out. The envelope would go under the rug in my hotel room. If I died suddenly, Spinner could come around and retrieve his property. He wouldn't need a key. He'd never needed one in the past.

We worked out details, the weekly phone call, the bland message if I wasn't in. I ordered another drink. Spinner still had plenty of milk left.

I asked him why he had picked me.

'Well, you were always straight with me, Matt. You been off the force how long? A couple of years?'

'Something like that.'

'Yeah, you quit. I'm not good on the details. You killed some kid or something?'

'Yeah. Line of duty, a bullet took a bad hop.'

'Catch a lot of static from on top?'

I looked at my coffee and thought about it. A summer night, the heat almost visible in the air, the air conditioning working overtime in the Spectacle, a bar in Washington Heights where a cop got his drinks on the house. I was off duty, except you never really are, and two kids picked that night to hold up the place. They shot the bartender dead on their way out. I chased them into the street, killed one of them, splintered the other one's thigh bone.

But one shot was off and took a ricochet that bounced it right into the eye of a seven-year-old girl named Estrellita Rivera. Right in the eye, and through soft tissue and on into the brain.

'I was out of line,' the Spinner said. 'I shouldn'ta brought it up.'

'No, that's all right. I didn't get any static. I got a commendation, as a matter of fact. There was a hearing, and I was completely exonerated.'

'And then you quit the force.'

'I sort of lost my taste for the work. And for other things. A house on the Island. A wife. My sons.'

'I guess it happens,' he said.

'I guess it does.'

'So what you're doing, you're sort of a private cop, huh?'

I shrugged. 'I don't have a license. Sometimes I do favors for people and they pay me for it.'

'Well, getting back to our little business ...' Spin. 'You'd be doing me a favor is what you'd be doing.'

'If you think so.'

He picked up the dollar in mid-spin, looked at it, set it down on the blue-and-white checkered tablecloth.

I said, 'You don't want to get killed, Spinner.'

'Fuck, no.'

'Can't you get out from under?'

'Maybe. Maybe not. Let's don't talk about that part of it, huh?'

'Whatever you say.

''Cause if somebody wants to kill you, what the fuck can you do about it? Nothin'.'

'You're probably right.'

'You'll handle this for me, Matt?'

'I'll hang on to your envelope. I'm not saying what I'll do if I have to open it, because I don't know what's in it.'

'If it happens, then you'll know.'

'No guarantees I'll do it, whatever it is.'

He took a long look at me, reading something in my face that I didn't know was there. 'You'll do it,' he said.

'Maybe.'

'You'll do it. And if you don't I won't know about it, so what the fuck. Listen, what do you want in front?'

'I don't know what it is I'm supposed to do.'

'I mean for keeping the envelope. How much do you want?'

I never know how to set fees. I thought for a moment. I said, 'That's a nice suit you're wearing.'

'Huh? Thanks.'

139

'Where'd you get it?'

'Phil Kronfeld's. Over on Broadway?'

'I know where it is.'

'You really like it?'

'It looks good on you. What did it set you back?'

'Three twenty.'

'Then that's my fee.'

'You want the fuckin' suit?'

'I want three hundred and twenty dollars.'

'Oh.' He tossed his head, amused. 'You had me goin' there for a minute. I couldn't understand what the fuck you'd want with the suit.'

'I don't think it would fit.'

'I guess not. Three twenty? Yeah, I guess that's as good a number as any.' He got out a fat alligator wallet and counted out six fifties and a twenty. 'Three – two – oh,' he said, handing them to me. 'If this drags on and on and you want more, you let me know. Good enough?'

'Good enough. Suppose I have to get in touch with you, Spinner?'

'Uh-uh.'

'Okay.'

'Like, you won't have to, and if I wanted to give you an address I couldn't anyway.'

'Okay.'

He opened the attaché and passed me a nine-by-twelve manila envelope sealed on both ends with heavy-duty tape. I took it from him and put it on the bench beside me. He gave the silver dollar a spin, picked it up, put it in his pocket, and beckoned to Trina for the check. I let him have it. He paid it and left a two-dollar tip.

'What's so funny, Matt?'

'Just that I never saw you grab a check before. And I've seen you pick up other people's tips.'

'Well, things change.'

'I guess they do.'

'I didn't do that often, dragging down somebody's tips. You do lots of things when you're hungry.'

'Sure.'

He got to his feet, hesitated, put out his hand. I shook it. He turned to go, and I said, 'Spinner?'

'What?'

'You said the kind of lawyers you know would open the envelope as soon as you left the office.'

'You bet your ass they would.'

'How come you don't think I will?'

He looked at me as though the question was a stupid one. 'You're honest,' he said.

'Oh, Christ. You know I used to take. I let you buy your way out of a collar or two, for Christ's sake.'

'Yeah, but you were always square with me. There's honest and there's honest. You're not gonna open that envelope until you have to.'

I knew he was right. I just didn't know how he knew it. 'Take care of yourself,' I said.

'Yeah, you too.'

'Watch yourself crossing the street.'

'Huh?'

'Watch out for buses.'

He laughed a little, but I don't think he thought it was funny.

Later that day, I stopped off at a church and stuffed thirty-two dollars into the poor box. I sat in a rear pew and thought about the Spinner. He'd given me easy money. All I had to do to earn it was nothing at all.

Back in my room, I rolled up the rug and put Spinner's envelope beneath it, centering it under the bed. The maid runs the vacuum cleaner occasionally but never moves the furniture around. I put the rug back in place and promptly forgot about the envelope, and every Friday a call or a message would assure me that Spinner was alive and the envelope could stay right where it was.

TWO

For the next three days I read the papers twice a day and waited for a phone call. Monday night I picked up the early edition of the *Times* on the way to my room. Under the heading of 'Metropolitan Briefs' there's always a batch of crime items tagged 'From the Police Blotter', and the last one was the one I was looking for. An unidentified male, white, height approximately five six, weight approximately one forty, age approximately forty-five, had been fished out of the East River with a crushed skull.

It sounded right. I'd have put his age a few years higher and his weight a few pounds lower, but otherwise it sounded very right. I couldn't know that it was Spinner. I couldn't even know that the man, whoever he was, had been murdered. The skull damage could have been done after he went into the water. And there was nothing in the item to indicate how long he'd been in the water. If it was more than ten days or so, it wasn't Spinner; I'd heard from him the Friday before.

I looked at my watch. It wasn't too late to call someone, but it was far too late to call someone and seem casual about it. And it was too early to open his envelope. I didn't want to do that until I was very certain he was dead.

I had a couple more drinks than usual, because sleep was a long time coming. In the morning I woke up with a headache and a bad taste in my mouth. I used aspirin and mouthwash and went down to the Red Flame for breakfast. I picked up a later *Times*, but there was nothing further on the floater. They had the same item as the earlier edition.

Eddie Koehler is a lieutenant now, attached to the Sixth Precinct in the West Village. I called from my room and managed to get through to him. 'Hey, Matt,' he said. 'It's been a while.'

It hadn't been all that long. I asked about his family and he asked about mine. 'They're fine,' I said.

'You could always go back there,' he said.

I couldn't, for far more reasons than I wanted to go into. I couldn't start carrying a badge again, either, but that didn't keep him from asking his next question.

'I don't suppose you're ready to rejoin the human race, huh?'

'That's not going to happen, Eddie.'

'Instead you got to live in a dump and scrounge for every buck. Listen, you want to drink yourself to death, that's your business.'

'That's right.'

'But what's the sense paying for your own drinks when you can drink free? You were born to be a cop, Matt.'

'The reason I called –'

'Yeah, there has to be a reason, doesn't there?'

I waited for a minute. Then I said, 'Something in the paper that caught my eye, and I thought maybe you could save me a trip to the morgue. They took a floater out of the East River yesterday. Little guy, middle-aged.'

'So?'

'Could you find out if they identified him yet?'

'Probably. What's your interest?'

'I got a missing husband I'm sort of looking for. He fits the description. I could go down and take a look at him, but I only know him from photographs and after a little while in the water –'

'Yeah, right. What's your guy's name and I'll find out.'

'Let's do it the other way around,' I said. 'It's supposed to be confidential, I don't want to spread the name if I don't have to.'

'I guess I could make a couple of calls.'

'If it's my guy, you'll get yourself a hat.'

'I figured as much. And if it's not?'

'You'll get my sincere gratitude.'

'Fuck you too,' he said. 'I hope it's your guy. I can use a hat. Hey, that's funny, come to think of it.'

'How?'

'You're looking for a guy and I'm hoping he's dead. You think about it, it's pretty funny.'

The phone rang forty minutes later. He said, 'It's a shame, I could've used a hat.'

'They didn't get a make?'

'Oh, they got a make, they made him on fingerprints, but he's not a guy anybody's gonna hire you to look for. He's a character,

143

we got a sheet on him a yard long. You must've run into him once or twice yourself.'

'What's his name?'

'Jacob Jablon. Did a little stooling, a little boosting, all kinds of dumb shit.'

'Name's familiar.'

'They called him the Spinner.'

'I did know him,' I said. 'Haven't run into him in years. He used to spin a silver dollar all the time.'

'Well, all he's gonna spin now is in his grave.'

I drew a breath. I said, 'He's not my guy.'

'I didn't think so. I don't think he was anybody's husband, and if he was she wouldn't want him found.'

'It's not the wife who's looking for my guy.'

'It's not?'

'It's his girlfriend.'

'I'll be a son of a bitch.'

'And I don't think he's in town in the first place, but I might as well string her for a few bucks. A guy wants to disappear, he's just going to do it.'

'That's the way it generally goes, but if she wants to hand you money –'

'That's my feeling,' I said. 'How long was the Spinner in the water? Do they know that yet?'

'I think they said four, five days. What's your interest?'

'Getting him on prints, I figured it had to be fairly recent.'

'Oh, prints'll hold a week, easy. Longer sometimes, depending on the fish. Imagine fingerprinting a floater – shit, if I did that I'd be a long time before I wanted anything to eat. Imagine doing the autopsy.'

'Well, that shouldn't be hard. Somebody must have hit him on the head.'

'Considering who he was, I'd say there's no question. He wasn't the type to go swimming and accidentally hit his head on a pier. What'll you bet they don't come up with a conclusive homicide tag for it, though?'

'Why's that?'

'Because they don't want this sitting in the open file for the next fifty years, and who wants to bust their balls finding out what happened to an asshole like the Spinner? So he's dead, so nobody's gonna cry for him.'

'I always got along with him.'

'He was a cheap little crook. Whoever bumped him did the world a favor.'

'I suppose you're right.'

I got the manila envelope out from under the rug. The tape didn't want to budge, so I got my penknife from the dresser and slit the envelope open along the fold. Then I just sat on the edge of the bed with the envelope in my hand for a few minutes.

I didn't really want to know what was in it.

After a while I opened it, and I spent the next three hours in my room going over the contents. They answered a few questions, but not nearly as many as they asked. Finally I put everything back in the envelope and returned it to its place under the rug.

The cops would sweep Spinner Jablon under the rug, and that's what I wanted to do with his envelope. There were a lot of things I could do, and what I most wanted to do was nothing at all, so until my options had time to sort themselves out in my head the envelope could stay in its hiding place.

I stretched out on the bed with a book, but after I'd gone through a few pages I realized I was reading without paying attention. And my little room was beginning to feel even smaller than usual. I went out and walked around for a while, and then I hit a few places and had a few drinks. I started out in Polly's Cage, across the street from the hotel, then Kilcullen's, then Spiro and Antares. Somewhere along the way I stopped at a deli for a couple of sandwiches. I wound up in Armstrong's, and I was still there when Trina ended her shift. I told her to sit down and I'd buy her a drink.

'But just one, Matt. I got places to go, people to see.'

'So do I, but I don't want to go there and I don't want to see them.'

'You could be just the slightest bit drunk.'

'It's not impossible.'

I went to the bar and got our drinks. Plain bourbon for me, a vodka and tonic for her. I came back to the table, and she picked up her glass.

She said, 'To crime?'

'You've really only got time for one?'

'I don't even have time for the one, but one's got to be the limit.'

'Then let's not make it to crime. Let's make it absent friends.'

145

THREE

I suppose I had a fair idea what was in the envelope before I opened it. When a man who sidesteps through life by keeping his ears open suddenly turns up wearing a three-hundred-dollar suit, it's not hard to figure out how he got it. After a lifetime of selling information, the Spinner had come up with something too good to sell. Instead of peddling information, he had turned to peddling silence. Blackmailers are richer than stool pigeons, because their commodity is not a one-time thing; they can rent it out to the same person over and over for a lifetime.

The only problem is that their lifetimes tend to shrink. The Spinner became a bad actuarial risk the day he got successful. First aggravation and ulcers, then a dented skull and a long swim.

A blackmailer needs insurance. He has to have some leverage that will convince his victim not to terminate the blackmail by terminating the blackmailer. Somebody – a lawyer, a girlfriend, anyone – sits in the background with whatever evidence has the victim squirming in the first place. If the blackmailer dies, the evidence goes to the cops and the shit hits the fan. Every blackmailer makes a point of letting the victim know about this added element. Sometimes there's no confederate, no envelope to be mailed, because evidence lying around is dangerous to all concerned, so the blackmailer just *says* that there is and figures the mark won't call his bluff. Sometimes the mark believes him, and sometimes he doesn't.

Spinner Jablon probably told his mark about the magic envelope from the beginning. But in February he had started to sweat. He had decided that somebody was trying to kill him, or was likely to try, so he had put his envelope together. An actual envelope wouldn't keep him alive if the idea of the envelope failed. He'd be just as dead, and he had known it.

But he had been, in the final analysis, a pro. Penny-ante for almost all his life, but professional just the same. And a professional doesn't get mad. He gets even.

He'd had a problem, though, and it became my problem when I cut his envelope open and checked its contents. Because Spinner had known that he would have to get even with somebody.

He just hadn't known who.

The first thing I looked at was the letter. It was typed, which suggested that at one time or another he had stolen one more typewriter than he could sell, so he'd kept it around. He hadn't used it a hell of a lot. His letter was full of xxxxxx'd out words and phrases, skips between letters, and enough misspelled words to make it interesting. But it added up to something like this:

Matt:
If you're reading this I'm a dead man. I hope it blows over but no bets on that. I think somebody tried for me yesterday. There was this car just about crawled up the curb coming at me.

What I got going is blackmail. I fell into some information worth good money. Years of scrounging around and I finally stepped right into it.

There is three of them. You'll see how it lays when you open the other envelopes. That is the problem, the three of them, because if I'm dead one of them did it and I don't know which. I got each one on a string and I don't know which one I'm choking.

This Prager, two years ago December his daughter ran down a kid on a tricycle and kept on going on account of she was driving on a suspended license and strung out on speed and grass and I don't know what else. Prager has more money than God and he spread it on everybody and his kid was never picked up. All the information is in the envelope. He was the first one, I overheard some shit in a bar and I fed this one guy drinks and he opened up for me. I'm not taking him for anything he can't afford and he just pays me like you pay rent the first of the month but who knows when a man is going to go crazy and maybe that's what happened. He wants me dead, shit, he could hire it done easy enough.

The Ethridge broad was just dumb luck. I hit on her picture in the newspapers, some society page hype, and I reckonized her from this fuck film I saw some years back. Talk about remembering a face, and who looks at the face, but maybe she was giving head to some dude and it caught in my mind. I read all these schools she went to and I couldn't add it up, so I did some homework, and there was a couple

147

years when she dropped out of sight and went into things a little heavy, and I got pictures and some other shit which you'll see. I been dealing with her and whether her husband knows what's happening or anything else I don't know. She is very hard and could kill a person without turning a hare. You look into her eyes and you know exactly what I mean.

Huysendahl came in third on the string and by this time I'm on the earie as a regular thing because it's all working so nice for me. What I pick up on is his wife is a lezzie. Well this is nothing spectacular Matt as you know. But he's rich as shit and he's thinking about pushing for governor so why not dig a little. The dyke thing is nothing, too many people know it in front, and you spread it around and all that happens is he gets the dyke vote which maybe puts him over the top, so I don't care about that, but why is he still married to this dyke, that's my question. Like is there something kinky about him. So I work my ass to the bone and it turns out there's something there, but getting a handle on it is something else again. He's not a normal queer but his thing is young boys, younger the better. It's a sickness and it is enough to turn your stomach. I got small things, like this kid hospitalized for internal injuries which Huysendahl paid the hospital bills, but I wanted to be able to sink the hook so the pictures were a set up. It don't matter how I set it up but there was other people involved. He must of shit when he saw the pictures. The deal cost me a packet but nobody ever made a better investment.

Matt the thing is if somebody hit me it was one of them, or they hired it out which adds up the same way, and what I want is for you to fuck them good. The one that did it, not the other two which played straight with me, which is why I can't leave this with a lawyer and send it all to the police, because the ones that played straight with me deserve to be off the hook, not to mention if it goes to the wrong cop he just works a shakedown and whoever kills me is home free, except he's still paying out money.

The fourth envelope has your name on it because it is for you. There is 3K in it and that is for you. I don't know if it should be more or what it should be, but there's always the chance you'll just put it in your pocket and shitcan the rest of the stuff, which if it happens I'll be dead and won't know about it. Why I think you'll follow through is something I noticed about you a long time ago, namely that you happen to think there is a difference between murder and other crimes. I am the same. I have done bad things all my life but never killed anybody and never would. I have known people who have killed which I've known for a fact or a rumor and would never get close to them. It is the way I am and I think you are that way too and that is why you might do something, and again if you don't I will not know it.

Your Friend,
Jake 'Spinner' Jablon

Wednesday morning I got the envelope out from under the carpet and took another long look at the evidence. I got out my notebook and jotted down a few details. I wasn't going to be able to keep the stuff on hand, because if I made any kind of move I would be making myself visible, and my room would no longer be a clever hiding place.

Spinner had nailed them down tight enough. There was very little hard evidence to prove that Henry Prager's daughter Stacy had left the scene of an accident in which three-year-old Michael Litvak was run down and killed, but in this instance hard evidence wasn't necessary. Spinner had the name of the garage where the Prager car had been repaired, the names of the people in the police department and Westchester D.A.'s officer who had been reached, and a few other bits and pieces which would do the job. If you handed the whole package to a good investigative reporter, he wouldn't be able to leave it alone.

The material on Beverly Ethridge was more graphic. The pictures alone might not have been enough. There were a couple of four-by-five color prints and half a dozen clips of film running a few frames each. She was clearly identifiable throughout, and there was no question what she was doing. This by itself might not have been so damaging. A lot of the things people do for a lark in their youth can be written off readily enough after a few years have passed, especially in those social circles where every other closet sports a skeleton.

But the Spinner had done his homework, just as he'd said. He traced Mrs Ethridge, then Beverly Guildhurst, from the time she left Vassar in her junior year. He turned up an arrest in Santa Barbara for prostitution, sentence suspended. There was a narcotics bust in Vegas, thrown out for lack of evidence, with a strong implication that some family money had pulled her ass out of the fire. In San Diego she was working a badger game with a partner who was a known pimp. It went sour one time; she turned state's evidence and picked up another suspension, while her partner pulled one-to-five in Folsom. The only time she

149

served, as far as Spinner had been able to make out, was fifteen days in Oceanside for drunk and disorderly.

Then she came back and married Kermit Ethridge, and if she hadn't gotten her picture in the paper at just the wrong time, she'd have been home free.

The Huysendahl material was hard to take. The documentary evidence was nothing special: the names of some prepubescent boys and the dates on which Ted Huysendahl had allegedly had sexual relations with them, a stat of hospital records indicating that Huysendahl had sprung for treatment of internal injuries and lacerations for one Jeffrey Kramer, age eleven. But the pictures did not leave you with the feeling that you were looking at the people's choice for the next governor of New York State.

There were an even dozen of them, and they portrayed a fairly full repertoire. The worst one showed Huysendahl's partner, a young and slender black boy, with his face contorted in pain while Huysendahl penetrated him anally. The kid was looking straight at the camera in that shot, as in several of the others, and it was certainly possible that the facial expression of agony was nothing but theater, but that possibility wouldn't prevent nine out of ten average citizens from gladly fitting a noose around Huysendahl's neck and hanging him from the nearest lamp-post.

FOUR

At four thirty that afternoon I was in a reception room on the twenty-second floor of a glass and steel office building on Park Avenue in the high Forties. The receptionist and I had the room to ourselves. She was behind a U-shaped ebony desk. She was a shade lighter than the desk, and she wore her hair in a tight-cropped Afro. I sat on a vinyl couch the same color as the desk. The small white parson's table beside it was sparsely covered with magazines: *Architectural Forum, Scientific American*, a couple of different golf magazines, last week's *Sports Illustrated*. I didn't think any of them would tell me anything I wanted to know, so I left them where they were and looked at the small oil on the far wall. It was an amateurish seascape with a great many small boats cavorting on a turbulent ocean. Men leaned over the sides of the boat in the foreground. They seemed to be vomiting, but it was hard to believe the artist had intended it that way.

'Mrs Prager painted that,' the girl said. 'His wife?'

'It's interesting.'

'All those in his office, she painted them, too. It must be wonderful to have a talent like that.'

'It must be.'

'And she never had a lesson in her life.'

The receptionist found this more remarkable than I did. I wondered when Mrs Prager had taken up painting. After her children were grown, I supposed. There were three Prager children: a boy in medical school at the University of Buffalo, a married daughter in California, and the youngest, Stacy. They had all left the nest now, and Mrs Prager lived in a land-locked house in Rye and painted stormy seascapes.

'He's off the phone now,' the girl said. 'I didn't get your name, I'm afraid.'

'Matthew Scudder,' I said.

She buzzed him to announce my presence. I hadn't expected the name would mean anything to him, and it evidently didn't, because she asked me what my visit was in reference to.

'I'm representing the Michael Litvak project.'

If that registered, Prager wasn't letting on. She conveyed his continued puzzlement. 'The Hit-and-Run Cooperative,' I said. 'The Michael Litvak project. It's a confidential matter, I'm sure he'll want to see me.'

I was sure he wouldn't want to see me at all, actually, but she repeated my words and he couldn't really avoid it. 'He'll see you now,' she said, and nodded her curly little head at a door marked PRIVATE.

His office was spacious, the far wall all glass with a rather impressive view of a city that looks better the higher up you go. The decor was traditional, in sharp contrast to the harsh modern furnishings of the reception room. The walls were paneled in dark wood – individual boards, not the plywood stuff. The carpet was the color of tawny port wine. There were a lot of pictures on the walls, all of them seascapes, all unmistakably the work of Mrs Henry Prager.

I had seen his picture in the papers I'd scanned in the microfilm room at the library. Just head-and-shoulder shots, but they had prepared me for a larger man than the one who now stood up behind the broad leather-topped desk. And the face in the Bachrach photo had beamed with calm assurance. Now it was lined with apprehension pinned in place by caution. I approached the desk, and we stood looking each other over. He seemed to be considering whether or not to offer his hand. He decided against it.

He said, 'Your name is Scudder?'

'That's right.'

'I'm not sure what you want.'

Neither was I. There was a red leather chair with wooden arms near the desk. I pulled it up and sat in it while he was still on his feet. He hesitated a moment, then seated himself. I waited for a few seconds on the off chance that he might have something to say. But he was pretty good at waiting.

I said, 'I mentioned a name before. Michael Litvak.'

'I don't know the name.'

'Then I'll mention another. Jacob Jablon.'

'I don't know that name, either.'

'Don't you? Mr Jablon was an associate of mine. We did some business together.'

'What kind of business would that be?'

'Oh, a little of this, a little of that. Nothing as successful as your line of work, I'm afraid. You're an architectural consultant?'

'That's correct.'

'Large-scale projects. Housing developments, office buildings, that sort of thing.'

'That's hardly classified information, Mr Scudder.'

'It must pay well.'

He looked at me.

'Actually, the phrase you just used. "Classified information." That's what I really wanted to talk to you about.'

'Oh?'

'My associate Mr Jablon had to leave town abruptly.'

'I don't see how –'

'He retired,' I said. 'He was a man who worked hard all his life, Mr Prager, and he came into a sum of money, you see, and he retired.'

'Perhaps you could come to the point.'

I took a silver dollar out of my pocket and gave it a spin, but, unlike Spinner, I kept my eyes on Prager's face instead of on the coin. He could have taken that face to any poker game in town and done just fine with it. Assuming he played his cards right.

'You don't see many of these,' I said. 'I went into a bank a couple of hours ago and tried to buy one. They just stared at me and then told me to go see a coin dealer. I thought a dollar was a dollar, you know? That's the way it used to be. It seems the silver content alone in these things is worth two or three bucks, and the collector value is even higher. I had to pay seven dollars for this thing, believe it or not.'

'Why did you want it?'

'Just for luck. Mr Jablon has a coin just like this one. Or at least it looked the same to me. I'm not a numismatist. That's a coin expert.'

'I know what a numismatist is.'

'Well, I only found that out today, while I was finding out that a dollar's not a dollar any more. Mr Jablon could have saved me seven bucks if he'd left his dollar with me when he went out of town. But he left me something else that's probably worth a little more than seven dollars. See, he gave me this envelope full of papers and things. Some of them have your name on them. And

153

your daughter's name, and some other names I mentioned. Michael Litvak, for example, but that's not a name you recognize, is it?'

The dollar had stopped spinning. Spinner had always snatched it up when it started to wobble, but I just let it drop. It landed heads.

'I thought since those papers had your name on them, along with those other names, I thought you might like to own them.'

He didn't say anything, and I couldn't think of anything else to say. I picked up the silver dollar and gave it another spin. This time we both watched it. It stayed spinning for quite a while on the leather desk top. Then it glanced off a photograph in a silver frame, wobbled uncertainly, and landed heads again.

Prager picked up his desk phone and pushed a buzzer. He said, 'That's all for today, Shari. Just put the machine on and go ahead home.' Then, after a pause: 'No, they can wait, I'll sign them tomorrow. You can head along home now. Fine.'

Neither of us spoke until the door of the outer office opened and closed. Then Prager leaned back in his chair and folded his hands on his shirt front. He was a rather plump man, but there was no spare flesh on his hands. They were slender, with long fingers.

He said, 'I gather you want to take up where – what was his name?'

'Jablon.'

'Where Jablon took off.'

'Something like that.'

'I'm not a rich man, Mr Scudder.'

'You're not starving.'

'No,' he agreed. 'I am not starving.' He looked past me for a moment, probably at a seascape. He said, 'My daughter Stacy went through a difficult period in her life. In the course of it, she had a very unfortunate accident.'

'A little boy died.'

'A little boy died. At the risk of sounding callous, I'll point out that that sort of thing happens all the time. Human beings – children, adults, what does it matter – people are killed accidentally every day.'

I thought of Estrellita Rivera with a bullet in her eye. I don't know if anything showed in my face.

'Stacy's situation – her culpability, if you want to call if that – stemmed not from the accident but from her response after the fact. She didn't stop. If she had stopped, it would not have helped the boy at all. He was killed instantly.'

'Did she know that?'

He closed his eyes for a moment. 'I don't know,' he said. 'Is that pertinent?'

'Probably not.'

'The accident ... if she had stopped as she should have done, I'm sure she would have been exonerated. The boy rode his tricycle right off the curb in front of her.'

'I understand she was on drugs at the time.'

'If you want to call marijuana a drug.'

'It doesn't matter what we call it, does it? Maybe she could have avoided the accident if she hadn't been stoned. Or maybe she would have had the judgment to stop once she hit the kid. Not that it matters any more. She was high, and she did hit the boy, and she didn't stop the car, and you managed to buy her off.'

'Was I wrong to do that, Scudder?'

'How do I know?'

'Do you have children?' I hesitated, then nodded. 'What would you have done?'

I thought about my sons. They weren't old enough to drive yet. Were they old enough to smoke marijuana? It was possible. And what would I do in Henry Prager's place?

'Whatever I had to do,' I said. 'To get them off.'

'Of course. Any father would.'

'It must have cost you a lot of money.'

'More than I could afford. But I couldn't have afforded not to, you see.'

I picked up my silver dollar and looked at it. The date was 1878. It was a good deal older than I was, and had held up a lot better.

'I thought it was over,' he said. 'It was a nightmare, but I managed to straighten everything out. The people I dealt with, they realized that Stacy was not a criminal. She was a good girl from a good family who went through a difficult period in life. That's not uncommon, you know. They recognized that there was no reason to ruin a second life because a horrible accident had taken one life. And the experience – it's awful to say this, but it helped Stacy. She grew as a result of it. She matured. She stopped using drugs, of course. And her life took on more purpose.'

'What's she doing now?'

'She's in graduate school at Columbia. Psychology. She plans to work with mentally retarded children.'

'She's what, twenty-one?'

'Twenty-two last month. She was nineteen at the time of the accident.'

'I suppose she has an apartment here in town?'

'That's correct. Why?'

'No reason. She turned out all right, then.'

'All my children turned out well, Scudder. Stacy had a difficult year or two, that's all.' His eyes sharpened their focus suddenly. 'And how long do I have to pay for that one mistake? That's what I'd like to know.'

'I'm sure you would.'

'Well?'

'How deep did Jablon have the hook in you?'

'I don't understand.'

'What were you paying him?'

'I thought he was your associate.'

'It was a loose association. How much?'

He hesitated, then shrugged. 'The first time he came I gave him five thousand dollars. He gave the impression that one payment would be the end of it.'

'It never is.'

'So I understand. Then he came back a while later. He told me he needed more money. We finally put things on a business basis. So much a month.'

'How much?'

'Two thousand dollars a month.'

'You could afford that.'

'Not all that easily.' He managed a small smile. 'I was hoping I could find a way to deduct it, you know. Charge it to the business in some fashion.'

'Did you find a way?'

'No. Why are you asking all this? Trying to determine just how much you can squeeze out of me?'

'No.'

'This whole conversation,' he said suddenly. 'There's something wrong with it. You don't seem like a blackmailer.'

'How so?'

'I don't know. That man was a weasel, he was calculating, slimy. You're calculating, but in a different way.'

'It takes all kinds.'

He stood up. 'I won't go on paying indefinitely,' he said. 'I can't live with a sword hanging over me. Damn it, I shouldn't *have* to.'

'We'll work something out.'

'I don't want my daughter's life ruined. But I won't be bled to death.'

I picked up the silver dollar and put it in my pocket. I couldn't make myself believe he had killed the Spinner, but at the same time I couldn't positively rule him out, and I was getting sick of the role I was playing. I pushed my chair back and got to my feet.

'Well?'

'I'll be in touch,' I said.

'How much is it going to cost me?'

'I don't know.'

'I'll pay you what I paid him. I won't pay any more than that.'

'And how long will you pay me? Forever?'

'I don't understand.'

'Maybe I can figure out something that'll make us both happy,' I said. 'I'll let you know when I do.'

'If you mean a single large payment, how could I trust you?'

'That's one of the things that has to be worked out,' I said. 'You'll hear from me.'

FIVE

I had arranged to meet Beverly Ethridge in the bar at the Hotel Pierre at seven o'clock. From Prager's office I walked to another bar, one on Madison Avenue. It turned out to be a hangout for advertising people, and the noise level was high and the tension unsettling. I had some bourbon and left.

On my way up Fifth Avenue, I stopped at St Thomas's and slipped into a pew. I discovered churches not long after I left the force and moved away from Anita and the boys. I don't know what it is about them, exactly. They are about the only place in New York where a person has room to think, but I'm not sure that's their sole attraction for me. It seems logical to assume that there's some sort of personal quest involved, although I've no real idea what it might be. I don't pray. I don't think I believe in anything.

But they are perfect places to sit and think things out. I sat in St Thomas's and thought about Henry Prager for a while. The thoughts didn't lead anywhere in particular. If he'd had a more expressive and less guarded face, I might have learned something one way or the other. He had done nothing to give himself away, but if he had been clever enough to nail the Spinner when the Spinner was already on guard, he'd be clever enough to give damned little away to me.

I had trouble seeing him as a murderer. At the same time, I had trouble seeing him as a blackmail victim. He didn't know it, and it was hardly time for me to tell him, but he should have told Spinner to take his dirt and shove it. So much money gets spread around to brush so many crimes under various rugs that no one really had anything resembling a hold on him. His daughter had committed a crime a couple of years ago. A really tough prosecutor might have gone for vehicular homicide, but more likely the charge would have been involuntary manslaughter and the sentence would have been suspended. Given those facts, there was really nothing much that could happen to her or to him this long after the fact. There might be a touch of scandal involved, but not enough to ruin either his business or his daughter's life.

So on the surface he had little motive for paying Spinner off, and less for killing him. Unless there was more to it than I knew about.

Three of them, Prager and Ethridge and Huysendahl, and they had all been paying silence money to Spinner until one of them decided to make the silence permanent. All I had to do was find out which was which.

And I really didn't want to.

For a couple of reasons. One of the best was that there was no way I could have as good a shot at the killer as the police could. All I had to do was dump Spinner's envelope on the desk of a good Homicide cop and let him play it out. The department's determination of time of death would be a lot more accurate than the vague estimate Koehler had given me. They could check alibis. They could put the three possibles through intensive interrogation, which all by itself would almost certainly be enough to open it all up.

There was just one thing wrong with that: The killer would wind up in slam, but the other two would come out with dirty faces. I came very close to passing it on to the cops anyway, figuring that none of the three had spotless faces to begin with. A hit-and-run killer, a hooker and con artist, a particularly nasty pervert – Spinner, with his personal code of ethics, had felt that he owed those innocent of his murder the silence they had purchased. But they had bought nothing from me, and I didn't owe them a thing.

The police would always be an option. If I never got a handle on things, they would remain as a last resort. But in the meantime I was going to make a try, and so I had made an appointment with Beverly Ethridge, I had dropped in on Henry Prager, and I would see Theodore Huysendahl sometime the next day. One way or another, they would all find out I was Spinner's heir and that the hook he'd had in them was in as deep as ever.

A group of tourists passed in the aisle, pointing out things to each other about the elaborate stone carvings above the high altar. I waited until they went by, sat for another minute or two, then got to my feet. On my way out I examined the offering boxes at the doors. You had your choice of furthering church work, overseas missions, or homeless children. I put three of Spinner's thirty hundred-dollar bills in the slot for homeless children.

There are certain things I do without knowing why. Tithing is one of them. A tenth of whatever I earn goes to whatever church I happen to visit after I've received the money. The Catholics get most of my business, not because I'm partial to them but because their churches are more apt to be open at odd times.

St. Thomas's is Episcopal. A plaque in front says they keep it open all week long so that passers-by will have a refuge from the turmoil of midtown Manhattan. I suppose the donations from tourists cover their overheads, Well, they now had a quick three hundred toward the light bill, courtesy of a dead blackmailer.

I went outside and headed uptown. It was time to let a lady know who was taking Spinner Jablon's place. Once they all knew, I would be able to take it easy. I could just sit back and relax, waiting for Spinner's killer to try killing me.

SIX

The cocktail lounge in the Pierre is illuminated by small candles set in deep blue bowls, one to a table. The tables are small and well separated from one another, round white tables with two or three blue velvet chairs at each. I stood blinking my eyes in the darkness and looking for a woman in a white pants suit. There were four or five unescorted women in the room, none of them wearing a pants suit. I looked instead for Beverly Ethridge, and found her at a table along the far wall. She was wearing a navy sheath and a string of pearls.

I gave my coat to the checkroom attendant and walked directly to her table. If she watched my approach, she did so out of the corner of her eye. Her head never turned in my direction. I sat down in the chair across from her, and only then did she meet my eyes. 'I am expecting someone,' she said, and her eyes slipped away, dismissing me.

'I'm Matthew Scudder,' I said.

'Is that supposed to mean something to me?'

'You're pretty good,' I said. 'I like your white pants suit, it becomes you. You wanted to see if I could recognize you so that you would know whether I had the pictures or not. I suppose that's clever, but why not just ask me to bring one along?'

Her eyes returned, and we took a few minutes to look at each other. It was the same face I'd seen in the pictures, but it was hard to believe it was the same woman. I don't know that she looked all that much older, but she did look a great deal more mature. More than that, there was an air of poise and sophistication that was quite incompatible with the girl in those pictures and on those arrest sheets. The face was aristocratic and the voice said good schools and good breeding.

Then she said, 'A fucking cop,' and her face and voice turned on the words and all the good breeding vanished. 'How did you come up with it, anyway?'

161

I shrugged. I started to say something, but a waiter was on his way over. I ordered bourbon and a cup of coffee. She nodded at him to bring her another of what she was drinking. I don't know what it was. It had a lot of fruit in it.

When he was gone I said, 'The Spinner had to leave town for a while. He wanted me to keep the business going in his absence.'

'Sure.'

'Sometimes things happen that way.'

'Sure. You collared him and he threw me to you as his own ticket out. He had to get himself picked up by a crooked cop.'

'Would you be better off with an honest one?'

She put one hand to her hair. It was straight and blonde, and styled in what I think they call a Sassoon cut. It had been considerably longer in the pictures, but the same color. Maybe the color was natural.

'An honest one? Where would I find one?'

'They tell me there's a couple around.'

'Yeah, working traffic.'

'Anyway, I'm not a cop. Just crooked.' Her eyebrows went up. 'I left the force a few years back.'

'Then I don't get it. How do you wind up with the stuff?'

Either she was honestly puzzled or she knew Spinner was dead and she was very good indeed. That was the whole problem. I was playing poker with three strangers and I couldn't even get them all around the same table.

The waiter came around with the drinks. I sipped a little bourbon, drank a half inch of coffee, poured the rest of the bourbon into the cup. It's a great way to get drunk without getting tired.

'Okay,' she said.

I looked at her.

'You'd better lay it out for me, Mr Scudder.' The well-bred voice now, and the face returning to its earlier planes. 'I gather this is going to cost me something.'

'A man has to eat, Mrs Ethridge.'

She smiled suddenly, whether spontaneously or not. Her whole face brightened with it. 'I think you really ought to call me Beverly,' she said. 'It strikes me as odd to be addressed formally by a man who's seen me with a cock in my mouth. And what do they call you – Matt?'

'Generally.'

'Put a price on it, Matt. What's it going to cost?'

'I'm not greedy.'

'I bet you tell that to all the girls. How greedy aren't you?'

'I'll settle for the same arrangement you had with Spinner. What's good enough for him is good enough for me.'

She nodded thoughtfully, a trace of a smile playing on her lips. She put the tip of one dainty finger to her mouth and gnawed it.

'Interesting.'

'Oh?'

'The Spinner didn't tell you much. We didn't have an arrangement.'

'Oh?'

'We were trying to work one out. I didn't want him to nickel me to death a week at a time. I did give him some money. I suppose it came to a total of five thousand dollars over the past six months.'

'Not very much.'

'I also went to bed with him. I would have preferred giving him more money and less sex, but I don't have much money of my own. My husband is a rich man, but that's not the same thing, you see, and I don't have very much money.'

'But you've got a lot of sex.'

She licked her lip in a very obvious way. That didn't make it any less provocative. 'I didn't think you noticed,' she said.

'I noticed.'

'I'm glad.'

I had some of my coffee. I looked around the room. Everybody was poised and well dressed, and I felt out of place. I was wearing my best suit, and I looked like a cop in his best suit. The woman across from me had made pornographic movies, prostituted herself, worked a confidence game. And she was completely at ease here, while I knew I looked out of place.

I said, 'I think I'd rather have money, Mrs Ethridge.'

'Beverly.'

'Beverly,' I agreed.

'Or Bev, if you prefer. I'm very good, you know.'

'I'm sure you are.'

'I'm told I combine a professional's skill and an amateur's zeal.'

'And I'm sure you do.'

'After all, you've seen photographic proof.'

'That's right. But I'm afraid I have a greater need for money than for sex.'

She nodded slowly. 'With Spinner,' she said, 'I was trying to arrange something. I don't have much cash available now. I sold some jewelry, things of that sort, but just to buy time. I could probably raise some money if I had a little time. I mean some substantial money.'

'How substantial?'

She ignored the question. 'Here's the problem. Look, I was on the game, you know that. It was temporary, it was what my psychiatrist calls a radical means of acting out inner anxieties and hostilities. I don't know what the fuck he's talking about, and I'm not sure he does either. I'm clean now, I'm a respectable woman, I'm a fucking jet-setter in a teensy way; but I know how the game works. Once you start paying, you wind up paying for the rest of your life.'

'That's the usual pattern, all right.'

'I don't want that pattern. I want to make one big buy and come up with everything. But it's hard to work out the mechanics of it.'

'Because I could always have copies of the pictures.'

'You could have copies. You could also just hold the information in your head, because the information is enough to wreck me.'

'So you'd need a guarantee that one payment was all you'd ever have to make.'

'That's right. I'd need to have a hook stuck in you so that you wouldn't even think about keeping any pictures. Or about coming back for another shot at me.'

'It's a problem,' I agreed. 'You were trying to work it that way with Spinner?'

'That's right. Neither of us could come up with an idea that the other liked, and in the meantime I stalled him with sex and small change.' She licked her lip. 'It was rather interesting sex. His perceptions of me and all. I don't suppose a little man like that got much experience with young attractive women. And of course the social thing, the Park Avenue goddess, and at the same time he had those pictures and he knew things about me, so I became a special person for him. I didn't find him attractive. And I didn't like him, I didn't like his manner and I hated the hold he had over me. And the same, we did interesting things together. He was surprisingly inventive. I didn't like *having* to do things with him, but I liked *doing* them, if you know what I mean.'

I didn't say anything.

'I could tell you some of the things we did.'

'Don't bother.'

'It might turn you on, listening.'

'I don't think so.'

'You don't like me much, do you?'

'Not too much, no. I can't really afford to like you, can I?'

She drank some of her drink, then licked her lips again. 'You wouldn't be the first cop I ever took to bed,' she said. 'When you're in the game, that's a part of it. I don't think I ever met a cop who wasn't worried about his cock. That it was too small, that he wasn't good at using it. I suppose that's part of carrying a gun and a nightstick and all the rest of it, don't you think?'

'Could be.'

'Personally, I always found cops to be built the same as anyone else.'

'I think we're getting off the subject, Mrs Ethridge.'

'Bev.'

'I think we ought to talk about money. One large sum of money, say, and then you can get off the hook and I can let go of the fishing rod.'

'How much money are we talking about?'

'Fifty thousand dollars.'

I don't know what sort of figure she was expecting. I don't know if she and Spinner had talked price while they rolled around on expensive sheets. She pursed her lips and gave a silent whistle, indicating that the sum I'd mentioned was a very large sum indeed.

She said, 'You have expensive ideas.'

'You pay it once and it's over.'

'Back on Square A. How do I know that?'

'Because when you pay over the money, I give you a handle on me. I did something a few years ago. I could go to jail for it for a long time. I can write out a confession giving all the details. I'll give it to you when you pay the fifty thou, along with the stuff Spinner has on you. That locks me in, keeps me from doing a thing.'

'It wasn't just something like police corruption.'

'No, it wasn't.'

'You made somebody dead.'

I didn't say anything.

She took her time thinking it over. She took out a cigarette, tapped its end on a well-manicured nail. I guess she was waiting for me to light it for her. I remained in character and let her light it for herself.

Finally she said, 'It might work.'

'I'd be putting my neck in a noose. You wouldn't have to worry about me running out and yanking on the rope.'

She nodded. 'There's only one problem.'

'The money?'

'That's the problem. Couldn't we lower the price a little?'

'I don't think so.'

'I just don't have that kind of money.'

'Your husband does.'

'That doesn't put it in my handbag, Matt.'

'I could always eliminate the middleman,' I said. 'Sell the goods directly to him. He'd pay.'

'You bastard.'

'Well? Wouldn't he?'

'I'll get the money somewhere. You bastard. He probably wouldn't pay, as a matter of fact, and then your hold's gone, isn't it? Your hold and my life, and we both wind up with nothing, and are you sure you want to risk that?'

'Not if I don't have to.'

'Meaning if I come up with the money. You've got to give me some time.'

'Two weeks.'

She shook her head. 'At least a month.'

'That's longer than I planned on staying in town.'

'If I can have it faster, I will. Believe me, the faster you're off my back the better I like it. But it might take me a month.'

I told her a month would be all right but I hoped it wouldn't take that long. She told me I was a bastard and a son of a bitch, and then she turned abruptly seductive again and asked me if I wouldn't like to take her to bed anyway for the hell of it. I liked it better when she called me names.

She said, 'I don't want you calling me. How can I get in touch with you?'

I gave her the name of my hotel. She tried not to show it, but it was obvious that my openness surprised her. Evidently the Spinner hadn't wanted her to know where she could find him.

I didn't blame him.

SEVEN

On his twenty-fifth birthday, Theodore Huysendahl had come into an inheritance of two and a half million dollars. A year later he'd added another million and change by marrying Helen Godwynn, and in the next five years or so he'd increased their total wealth to somewhere in the neighborhood of fifteen million dollars. At age thirty-two he sold his business interests, moved from a waterfront estate in Sands Point to a co-op apartment on Fifth Avenue in the Seventies, and devoted his life to public service. The President appointed him to a commission. The Mayor installed him as head of the Parks and Recreation Department. He gave good interviews and made good copy and the press loved him, and as a result he got his name in the papers a lot. For the past few years he'd been making speeches all over the state, turning up at every Democratic fund-raising dinner, calling press conferences all over the place, guesting occasionally on television talk shows. He always said that he was not running for governor, and I don't think even his own dog was dumb enough to buy that one. He was running, and running very hard, and he had a lot of money to spend and a lot of political favors to call, and he was tall and good-looking and radiantly charming, and if he had a political position, which was doubtful, it was not far enough to either the left or the right to alienate voters in the great middle.

The smart money gave him one shot in three at the nomination, and if he got that far he had a very strong chance for election. And he was only forty-one. He was probably already looking beyond Albany in the direction of Washington.

A handful of nasty little photographs could end all that in a minute.

He had an office in City Hall. I took the subway down to Chambers Street and headed over there, but first I detoured and walked up Center Street and stood in front of Police Headquarters for a few minutes. There was a bar across the street where we used to go before or after appearing in the Criminal Courts Building. It was a little early for a drink, though, and I didn't much want to run into anyone, so I went over to City Hall and managed to find Huysendahl's office.

His secretary was an older woman with wiry gray hair and sharp blue eyes. I told her I wanted to see him, and she asked my name.

I took out my silver dollar. 'Watch closely,' I said, and set it spinning on the corner of her desk. 'Now just tell Mr Huysendahl exactly what I've done, and that I'd like to see him in private. Now.'

She scrutinized my face for a moment, probably in an attempt to assess my sanity. Then she reached for the telephone, but I put my hand gently atop hers.

'Ask him in person,' I said.

Another long sharp look, with her head cocked slightly to one side. Then, without quite shrugging, she got up and went into his office, closing the door after her.

She wasn't in there long. She came out looking puzzled and told me Mr Huysendahl would see me. I'd already hung my coat on a metal rack. I opened Huysendahl's door, went in, closed it after me.

He started talking before he raised his eyes from the paper he was reading. He said, 'I thought it was agreed that you were not to come here. I thought we established –'

Then he looked up and saw me, and something happened to his face.

He said, 'You're not –'

I flipped the dollar into the air and caught it. 'I'm not George Raft, either,' I said. 'Who were you expecting?'

He looked at me, and I tried to get something out of his face. He looked even better than his newspaper photos, and a lot better than the candid shots I had of him. He was sitting behind a gray steel desk in an office furnished with standard City-issue goods. He could have afforded to redecorate it himself – a lot of people in his position did that. I don't know what it said about him that he hadn't, or what it was supposed to say.

I said, 'Is that today's *Times*? If you were expecting a different man with a silver dollar, you couldn't have read the paper very carefully. Third page of the second section, toward the bottom of the page.'

'I don't understand what this is all about.'

I pointed at the paper. 'Go ahead. Third page, second section.'

I stayed on my feet while he found the story and read it. I'd seen it myself over breakfast, and I might have missed it if I hadn't been looking for it. I hadn't known whether it would make the paper or not, but there were three paragraphs identifying the corpse from the East River as Jacob 'Spinner' Jablon and giving a few of the highlights of his career.

I watched carefully while Huysendahl read the squib. There was no way his reaction could have been anything other than legitimate. The color drained instantly from his face, and a pulse hammered in his temple. His hands clenched so violently that the paper tore. It certainly seemed to mean that he hadn't known Spinner was dead, but it could also mean he hadn't expected the body to come up and was suddenly realizing what a pot he was in.

'God,' he said. 'That's what I was afraid of. That's why I wanted – oh, *Christ!*'

He wasn't looking at me and he wasn't talking to me. I had the feeling that he didn't remember I was in the room with him. He was looking into the future and watching it go down the drain.

'Just what I was afraid of,' he said again. 'I kept telling him that. If anything happened to him, he said, a friend of his would know what to do with those ... those pictures. But he had nothing to fear from me, I told him he had nothing to fear from me. I would have paid anything, and he knew that. But what would I do if he died? 'You better hope I live forever,' that's what he said.' He looked up at me. 'And now he's dead,' he said. 'Who *are* you?'

'Matthew Scudder.'

'Are you from the police?'

'No. I left the department a few years ago.'

He blinked. 'I don't know ... I don't know why you're here,' he said. He sounded lost and helpless, and I wouldn't have been surprised if he had started to weep.

'I'm sort of a freelance,' I explained. 'I do favors for people, pick up the odd dollar here and there.'

'You're a private detective?'

'Nothing that formal. I keep my eyes and ears open, that sort of thing.'

169

'I see.'

'Here I read this item about my old friend Spinner Jablon, and I thought it might put me in a position to do a favor for a person. A favor for you, as a matter of fact.'

'Oh?'

'I figured that maybe Spinner had something that you'd like to have your hands on. Well, you know, keeping my eyes and ears open and all that, you never know what I might come up with. What I figured was that there might be some kind of a reward offered.'

'I see.' he said. He started to say something else, but the phone rang. He picked it up and started to tell the secretary that he wasn't taking any calls, but this one was from His Honor and he decided not to duck it. I pulled up a chair and sat there while Theodore Huysendahl talked with the Mayor of New York. I didn't really pay much attention to the conversation. When it ended, he used the intercom to stress that he was out to all callers for the time being. Then he turned to me and sighed heavily.

'You thought there might be a reward.'

I nodded. 'To justify my time and expenses.'

'Are you the ... friend Jablon spoke of?'

'I was a friend of his,' I admitted.

'Do you have those pictures?'

'Let's say I might know where they are.'

He rested his forehead on the heel of his hand and scratched his hair. The hair was a medium brown, not too long and not too short; like his political position, it was designed to avoid irritating anyone. He looked at me over the tops of his glasses and sighed again.

Levelly he said, 'I would pay a substantial sum to have those pictures in hand.'

'I can understand that.'

'The reward would be ... a generous one.'

'I thought it probably would be.'

'I can afford a generous reward, Mr ... I don't think I got your name.'

'Matthew Scudder.'

'Of course. I'm usually quite good at names, actually.' His eyes narrowed. 'As I said, Mr Scudder, I can afford a generous reward. What I cannot afford is for that material to remain in existence.'

170

He drew a breath and straightened up in his chair. 'I am going to be the next governor of the State of New York.'

'So a lot of people say.'

'More people will say it. I have scope, I have imagination, I have vision. I'm not a party hack in debt to the bosses. I'm independently wealthy, I'm not looking to enrich myself out of the public till. I could be an excellent governor. The state needs leadership. I could –'

'Maybe I'll vote for you.'

He smiled ruefully. 'I don't suppose it's time for a political speech, is it? Especially at a time when I'm so careful to deny that I'm a candidate. But you must see the importance of this to me, Mr Scudder.'

I didn't say anything.

'Did you have a specific reward in mind?'

'You'd have to set that figure. Of course, the higher it is, the more of an incentive it would be.'

He put his fingertips together and thought it over. 'One hundred thousand dollars.'

'That's quite generous.'

'That's what I would pay as a reward. For the return of absolutely everything.'

'How would you know you got everything back?'

'I've thought of that. I had that problem with Jablon. Our negotiations were complicated by the difficulty I found in being in the same room with him. I knew instinctively that I would be at his mercy on a permanent basis. If I gave him substantial funds, he'd run through them sooner or later and be back for more money. Blackmailers always are, from what I understand.'

'Usually.'

'So I paid him so much a week. A weekly envelope, old bills out of sequence, as if I were paying ransom. As in a sense I was. I was ransoming all my tomorrows.' He leaned back in his wooden swivel chair and closed his eyes. He had a good head, a strong face. I suppose there must have been weakness in it, because he had shown this weakness in his behavior, and sooner or later your character shows up in your face. It takes longer in some faces than in others; if there was weakness there, I couldn't spot it.

'All my tomorrows,' he said. 'I could afford that weekly payment. I could think of it' – that quick, rueful smile – 'as a campaign expense. An ongoing one. What worried me was my continued vulnerability, not to Mr Jablon but to what might come to pass should he die. My God, people die every day. Do you know how many New Yorkers are murdered in the average day?'

'It used to be three,' I said. 'A homicide once every eight hours, that was the average. I suppose it's higher now.'

'The figure I heard was five.'

'Higher in the summer. One week last July the tally ran over ·fifty. Fourteen of them in one day.'

'Yes, I remember that week.' He looked away for a moment, evidently lost in thought. I didn't know whether he was planning how to reduce homicide rates when he was governor or how to add my name to the list of victims. He said, 'Can I assume that Jablon was murdered?'

'I don't see how you can assume anything else.'

'I thought that might happen. I worried about it, that is. That sort of man, his kind runs a higher-than-average risk of being murdered. I'm sure I wasn't his only victim.' His voice rose in pitch on the last words of the sentence, and he waited for me to confirm or deny his guess. I outwaited him, and he went on. 'But even if he weren't murdered, Mr Scudder, men die. They don't live forever. I didn't like paying that slimy gentleman every week, but the prospect of ceasing to pay him was significantly worse. He could die in any number of ways, anything at all. A drug overdose, say.'

'I don't think he used anything.'

'Well, you understand my point.'

'He could have been hit by a bus,' I said.

'Exactly.' Another long sigh. 'I can't go through this again. Let me state my case quite plainly. If you ... recover the material. I'll pay you the figure I stated. One hundred thousand dollars, paid in any fashion you care to specify. Paid into a private Swiss account, if you prefer. Or handed over to you in cash. For that I'll expect the return of absolutely everything and your continued silence.'

'That makes sense.'

'I should think so.'

'But what guarantee would you have that you're getting what you pay for?'

His eyes studied me keenly before he spoke. 'I think I'm rather good at judging men.'

'And you've decided I'm honest?'

'Hardly that. No insult intended, Mr Scudder, but such a conclusion would be naive on my part, wouldn't it?'

'Probably.'

'What I have decided,' he said, 'is that you are intelligent. So let me spell things out. I will pay you the sum I've mentioned. And if, at any time in the future, you should attempt to extort further funds from me, on whatever pretext, I would make contact with … certain people. And have you killed.'

'Which might put you right on the spot.'

'It might,' he agreed. 'But in a certain position I would have to take just that chance. And I said before that I believe you are intelligent. What I meant was that I feel you would be intelligent enough to avoid finding out whether or not I'm bluffing. One hundred thousand dollars should be a sufficient reward. I don't think you'd be foolish enough to push your luck.'

I thought it over, gave a slow nod. 'One question.'

'Ask it.'

'Why didn't you think of making this offer to the Spinner?'

'I did think of it.'

'But you didn't make it.'

'No, Mr Scudder, I did not.'

'Why?'

'Because I didn't think he was sufficiently intelligent.'

'I guess you were right about that.'

'Why do you say that?'

'He wound up in the river,' I said. 'That wasn't very bright of him.'

EIGHT

That was Thursday. I left Huysendahl's office a little before noon and tried to figure out what to do next. I'd seen all three of them now. They were all on notice, they all knew who I was and where to find me. I in turn had picked up a handful of facts about Spinner's operation and not very much more. Prager and Ethridge had given no indication of knowing the Spinner was dead. Huysendahl had seemed genuinely shocked and dismayed when I pointed it out to him. So far as I could tell, I'd accomplished nothing beyond making a target out of myself, and I wasn't even certain I'd done that right. It was conceivable I'd made myself all too reasonable a blackmailer. One of them had tried murder once, and it hadn't worked too well, so he might not be inclined to try it again. I could pick up fifty grand from Beverly Ethridge and twice that from Ted Huysendahl and some as yet undetermined sum from Henry Prager, and that would be just perfect except for one thing. I wasn't looking to get rich. I was looking to trap a killer.

The weekend floated on by. I spent a little time in the microfilm room at the library, scanning old issues of the *Times* and picking up useless information on my three possibles and their various friends and relations. On the same page with an old story about a shopping center with which Henry Prager had been involved. I happened to see my own name. There was a story about a particularly good collar I had made about a year before I left the force. A partner and I had tagged a heroin wholesaler with enough pure smack to give the world an overdose. I would have enjoyed the story more if I hadn't known how it turned out. The dealer had a good lawyer, and the whole thing got thrown out on a technicality. The word at the time was that it had taken an even twenty-five thou to put the judge in the proper frame of mind.

You learn to get philosophical about things like that. We didn't manage to put the prick away, but we hurt him pretty good. Twenty-five for the judge, ten or fifteen easy for the lawyer, and on top of that he'd lost the smack, which left him out what he'd paid the importer plus what he could have expected to clear when he turned it over. I'd have been happier to see him in slam, but you take what you can get. Like the judge.

Sometime Sunday I called a number I didn't have to look up. Anita answered, and I told her a money order was on its way to her. 'I came up with a couple of bucks,' I said.

'Well, we can find a use for it,' she said. 'Thanks. Do you want to talk to the boys?'

I did and I didn't. They're getting to an age where it's a little easier for me to talk to them, but it's still awkward over the phone. We talked about basketball.

Right after I hung up, I had an odd thought. It occurred to me that I might not be talking to them again. Spinner had been a careful man by nature, a man who had made himself inconspicuous reflexively, a man who had felt most comfortable in deep shadows, and he still had not been careful enough. I was accustomed to open spaces, and in fact had to stay enough in the open to invite a murder attempt. If Spinner's killer decided to take a shot at me, he just might make it work.

I wanted to call back and talk to them again. It seemed that there ought to be something important for me to say, just on the off chance that I'd taken on more than I could carry. But I couldn't manage to think what it might be, and a few minutes later the impulse went away.

I had a lot to drink that night. It was just as well no one took a crack at me then. I'd have been easy.

Monday morning I called Prager. I'd left him on a very loose leash, and I had to give it a yank. His secretary told me he was busy on another line and asked if I would hold. I held for a minute or two. Then she came back to establish that I was still hanging in there, and then she put me through to him.

I said, 'I've decided how we'll work this so that you're covered. There's something the police tried to hang on me that they could never make stick.' He didn't know I'd been a cop myself. 'I can write out a confession, include enough evidence to make it airtight. I'll give that to you as part of our deal.'

It was basically the arrangement I'd tried out on Beverly Ethridge, and it made the same kind of sense to him that it had to her. Neither of them had managed to spot the joker in it, either: All I had to do was confess at great length to a crime that had never happened, and while my confession might make interesting reading, it would hardly enable anyone to hold a gun to my head. But Prager didn't figure out that part of it, so he liked the idea.

What he didn't like was the price I set.

'That's impossible,' he said.

'It's easier than paying it in bits and pieces. You were paying Jablon two thousand a month. You'll pay me sixty in one chunk, that's less than three years' worth, and it'll all be over once and for all.'

'I can't raise that kind of money.'

'You'll find a way, Prager.'

'I can't manage it.'

'Don't be silly,' I said. 'You're an important man in your field, a success. If you don't have it in cash, you certainly have assets you can borrow against.'

'I can't do it.' His voice almost broke. 'I've had ... financial difficulties. Some investments haven't turned out to be what they should have been. The economy, there's less building, the interest rates are going crazy, just last week somebody raised the prime rate to ten percent –'

'I don't want an economics lesson, Mr Prager. I want sixty thousand dollars.'

'I've borrowed every cent I could.' He paused for a moment. 'I can't, I have no source –'

'I'll need the money fairly soon,' I cut in. 'I don't want to stay in New York any longer than I have to.'

'I don't –'

'You do some creative thinking,' I said. 'I'll be in touch with you.'

I hung up and sat in the phone booth for a minute or two, until someone waiting to use it gave an impatient knock on the door. I opened the door and stood up. The man who wanted to use the phone looked as though he was going to say something, but he looked at me and changed his mind.

I wasn't enjoying myself. I was putting Prager through a wringer. If he'd killed Spinner, then maybe he had it coming. But

176

if he hadn't, I was torturing him to no purpose, and the thought did not sit well with me.

But one thing had come out of the conversation: He was hurting for money. And if Spinner, too, had been pushing for the fast final settlement, the big bite so that he could get out of town before someone killed him, that might have been enough to put the last bit of pressure on Henry Prager.

I'd been on the verge of ruling him out when I saw him in his office. I just didn't see that he had enough of a motive, but now he seemed to have a pretty good one after all.

And I'd just given him another.

I called Huysendahl a little later. He was out, so I left my number, and he called around two.

'I know I wasn't supposed to call you,' I said 'but I have some good news for you.'

'Oh?'

'I'm in a position to claim my reward.'

'You managed to turn up that material?'

'That's right.'

'Very quick work,' he said.

'Oh, just sound detective procedure and a little bit of luck.'

'I see. It may take some time to, uh, assemble the reward.'

'I don't have very much time, Mr Huysendahl.'

'You have to be reasonable about this, you know. The sum we discussed is substantial.'

'I understand you have substantial assets.'

'Yes, but hardly in cash. Not every politician has a friend in Florida with that kind of money in a wall safe.' He chuckled over the line, and seemed disappointed when I didn't join in. 'I'll need some time.'

'How much time?'

'A month at the outside. Perhaps less than that.'

The role was easy enough, since I kept getting to rehearse it. I said, 'That's not soon enough.'

'Really? Just how much of a hurry are you in?'

'A big one. I want to get out of town. The climate doesn't agree with me.'

'Actually, it's been rather mild the past few days.'

'That's just the trouble. It's too hot.'

'Oh?'

'I keep thinking about what happened to our mutual friend, and I wouldn't want it to happen to me.'

'He must have made someone unhappy.'

'Yeah, well, I've made a few people unhappy myself, Mr Huysendahl, and what I want to do is get the hell out of here within the week.'

'I don't see how that would be possible.' He paused for a moment. 'You could always go and come back for the reward when things have had a chance to cool down somewhat.'

'I don't think I'd like to do it that way.'

'That's rather an alarming statement, don't you think? The sort of venture we've discussed requires a certain amount of give-and-take. It has to be a cooperative venture.'

'A month is just too long.'

'I might be able to manage it in two weeks.'

'You might have to,' I said.

'That sounds disturbingly like a threat,'

'The thing is, you're not the only person furnishing a reward.'

'I'm not surprised.'

'Right. And if I have to leave town before I can collect the reward from you, well, you never know what might happen.'

'Don't be foolish, Scudder.'

'I don't want to be. I don't think either of us should be foolish.' I took a breath. 'Look, Mr Huysendahl, I'm sure it's nothing we can't work out.'

'I certainly hope you're right.'

'How does two weeks sound to you?'

'Difficult.'

'Can you manage it?'

'I can try. I *hope* I can manage it.'

'So do I. You know how to reach me.'

'Yes,' he said. 'I know how to reach you.'

I hung the phone up and poured a drink. Just a small one. I drank half of it and nursed the rest of it. The phone rang. I tossed down the last of the bourbon and picked it up. I thought it would be Prager. It was Beverly Ethridge.

She said, 'Matt, it's Bev. I hope I didn't wake you?'

'You didn't.'

'Are you alone?'

'Yes. Why?'

'I'm lonesome.'

I didn't say anything. I remembered sitting across the table from her, making it obvious that she wasn't getting to me. The performance had evidently convinced her. But I knew better. The woman was good at getting to people.

'I hoped we could get together, Matt. There are things we ought to talk about.'

'All right.'

'Would you be free around seven this evening? I've appointments until then.'

'Seven's fine.'

'The same place?'

I remembered how I had felt in the Pierre. This time we would meet on my turf. But not Armstrong's; I didn't want to take her there.

'There's a place called Polly's Cage,' I said. 'Fifty-seventh between Eighth and Ninth, middle of the block, the downtown side.'

'Polly's Cage? It sounds charming.'

'It's better than it sounds.'

'Then I'll see you there at seven. Fifty-seventh between Eighth and Ninth – that's very near your hotel, isn't it?'

'It's across the street.'

'That's very convenient,' she said.

'It's handy for me.'

'It might be handy for both of us, Matt.'

I went out and had a couple of drinks and something to eat. Around six I got back to my hotel. I checked with the desk, and Benny told me I'd had three calls and there had been no messages.

I wasn't in my room ten minutes before the phone rang. I picked it up, and a voice I didn't recognize said, 'Scudder?'

'Who's this?'

'You ought to be very careful. You go off half-cocked and upset people.'

'I don't think I know you.'

'You don't want to know me. All you gotta know is it's a big river, plenty of room in it, you don't want to try and fill it up all by yourself.'

'Who wrote that line for you, anyway?'

The phone clicked.

NINE

I got to Polly's a few minutes early. There were four men and two women drinking at the bar. Behind it, Chuck was laughing politely at something one of the women had said. On the jukebox Sinatra was asking them to send in the clowns.

The room is a small one, with the bar on the right side as you enter. A railing runs the length of the room, and on the left of it there is an area a few steps up that contains about a dozen tables. They were all unoccupied now. I walked to the break in the railing, climbed the steps, and took the table that was farthest from the door.

Polly's gets most of its play around five, when thirsty people leave their offices. The really thirsty ones stick around longer than the rest, but the place doesn't pick up much passer-by trade, and almost always closes fairly early. Chuck pours generous drinks, and the five-o'clock drinkers usually tap out early on. On Fridays the TGIF crowd shows a certain amount of perseverance, but other times they generally lock up by midnight, and they don't even bother opening up on Saturdays or Sundays. It's a bar in the neighborhood without being a neighborhood bar.

I ordered a double bourbon, and had put half of it away by the time she walked in. She hesitated in the doorway, not seeing me at first, and some conversations died as heads turned her way. She seemed unaware of the attention she was drawing, or too accustomed to it to take notice of it. She spotted me, came over, and sat opposite me. The bar conversations resumed once it was established that she wasn't up for grabs.

She slid her coat off her shoulders and onto the back of her chair. She was wearing a hot-pink sweater. It was a good color for her, and an excellent fit. She took a pack of cigarettes and a lighter from her handbag. This time she didn't wait for me to light her cigarette. She drew in a lot of smoke, blew it out in a thin column, and watched with evident interest as it ascended toward the ceiling.

When the waitress came over she ordered gin and tonic. 'I'm rushing the season,' she said. 'It's really too cold out for summer drinks. But I'm such a warm person emotionally that I can carry it off, don't you think?'

'Whatever you say, Mrs Ethridge.'

'Why do you keep forgetting my first name? Blackmailers shouldn't be so formal with their victims. It's easy for me to call you Matt. Why can't you call me Beverly?'

I shrugged. I didn't really know the answer myself. It was hard to be sure what was my own reaction to her and what was a part of the role I was playing. I didn't call her Beverly largely because she wanted me to, but that was an answer that only led to another question.

Her drink came. She put out her cigarette, sipped her gin and tonic. She breathed deeply, and her breasts rose and fell within the pink sweater.

'Matt?'

'What?'

'I've been trying to figure out a way to raise the money.'

'Good.'

'It's going to take me some time.'

I played them all the same way, and they all came back with the same response. Everybody was rich and nobody could get a few dollars together. Maybe the country was in trouble, maybe the economy was as bad as everybody said it was.

'Matt?'

'I need the money right away.'

'You son of a bitch, don't you think I'd like to get this over with as soon as possible? The only way I could get the money is from Kermit, and I can't tell him what I need it for.' She lowered her eyes. 'Anyway, he hasn't got it.'

'I thought he had more money than God.'

She shook her head. 'Not yet. He has an income, and it's substantial, but he doesn't come into the principal until he's thirty-five.'

'When does that happen?'

'In October. That's his birthday. The Ethridge money is all tied up in a trust that terminates when the youngest child turns thirty-five.'

'He's the youngest?'

181

'That's right. He'll come into the money in October. That's in six months. I've decided, I've even mentioned it to him, that I'd like to have some money of my own. So that I won't be dependent upon him to the extent that I am now. That's the kind of request he can understand, and he's more or less agreed to it. So in October he'll give me money. I don't know how much, but it will certainly be more than fifty thousand dollars, and then I'll be able to work things out with you.'

'In October.'

'Yes.'

'You won't have money in your hands then, though. There'll be a lot of paperwork involved. October's six months from now, and it'll be another six months easy before you've got cash in hand.'

'Will it really take that long?'

'Easily. So we're not talking about six mouths, we're talking about a year, and that's too long. Even six months is too long. Hell, *one* month is too long, Mrs Ethridge. I want to get out of this town.'

'Why?'

'I don't like the climate.'

'But spring's here. These are New York's best months, Matt.'

'I still don't like it.'

She closed her eyes, and I studied her face in repose. The lighting in the room was perfect for her, paired electric candles glowing against the red flecked wallpaper. At the bar, one of the men got to his feet picked up some of the change in front of him, and headed for the door. On the way out he said something, and one of the women laughed loudly. Another man entered the bar. Somebody put money in the jukebox, and Lesley Gore said it was her party and she would cry if she wanted to.

'You've got to give me time,' she said.

'I haven't got it to give.'

'Why do you have to get out of New York? What are you afraid of, anyway?'

'The same thing the Spinner was afraid of.'

She nodded thoughtfully. 'He was very nervous toward the end,' she said. 'It made the bed part very interesting.'

'It must have.'

'I wasn't the only one on his string. He made that fairly obvious. Are you playing his whole string, Matt? Or just me?'

'It's a good question, Mrs Ethridge.'

'Yeah, I like it myself. Who killed him, Matt? One of his other customers?'

'You mean he's dead?'

'I read newspapers.'

'Sure. Sometimes your picture's in them.'

'Yeah, and wasn't that just my lucky day. Did you kill him, Matt?'

'Why would I do that?'

'So that you could take his nice little number away from him. I thought you shook him down. Then I read how they fished him out of the river. Did you kill him?'

'No. Did you?'

'Sure, with my little bow and arrow. Listen, wait a year for your money and I'll double it. A hundred thousand dollars. That's nice interest.'

'I'd rather take the cash and invest it myself.'

'I told you I can't get it.'

'How about your family?'

'What about them? They don't have any money.'

'I thought you had a rich daddy.'

She winced, and covered it by lighting another cigarette. Both our drinks were empty. I motioned to the waitress, and she brought fresh ones. I asked if there was any coffee made. She said there wasn't but she'd make a pot if I wanted. She sounded as though she really hoped I wouldn't want her to. I told her not to bother.

Beverly Ethridge said, 'I had a rich great-grandfather.'

'Oh?'

'My own father followed in his father's footsteps. The gentle art of turning a million dollars into a shoestring. I grew up thinking the money would always be there. That's what made everything that happened in California so easy. I had a rich daddy and I never really had to worry about anything. He could always bail me out. Even the serious things weren't serious.'

'Then what happened?'

'He killed himself.'

'How?'

'Sat in the car in a closed garage with the motor running. What's the difference?'

'None, I guess. I always wonder how people do it, that's all. Doctors usually use guns, did you know that? They have access to the simplest, cleanest ways in the world, an O.D. of morphine, anything like that, and instead they generally blow their brains out and make a hell of a mess. Why did he kill himself?'

'Because the money was gone.' She picked up her glass, but paused with it halfway to her mouth. 'That was why I came back east. All of a sudden he was dead, and instead of money there were debts. There was enough insurance so that my mother can live decently. She sold the house, moved to an apartment. With that and Social Security, she gets along.' She took a long drink now. 'I don't want to talk about it.'

'All right.'

'If you took those pictures to Kermit, you wouldn't get anything. You'd just queer your own pitch. He wouldn't buy them, because he wouldn't care about my good name. He'd just care about his own, which would mean getting rid of me and finding a wife as bloodless as he is.'

'Maybe.'

'He's playing golf this week. A pro-am tournament, they have them the day before the regular tournaments. He gets a professional golfer for a partner, and if they finish in the money the pro gets a few dollars out of it. Kermit gets the glory. It's his chief passion, golf.'

'I thought you were.'

'I'm nicely ornamental. And I can act like a lady. When I have to.'

'When you have to.'

'That's right. He's out of town now, getting ready for this tournament. So I can stay out as late as I want. I can do as I please.'

'Handy for you.'

She sighed. 'I guess I can't use sex this time, can I?'

'I'm afraid not.'

'It's a shame. I'm used to using it, I'm damned good at it. Hell. A hundred thousand dollars a year from now is a lot of money.'

'It's also a bird in the bush.'

'I wish to hell I had something to use on you. Sex doesn't work, and I don't have money. I have a couple of dollars in a savings account, my own money.'

'How much?'

'About eight thousand. I haven't had the interest entered in a long time. You're supposed to take the book in once a year. Somehow I never got around to it. I could give you what I've got, a down payment.'

'All right.'

'A week from today?'

'What's wrong with tomorrow?'

'Uh-uh.' She shook her head emphatically. 'No. All I can buy for my eight thousand is time, right? So I'm going to buy a week with it right off. A week from today you'll have the money.'

'I don't even know you've got it.'

'No, you don't.'

I thought it over. 'All right,' I said finally. 'Eight thousand dollars a week from today. But I'm not going to wait a year for the rest of it.'

'Maybe I could turn some tricks,' she said. 'Like four hundred and twenty of 'em at a hundred dollars a throw.'

'Or forty-two hundred at ten.'

'You fucker,' she said.

'Eight thousand. A week from today.'

'You'll get it.'

I offered to put her in a cab. She said she'd get her own and that I could pay for the drinks this time. I stayed at the table for a few minutes after she left, then paid the check and went out. I crossed the street and asked Benny if there were any messages. There weren't, but a man had called and not left his name. I wondered if it was the man who had threatened to put me in the river.

I went over to Armstrong's and took my usual table. The place was crowded for a Monday. Most of the faces were familiar. I had bourbon and coffee, and the third time around I caught a glimpse of a face that looked familiar in an unfamiliar way. On her next circuit of the tables, I crooked a finger at Trina. She came over to me with her eyebrows up, and the expression accented the feline cast to her features.

'Don't turn around,' I said. 'At the bar in front, right between Gordie and the guy in the denim jacket.'

'What about him?'

'Probably nothing. Not right away, but in a couple of minutes, why don't you walk past him and get a look at him?'

'And then what, Cap'n?'

'Then report back to Mission Control.'

'Aye-aye, sir.'

I kept my eyes facing toward the door but concentrated on what I could see of him at the periphery of my vision, and it

185

wasn't my imagination. He did keep glancing my way. It was hard to gauge his height, because he was sitting down, but he looked almost tall enough to play basketball. He had an outdoor face and modishly long sand-colored hair. I couldn't make out his features very well – he was the length of the room away from me – but I got an impression of cool, competent toughness.

Trina drifted back with a drink I hadn't gotten around to ordering. 'Camouflage,' she said, setting it before me. 'I have given him the old once-over. What did he do?'

'Nothing that I know of. Have you seen him before?'

'I don't think so. In fact, I'm sure I haven't, because I would remember him.'

'Why?'

'He tends to stand out in a crowd. You know who he looks like? The Marlboro man.'

'From the commercials? Didn't they use more than one guy?'

'Sure. He looks like all of them. You know, high rawhide boots and a wide-brimmed hat and smelling of horseshit, and the tattoo on his hand. He's not wearing boots or a hat, and he doesn't have the tattoo, but it's the same image. Don't ask me if he smells of horseshit. I didn't get close enough to tell.'

'I wasn't going to ask.'

'What's the story?'

'I'm not sure there is one. I think I saw him a little while ago in Polly's.'

'Maybe he's making the rounds.'

'Uh-huh. Same rounds I'm making.'

'So?'

I shrugged. 'Probably nothing. Thanks for the surveillance work, away.'

'Do I get a badge?'

'And a decoder ring.'

'Neat,' she said.

I waited him out. He was definitely paying attention to me. I couldn't tell whether he knew I was taking an interest in him as well. I didn't want to look straight at him.

He could have tagged me from Polly's. I wasn't sure I'd seen him there, just felt I'd noticed him somewhere or other. If he'd picked me up at Polly's, then it wasn't hard to tie him to Beverly Ethridge; she could have set up the date in the first place in order to put a tag on me. But even if he had been at Polly's, that didn't prove anything; he could have picked me up earlier and tailed me there. I hadn't been making myself hard to find. Everybody knew where I lived, and I'd spent the whole day in the neighborhood.

It was probably around nine thirty when I noticed him, maybe closer to ten. It was almost eleven when he packed it in and left. I had decided he was going to leave before I did, and I would have sat there until Billie closed the place if necessary. It didn't take that long, and I hadn't thought it would. The Marlboro man didn't look like the sort who enjoyed biding his time in a Ninth Avenue gin mill, even as congenial a gin mill as Armstrong's. He was too active and western and outdoorsy, and by eleven o'clock he had mounted his horse and ridden off into the sunset.

A few minutes after he left, Trina came over and sat down across from me. She was still on duty, so I couldn't buy her a drink. 'I have more to report,' she said. 'Billie has never seen him before. He hopes he never sees him again, he says, because he does not like to serve alcoholic beverages to men with eyes like that.'

'Eyes like what?'

'He did not go into detail. You could probably ask him. What else? Oh, yes. He ordered beer. Two of them, in about as many hours. Wurzburger dark, if you care.'

'Not awfully.'

'He also said –'

'Shit.'

'Billie rarely says "shit." He says "fuck" a lot, but rarely "shit," and he didn't say it now. What's the matter?'

But I was up from the table and on my way to the bar. Billie ambled over, polishing a glass with a towel. He said, 'You move fast for a big man, stranger.'

'My mind moves slow. That customer you had –'

'The Marlboro man, Trina calls him.'

'That's the one. I don't suppose you got around to washing his glass yet, did you?'

'Yes, as a matter of fact I did. This is it here, as best I recall.' He held it up for my inspection. 'See? Spotless.'

'Shit.'

'That's what Jimmie says when I *don't* wash them. What's the matter?'

'Well, unless the bastard was wearing gloves, I have just done something stupid.'

'Gloves. Oh. Fingerprints?'

'Uh-huh.'

187

'I thought that only worked on the tube.'

'Not, when they come as a gift. Like on a beer glass. Shit. If he ever comes in again, which would be too much to hope for –'

'I pick up the glass with a towel and put it some place very safe.'

'That's the idea.'

'If you'd told me ...'

'I know. I should have thought of it.'

'All I was interested in was seeing the last of him. I don't like people like him anywhere, and especially in bars. He made two beers last an hour apiece, and that was just fine with me. I was not about to push drinks on him. The less he drank and the sooner he left, the happier he made me.'

'Did he talk at all?'

'Just to order the beers.'

'You catch any kind of an accent?'

'Didn't notice it at the time. Let me think.' He closed his eyes for a few seconds. 'No. Standard American nondescript. I usually notice voices, and I can't dredge up anything special about his. I can't believe he's from New York, but what does that prove?'

'Not too much. Trina said you didn't like his eyes.'

'I didn't like them at all.'

'How so?'

'The feeling they gave me. It's hard to describe. I couldn't even tell you what color they were, although I think they were light rather than dark. But there was something about them, they stopped at the surface.'

'I'm not sure I know what you mean.'

'There was no depth to them. They could have been glass eyes, almost. Did you happen to watch Watergate?'

'Some of it. Not much.'

'One of those pricks, one of the ones with a German name –'

'They all had German names, didn't they?'

'No, but there were two of them. Not Haldeman. The other one.'

'Ehrlichman.'

'That's the prick. Did you happen to see him? Did you notice his eyes? No depth to them.'

'A Marlboro man with eyes like Ehrlichman.'

'This isn't connected with Watergate or anything, is it, Matt?'

'Only in spirit.'

I went back to my table and had a cup of coffee. I'd have liked to sweeten it with bourbon, but I decided it wasn't sensible. The Marlboro man didn't figure to try to take me tonight. There were too many people who could place him at the scene. This was simple reconnaissance. If he was going to try anything on, it would be some other time.

That was the way it looked to me, but I wasn't sure enough by my reasoning to walk home with too much bourbon in my bloodstream. I was probably right, but I didn't want to risk being very wrong.

I took what I'd seen of the guy and pasted in Ehrlichman's eyes and Billie's general impression of him, and I tried to match up the picture with my three angels. I couldn't make anything work. He could be some construction roughneck off one of Prager's projects, he could be a healthy young stud Beverly Ethridge liked to have around, he could be pro talent Huysendahl had hired for the occasion. Fingerprints would have given me a make on him, but my mental reflexes had been too slow for me to take advantage of the opportunity. If I could find out who he was I could come up around him from behind, but now I had to let him make his play and meet him head on.

I guess it was about twelve thirty when I paid my tab and left. I eased the door open carefully, feeling a little foolish, and I scanned both sides of Ninth Avenue in both directions. I didn't see my Marlboro man, or anything else that looked at all menacing.

I started toward the corner of Fifty-seventh Street, and for the first time since it all started I had the feeling of being a target. I had set myself up this way quite deliberately, and it had certainly seemed like a good idea at the time, but ever since the Marlboro man had turned up things had become very different. It was real now, and that was what made all the difference.

There was movement in a doorway ahead of me, and I was up on the balls of my feet before I recognized the old woman. She was in her usual spot in the doorway of the boutique called Sartor Resartus. She's always there when the weather's decent. She always asks for money. Most of the time I give her something.

She said, 'Mister, if you could spare –' and I found some coins in my pocket and gave them to her. 'God will bless you,' she said.

I told her I hoped she was right. I walked on toward the corner, and it's a good thing it wasn't raining that night, because I heard her scream before I heard the car. She let out a shriek, and I spun

189

around in time to see a car with its high beams on vault the curb at me.

TEN

I didn't have time to think it over. I guess my reflexes were good. At least they were good enough. I was off balance from spinning around when the woman screamed, but I didn't stop to get my balance. I just threw myself to the right. I landed on a shoulder and rolled up against the building.

It was barely enough. If a driver has the nerve, he can leave you no room at all. All he has to do is bounce his car off the side of the building. That can be rough on the car and rough on the building, but it's roughest of all on the person caught between the two. I thought he might do that, and then when he yanked the wheel at the last minute I thought he might do it accidentally, fishtailing the car's rear end and swatting me like a fly.

He didn't miss by much. I felt a rush of air as the car hurtled past me. Then I rolled over and watched him cut back off the sidewalk and onto the avenue. He snapped off a parking meter on his way, bounced when he hit the asphalt, then put the pedal on the floor and hit the corner just as the light turned red. He sailed right through the light, but then, so do half the cars in New York. I don't remember the last time I saw a cop ticket anybody for a moving violation. They just don't have the time.

'These crazy, crazy drivers!'

It was the old woman, standing beside me now, making *tsk* sounds.

'They just *drink* their whiskey,' she said, 'and they *smoke* their reefers, and then they go out for a *joy* ride. You could have been killed.'

'Yes.'

'And after all that, he didn't even stop to see if you were all right.'

'He wasn't very considerate.'

'People are not considerate any more.'

I got to my feet and brushed myself off. I was shaking, and

badly rattled. She said, 'Mister, if you could spare ...' and then her eyes clouded slightly and she frowned at some private puzzlement. 'No,' she said. 'You just gave me money, didn't you? I'm very sorry. It's difficult to remember.'

I reached for my wallet. 'Now this is a ten-dollar bill,' I said, pressing it into her hand. 'You make sure you remember, all right? Make sure you get the right amount of change when you spend it. Do you understand?'

'Oh, dear,' she said.

'Now you'd better go home and get some sleep. All right?'

'Oh, dear,' she said. 'Ten dollars. A ten-dollar bill. Oh, God bless you, sir.'

'He just did,' I said.

Jacob was behind the desk when I got back to the hotel. He's a light-skinned West Indian with bright blue eyes and kinky rust-colored hair. He has large dark freckles on his cheeks and on the backs of his hands. He likes the midnight-to-eight shift because it's quiet and he can sit behind the desk working double-acrostics, toking periodically from a bottle of cough syrup with codeine in it.

He does the puzzles with a nylon-tipped pen. I asked him once if it wasn't more difficult that way. 'Otherwise there is no pride in it, Mr Scudder,' he'd said.

What he said now was that I'd had no calls. I went upstairs and walked down the hall to my room. I checked to see if there was any light coming from under the door, and there wasn't, and I decided that didn't prove anything. Then I looked for scratch marks around the lock, and there weren't any, and I decided that that didn't prove anything either, because you could pick those hotel locks with dental floss. Then I opened the door and found there was nothing in the room but the furniture, which stood to reason, and I turned on the light and closed and locked the door and held my hands at arm's length and watched the fingers tremble.

I made myself a stiff drink and then I made myself drink it. For a moment or two my stomach picked up the shakes from my hands and I didn't think the whiskey was going to stay down, but it did. I wrote some letters and numbers on a piece of paper and put it in my wallet. I got out of my clothes and stood under the shower to wash off a coating of sweat. The worst sort of sweat, composed of equal parts of exertion and animal fear.

I was toweling dry when the phone rang. I didn't want to pick it up. I knew what I was going to hear.

'That was just a warning, Scudder.'

'Bullshit. You were trying. You're just not good enough.'

'When we try, we don't miss.'

I told him to fuck off and hung up. I picked it up a few seconds later and told Jacob no calls before nine, at which time I wanted a wake-up call.

Then I got into bed to see whether I could sleep.

I slept better than I'd expected. I woke up only twice during the night, and both times it was the same dream, and it would have bored a Freudian psychiatrist to tears. It was a very literal dream, no symbols to it at all. Pure reenactment, from the moment I left Armstrong's to the moment the car closed on me, except that in the dream the driver had the necessary skill and balls to go all the way, and just as I knew he was going to put me between the rock and the hard place, I woke up, with my hands in fists and my heart hammering.

I guess it's a protective mechanism, dreaming like that. Your unconscious mind takes the things you can't handle and plays with them while you sleep until some of the sharp corners are worn off. I don't know how much good those dreams did, but when I awoke for the third and last time a half-hour before I was supposed to get my wake-up call, I felt a little better about things. It seemed to me that I had a lot to feel good about. Someone had tried for me, and that's what I had been looking to provoke all along. And someone had missed, and that was also as I wanted it.

I thought about the phone call. It had not been the Marlboro man. I was reasonably certain of that. The voice I'd heard was older, probably around my own age, and it had had the flavor of New York streets in its tones.

So there looked to be at least two of them in on it. That didn't tell me much, but it was something else to know, another fact to file and forget. Had there been more than one person in the car? I tried to remember what I had seen in the brief glimpse I'd had while the car was bearing down on me. I hadn't seen much, not with the headlights pitched right at my eyes. And by the time I'd turned for a look at the departing car, it was already a good distance past me and moving fast. And I'd been more intent on catching the plate number than counting heads.

I went downstairs for breakfast, but couldn't manage more than a cup of coffee and a piece of toast. I bought a pack of cigarettes out of the machine and smoked three of them with my coffee. They were the first I'd had in almost two months, and I couldn't have gotten a better hit if I'd punched them right into a vein. They made me dizzy but in a nice way. After I'd finished the three, I left the pack on the table and went outside.

I went down to Centre Street and found my way to the Auto Squad room. A pink-cheeked kid who looked to be fresh out of John Jay asked if he could help me. There were half a dozen cops in the room, and I didn't recognize any of them. I asked if Ray Landauer was around.

'Retired a few months ago,' he said. To one of the others he called, 'Hey, Jerry, when did Ray retire anyway?'

'Musta been October.'

He turned to me. 'Ray retired in October,' he said. 'Can I help you?'

'It was personal,' I said.

'I can find his address if you want to give me a minute.'

I told him it wasn't important. It surprised me that Ray had packed it in. He didn't seem old enough to retire. But he was older than me, come to think of it, and I had had fifteen years on the force and had been off it for more than five, so that made me retirement age myself.

Maybe the kid would have given me a peek at the hot-car sheet. But I would have had to tell him who I was and go through a lot of bullshit that wouldn't be necessary with someone I knew. So I left the building and started walking toward the subway. When an empty cab came along, I changed my mind and grabbed it. I told the driver I wanted the Sixth Precinct.

He didn't know where it was. A few years ago, if you wanted to drive a cab you had to be able to name the nearest hospital or police station or firehouse from any point in the city. I don't know when they dropped the test, but now all you have to do is be alive.

I told him it was on West Tenth, and he got there without too much trouble. I found Eddie Koehler in his office. He was reading something in the *News*, and it wasn't making him happy.

'Fucking Special Prosecutor,' he said. 'What's a guy like this accomplish except aggravate people?'

'He gets his name in the papers a lot.'

'Yeah. Figure he wants to be governor?'

I thought of Huysendahl. 'Everybody wants to be governor.'

'That's the fucking truth. Why do you figure that is?'

'You're asking the wrong person, Eddie. I can't figure out why anybody wants to be anything.'

His cool eyes appraised me. 'Shit, you always wanted to be a cop.'

'Since I was a kid. I never wanted to be anything else, as far back as I can remember.'

'I was the same way. Always wanted to carry a badge. I wonder why. Sometimes I think it was how we were brought up, the cop on the corner, everybody respecting him. And the movies we saw as a kid. The cops were the good guys.'

'I don't know. They always shot Cagney in the last reel.'

'Yeah, but the fucker had it coming. You'd watch and you'd be crazy about Cagney but you wanted him to buy the farm at the end. He couldn't fucking get away with it. Sit down, Matt. I don't see you much lately. You want some coffee?'

I shook my head but I sat down. He took a dead cigar from his ashtray and put a match to it. I took two tens and a five from my wallet and put them on his desk.

'I just earned a hat?'

'You will in a minute.'

'Just so the Special Prosecutor don't get wind of it.'

'You don't have anything to worry about, do you?'

'Who knows? You get a maniac like that and everybody's got something to worry about.' He folded the bills and put them in his shirt pocket. 'What can I do for you?'

I got out the slip of paper I'd written on before going to bed. 'I've got part of a license number,' I said.

'Don't you know anybody at Twenty-sixth Street?'

That was where the Motor Vehicle people had their offices. I said, 'I do, but it's a Jersey plate. I'm guessing the car was stolen and that you can turn it up on the G.T.A. sheet. The three letters are either LKJ or LJK. I only got a piece of the three numbers. There's a nine and a four, possibly a nine and two fours, but I don't even know the order.'

'That should be plenty, if it's on the sheet. All this towing, sometimes people don't report thefts. They just assume we towed it, and they don't go down to the pound if they don't happen to have the fifty bucks, and then it turns out it was stolen. Or by then the thief dumped it and we *did* tow it away, and they wind up paying for a tow, but not from where they parked it. Hang on, I'll get the sheet.'

He left his cigar in the ashtray, and it was out again by the time he got back. 'Grand Theft Auto,' he said. 'Give me those letters again.'

'LKJ or LJK.'

'Uh-huh. You got a make and model on it?'

'Nineteen forty-nine Kaiser-Frazer.'

'Huh?'

'Late-model sedan, dark. That's about as much as I got. They all look about the same.'

'Yeah. Nothing on the main sheet. Let's see what came in last night. Oh, hello, LJK nine one four.'

'That sounds like it.'

'Seventy-two Impala two-door, dark green.'

'I didn't count the doors, but that's got to be it.'

'Belongs to a Mrs William Raiken from Upper Montclair. She a friend of yours?'

'I don't think so. When did she report it?'

'Let's see. Two in the morning, it says here.'

I had left Armstrong's around twelve thirty, so Mrs Raiken hadn't missed her car right away. They could have put it back and she never would have known it was gone.

'Where did it come from, Eddie?'

'Upper Montclair, I suppose.'

'I mean where did she have it parked when they swiped it?'

'Oh.' He had closed the list; now he flipped it open to the last page. 'Broadway and a Hundred Fourteenth. Hey, that leads to an interesting question.'

It damn well did, but how did he know that? I asked him what question it led to.

'What was Mrs Raiken doing on Upper Broadway at two in the morning? And did Mr Raiken know about it?'

'You've got a dirty mind.'

'I shoulda been a Special Prosecutor. What's Mrs Raiken got to do with your missing husband?'

I looked blank, then remembered the case I'd invented to explain my interest in Spinner's corpse. 'Oh,' I said. 'Nothing. I wound up telling his wife to forget it. I got a couple days' work out of it.'

'Uh-huh. Who took the car and what did they do with it last night?'

'Destroyed public property.'

'Huh?'

'They knocked over a parking meter on Ninth Avenue, then got the hell away in a hurry.'

'And you just happened to be there, and so you just happened to catch the license number, and naturally you figured the car was stolen but you wanted to check because you're a public-spirited citizen.'

'That's close.'

'It's crap. Sit down, Matt. What are you into that I oughta know about?'

'Nothing.'

'How does a stolen car tie into Spinner Jablon?'

'Spinner? Oh, the guy they took out of the river. No connection.'

'Because you were just looking for this woman's husband.' I saw my slip then, but waited to see if he'd caught it, and he had. 'It was his girlfriend looking for him last time I heard it. You're being awful cute with me, Matt.'

I didn't say anything. He picked his cigar out of the ashtray and studied it, then leaned over and dropped it in his wastebasket. He straightened up and looked at me, then away, then at me again.

'What are you holding out?

'Nothing you have to know.'

'How do you get tied into Spinner Jablon?'

'It's not important.'   •

'And what's with the car?'

'That's not important either.' I straightened up. 'Spinner got dropped in the East River, and the car sheared off a parking meter on Ninth between Fifty-seventh and Fifty-eighth. And the car was stolen up-town, so none of this has been going on in the Sixth Precinct. There's nothing you've got to know, Eddie.'

'Who killed Spinner?'

'I don't know.'

'Is that straight?'

'Of course it's straight.'

'Are you playing tag with somebody?'

'Not exactly.'

'Jesus Christ, Matt.'

I wanted to get out of there. I wasn't holding out anything he had a claim on, and I really couldn't give him or anybody .else what I had. But I was playing a lone hand and ducking his questions, and I could hardly expect him to like it.

'Who's your client, Matt?'

Spinner was my client, but I could see no profit in saying so. 'I don't have one,' I said.

'Then what's your angle?'

'I'm not sure I have an angle, either.'

'I hear things to the effect that Spinner was in the dollars lately.'

'He was well dressed the last time I saw him.'

'That so?'

'His suit set him back three hundred and twenty dollars. He happened to mention it.'

He looked at me until I averted my own gaze. In a low voice he said, 'Matt, you don't want people driving cars at you. It's unhealthy. You sure you don't want to lay it all out for me?'

'As soon as it's time, Eddie.'

'And you're sure it's not time yet?'

I took my time answering. I remembered the feel of that car rolling at me, remembered what actually happened, and then remembered how I dreamed it, with the driver taking the big car all the way to the wall.

'I'm sure,' I said.

At the Lion's Head I had a hamburger and some bourbon and coffee. I was a little surprised that the car had been stolen so far uptown. They could have picked it up early on and parked it in my neighborhood, or the Marlboro man could have made a phone call between the time I left Polly's and the time he found his way into Armstrong's. Which would mean there were at least two people in the thing, which I had already decided on the basis of the voice I'd heard over the telephone. Or he could have –

No, it was pointless. There were too many possible scenarios I could write for myself, and none of them was going to get me anywhere but confused.

I signaled for another cup of coffee and another shot, mixed them together, and worked on it. The tail end of my conversation with Eddie had gotten in the way. There was something I had learned from him, but the problem was that I didn't know that I knew it. He had said something that had rung a very muted bell, and I couldn't get it to ring again.

I got a dollar's worth of change and went over to the phone.

Jersey Information gave me William Raiken's number in Upper Montclair. I called it and told Mrs Raiken I was from the Auto Theft Squad, and she said was surprised we had recovered her car so soon and did I happen to know if it was at all damaged.

I said, 'I'm afraid we haven't recovered your car yet, Mrs Raiken.'

'Oh.'

'I just wanted to get some details. Your car was parked at Broadway and One Hundred Fourteenth Street?'

'That's right. On One Hundred Fourteenth, not on Broadway.'

'I see. Now, our records indicate that you reported the theft at approximately two A.M. Was that immediately after you noticed the car was missing.

'Yes. Well, just about. I went to where I parked the car and it wasn't there, of course, and my first thought was it was towed away. I was parked legally, but sometimes there are signs you don't see, different regulations, but anyway they don't do any towing that far uptown, do they?'

'Not above Eighty-sixth Street.'

'That's what I thought, although I always manage to find a legal space. Then I thought maybe I'd made a mistake and I actually left the car on a Hundred Thirteenth, so I went and checked, but of course it wasn't there either, so then I called my husband to have him pick me up, and he said to report the theft, so that was when I called you. Maybe there was fifteen or twenty minutes between when I missed the car and when I actually placed the call.'

'I see.' I was sorry now that I'd asked. 'And when did you park the car, Mrs Raiken?'

'Let me see. I had the two classes, an eight-o'clock short-story workshop and a ten-o'clock course in Renaissance history, but I was a little early, so I guess I parked a little after seven. Is that important?'

'Well, it won't aid in recovering the vehicle, Mrs Raiken, but we try to develop data to pinpoint the times when various crimes are likely to occur.'

'That's interesting,' she said. 'What good does that do?'

I had always wondered that myself. I told her it was part of the overall crime picture, which is what I generally had been told when I'd asked similar questions. I thanked her and assured her that her car would probably be recovered shortly, and she thanked me, and we said good-bye to each other and I went back to the bar.

I tried to determine what I'd learned from her and decided I'd learned nothing. My mind wandered, and I found myself wondering just what Mrs Raiken had been doing on the Upper West Side in the middle of the night. She hadn't been with her husband, and her last class must have let out around eleven. Maybe she'd just had a few beers at the West End or one of the other bars around Columbia. Quite a few beers, maybe, which would explain why she'd walked around the block looking for her car. Not that it mattered if she'd had enough beer to float a battleship, because Mrs Raiken didn't have a whole hell of a lot to do with Spinner Jablon or anybody else, and whether or not she had anything to do with Mr Raiken was their business and none of my own, and—

Columbia.

Columbia is at One Hundred Sixteenth and Broadway, so that's where she would have been taking courses. And someone else was studying at Columbia, taking graduate courses in psychology and planning to work with retarded children.

I checked the phone book. No Prager, Stacy, because single women know better than to put their first names in telephone books. But there was a Prager, S., on West One Hundred Twelfth between Broadway and Riverside.

I went back and finished my coffee. I left a bill on the bar. At the doorway I changed my mind, looked up Prager, S., again, and made a note of the address and phone number. On the chance that S. stood for Seymour or anything other than Stacy, I dropped a dime in the slot and dialed the number. I let it ring seven times, then hung up and retrieved my dime. There were two other dimes with it.

Some days you get lucky.

ELEVEN

By the time I got off the subway at Broadway and One Hundred Tenth, I was a lot less impressed by the coincidence I had turned up. If Prager had decided to kill me, either directly or through hirelings, there was no particular reason why he would have stolen a car two blocks away from his daughter's apartment. It looked at first glance as though it ought to add up to something, but I wasn't sure that it did.

Of course, if Stacy Prager had a boyfriend, and if he turned out to be the Marlboro man ...

It looked to be worth a try. I found her building, a five-story brownstone which now held four apartments to a floor. I rang her bell, and there was no answer. I rang a couple of other bells on the top floor – it's surprising how often people buzz you in that way – but no one was home, and the vestibule lock looked very easy. I used a pick on it, and I couldn't have opened it much faster with a key. I climbed three steep flights of stairs and knocked on the door of 4-C. I waited and knocked again, and then I opened both the locks on her door and made myself at home.

There was one fairly large room with a convertible sofa and a sprinkling of Salvation Army furniture. I checked the closet and the dresser, and all I learned was that if Stacy had a boyfriend he lived elsewhere. There were no signs of male occupancy.

I gave the place a very casual toss, just trying to get some sense of the person who lived there. There were a lot of books, most of them paperbacks, most of them dealing with some aspect of psychology. There was a stack of magazines: *New York* and *Psychology Today* and *Intellectual Digest*. There was nothing stronger than aspirin in the medicine chest. Stacy kept her apartment in good order, and it in turn gave the impression that her life was also in good order. I felt a violator standing there in her apartment, scanning the titles of her books, rummaging through the clothes in her closet. I grew increasingly uncomfortable in the role, and my failure to find anything to justify my presence augmented the feeling. I got out of there and closed up after myself. I locked one of the locks; the other had to be locked with a key, and I figured she would simply decide she had failed to lock it on the way out.

I could have found a nice framed photo of the Marlboro man. That would have been handy, but it just hadn't happened. I left the building and went around the corner and had a cup of coffee at a lunch counter. Prager and Ethridge and Huysendahl, and one of them had killed Spinner and had tried to kill me, and I didn't seem to be getting anywhere.

Suppose it was Prager. Things seemed to form a pattern, and although they didn't really lock in place, they had the right sort of feel to them. He was on the hook in the first place because of a hit-and-run case, and so far a car had been used twice. Spinner's letter mentioned a car jumping a curb at him, and one had certainly taken a shot at me last night. And he was the one who seemed to be feeling the bite financially. Beverly Ethridge was stalling for time, Theodore Huysendahl had agreed to my price, and Prager said he didn't know how he could raise the money.

So suppose it was him. If so, he had just tried to commit murder, and he hadn't made it work, and he was probably a little shaky about it. If it was him, now was a good time to rattle the bars of his cage. And if it wasn't him, I'd be in a better position to know it if I dropped in on him.

I paid for my coffee and went out and flagged a cab.

The black girl looked up at me when I entered his office. It took her a second or two to place me, and then her dark eyes took on a wary expression.

'Matthew Scudder,' I said.

'For Mr Prager?'

'That's right.'

'Is he expecting you, Mr Scudder?'

'I think he'll want to see me, Shari.'

She seemed startled that I remembered her name. She got hesitantly to her feet and stepped out from behind the U-shaped desk.

'I'll tell him you're here,' she said.

'You do that.'

She slipped through Prager's door, drawing it swiftly shut

behind her. I sat on the vinyl couch and looked at Mrs Prager's seascape. I decided that the men were vomiting over the sides of the boat. There was no question about it.

The door opened and she returned to the reception room, again closing the door after her. 'He'll see you in about five minutes,' she said.

'All right.'

'I guess you got important business with him.'

'Fairly important.'

'I just hope things go right. That man has not been himself lately. It just seems the harder a man works and the more successful he grows, that's all the more pressure he has bearing down upon him.'

'I guess he's been under a lot of pressure lately.'

'He has been under a strain,' she said. Her eyes challenged me, holding me responsible for Prager's difficulty. It was a charge I could not deny.

'Maybe things will clear up soon,' I suggested.

'I truly hope so.'

'I suppose he's a good man to work for?'

'A very good man. He has always been –'

But she didn't get to finish the sentence, because just then there was the sound of a truck backfiring, except trucks do that at ground level, not on the twenty-second floor. She had been standing beside her desk, and she stayed frozen there for a moment, eyes wide, the back of her hand pressed to her mouth. She held the pose long enough for me to get out of my chair and beat her to his door.

I yanked it open, and Henry Prager was seated at his desk, and of course it had not been a truck backfiring. It had been a gun. A small gun, .22 or .25 caliber from the look of it, but when you put the barrel in your mouth and tilt it up toward the brain, a small gun is all you really need.

I stood in the doorway, trying to block it, and she was at my shoulder, small hands hammering at my back. For a moment I didn't yield, and then it seemed to me that she had at least as much right as I to look at him. I took a step into the room and she followed me and saw what she'd known she was going to see.

Then she started to scream.

TWELVE

If Shari hadn't known my name, I might have left. Perhaps not; cop instincts die hard if they die at all, and I had spent too many years despising those reluctant witnesses who slipped off into the shadows to feel comfortable playing the role myself. Nor would it have sat well to duck out on a girl in her condition.

But the impulse was surely present. I looked at Henry Prager, his body slumped over his desk, his features contorted in death, and I knew that I was looking at a man I had killed. His finger had pulled the trigger, but I'd put the gun in his hand by playing my game a little too well.

I had not asked to have his life intertwined with mine, nor had I sought to be a factor in his death. Now his corpse confronted me; one hand was stretched across the desk, as if pointing at me.

He had bribed his daughter's way out of an unintentional homicide. The bribery had laid him open to blackmail, which had provoked another homicide, this one intentional. And that first murder had only sunk the barb deeper – he was still being blackmailed, and he could always be tagged for Spinner's murder.

And so he had tried to murder again, and had failed. And I turned up in his office the next day, and so he told his secretary he wanted five minutes, but he'd taken only two or three of them.

He'd had the gun at hand. Perhaps he'd checked it earlier in the day to make sure it was loaded. And perhaps, while I waited in the outer office, he entertained thoughts of greeting me with a bullet.

But it is one thing to run a man down on a dark street at night or to knock a man unconscious and throw him in the river. And it is something else again to shoot a man in your own office with your secretary a few yards away. Perhaps he had measured out these considerations in his mind. Perhaps he had already resolved on suicide. I couldn't ask him now, and what did it matter?

Suicide protected his daughter, while murder would have exposed everything. Suicide got him off a treadmill that turned faster than his legs could travel.

I had some of these thoughts as I stood there regarding his corpse, others in the hours that followed. I don't know how long I looked at him while Shari sobbed against my shoulder. Not all that long, I suppose. Then reflexes took over, and I steered the girl back to the outer office and made her sit on the couch. I picked up her phone and dialed 911.

The crew that caught it were from the Seventeenth Precinct over on East Fifty-first. The two detectives were Jim Heaney and a younger man named Finch – I didn't catch his first name. I had known Jim enough to nod to, and that made it a little easier, but even with total strangers I didn't look to be in for much trouble. Everything added up to suicide to begin with, and the girl and I could both confirm that Prager was all alone when the gun went off.

The lab boys went through the motions all the same, although their hearts weren't in it. They took a lot of pictures and made a lot of chalk marks, wrapped and bagged the gun, and finally zipped Prager into a body bag and got him out of there. Heaney and Finch took Shari's statement first so that she could go home and collapse on her own time. All they really wanted was for her to plug the standard gaps so that the coroner's inquest could return a verdict of suicide, so they fed her questions and confirmed that her boss had been depressed and edgy lately, that he had been evidently worried about business, that his moods had been abnormal and out of character, and, on the mechanical side, that she had seen him a few minutes before the shot sounded, that she and I had been sitting in the outer office at the time, and that we had entered simultaneously to find him dead in his chair.

Heaney told her that was fine. Someone would be around for a formal statement in the morning, and in the meantime Detective Finch would see her home. She said that wasn't necessary, she'd get a cab, but Finch insisted.

Heaney watched the two of them leave. 'You bet Finch'll take her home,' he said. 'That's quite an ass on that little lady.'

'I didn't notice.'

'You're getting old. Finch noticed. He likes the black ones, especially built like that. Myself, I don't fool around, but I got to admit I get a kick out of working with Finch. If he gets half the ass he tells me about, he's gonna fuck himself to death. Tell you the truth, I don't think he makes any of it up, either. The broads go for him.' He lit a cigarette and offered the pack to me. I passed. He said, 'That girl now, Shari, I'll give you odds he nails her.'

'Not today he won't. She's pretty shaky.'

'Hell, that's the best time. I don't know what the hell it is, but that's when they want it the most. Go tell a woman her husband got killed, like breaking the news, now would you make a pass at a time like that? Whatever she looks like, would you do it? Neither would I. You should hear the stories that son of a bitch tells. Couple of months ago we had this ironworker falls off a girder, Finch has to break the news to the wife. He tells her, she cracks up, he gives her a hug to comfort her, pets her a little, and the next thing he knows she's got his zipper down and she's blowing him.'

'That's if you take Finch's word for it.'

'Well, if half what he says is true, and I think he's straight about it. I mean, he tells me when he strikes out, too.'

I didn't much want to have this conversation, but neither did I want to make my feelings obvious, so we went through a few more stories of Finch's love life and then wasted a few minutes reviewing mutual friends. This might have taken longer had we known each other better. Finally he picked up his clipboard and concentrated on Prager. We went through the automatic questions, and I confirmed what Shari had told him.

Then he said, 'Just for the record, any chance he could've been dead before you got here?' When I looked blank, he spelled it out. 'This is off the wall, but just for the record. Suppose she killed him, don't ask me how or why, and then she waits for you or somebody else to come in, and then she fakes talking to him, and she's sitting with you, and she triggers a gun, I don't know, a thread or something, and then the two of you discover the body together and she's covered.'

'You better cut out all that television, Jim. It's affecting your brain.'

'Well, it *could* happen that way.'

'Sure. I heard him talking to her when she went inside. Of course, she could have set up a tape recorder –'

'All right, for Christ's sake.'

'If you want to explore all the possibilities –'

'I said it was just off the wall. You watch what they do on

Mission Impossible and you wonder how criminals are so stupid in real life. So what the hell, a crook can watch television too, and maybe he picks up an idea. But you heard him talking, and we can forget tape recorders, and that settles that.'

Actually, I hadn't heard Prager talking, but it was a lot simpler to say that I had. Heaney wanted to explore possibilities; all I wanted to do was get out of there.

'How do you fit into this, Matt? You working for him?'

I shook my head. 'Checking out some references.'

'Checking on Prager?'

'No. On somebody who used him for a reference, and my client wanted a fairly intensive check. I saw Prager last week and I was in the neighborhood so I dropped in to clear up a couple of points.'

'Who's the subject of the investigation?'

'What's the difference? Somebody who worked with him eight or ten years ago. Nothing to do with him knocking himself off.'

'You didn't really know him, then. Prager.'

'Met him twice. Once, come to think of it, since I didn't really get to see much of him today. And I talked briefly with him on the phone.'

'He in some kind of trouble?'

'Not any more. I can't tell you much, Jim. I didn't know the guy or much about his situation. He seemed depressed and agitated. As a matter of fact, he impressed me as thinking the world was after him. He was very suspicious the first time I saw him, as if I was part of a plot to harm him.'

'Paranoia.'

'Like that, yes.'

'Yeah, it all fits together. Business troubles and the feeling everything's closing in on you, and maybe he thought you were going to hassle him today, or maybe he reached a point, you know, he's had it up to here and he just can't stand to see one more person. So he takes the gun out of the drawer and there's a bullet in his brain before he has time to think it over. I wish to God they'd keep those handguns off the market. They truck 'em in by the ton out of the Carolinas. What do you bet that was an unregistered gun?'

'No bet.'

'He probably thought he was buying it for protection. Little rinky-dink Spanish gun, you could hit a mugger six times in the chest and not stop him, and all it's good for is blowing your brains out. Had a guy about a year ago, it wasn't even good for that. Decided to kill himself and only did half the job and he's a vegetable now. Now he *oughta* kill himself, the life he's got left to him, but he can't even move his hands.' He lit another cigarette. 'You want to drop around tomorrow and dictate a statement?'

I told him I could do better than that. I used Shari's typewriter and knocked out a short statement with all the facts in the right places. He read it over and nodded. 'You know the form,' he said. 'Saves us all some time.'

I signed what I'd typed up, and he added it to the papers on his clipboard. He shuffled through them and said, 'His wife's where? Westchester. Thank Christ for that. I'll phone the cops up there and let them have the fun of telling her her husband's dead.'

I caught myself just in time to keep from volunteering the information that Prager had a daughter in Manhattan. It wasn't something I was likely to know. We shook hands, and he said he wished Finch would get back. 'The bastard scored again,' he said. 'He figured to. Just so he don't stick around for seconds. And he might. He really likes the spades.'

'I'm sure he'll tell you all about it.'

'He always does.'

THIRTEEN

I went to a bar, but stayed only long enough to throw down two double shots, one right after the other. There was a time factor involved. Bars remain open until four in the morning, but most churches close up shop by six or seven. I walked over to Lexington and found a church I couldn't remember having been to before. I didn't notice the name of it. Our Lady of Perpetual Bingo, probably.

They were having some sort of service, but I didn't pay any attention to it. I lit a few candles and stuffed a couple of dollars in the slot, then took a seat in the rear and silently repeated three names over and over. Jacob Jablon, Henry Prager, Estrellita Rivera, three names, three candles for three corpses.

During the worst times after I shot and killed Estrellita Rivera, I had been unable to keep my mind from going over and over what had happened that night. I kept trying to repeal time and change the ending, like an antic projectionist reversing the film and drawing the bullet back into the barrel of the gun. In the new version that I wanted to superimpose on reality, all my shots were on target. There were no ricochets, or if there were they spent themselves harmlessly, or Estrellita spent an extra minute picking out peppermints in the candy store and wasn't in the wrong place at the wrong time, or –

There was a poem I'd had to read in high school, and it had nagged at me from somewhere in the back of my mind until one day I went to the library and ran it down. Four lines from Omar Khayyam:

> The moving finger writes, and having writ
> Moves on. Nor all your piety and wit
> Can call it back to cancel half a line
> Nor all your tears wash out a word of it.

I had tried hard to blame myself for Estrellita Rivera, but in a certain sense it wouldn't stick. I had been drinking, certainly, but not heavily, and my overall marksmanship that night could not be faulted. And it was proper for me to shoot at the robbers. They were armed, they were fleeing from one killing already, and there were no civilians in the line of fire. A bullet ricocheted. Those things happen.

Part of the reason I left the force was that those things happen and I did not want to be in a position where I could do wrong things for right reasons. Because I had decided that, while it might be true that the end does not justify the means, neither does the means justify the end.

And now I had deliberately programmed Henry Prager to kill himself.

I hadn't seen it that way, of course. But I couldn't see that it made too much difference. I had begun by pressuring him into attempting a second murder, something he would never have done otherwise. He had killed Spinner, but if I had simply destroyed Spinner's envelope I'd have left Prager with no need ever to kill again. But I'd given him reason to try, and he had tried and failed, and then he'd been backed into a corner and chosen, impulsively or deliberately, to kill himself.

I could have destroyed that envelope. I had no contract with Spinner. I'd agreed only to open the envelope if I failed to hear from him. I could have given away the whole three thousand instead of a tenth of it. I had needed the money, but not that badly.

But Spinner had made a bet, and he'd turned out a winner. He had spelled it all out: 'Why I think you'll follow through is something I noticed about you a long time ago, namely that you happen to think there is a difference between murder and other crimes. I am the same. I have done bad things all my life but never killed anybody and never would. I have known people who have killed which I've known for a fact or a rumor and would never get close to them. It is the way I am and I think that you are that way too ...'

I could have done nothing, and then Henry Prager would not have wound up in a body bag. But there *is* a difference between murder and other crimes, and the world is a worse place for the murderers it allows to walk unpunished, as Henry Prager would have walked had I would have walked had I done nothing.

There should have been another way. Just as the bullet should not have ricocheted into a little girl's eye. And try telling all that to the moving finger.

Mass was still going on when I left. I walked a couple of blocks, not paying much attention to where I was, and then I stopped at a Blarney Stone and took communion.

It was a long night.

The bourbon kept refusing to do its job. I moved around a lot, because every bar I hit had one person in it whose company put me on edge. I kept seeing him in the mirror and taking him with me wherever I went. The activity and the nervous energy probably burned off a lot of the alcohol before it had a chance to get to me, and the time I spent walking around was time I could have more profitably spent sitting in one place and drinking.

The kind of bars I chose had something to do with keeping me relatively sober. I usually drink in dark quiet places where a shot is two ounces, three if they know you. Tonight I was hitting Blarney Stones and White Roses. The prices were considerably lower but the shot glasses were small, and when you paid for an ounce that's what you got, and even so it was apt to be about thirty percent water.

At one place on Broadway they had the basketball game on. I watched the last quarter on a big color set. The Knicks were down by a point when the quarter started, and wound up dropping it by twelve or thirteen. That was the fourth game for the Celtics.

The guy next to me said, 'And next year they lose Lucas and DeBusschere, and Reed's knees are still gonna be shit, and Clyde can't do it all, so where the fuck are we?'

I nodded. What he said sounded reasonable to me.

'Even at the end of three, dead even for three periods, and they got Cowens and What's-his-name with five fouls, and then they can't find the basket. I mean, they don't fucking try, you know?'

'Must be my fault,' I said.

'Huh?'

'They started falling apart when I started watching. It must be my fault.'

He looked me over and backed off a step. He said, 'Easy, guy. I didn't mean nothing.'

But he'd read me wrong. I'd been absolutely serious.

I wound up at Armstrong's, where they pour perfectly fine

drinks, but by then I'd lost my taste for it. I sat in the corner with a cup of coffee. It was a quiet night, and Trina had time to join me.

'I kept a weather eye open,' she said, 'but saw of him neither hide nor hair.'

'How's that?'

'The cowboy. Just my cute little way of saying he hasn't been around tonight. Wasn't I supposed to keep watch, like a good Junior G-Man?'

'Oh, the Marlboro man. I thought *I* saw him tonight.'

'Here?'

'No, earlier. I've been seeing a lot of shadows tonight.'

'Is something wrong?'

'Yeah.'

'Hey.' She covered my hand with one of hers. 'What's the matter, baby?'

'I keep finding new people to light candles for.'

'I don't get you. You're not drunk, are you, Matt?'

'No, but not for lack of trying. I have had better days.' I sipped coffee, put the cup down on the checkered cloth. I took out Spinner's silver dollar – correction, *my* dollar, I'd bought and paid for it – and I gave it a spin. I said, 'Last night somebody tried to kill me.'

'God! Around here?'

'A few doors down the block.'

'No wonder you're –'

'No, that's not it. This afternoon I got even. I killed a man.' I thought she would take her hand from atop mine, but she didn't. 'I didn't exactly kill him. He stuck a gun in his mouth and pulled the trigger. A little Spanish gun, they truck them in by the ton from the Carolinas.'

'Why do you say you killed him?'

'Because I put him in a room and the gun was the only door out of it. I boxed him in.'

She looked at her watch. 'Fuck it,' she said. 'I can leave early for a change. If Jimmie wants to sue me for half an hour, then the hell with him.' She reached behind her neck with both hands to unfasten her apron. The movement emphasized the swell of her breasts.

She said, 'Like to walk me home, Matt?'

We had used each other a few times over the months to keep the lonelies away. We liked each other in and out of bed, and both of us had the vital security of knowing it could never lead to anything.

'Matt?'

'I couldn't do you much good tonight, kid.'

'You could keep me from getting mugged on the way home.'

'You know what I mean.'

'Yeah, Mr Detective, but you don't know what *I* mean.' She touched my cheek with her forefinger. 'I wouldn't let you near me tonight anyway. You need a shave.' Her face softened into a smile. 'I was offering a little coffee and company,' she said. 'I think you could use it.'

'Maybe I could.'

'Plain old coffee and company.'

'All right.'

'Not tea and sympathy, nothing like that.'

'Just coffee and company.'

'Uh-huh. Now tell me it's the best offer you've had all day.'

'It is,' I said. 'But that's not saying a hell of a lot.'

She made good coffee, and she managed to come up with a pint of Harper's to flavor it with. By the time I was done talking, the pint had gone from mostly full to mostly empty.

I told her most of it. I left out anything that would make Ethridge or Huysendahl identifiable, and I didn't spell out Henry Prager's smarmy little secret. I didn't mention his name, either, although she figured to dope it out for herself if she bothered to read the morning papers.

When I was finished she sat there for a few minutes, head tilted to one side, eyes half lidded, smoke drifting upward from her cigarette. At length she said she didn't see how I could have done things differently.

'Because suppose you managed to let him know that you weren't a blackmailer, Matt. Suppose you got a little more evidence together and went to him. You would have exposed him, wouldn't you?'

'One way or another.'

'He killed himself because he was afraid of exposure, and that was while he thought you were a blackmailer. If he knew you were going to hand him over to the cops, wouldn't he have done the same thing?'

'He might not have had the chance.'

'Well, maybe he was better off having the chance. Nobody forced him to take it, it was his decision.'

I thought it over. 'There's still something wrong.'

'What?'

'I don't exactly know. Something doesn't fit together the way it should.'

'You just have to have something to feel guilty about.' I guess the line hit home enough to show in my face, because she blanched. 'I'm sorry,' she said. 'Matt, I'm sorry.'

'For what?'

'I was just, you know, being cute.'

'Many a true word is et cetera.' I stood up. 'It'll look better in the morning. Things generally do.'

'Don't leave.'

'I had the coffee and company, and thanks for both. Now I'd better get on home.'

She was shaking her head. 'Stay over.'

'I told you before, Trina –'

'I know you did. I don't particularly want to fuck either, as a matter of fact. But I really don't want to sleep alone.'

'I don't know if I can sleep.'

'Then hold me until I fall asleep, Please, baby?'

We went to bed together and held each other. Maybe the bourbon finally got around to working, or maybe I was more exhausted than I'd realized, but I fell asleep like that, holding her.

FOURTEEN

I woke up with my head throbbing and a liverish taste in the back of my throat. A note on her pillow advised me to help myself to breakfast. The only breakfast I could face was in the bottle of Harper's, and I helped myself to it, and, along with a couple of aspirins from her medicine cabinet and a cup of lousy coffee from the deli downstairs, it took some of the edge off the way I felt.

The weather was good and the air pollution lighter than usual. You could actually see the sky. I headed back to the hotel, picking up a paper on the way. It was almost noon. I don't usually get that much sleep.

I would have to call them, Beverly Ethridge and Theodore Huysendahl. I had to let them know that they were off the hook, that in fact they'd never actually been on it in the first place. I wondered what their reactions would be. Probably a combination of relief and some indignation about having been gulled. Well, that would be their problem. I had enough of my own.

I'd have to see them in person, obviously. I couldn't manage it over the phone. I didn't look forward to it, but did look forward to having it behind me. Two brief phone calls and two brief meetings and I would never have to see either of them again.

I stopped at the desk. There was no mail for me, but there was a phone message. Miss Stacy Prager had called. There was a number where I was to call her as soon as possible. It was the number I had dialed from the Lion's Head.

In my room I checked through the *Times*. Prager was on the obit page under a two-column headline. Just his obituary, with the statement that he had died of an apparently self-inflicted gunshot wound. It was apparent, all right. I was not mentioned in the article. I'd thought that was how his daughter might have gotten my name. Then I looked at the message slip again. She had called around nine the night before, and the first edition of the *Times* wouldn't have hit the street before eleven or twelve.

So that meant she'd learned my name from the police. Or that she had heard it earlier, from her father.

I picked up the phone, then put it down again. I did not much want to talk to Stacy Prager. I couldn't imagine that there was anything I wanted to hear from her, and I knew there was nothing I wanted to say to her. The fact that her father was a murderer was not something she would learn from me, nor would anyone else. Spinner Jablon had had the revenge he'd purchased from me. So far as the rest of the world was concerned, his case could remain in the Open file forever. The police didn't care who had killed him, and I didn't feel obliged to tell them.

I picked up the phone again and called Beverly Ethridge. The line was busy. I broke the connection and tried Huysendahl's office. He was out to lunch. I waited a few minutes and tried the Ethridge number again, and it was still busy. I stretched out on the bed and closed my eyes, and the phone rang.

'Mr Scudder? My name is Stacy Prager.' A young and earnest voice. 'I'm sorry I haven't been in. After I called last night I wound up taking the train so I could be with my mother.'

'I just got your message a few minutes ago.'

'I see. Well, would it be possible for me to talk with you? I'm at Grand Central, I could come to your hotel or meet you wherever you say.'

'I'm not sure how I could help you.'

There was a pause. Then she said, 'Maybe you can't. I don't know. But you were the last person to see my father alive, and I –'

'I didn't even see him yesterday, Miss Prager. I was waiting to see him at the time it happened.'

'Yes, that's right. But the thing is … listen, I'd really like to meet with you, if that's all right.'

'If there's anything I could help you with over the telephone –'

'Couldn't I meet you?'

I asked her if she knew where my hotel was. She said she did, and that she could be there in ten or twenty minutes and she would phone me from the lobby. I hung up and wondered how she had known how to reach me. I'm not in the telephone book. And I wondered if she'd known about Spinner Jablon, and if she'd known about me. If the Marlboro man was her boyfriend, and if she'd been in on the planning …

If so, it was logical to believe that she'd hold me responsible for her father's death. I couldn't even argue the point – I felt responsible myself. But I couldn't really believe she'd have a cute little gun in her handbag. I'd ragged Heaney about watching television. I don't watch all that much television myself.

It took her fifteen minutes, during which time I tried Beverly Ethridge again and got another busy signal. Then Stacy called from the lobby, and I went downstairs to meet her.

Long dark hair, straight, parted in the middle. A tall, slender girl with a long, narrow face and dark, bottomless eyes. She wore clean well-tailored blue jeans and a lime-green cardigan sweater over a simple white blouse. Her handbag had been made by cutting the legs off another pair of jeans. I decided it was highly unlikely there was a gun in it.

We confirmed that I was Matthew Scudder and she was Stacy Prager. I suggested coffee, and we went to the Red Flame and took a booth. After they gave us the coffee, I told her I was very sorry about her father but that I still couldn't imagine why she wanted to see me.

'I don't know why he killed himself,' she said.

'Neither do I.'

'Don't you?' Her eyes searched my face. I tried to imagine her as she had been a few years ago, smoking grass and dropping pills, running down a child and freaking out sufficiently to drive away from what she'd done. That image failed to jibe with the girl seated across the Formica table from me. She now seemed alert and aware and responsible, wounded by her father's death but strong enough to ride it out.

She said, 'You're a detective.'

'More or less.'

'What does that mean?'

'I do some private work on a free-lance basis. None of it as interesting as it may sound.'

'And you were working for my father?'

I shook my head. 'I'd seen him once last week,' I said, and went on to repeat the cover story I'd given Jim Heaney. 'So I really didn't know your father at all.'

'That's very strange,' she said.

She stirred her coffee, added more sugar, stirred it again. She took a sip and put the cup back in the saucer. I asked her why it was strange.

She said, 'I saw my father the night before last. He was waiting at my apartment when I got home from classes. He took me out

217

for dinner. He does that – did that – once or twice a week. But usually he would call me first to arrange it. He said he just had the impulse and took the chance that I'd be coming home.'

'I see.'

'He was very upset. Is that the right word? He was agitated, he was unsettled about something. He was always inclined to be a moody man, very exuberant when things were going right, very depressed when they weren't. When I was first getting into Abnormal Psych and studied the manic-depressive syndrome I got tremendous echoes of my father. I don't mean that he was insane in any sense of the word, but that he had the same kind of mood swings. They didn't interfere with his life, it was just that he had that type of personality.'

'And he was depressed the night before last?'

'It was more than depression. It was a combination of depression and the kind of hyperactive nervousness you can get on speed. I would have thought he had taken some amphetamines except I know how he feels about drugs. I had a period of drug use a few years ago and he made it pretty clear how he felt, so I didn't really believe he was on anything.'

She drank some more coffee. No, there was no gun in her purse. This was a very open girl. If she had a gun she'd have used it immediately.

She said, 'We had dinner in a Chinese restaurant in the neighborhood. That's the Upper West Side, that's where I live. He hardly touched his food. I was very hungry myself, but I kept picking up his vibrations and I wound up not eating very much either. His conversation kept rambling all over the place. He was very concerned about me. He asked several times if I ever used drugs any more. I don't, and I told him so. He asked about my classes, if I was happy with my coursework and if I felt I was on the right track so far as how I would be earning a living. He asked if I was involved with anybody romantically, and I said I wasn't, nothing serious. And then he asked me if I knew you.'

'He did?'

'Yes. I said the only Scudder I knew was the Scudder Falls Bridge. He asked if I had ever been to your hotel – he named the hotel and asked if I had been there – and I said I hadn't. He said that was where you lived. I didn't really understand what he was driving at.'

'Neither do I.'

'He asked if I ever saw a man spin a silver dollar. He took a

218

quarter and spun it on the top of the table and asked if I had ever seen a man do that with a silver dollar. I said no, and I asked him if he was feeling all right. He said he was fine, and that it was very important that I shouldn't worry about him. He said if anything happened to him that I would be all right and not to worry.'

'Which made you more concerned than ever.'

'Of course. I was afraid ... I was afraid of all kinds of things, and scared even to think of them. Like I thought he might have been to the doctor and found out there was something wrong with him. But I called the doctor he always goes to, I did that last night, and he hadn't been there since his annual physical last November, and there was nothing wrong with him then except slightly high blood pressure. Of course, maybe he went to some other doctor, there's no way of knowing unless it shows up in the autopsy. They have to do an autopsy in cases like this. Mr Scudder?'

I looked at her.

'When they called me, when I found out he had killed himself, I wasn't surprised.'

'You expected it?'

'Not consciously. I didn't really expect it, but once I heard, it all seemed to fit. In some way or other, I guess I knew he was trying to tell me he was going to die, trying to tie off the ends before he did it. But I don't know why he did it. And then I heard that you were there when he did it, and I remembered his asking me about you, if I knew you, and I wondered how you fit into it all. I thought maybe there was some problem in his life and you were investigating it for him, because the policeman said you were a detective, and I wondered ... I just don't understand what it was all about.'

'I can't imagine why he mentioned my name.'

'You really weren't working for him?'

'No, and I hadn't had very much contact with him, it was just a superficial matter of confirming another man's references.'

'Then it doesn't make sense.'

I considered. 'We did talk for a while last week,' I said. 'I suppose it's possible something I said seemed to have a special impact on his thinking. I can't imagine what it might have been, but we had one of those rambling conversations, and he might have picked up on something without my noticing it.'

'I suppose that would have to be the explanation.'

'I can't conceive of anything else.'

'And then, whatever it was, it stayed on his mind. So he brought up your name because he couldn't bring himself to mention what it was that you said, or what it meant to him. And then when his secretary said you were there it must have sort of triggered things in his mind. *Triggered*. That's an interesting choice of word, isn't it?'

It had triggered things, the girl's announcing my presence. There was no question about it.

'I can't make anything out of the silver dollar. Unless it's the song. 'You can spin a silver dollar on a barroom floor and it'll roll because it's round.' What's the next line? Something about a woman never knows what a good man she has until she loses him, something like that. Maybe he meant he was losing everything now, I don't know. I guess his mind, I guess it wasn't terribly clear at the end.'

'He must have been under a strain.'

'I guess so.' She looked away for a moment. 'Did he ever say anything to you about me?'

'No.'

'Are you sure?'

I pretended to concentrate, then said I was sure.

'I just hope he realized that everything's all right with me now. That's all. If he had to die, if he thought he had to die, I at least hope he knew I'm okay.'

'I'm sure he did.'

She'd been going through a lot since they called her and told her. Longer than that: since that dinner at the Chinese place. And she was going through plenty now. But she wasn't going to cry. She wasn't a crier. She was a strong one. If he'd had half her strength, he wouldn't have had to kill himself. He would have told Spinner to go screw himself in the first place, and he wouldn't have paid blackmail money, wouldn't have killed once, wouldn't have had to try to kill a second time. She was stronger that he had been. I don't know how much pride you can take in that kind of strength. You either have it or you don't.

I said, 'So that was the last time you saw him. At the Chinese restaurant.'

'Well, he walked me back to my apartment. Then he drove home.'

'What time was that? That he left your place.'

'I don't know. Probably around ten or ten thirty, maybe a little later. Why do you ask?'

I shrugged. 'No reason. Call it habit. I was a cop for a lot of years. When a cop runs out of things to say, he finds himself asking questions. It hardly matters what the questions are.'

'That's interesting. A kind of a learned reflex.'

'I suppose that's the term for it.'

She drew a breath. 'Well,' she said. 'I want to thank you for meeting with me. I wasted your time –'

'I have plenty of time. I don't mind wasting some of it now and then.'

'I just wanted to learn whatever I could about ... about him. I thought there might be something, that he would have had some last message for me. A note, or a letter he might have mailed. I guess it's part of not really believing he's dead, that I can't believe I'll never hear from him one way or the other. I thought – well, thank you, anyway.'

I didn't want her to thank me. She had no reason on earth to thank me.

An hour or so later, I reached Beverly Ethridge. I told her I had to see her.

'I thought I had until Tuesday. Remember?'

'I want to see you tonight.'

'Tonight's impossible. And I don't have the money yet, and you agreed to give me a week.'

'It's something else.'

'What?'

'Not over the phone.'

'Jesus,' she said. 'Tonight is absolutely impossible, Matt. I have an engagement.'

'I thought Kermit was out playing golf.'

'That doesn't mean I sit home alone.'

'I can believe that.'

'You really are a bastard, aren't you? I was invited to a party. A perfectly respectable party, the kind where you keep your clothes on. I could meet you tomorrow if it's absolutely necessary.'

'It is.'

'Where and when?'

'How about Polly's? Say around eight o'clock.'

'Polly's Cage. It's a little tacky, isn't it?'

'A little,' I agreed.

'And so am I, huh?'

'I didn't say that.'

'No, you're always the perfect gentleman. Eight o'clock at Polly's. I'll be there.'

I could have told her to relax, that the ball game was over, instead of letting her spend another day under pressure. But I figured she could handle the pressure. And I wanted to see her face when I let her off the hook. I don't know why. Maybe it was the particular kind of spark we struck off each other, but I wanted to be there when she found out that she was home free.

'Huysendahl and I didn't strike those sparks. I tried him at his office and couldn't reach him, and on a hunch I tried him at home. He wasn't there, but I managed to talk to his wife. I left a message that I would be at his office at two the next afternoon and that I would call again in the morning to confirm the appointment.

'And one other thing,' I said. 'Please tell him that he has absolutely nothing to worry about. Tell him everything's all right now and everything will work out fine.'

'And he'll know what that means?'

'He'll know,' I said.

I napped for a while, had a late bite at the French place down the block, then went back to my room and read for a while. I came very close to making an early night of it, but around eleven my room started to feel a little bit more like a monastic cell than it generally does. I'd been reading *The Lives of the Saints*, which may have had something to do with it.

Outside it was trying to make up its mind to rain. The jury was still out. I went around the corner to Armstrong's. Trina gave me a smile and brought me a drink.

I was only there for an hour or so. I did quite a bit of thinking about Stacy Prager, and even more about her father. I liked myself a little less now that I'd met the girl. On the other hand, I had to agree with what Trina had suggested the night before. He had indeed had the right to pick that way out of his trouble, and now at least his daughter was spared the knowledge that her father had killed a man. The fact of his death was horrible, but I could not easily construct a scenario which would have worked out better.

When I asked for the check Trina brought it over and perched on the edge of my table while I counted out bills. 'You're looking a little cheerier,' she said.

'Am I?'

'Little bit.'

'Well, I had the best night's sleep I've had in a while.'

'Is that so? So did I, strangely enough.'

'Good.'

'Quite a coincidence, wouldn't you say?'

'Hell of coincidence.'

'Which proves there are better sleeping aids than Seconal.'

'You've got to use them sparingly, though.'

'Or you get hooked on them?'

'Something like that.'

A guy two tables away was trying to get her attention. She gave him a look, then turned back to me. She said, 'I don't think it'll ever get to be a habit. You're too old and I'm too young and you're too withdrawn and I'm too unstable and we're both generally weird.'

'No argument.'

'But once in a while can't hurt, can it?'

'No.'

'It's even kinda nice.'

I took her hand and gave it a squeeze. She grinned quickly, scooped up my money, and went off to find out what the pest two tables down wanted. I sat there watching her for a moment, then got up and went out the door.

It was raining now, a cold rain with a nasty wind behind it. The wind was blowing uptown and I was walking downtown, which didn't make me particularly happy. I hesitated, wondering if I ought to go back inside for one more drink and give it a chance for the worst of it to blow over. I decided it wasn't worth it.

So I started walking toward Fifty-seventh Street, and I saw the old beggarwoman in the doorway of Sartor Resartus. I didn't know whether to applaud her industry or worry about her; she wasn't usually out on nights like this. But it had been clear until recently, so I decided she must have taken her post and then found herself caught in the rain.

I kept walking, reaching into my pocket for change. I hoped she wouldn't be disappointed, but she couldn't expect ten dollars from me every night. Only when she saved my life.

I had the coins ready, and she came out of the doorway as I reached it. But it wasn't the old woman.

It was the Marlboro man, and he had a knife in his hand.

FIFTEEN

He came at me in a rush, the knife held underhand and arcing upward, and if it hadn't been raining he would have had me cold. But I got a break. He lost his footing on the wet pavement and had to check the knife thrust in order to regain his balance, and that gave me time to react enough to duck back from him and set myself for his next try.

I didn't have to wait long. I was up on the balls of my feet, arms loose at my sides, a tingling sensation in my hands and a pulse working in my temple. He rocked from side to side, his broad shoulders hinting and feinting, and then he came at me. I'd been watching his feet and I was ready. I dodged to the left, pivoted, threw a foot at his kneecap. And missed, but bounced back and squared off again before he could set himself for another lunge.

He began circling to his left, circling like a prize-fighter stalking an opponent, and when he'd completed a half circle and had his back to the street, I figured out why. He wanted to corner me so that I couldn't make a run for it.

He needn't have bothered. He was young and trim and athletic and outdoorsy. I was too old and carried too much weight, and for too many years the only exercise I had got was bending my elbow. If I tried to run, all I'd manage to do would be to give him my back for a target.

He leaned forward and began transferring the knife from hand to hand. That looks good in the movies, but a really good man with a knife doesn't waste his time that way. Very few people are really ambidextrous. He had started off with the knife in his right hand, and I knew it would be in his right hand when he made his next pass, so all he did with his hand-to-hand routine was give me breathing space and let me tune in on his timing.

He also gave me a little hope. If he'd waste energy with games like that, he wasn't all that great with a knife, and if he was amateur enough I had a chance.

I said, 'I don't have much money on me, but you're welcome to it.'

'Don't want your money, Scudder. Just you.'

Not a voice I'd heard before, and certainly not a New York voice. I wondered where Prager had found him. After having met Stacy, I was fairly sure he wasn't her type.

'You're making a mistake,' I said.

'It's your mistake, man. And you already made it.'

'Henry Prager killed himself yesterday.'

'Yeah? I'll have to send him some flowers.' Back and forth with the knife, knees tensing, relaxing. 'I'm gonna cut you up pretty, man.'

'I don't think so.'

He laughed. I could see his eyes now by the light of the street lamps, and I knew what Billie meant. He had killer eyes, psychopath eyes.

I said, 'I could take you if we both had knives.'

'Sure you could, man.'

'I could take you with an umbrella.' And what I really wished I had was an umbrella or a walking stick. Anything that gives you a little reach is a better defense against a knife than another knife. Better than anything short of a gun.

I wouldn't have minded a gun just then, either. When I left the police department, one immediate benefit was that I no longer had to carry a gun every waking moment. It was very important to me at the time not to carry a gun. Even so, for months I'd felt naked without one. I had carried one for fifteen years, and you sort of get used to the weight.

If I'd had a gun now, I'd have had to use it. I could tell that about him. The sight of a gun wouldn't make him drop the knife. He was determined to kill me, and nothing would keep him from trying. Where had Prager found him? He wasn't professional talent, certainly. Lots of people hire amateur killers, of course, and unless Prager had some mob connections I didn't know about, he wouldn't be likely to have access to any of the pro hit men.

Unless –

That almost started me on a whole new train of thought, and the one thing I couldn't afford to do was let my mind wander. I came back to reality in a hurry when I saw his feet change their shuffling pattern, and I was ready when he closed in on me. I had my moves figured and I had him timed, and I started my kick just as he was getting into his thrust, and I was lucky enough to get his wrist. He lost his balance but managed not to take a spill, and while I managed to jar the knife loose from his hand, it didn't sail far enough to do me much good. He caught his balance and reached for the knife, and got it before my foot did. He scrambled backward almost to the edge of the curb, and before I could jump him he had the knife at his side and I had to back off.

'Now you're dead, man.'

'You talk a good game. I almost had you that time.'

'I think I'll cut you in the belly, man. Let you go out nice and slow.'

The more I kept talking, the more time he'd take between rushes. And the more time he took, the better chance there was that someone would join the party before the guest of honor wound up on the end of the knife. Cabs cruised by periodically, but not many of them, and the weather had cut the pedestrian traffic down to nothing. A patrol car would have been welcome, but you know what they say about cops, they're never around when you want 'em.

He said, 'Come on, Scudder. Try and take me.'

'I've got all night.'

He rubbed his thumb across the blade of the knife. 'It's sharp,' he said.

'I'll take your word for it.'

'Oh, I'll prove it to you, man.'

He backed off a little, moving in the same shuffling gait, and I knew what was coming. He was going to commit himself to one headlong rush, and that meant it wouldn't be a fencing match any more, because if he didn't stab me on the first lunge he'd wind up tumbling me to the ground and we'd wrestle around there until only one of us got up. I watched his feet and avoided getting taken in by the shoulder fakes, and when he came I was ready.

I dropped to one knee and went way down after he'd already committed himself, and his knife hand went over my shoulder and I came up under him, my arms around his legs, and in one motion I spun and heaved. I got my legs into it and threw him as high and as far as I could, knowing he'd drop the knife when he landed, knowing I'd be on him in time to kick it away and put a toe into the side of his head.

But he never did drop the knife. He went high into the air and his legs kicked at nothing and he turned lazily in midair like an

Olympic diver, but when he came down there was no water in the swimming pool. He had one hand extended to break the fall, but he didn't land right. The impact of his head on the concrete was like that of a melon dropped from a third-floor window. I was fairly sure he'd have a skull fracture, and that can be enough to kill you.

I went over and looked at him and knew it didn't matter if his skull was fractured or not, because he had landed on the back of his head while falling forward, and he was now in a position you can't achieve unless your neck is broken. I looked for a pulse, not expecting to find one, and I couldn't get a beat. I rolled him over and put my ear to his chest and didn't hear anything. He still had the knife in his hand, but it wouldn't do him any good now.

'Holy shit.'

I looked up. It was one of the neighborhood Greeks who did his drinking at Spiro and Antares. We would nod at each other now and then. I didn't know his name.

'I saw what happened,' he said. 'Bastard was tryin' to kill you.'

'That's just what you can help me explain to the police.'

'Shit, no. I didn't see nothin', you know what I mean?'

I said, 'I don't care what you mean. How hard do you think it'll be for me to find you if I want to? Go back into Spiro's and pick up the phone and dial 911. You don't even need a dime to do it. Tell 'em you want to report a homicide in the Eighteenth Precinct and give 'em the address.'

'I don't know about that.'

'You don't have to know anything. All you have to do is what I just told you.'

'Shit, there's a knife in his hand, anybody can see it was self-defense. He's dead, huh? You said homicide, and the way his neck's bent. Can't walk the fuckin' streets any more, the whole fuckin' city's a fuckin' jungle.'

'Make the call.'

'Look –'

'You dumb son of bitch, I'll give you more aggravation than you'd ever believe. You want cops driving you crazy for the rest of your life? Go make the call.'

He went.

I kneeled down next to the body and gave it a fast but thorough frisk. What I wanted was a name, but there was nothing on him to identify him. No wallet, just a money clip in the shape of a dollar sign. Sterling silver, it looked like. He had a little over

228

three hundred dollars. I put the ones and fives back into the clip and returned it to his pocket. I stuffed the rest into my own pocket. I had more of a use for it than he did.

Then I stood there waiting for the cops to show and wondering if my little friend had called them. While I was waiting, a couple of cabs stopped from time to time to ask what had happened and if they could help. Nobody'd taken the trouble while the Marlboro man was waving the knife at me, but now that he was dead everybody wanted to live dangerously. I shooed them all away and waited some more, and finally a black-and-white turned at Fifty-seventh Street and ignored the fact that Ninth Avenue runs one way downtown. They cut the siren and trotted over to where I was standing over the body. Two men in plainclothes; I didn't recognize either of them.

I explained briefly who I was and what had happened. The fact that I was an ex-cop myself didn't hurt a bit. Another car pulled up while I was talking, with a lab crew, and then an ambulance.

To the lab crew I said, 'I hope you're going to print him. Not after you get him to the morgue. Take a set of prints now.'

They didn't ask who I was to be giving orders. I guess they assumed I was a cop and that I probably ranked them pretty well. The plainclothes guy I'd been talking to raised his eyebrows at me.

'Prints?'

I nodded. 'I want to know who he is, and he wasn't carrying any I.D.'

'You bothered to look?'

'I bothered to look.'

'Not supposed to, you know.'

'Yes, I know. But I wanted to know who would take the trouble to kill me.'

'Just a mugger, no?'

I shook my head. 'He was following me around the other day. And he was waiting for me tonight, and he called me by name. Your average mugger doesn't research his victims all that carefully.'

'Well, they're printing him, so we'll see what we come up with. Why would anybody want to kill you?'

I let the question go by. I said, 'I don't know if he's local or not. I'm sure somebody'll have a sheet on him, but he may never have taken a fall in New York.'

'Well, we'll take a look and see what we got. I don't think he's a virgin, do you?'

'Not likely.'

'Washington'll have him if we don't. Want to come over to the station? Probably a few of the boys you know from the old days.'

'Sure,' I said. 'Gagliardi still making the coffee?'

His face clouded. 'He died,' he said. 'Just about two years ago. Heart attack, he was just sitting at his desk and he bought it.'

'I never heard. That's a shame.'

'Yeah, he was all right. Made good coffee, too.'

SIXTEEN

My preliminary statement was sketchy. The man who took it, a detective named Birnbaum, noticed as much. I'd simply said that I had been assaulted by a person unknown to me at a specific place and time, that my assailant had been armed with a knife, that I had been unarmed, and that I had taken defensive measures which had involved throwing my assailant in such a way that, though I had not so intended, the ensuing fall had resulted in his death.

'This punk knew you by name,' Birnbaum said. 'That's what you said before.'

'Right.'

'That's not in here.' He had a receding hairline, and he paused to rub where the hair had previously been. 'You also told Lacey he'd been following you around past couple of days.'

'I noticed him once I'm sure of, and I think I saw him a few other times.'

'Uh-huh. And you want to hang around while we trace the prints and try to figure out who he was.'

'Right.'

'You didn't wait to see if we turned up any I.D. on him. Which means you probably looked and saw he wasn't carrying any-thing.'

'Maybe it was just a hunch,' I suggested. 'Man goes out to murder somebody, he doesn't carry identification around. Just an assumption on my part.'

He raised his eyebrows for a minute, then shrugged. 'We can let it go at that, Matt. Lot of times I check out an apartment when nobody's home, and wouldn't you know it that they got careless and left the door open, because of course I wouldn't think of letting myself in with a loid.'

'Because that would be breaking-and-entering.'

'And we wouldn't want that, would we?' He grinned, then

picked up my statement again. 'There's things you know about this bird that you don't want to tell. Right?'

'No. There's things I *don't* know.'

'I don't get it.'

I took one of his cigarettes from the pack on the desk. If I wasn't careful I'd get the habit again. I spent some time lighting up, getting the words in the right order.

I said, 'You're going to be able to clear a case off the books, I think. A homicide.'

'Give me a name.'

'Not yet.'

'Look, Matt —'

I drew on the cigarette. I said, 'Let me do it my way for a little while. I'll fill in part of it for you, but nothing goes on paper for the time being. You've got enough already to wrap what happened tonight as justifiable homicide, don't you? You got a witness and you've got a corpse with a knife in his hand.'

'So?'

'The corpse was hired to tag me. When I know who he is I'm probably going to know who hired him. I think he was also hired to kill somebody else a while ago, and when I know his name and back-ground I'll be able to come up with evidence that should lock right into the person who's paying the check.'

'And you can't open up on any of this in the meantime?'

'No.'

'Any particular reason?'

'I don't want to get the wrong person in trouble.'

'You play a very lone hand, don't you?'

I shrugged.

'They're checking downtown right now. If he doesn't show there, we'll wire the prints down to the Bureau in D.C. It could add up to a long night.'

'I'll hang around, if it's all right.'

'I'd just as soon you did, matter of fact. There's a couch in the loot's office if you want to close your eyes for a while.'

I said I'd wait until the word came back from downtown. He found something to do, and I went into an empty office and picked up a newspaper. I guess I fell asleep, because the next thing I knew, Birnbaum was shaking my shoulder. I opened my eyes.

'Nothing downtown, Matt. Our boy's never taken a bust in New York.'

'That's what I thought.'

'I thought you didn't know anything about him.'

'I don't. I'm running hunches, I told you that.'

'You could save us trouble if you told us where to look.'

I shook my head. 'I can't think of anything faster than wiring Washington.'

'His prints are already on the wire. Might be a couple of hours anyway, and it's getting light outside already. Why don't you go home, and I'll give you a call soon as anything comes in.'

'You got a full set. Doesn't the Bureau do this sort of things by computer these days?'

'Sure. But somebody has to tell the computer what to do, and they tend to take their time down there. Go home and get some sleep.'

'I'll wait.'

'Suit yourself.' He started for the door, then turned to remind me about the couch in the lieutenant's office. But the time I'd dozed in the chair had taken the edge off the urge to sleep. I was exhausted, certainly, but sleep was no longer possible. Too many mental wheels were starting to turn, and I couldn't shut them off.

He had to be Prager's boy. It just had to add up that way. Either he had somehow missed the news that Prager was dead and out of the picture, or he was tied in close to Prager and wanted me dead out of spite. Or he had been hired through an intermediary, somehow, and didn't know that Prager was a part of it. Something, anything, because otherwise –

I didn't want to think about the otherwise.

I had been telling Birnbaum the truth. I had a hunch, and the more I thought about it the more I believed in it, and at the same time I kept wanting to be wrong. So I sat around the station house and read newspapers and drank endless cups of weak coffee and tried not to think about all of the things I couldn't possibly avoid thinking about. Somewhere along the line Birnbaum went home, after he'd briefed another detective named Guzik, and around nine thirty Guzik came over to me and said they had a make from Washington.

He read it off the teletype sheet. 'Lundgren, John Michael. Date of birth fourteen March 'forty-three. Place of birth San Bernardino, California. Whole trail of arrests here, Matt. Living off immoral earnings, assault, assault with a deadly weapon, grand theft auto, grand larceny. He did local bits all up and down the West Coast, pulled some hard time in Quentin.'

'He pulled a one-to-five in Folsom,' I said. 'I don't know whether they called it extortion or larceny. That would have been fairly recent.'

He looked up at me. 'I thought you didn't know him.'

'I don't. He was working a badger game. Arrested in San Diego, and his partner turned state's evidence and got off. Sentence suspended.'

'That's more detail than I've got here.'

I asked him if he had a cigarette. He said he didn't smoke. He turned to ask if anybody had a cigarette, but I told him to forget it. 'Get somebody with a steno pad,' I said. 'There's a lot to tell.'

I gave them everything I could think of. How Beverly Ethridge had worked her way in and out of the world of crime. How she had married well and turned herself back into the society type she had been in the first place. How Spinner Jablon had pieced it all together on the strength of a newspaper photo and turned it into a neat little blackmail operation.

'I guess she stalled him for a while,' I said. 'But it kept being expensive, and he kept pushing for bigger money. Then her old boyfriend Lundgren came east and showed her a way out. Why pay blackmail when it's so much easier to kill the blackmailer? Lundgren was a pro as a criminal but an amateur as a killer. He tried a couple of different methods on Spinner. Tried to get him with a car, then wound up hitting him over the head and putting him in the East River. Then he tried for me with the car.'

'And then with the knife.'

'That's right.'

'How did you get into it?'

I explained, leaving out the names of Spinner's other blackmail victims. They didn't like that much, but there wasn't anything much they could do about it. I told them how I had staked myself out as a target and how Lundgren had taken the bait.

Guzik kept interrupting to tell me I should have given everything to the cops right off, and I kept telling him it was something I had not been willing to do.

'We'd've handled it right, Matt. Jesus, you talk about Lundgren's an amateur, shit, you ran around like an amateur yourself and almost got your ass in the wringer. You wound up going up against a knife with nothing but your hands, and it's dumb luck you're alive this minute. The hell, you ought to know better, you were a cop fifteen years, and you act like you don't know what the department's all about.'

'How about the people who didn't kill Spinner? What happens to them if I hand you the whole thing right off the bat?'

'That's their lookout, isn't it? They come into it with dirty hands. They got something to hide, that shouldn't be getting in the way of a murder investigation.'

'But there was no investigation. Nobody gave a shit about Spinner.'

'Because you were withholding evidence.'

I shook my head. 'That's horseshit,' I said. 'I didn't have evidence that anybody killed Spinner. I had evidence that he was blackmailing several people. That was evidence against Spinner, but he was dead, and I didn't think you were particularly anxious to take him out of the morgue and throw him in a cell. The minute I had murder evidence I put it in your hand. Look, we could argue all day. Why don't you put out a pickup order on Beverly Ethridge?'

'And charge her with what?'

'Two counts of conspiracy to murder.'

'You've got the blackmail evidence?'

'In a safe place. A safe-deposit box. I can bring it here in an hour.'

'I think I'll come along with you and get it.'

I looked at him.

'Maybe I want to see just what's in the envelope, Scudder.'

It had been *Matt* up until then. I wondered what kind of a number he wanted to run. Maybe he was just fishing, but he had visions of something or other. Maybe he wanted to take my place in the blackmail dodge, only he'd want real money, not the name of a murderer. Maybe he figured the other pigeons had committed real crimes and he could buy himself a commendation by knocking them off. I didn't know him well enough to guess which motivation would be consistent with the man, but it didn't really make very much difference.

'I don't get it,' I said. 'I give you a homicide collar on a silver platter and you want to melt down the platter.'

'I'm sending a couple boys over to pick up Ethridge. In the meantime, you and me are going to open up a safe-deposit box.'

'I could forget where I left the key.'

'And I could make your life difficult.'

235

'It's not that much of a cinch as it is. It's just a few blocks from here.'

'Still raining,' he said. 'We'll take a car.'

We drove over to the Manufacturers Hanover branch at Fifty-seventh and Eighth. He left the black-and-white in a bus stop. All that to save a three-block walk, and it wasn't raining all that hard any more. We went inside and went down the stairs to the vault, and I gave my key to the guard and signed the signature card.

'Had the damnedest thing you ever heard of a few months back,' Guzik said. He was friendly now that I was going along with him. 'This girl rented a box over at Chemical Bank, and she paid her eight bucks for a year, and she was visiting the box three or four times a day. Always with a guy, always a different guy. So the bank got suspicious and asked us to check it out, and wouldn't you know, the chick is a pross. Instead of taking a hotel room for ten bucks, she's picking up her tricks on the street and taking them to the fucking bank, for Christ's sake. Then she gets her box out and they show her to the little room, and she locks the door and gives the guy a quick blow job in complete privacy, and then she sticks the money in the box and locks it up again. And all it runs her is eight bucks for the year instead of ten bucks a trick, and it's safer than a hotel because if she gets a crazy he's not going to try beating her up in the middle of a fucking bank, is he? She can't get beaten up and she can't get robbed, and it's perfect.'

By this time the guard had used his key and mine to get the box from the vault. He handed it to me and led us to a cubicle. We entered together, and Guzik closed and locked the door. The room struck me as rather cramped for sex, but I understand people do it in airplane lavatories, and this was spacious in comparison.

I asked Guzik what had happened to the girl.

'Oh, we told the bank not to press charges, or all it would do was give every streetwalker in the business the same idea. We told them to refund her boxrental fee and tell her they didn't want her business, so I guess that's what they did. She probably walked across the street and started doing business with another bank.'

'But you never got any more complaints.'

'No. Maybe she's got a friend at Chase Manhattan.' He laughed hard at his own line, then chopped it off abruptly. 'Let's see what's in the box, Scudder.'

I handed it to him. 'Open it yourself,' I said.

He did, and I watched his face while he looked through everything. He had some interesting comments on the pictures he saw, and he gave the written material a fairly careful reading. Then he looked up suddenly.

'This is all the stuff on the Ethridge dame.'

'Seems that way,' I said.

'What about the others?'

'I guess these safe-deposit vaults aren't as foolproof as they're supposed to be. Somebody must have come in and taken everything else.'

'You son of a bitch.'

'You've got everything you need, Guzik. No more and no less.'

'You took a different box for each one. How many others are there?'

'What difference does it make?'

'You son of a bitch. So we'll walk back and ask the guard how many other boxes you have here, and we'll take a look at all of them.'

'If you want. I can save you a little time.'

'Oh?'

'Not just three different boxes, Guzik. Three different banks. And don't even think about shaking me for the other keys, or running a check on the banks, or anything else you might have in mind. In fact, it might be a good idea if you stopped calling me a son of a bitch, because I might get unhappy, and I might decide not to cooperate in your investigation. I don't have to cooperate, you know. And if I don't, your case goes down the drain. You can possibly tie Ethridge to Lundgren without me, but you'll have a hell of a time finding anything a D.A. is going to want to take to court.'

We looked at each other for a while. A couple of times he started to say something, and a couple of times he figured out that it wasn't a particularly good idea. Finally something changed in his face, and I knew he'd decided to let it go. He had enough, and he had all he was going to get, and his face said he knew it.

'The hell,' he said, 'it's the cop in me, I want to get to the bottom of things. No offense, I hope.'

'None at all,' I said. I don't suppose I sounded very convincing.

'They probably hauled Ethridge out of bed by now. I'll get back and see what she's got to say. It should make good listening. Or maybe they didn't haul her out of bed. These pictures, you'd have more fun hauling her into bed than out. Ever get any of that, Scudder?'

'No.'

'I wouldn't mind a taste myself. Want to come back to the station house with me?'

I didn't want to go anywhere with him. I didn't want to see Beverly Ethridge.

'I'll pass,' I said. 'I've got an appointment.'

SEVENTEEN

I spent half an hour under the shower with the spray as hot as I could stand it. It had been a long night, and the only sleep I'd had had been when I dozed off briefly in Birnbaum's chair. I had come close to being killed, and I had killed the man who'd been trying for me. The Marlboro man, John Michael Lundgren. He'd have been thirty-one next month. I would have guessed him at younger than that, twenty-six or so. Of course, I'd never seen him in particularly good light.

It didn't bother me that he was dead. He had been trying to kill me and had seemed pleased at the prospect. He had killed Spinner, and it wasn't unlikely that he'd killed other people before. He might not have been a pro at killing, but it seemed to be something he enjoyed. He certainly liked working with the knife, and the boys who like to use knives usually get a sexual thrill out of their weaponry. Edged weapons are even more phallic that guns.

I wondered if he'd used a knife on Spinner. It wasn't inconceivable. The Medical Examiner's office doesn't catch everything. There was a case a while ago, a then-unidentified floater they fished out of the Hudson, and she was processed and buried without anyone's noticing that there was a bullet in her skull. They found out only because some yoyo severed her head before burial. He wanted the skull for a desk ornament, and ultimately they found the bullet and identified the skull from dental records and found out the woman had been missing from her home in Jersey for a couple of months.

I let my mind wander with all these thoughts because there were other thoughts I wanted to avoid, but after half an hour I turned off the shower and toweled myself off and picked up the phone and told them to hold my calls, and to put me down for a wake-up call at one sharp.

Not that I expected to need the call, because I knew I wasn't going to be able to sleep. All I could do was stretch out on the bed and close my eyes and think about Henry Prager and how I had murdered him.

Henry Prager.

John Lundgren was dead and I had killed him, had broken his neck, and it did not bother me at all, because he had done everything possible to earn that death. And Beverly Ethridge was being grilled by the police, and it was very possible that they would wind up with enough on her to put her away for a couple of years. It was also possible that she would beat it, because there probably wasn't all that much of a case, but either way it didn't matter much, because Spinner would have his vengeance. She could forget about her marriage and her social position and cocktails at the Pierre. She could forget about most of her life, and that didn't bother me either, because it was nothing she didn't deserve.

But Henry Prager had never killed anybody, and I had pressured him enough to make him blow his brains out, and there was really no way I could justify that. It had bothered me enough when I'd believed him guilty of murder. Now I knew he was innocent, and it bothered me infinitely more.

Oh, there were ways to rationalize it. Evidently his business had turned sour. Evidently he had made a lot of bad financial judgments recently. Evidently he had been up against several different kinds of walls, and evidently he had been a marginal manic-depressive with suicidal tendencies, and that was all well and good, but I had put extra pressure on a man who was in no position to handle it and that had been the last straw, and there was no rationalizing my way out of that one, because it was more than coincidence that he had picked my visit to his office to put the gun in his mouth and pull the trigger.

I lay there with my eyes closed and I wanted a drink. I wanted a drink very badly.

But not yet. Not until I kept my appointment and told an up-and-coming young pederast that he didn't have to pay me a hundred thousand dollars, and that if he could just fool enough of the people enough of the time he could go right ahead and be governor.

By the time I was done talking to him, I had the feeling he might not make bad governor at that. He must have realized the minute

I sat down across the desk from him that it would be to his advantage to listen to what I had to say without interrupting. What I had to say must have come as a complete surprise to him, but he just sat there looking absorbed, listening intently, nodding from time to time as a way of punctuating my sentences for me. I told him that he was off the hook, that he had never really been on it, that it had all been a device designed to trap a killer without washing other people's dirty laundry in public. I took my time telling him, because I wanted to get it all said on the first try.

When I was done, he leaned back in his chair and looked at the ceiling. Then he turned his eyes to meet mine and said his first word.

'Extraordinary.'

'I had to pressure you the same as I had to pressure everyone else,' I said. 'I didn't like it, but it was what I had to do.'

'Oh, I wasn't even feeling all that much pressure, Mr Scudder. I recognized that you were a reasonable sort of man and that it was only a question of raising the money, a task which did not seem by any means impossible.' He folded his hands on the desk top. 'It's hard for me to digest all of this at once. You were quite the perfect blackmailer, you know. And now it seems you were never a blackmailer at all. I've never been more pleased at being gulled. And the, uh, photographs –'

'They've all been destroyed.'

'I'm to take your word for that, I take it. But isn't that a silly objection? I'm still thinking of you as a blackmailer, and that's absurd. If you were a blackmailer, I'd still have to take your word that you hadn't retained copies of the pictures, it would always come to that in the end, but since you haven't extorted money from me to begin with, I can hardly worry that you will do so in the future, can I?'

'I thought of bringing you the pictures. I also figured I might get hit by a bus on the way over here, or leave the envelope in a cab.' Spinner, I thought, had worried about getting hit by a bus. 'It seemed simpler to burn them.'

'I assure you, I had no desire to see them. Just the knowledge that they cease to exist, that's all I need to feel very much better about things.' His eyes probed mine. 'You took an awful chance, didn't you? You could have been killed.'

'I almost was. Twice.'

'I can't understand why you put yourself on the spot like that.'

'I'm not sure I understand it myself. Let's say I was doing a favor for a friend.'

'A friend?'

'Spinner Jablon.'

'An odd sort of person for you to select as a friend, don't you think?'

I shrugged.

'Well, I don't suppose your motives matter very much. You certainly succeeded admirably.'

I wasn't so sure of that.

'When you first suggested that you might be able to get those photographs of me, you couched a blackmail demand in terms of a reward. Rather a nice touch, actually.' He smiled. 'I do think you deserve a reward, however. Perhaps not a hundred thousand dollars, but something substantial, I should say. I don't have much cash on me at the moment –'

'A check will be fine.'

'Oh?' He looked at me for a moment, then opened a drawer and took out a checkbook, the large sort with three checks to the page. He uncapped a pen, filled in the date, and looked up at me.

'Can you suggest an amount?'

'Ten thousand dollars,' I said.

'It didn't take you long to think of a figure.'

'It's a tenth of what you were prepared to pay a blackmailer. It seems a reasonable figure.'

'Not unreasonable, and a bargain from my point of view. Shall I make it out to cash or to you personally?'

'Neither.'

'Pardon me?'

It wasn't my province to pardon him. I said, 'I don't want any money for myself. Spinner hired me and paid me well enough for my time.'

'Then –'

'Make it payable to Boys Town. Father Flanagan's Boys Town. I think it's in Nebraska, isn't it?'

He put the pen down and stared at me. His face reddened slightly, and then either he saw the humor in it or the politician in him took over, because he put his head back and laughed. It was a pretty good laugh. I don't know if he meant it or not, but it certainly sounded authentic.

He made out the check and handed it to me. He told me I had a marvelous sense of poetic justice. I folded the check and put it in my pocket.

He said, 'Boys Town indeed. You know, Scudder, that's all very much in the past. The subject of those photographs. It was a weakness, a very disabling and unfortunate weakness, but it's all in the past.'

'If you say so.'

'As a matter of fact, even the desire is completely over and done with, the particular demon exorcised. Even if it were not, I would have no difficulty in resisting the impulse. I have a career that's far too important for me to place it in jeopardy. And these past few months I have truly learned the meaning of jeopardy.'

I didn't say anything. He got up and walked around a little and told me all the plans he had for the great State of New York. I didn't pay too much attention. I just listened to the tone, and I decided I believed he was sincere enough. He really wanted to be governor, that was always obvious, but he seemed to want to be governor for reasonably good reasons.

'Well,' he said at length, 'I seemed to have found an opportunity to make a speech, haven't I? Will I be able to count on your vote. Scudder?'

'No.'

'Oh? I thought that was rather a good speech.'

'I won't vote against you, either, I don't vote.'

'Your duty as a citizen, Mr Scudder.'

'I'm a rotten citizen.'

He smiled broadly at that, for reasons that escaped me. 'You know,' he said, 'I like your style, Scudder. For all the bad moments you gave me, I still like your style. I even liked it before I knew the blackmail pose was a charade.' He lowered his voice confidentially. 'I could find a very good place for someone like you in my organization.'

'I'm not interested in organizations. I was in one for fifteen years.'

'The Police Department.'

'That's right.'

'Perhaps I stated it poorly. You wouldn't be part of an organization per se. You'd be working for me.'

'I don't like to work for people.'

'You're contented with your life as it is.'

'Not particularly.'

'But you don't want to change it.'

243

'No.'

'It's your life,' he said. 'I'm surprised, though. You have a great deal of depth to you. I should think you would want to accomplish more in the world. I would think you would be more ambitious, if not for your own personal advancement then in terms of your potential for doing some good in the world.'

'I told you I was a rotten citizen.'

'Because you don't exercise your right to vote, yes. But I would think – Well, if you should change your mind, Mr Scudder, the offer will hold.'

I got to my feet. He stood and extended his hand. I didn't really want to shake hands with him, but I couldn't see how to avoid it. His grip was firm and sure, which boded well for him. He was going to have to shake a lot of hands if he wanted to win elections.

I wondered if he'd really lost his passion for young boys. It didn't matter much to me one way or the other. The photos I'd seen had turned my stomach, but I don't know that I had all that much moral objection to them. The boy who'd posed for them had been paid, and undoubtedly knew what he was doing. I didn't like shaking hands with him, and he would never be my choice for a drinking buddy, but I figured he wouldn't be too much worse in Albany than any other son of a bitch who would want the job.

EIGHTEEN

It was around three when I left Huysendahl's office. I thought of calling Guzik and finding out how they were doing with Beverly Ethridge, but I decided to save a dime. I didn't want to talk to him, and I didn't much care how they were doing anyway. I walked around for a while and stopped at a lunch counter on Warren Street. I didn't have an appetite, but it had been a while since I'd had anything to eat, and my stomach was starting to tell me I was mistreating it. I had a couple of sandwiches and some coffee.

I walked around some more. I'd wanted to go to the bank where the data on Henry Prager was tucked away, but it was too late now, they were closed. I decided I'd do that in the morning so that I could destroy all that material. Prager couldn't be hurt any more, but there was still the daughter, and I would feel better when the stuff Spinner had willed to me had ceased to exist.

After a while I got on the subway, and got off at Columbus Circle. There was a message for me at the hotel desk. Anita had called and wanted me to call her back.

I went upstairs and addressed a plain white envelope to Boys Town. I enclosed Huysendahl's check, put a stamp on the envelope, and, in a monumental expression of faith, dropped the letter in the hotel's mail chute. Back in my room, I counted the money I'd taken from the Marlboro man. It came to two hundred and eighty dollars. Some church or other had twenty-eight dollars coming, but at the moment I didn't feel like going to a church. I didn't really feel like much of anything.

It was over now. There was really nothing more to do, and all I felt was empty. If Beverly Ethridge ever stood trial, I would probably have to testify, but that wouldn't be for months, if ever, and the prospect of testifying didn't bother me. I'd given testimony on enough occasions in the past. There was nothing more to do. Huysendahl was free to become governor or not, depending upon the whims of political bosses and the public at large, and Beverly Ethridge was up against the wall, and Henry Prager was going to be buried in a day or so. The moving finger had written and he had written himself off, and my role in his life was as finished as his life itself. He was another person to light meaningless candles for, that was all.

I called Anita.

'Thanks for the money order,' she said. 'I appreciated it.'

'I'd say there's more where that came from,' I said. 'Except there isn't.'

'Are you all right?'

'Sure. Why?'

'You sound different. I don't know how exactly, but you sound different.'

'It's been a long week.'

There was a pause. Our conversations are usually marked by pauses. Then she said, 'The boys were wondering if you wanted to take them to a basketball game.'

'In Boston?'

'Pardon me?'

'The Knicks are out of it. The Celtics destroyed them a couple of nights ago. It was the highlight of my week.'

'The Nets,' she said.

'Oh.'

'I think they're in the finals. Against Utah or something.'

'Oh.' I can never remember that New York has a second basketball team. I don't know why. I've taken my sons to the Nassau Coliseum to watch the Nets and I still tend to forget they exist. 'When are they playing?'

'There's a home game Saturday night.'

'What's today?'

'Are you serious?'

'Look, I'll get a calendar watch next time I think of it. What's today?'

'Thursday.'

'Tickets will probably be hard to get.'

'Oh, they're all sold out. They thought you might know somebody.'

I thought of Huysendahl. He could probably swing tickets without much trouble. He would also probably have enjoyed meeting my sons. Of course, there were enough other people who could manage to obtain last-minute tickets, and who wouldn't mind doing me a favor.

I said, 'I don't know. It's cutting it kind of close.' But what I was thinking was that I didn't want to see my sons, not in just two days' time, and I didn't know why. And I was also wondering if they really wanted me to take them to the game or if they simply wanted to go to it and knew that I would be able to root out a source of tickets.

I asked if there were any other home games.

'Thursday. But that's a school night.'

'It's also a lot more possible than Saturday.'

'Well, I hate to see them stay out late on a school night.'

'I could probably get tickets for the Thursday game.'

'Well –'

'I couldn't get tickets for Saturday, but I could probably get something for Thursday. It'll be later in the series, a more important game.'

'Oh, so that's the way you want to do it. If I say no because it's a school night, then I'm the heavy.'

'I think I'll hang up.'

'No, don't do that. All right, Thursday is fine. You'll call if you can get tickets?'

I said I would.

It was odd – I wanted to be drunk but didn't much want a drink. I sat around the room for a while, then walked over to the park and sat on a bench. A couple of kids ambled rather purposefully to a bench nearby. They sat down and lit cigarettes, and then one of them noticed me and nudged his companion, who looked carefully toward me. They got up and walked off, glancing back periodically to make sure I was not following them. I stayed where I was. I guessed that one of them had been about to sell drugs to the other, and that they had looked at me and decided not to conduct the transaction under the eyes of someone who looked like a policeman.

I don't know how long I sat there. A couple of hours, I suppose. Periodically a panhandler would brace me. Sometimes I'd contribute toward the next bottle of sweet wine. Sometimes I'd tell the bum to fuck off.

By the time I left the park and walked over to Ninth Avenue, St Paul's was closed for the day. The downstairs was opening up, however. It was too late to pray but just the right hour for bingo.

Armstrong's was open, and it had been a long dry night and day. I told them to forget the coffee.

The next forty hours or so were pretty much of a blur. I don't know how long I stayed in Armstrong's or where I went after that. Sometime Friday morning I woke up alone in a hotel room in the Forties, a squalid room in the king of hotel to which Times Square streetwalkers take their johns. I had no memory of a woman and my money was all still there, so it looked as though I had probably checked in alone. There was a pint bottle of bourbon on the dresser, about two-thirds empty. I killed it and left the hotel and went on drinking, and reality faded in and out, and sometime during that night I must have decided I was done, because I managed to find my way back to my hotel.

Saturday morning the telephone woke me. It seemed to ring for a long time before I roused myself enough to reach for it. I managed to knock it off the little nightstand and onto the floor, and by the time I managed to pick it up and get it to my ear I was reasonably close to consciousness.

It was Guzik.

'You're hard to find,' he said. 'I been trying to reach you since yesterday. Didn't you get my messages?'

'I didn't stop at the desk.'

'I gotta talk to you.'

'What about?'

'When I see you. I'll be over in ten minutes.'

I told him to give me half an hour. He said he'd meet me in the lobby. I said that would be fine.

I stood under the shower, first hot, then cold. I took a couple of aspirin and drank a lot of water. I had a hangover, which I had certainly earned, but aside from that I felt reasonably good. The drinking had purged me. I would still carry Henry Prager's death around with me – you cannot entirely shrug off such burdens – but I had managed to drown some of the guilt, and it was no longer as oppressive as it had been.

I took the clothes I'd been wearing, wadded them up, and stuffed them into the closet. Eventually I'd decide whether the cleaner could restore them, but for the moment I didn't even want to think about it. I shaved and put on clean clothes and drank two more glasses of tap water. The aspirin had polished off the headache, but I was dehydrated from too many hours of hard drinking, and every cell in my body had an unquenchable thirst.

I got down to the lobby before he arrived. I checked the desk and found that he'd called four times. There were no other messages, and no mail of any importance. I was reading one of the unimportant letters – an insurance company would give me a leather-covered memorandum book absolutely free if I would tell my date of birth – when Guzik came in. He was wearing a well-tailored suit; you had to look carefully to see he was carrying a gun.

He came over and took a chair next to me. He told me again that I was hard to find. 'Wanted to talk to you after I saw Ethridge,' he said. 'Jesus, she's something, isn't she? She turns the class on and off. One minute you can't believe she was ever a pross, and the next minute you can't believe she was anything else but.'

'She's an odd one, all right.'

'Uh-huh. She's also getting out sometime today.'

'She made bail? I thought they'd book her for Murder One.'

'Not bail. Not booking her for anything, Matt. We got nothing to hold her on.'

I looked at him. I could feel the muscles in my forearms tightening. I said, 'How much did it cost her?'

'I told you, no bail. We –'

'What did it cost her to buy out of a murder charge? I always heard you could wash homicide if you had enough cash. Never saw it done, but I heard about it, and –'

He was almost ready to swing, and I was by God hoping he would do it, because I wanted an excuse to put him through the wall. A tendon stood out on his neck, and his eyes narrowed to slits. Then he relaxed suddenly, and his face regained its original color.

He said, 'Well, you would have to figure it that way, wouldn't you?'

'Well?'

He shook his head. 'Nothing to hold her on,' he said again. 'That's what I was trying to tell you.'

'How about Spinner Jablon?'

'She didn't kill him.'

'Her bully boy did. Her pimp, whatever the hell he was. Lundgren.'

'No way.'

'The hell.'

249

'No way,' Guzik said. 'He was in California. Town called Santa Paula, it's halfway between L.A. and Santa Barbara.'

'He flew here and then flew back.'

'No way. He was there from a few weeks before we fished Spinner out of the river until a couple of days afterward, and nobody's gonna shake that alibi. He did thirty days in Santa Paula city jail. They tagged him for assault and let him plead to drunk and disorderly. He did the whole thirty days. Just no way on earth that he was in New York when Spinner got it.'

I stared at him.

'So maybe she had another boyfriend,' he went on. 'We figured that was possible. We could try to turn him up, but does it make any sense that way? She wouldn't use one guy to hit Spinner and another to go after you. It doesn't make sense.'

'What about the assault on me?'

'What about it?' He shrugged. 'Maybe she put him up to it. Maybe she didn't. She swears she didn't. Her story is she called him for advice when you put the screws to her and he flew out to see if he could help. She said she told him not to get rough, that she thought she would be able to buy you off. That's her story, but what can you expect her to say? Maybe she wanted him to kill you and maybe she didn't, but how can you put enough together to make a case out of it? Lundgren is dead, and nobody else has any information that absolutely implicates her. There's no evidence to tie her to the attack on you. You can prove she knew Lundgren and you can prove she had a motive for wanting you dead. You can't prove any kind of an accessory or conspiracy charge. You can't come up with anything that an indictment returned, you can't even get anything that would make anybody in the District Attorney's office take the whole thing seriously.'

'There's no way the Santa Paula records are wrong?'

'No way. Spinner would have had to spend a month in the river, and it didn't happen that way.'

'No. He was alive within ten days of the time the body was found. I spoke to him on the telephone. I don't get it. She had to have another accomplice.'

'Maybe. Polygraph says no.'

'She agreed to take a lie-detector test?'

'We never asked her to. She demanded it. It gets her completely off the hook as far as Spinner was concerned. It's not quite as clear as far as the attack on you was concerned. The expert who administered the test says there's a little stress involved, that his

250

guess would be she did and didn't know Lundgren was going to try to take you out. Like she suspected it but they hadn't talked about it and she'd been able to avoid thinking about it.'

'Those tests aren't always a hundred percent.'

'They come close enough, Matt. Sometimes they'll make a person look guilty when he's not, especially if the operator isn't very good at what he's doing. But if they say you're innocent, it's a pretty good bet you are. I think they ought to be admissible in court.'

I had always felt that way myself. I sat there for a while trying to run it all through my mind until everything fell into place. It took its time. Meanwhile, Guzik went on talking about the interrogation of Beverly Ethridge, pointing up his remarks with observations on what he would like to do with her. I didn't pay him much attention.

I said, 'The car wasn't him. I should have realized that.'

'How's that?'

'The car,' I said. 'I told you a car took a shot at me one night. The same night I spotted Lundgren for the first time, and the place was the same as where he came at me with the knife, so I had to think it was the same man both times.'

'You never saw the driver?'

'No. I figured it was Lundgren because he'd been dogging me earlier that night and I thought he'd been setting me up. But it couldn't have been that way. It wouldn't be his style. He liked that knife too much.'

'Then who was it?'

'Spinner said somebody ran up onto a curb after him. The same bit.'

'Who?'

'Plus the voice on the phone. Then there were no calls any more.'

'I don't follow you, Matt.'

I looked at him. 'Trying to make the pieces fit. That's all. Somebody killed Spinner.'

'The question is who.'

I nodded. 'That's the question,' I said.

'One of the other people he gave you the dope on?'

'They all check out,' I said. 'Maybe he had more people after him than he ever told me about. Maybe he added somebody to the string after he gave me the envelope. The hell, maybe somebody rolled him for his cash, hit him too hard, panicked, and threw the body in the river.'

'It happens.'

'Sure it happens.'

'You think we'll ever find out who did him?'

I shook my head. 'Do you?'

'No,' Guzik said. 'No, I don't think we ever will.'

NINETEEN

I had never been in the building before. There were two doormen on duty, and the elevator was manned. The doormen made sure that I was expected, and the elevator operator whisked me up eighteen floors and indicated which door was the one I was looking for. He didn't budge until I had rung the bell and been admitted.

The apartment was as impressive as the rest of the building. There was a stairway leading to a second floor. An olive-skinned maid led me into a large den with oak-paneled walls and a fireplace. About half the books on the shelves were bound in leather. It was a very comfortable room in a very spacious apartment. The apartment had cost almost two hundred thousand dollars, and the monthly maintenance charge came to something like fifteen hundred.

When you've got enough money, you can buy just about anything you want.

'He will be with you in a moment,' the maid said. 'He said for you to help yourself to a drink.'

She pointed to a serving bar alongside the fireplace. There was ice in a silver bucket, and a couple of dozen bottles. I sat in a red leather chair and waited for him.

I didn't have to wait very long. He entered the room. He was wearing white flannel slacks and a plaid blazer. He had a pair of leather house slippers on his feet.

'Well, now,' he said. He smiled to show how genuinely glad he was to see me. 'You'll have something to drink, I hope.'

'Not just now.'

'It's a little early for me too, as a matter of fact. You sounded quite urgent on the phone, Mr Scudder. I gather you've had second thoughts about working for me.'

'No.'

'I received the impression –'

'That was to get in here.'

'He frowned. 'I'm not sure I understand.'

'I'm really not sure whether you do or not, Mr Huysendahl. I think you'd better close the door.'

'I don't care for your tone.'

'You're not going to care for any of this,' I said. 'You'll like it less with the door open. I think you should close it.'

He was about to say something, perhaps another observation about my tone of voice and how little he cared for it, but instead he closed the door.

'Sit down, Mr Huysendahl.'

He was used to giving orders, not taking them, and I thought he was going to make an issue out of it. But he sat down, and his face wasn't quite enough of a mask to keep me from knowing that he knew what it was all about. I'd known anyway, because there was just no other way the pieces could fit together, but his face confirmed it for me.

'Are you going to tell me what this is all about?'

'Oh, I'm going to tell you. But I think you already know. Don't you?'

'Certainly not.'

I looked over his shoulder at an oil painting of somebody's ancestor. Maybe one of his. I didn't notice any family resemblance, though.

I said, 'You killed Spinner Jablon.'

'You're out of your mind.'

'No.'

'You already found out who killed Jablon. You told me that the day before yesterday.'

'I was wrong.'

'I don't know what you're driving at, Scudder –'

'A man tried to kill me Wednesday night,' I said. 'You know about that. I assumed he was the same man who killed Spinner, and I managed to tie him to one of Spinner's other suckers, so I thought that cleared you. But it turns out that he couldn't have killed Spinner, because he was on the other side of the country at the time. His alibi for Spinner's death was as solid as they come. He was in jail at the time.'

I looked at him. He was patient now, hearing me out with the same intent stare he had fixed on me Thursday afternoon when I told him he was in the clear.

I said, 'I should have known he wasn't the only one involved, that more than one of Spinner's victims had decided to fight back. The man who tried to kill me was a loner. He liked to use a knife. But I'd been attacked earlier by one or more men in a car, a stolen car. And a few minutes after that attack I had a phone call from an older man with a New York accent. I'd had a call from that man before. It didn't make sense that the knife artist would have had anybody else in on it. So somebody else was behind the dodge with the car, and somebody else was responsible for knocking Spinner on the head and dumping him in the river.'

'That doesn't mean I had anything to do with it.'

'I think it does. As soon as the man with the knife is taken out of the picture, it's obvious that everything was pointing to you all along. He was an amateur, but in other respects the operation was all quite professional. A car stolen from another neighborhood with a very good man at the wheel. Some men who were good enough to find Spinner when he didn't want to be found. You had the money to hire that kind of talent. And you had the connections.'

'That's nonsense.'

'No,' I said. 'I've been thinking about it. One thing that threw me was your reaction when I first came to your office. You didn't know Spinner was dead until I showed you the item in the paper. I almost ruled you out, because I couldn't believe you could fake a reaction that well. But of course it wasn't a fake. You really didn't know he was dead, did you?'

'Of course not.' He drew his shoulders back. 'And I think that's fairly good evidence that I had nothing to do with his death.'

I shook my head. 'It just means you didn't know about it yet. And you were stunned by the realization both that Spinner was dead and that the whole game didn't end with his death. I not only had the evidence on you, I also knew you were tied to Spinner and a possible suspect in his death. Naturally that shook you up a little.'

'You can't prove anything. You can say that I hired someone to kill Spinner. I didn't, and I can swear to you that I didn't, but it's hardly something I can prove either. But the point is that it's not incumbent upon me to prove it, is it?'

'No.'

'And you can accuse me of whatever you want, but you don't have a shred of proof either, do you?'

'No, I don't.'

'Then perhaps you'll tell me why you decided to come here this afternoon, Mr Scudder.'

'I don't have proof. That's true. But I have something else, Mr Huysendahl.'

'Oh?'

'I have those photographs.'

He gaped. 'You distinctly told me –'

'That I had burned them.'

'Yes.'

'I'd intended to. It was simpler to tell you it had already been done. I've been busy since then, and didn't get around to it. And then this morning I found out that the man with the knife was not the man who killed Spinner, and I sifted through some of the things that I already knew, and I saw that it had to be you. So it was just as well that I didn't burn those pictures, wasn't it?'

He got slowly to his feet. 'I think I'll have that drink after all,' he said.

'Go right ahead.'

'Will you join me?'

'No.'

He put ice cubes in a tall glass, poured Scotch, added soda from a siphon. He took his time building the drink, then walked over to the fireplace and rested with his elbow on the burnished oak mantel. He took a few small sips of his drink before he turned to look at me again.

'Then we're back to the beginning,' he said. 'And you've decided to blackmail me.'

'No.'

'Why else is it so fortunate for you that you didn't burn the pictures?'

'Because it's the only hold I've got on you.'

'And what are you going to do with it?'

'Nothing.'

'Then –'

'It's what you're going to do, Mr Huysendahl.'

'And what am I going to do?'

'You're not going to run for governor.'

He stared at me. I didn't really want to look at his eyes, but I forced myself. He was no longer trying to keep his face a mask, and I was able to watch as he tried one one of thought after another and found that none of them led anywhere.

'You've thought this out, Scudder.'

'Yes.'

'At length, I would suppose.'

'Yes.'

'And there's nothing you want, is there? Money, power, the things most people want. It wouldn't do any good for me to send another check to Boys Town.'

'No.'

He nodded. He worried the tip of his chin with a finger. He said, 'I don't know who killed Jablon.'

'I assumed as much.'

'I didn't order him killed.'

'The order originated with you. One way or the other, you're the man at the top.'

'Probably.'

I looked at him.

'I'd prefer to believe otherwise,' he said. 'When you told me the other day that you'd found the man who killed Jablon, I was enormously relieved. Not because I felt the killing could possibly be attributed to me, that any sort of trail would lead back to me. But because I honestly did not know whether I was in any way responsible for his death.'

'You didn't order it directly.'

'No, of course not. I didn't want the man killed.'

'But somebody in your organization –'

He sighed heavily. 'It would seem that someone decided to take matters into his own hands. I ... confided in several people that I was being blackmailed. It appeared that it might be possible to recover the evidence without acceding to Jablon's demands. More important, it was necessary to devise some way in which Jablon's silence could be purchased on a permanent basis. The trouble with blackmail is that one never ceases to pay it. The cycle can go on forever, there's no control.'

'So somebody tried to scare Spinner once with a car.'

'So it would seem.'

'And when that didn't work, somebody hired somebody to hire somebody to kill him.'

'I suppose so. You can't prove it. What's perhaps more to the point, I can't prove it.'

'But you believed it all along, didn't you? Because you warned me that one payment was all I was going to get. And if I tried to tap you again, you'd have me killed.'

'Did I really say that?'

'I think you remember saying it, Mr Huysendahl. I should have seen the significance in that at the time. You were thinking of murder as a weapon in your arsenal. Because you'd already used it once.'

'I never intended for a moment that Jablon should die.'

I stood up. I said, 'I was reading something the other day about Thomas à Becket. He was very close to one of the kings of England. One of the Henrys, I think Henry the Second.'

'I believe I see the parallel.'

'Do you know the story? When he became Archbishop of Canterbury he stopped being Henry's buddy and played the game according to his conscience. It rattled Henry, and he let some of his underlings know it. 'Oh, that someone might rid me of that rebellious priest!'

'But he never intended that Thomas be murdered.'

'That was his story,' I agreed. 'His subordinates decided Henry had issued Thomas's death warrant. Henry didn't see it that way at all, he'd just been thinking out loud, and he was very upset to learn that Thomas was dead. Or at least he pretended to be very upset. He's not around, so we can't ask him.'

'And you're taking the position that Henry was responsible.'

'I'm saying I wouldn't vote for him for governor of New York.'

He finished his drink. He put the glass on the bar and sat down in his chair again, crossing one leg over the other.

He said, 'If I run for governor –'

'Then every major newspaper in the state gets a full set of those photographs. Until you announce for governor, they stay where they are.'

'Where is that?'

'A very safe place.'

'And I have no option.'

'No.'

'No other choice.'

'None.'

'I might be able to determine the man responsible for Jablon's death.'

'Perhaps you could. It's also possible you couldn't. But what good would that do? He's sure to be a professional, and there would be no evidence to link him to either you or Jablon, let alone enough to bring him to trial. And you couldn't do anything with him without exposing yourself.'

'You're making this terribly difficult, Scudder.'

'I'm making it very easy. All you have to do is forget about being governor.'

'I would be an excellent governor. If you're so fond of historical parallels, you might consider Henry the Second a bit further. He's regarded as one of England's better monarchs.'

'I wouldn't know.'

'I would.' He told me some things about Henry. I gather he knew quite a bit about the subject. It might have been interesting. I didn't pay much attention to it. Then he went on to tell me some more about what a good governor he would make, what he would accomplish for the people of the state.

I cut him short. I said, 'You have a lot of plans, but that doesn't mean anything. You wouldn't be a good governor. You won't be any kind of governor, because I'm not going to let you, but you wouldn't be a good one because you're capable of picking people to work for you who are capable of murder. That's enough to disqualify you.'

'I could discharge those people.'

'I couldn't know if you did or not. And the individuals aren't even that important.'

'I see.' He sighed again. 'He wasn't much of a man, you know. I'm not justifying murder when I say that. He was a petty crook and a shoddy blackmailer. He began by entrapping me, preying on a personal weakness, and then he tried to bleed me.'

'He wasn't much of a man at all,' I agreed.

'Yet his murder is that significant to you.'

'I don't like murder.'

'You believe that human life is sacred, then.'

'I don't know if I believe that anything is sacred. It's a very complicated question. I've taken human life. A few days ago I killed a man. Not long before that, I contributed to a man's death. My contribution was unintentional. That hasn't made me feel all that much better about it. I don't know if human life is sacred. I just don't like murder. And you're in the process of getting away with murder, and that bothers me, and there's just one thing I'm going to do about it. I don't want to kill you, I don't want to expose you, I don't want to do any of those things. I'm sick of playing an incompetent version of God. All I'm going to do is keep you out of Albany.'

'Doesn't that constitute playing God?'

'I don't think so.'

'You say human life is sacred. Not in so many words, but that seems to be your position. What about my life, Mr Scudder? For years now only one thing has been important to me, and you're presuming to tell me I can't have it.'

I looked around the den. The portraits, the furnishings, the service bar. 'It looks to me as though you're doing pretty well,' I said.

'I have material possessions. I can afford them.'

'Enjoy them.'

'Is there no way I can buy you? Are you that devoutly incorruptible?'

'I'm probably corrupt, by most definitions. But you can't buy me, Mr Huysendahl.'

I waited for him to say something. A few minutes went by, and he just remained where he was, silent, his eyes looking off into the middle distance. I found my own way out.

TWENTY

This time I got to St Paul's before it closed. I stuffed a tenth of what I'd taken from Lundgren into the poor box. I lit a few candles for various dead people who came to mind. I sat for a while and watched people take their turns in the confessional. I decided that I envied them, but not enough to do anything about it.

I went across the street to Armstrong's and had a plate of beans and sausage, then a drink and a cup of coffee. It was over now, it was all over, and I could drink normally again, never getting drunk, never staying entirely sober. I nodded at people now and then, and some of them nodded back to me. It was Saturday, so Trina was off, but Larry did just as good a job of bringing more coffee and bourbon when my cup was empty.

Most of the time I just let my mind wander, but from time to time I would find myself going over the events since Spinner had walked in and given me his envelope. There were probably ways I could have handled things better. If I'd pushed it a little and taken an interest at the beginning, I might even have been able to keep Spinner alive. But it was over and I was done with it, and I even had some of his money left after what I'd paid to Anita and the churches and various bartenders, and I could relax now.

'This seat taken?'

I hadn't even noticed when she came in. I looked up and there she was. She sat down across from me and took a pack of cigarettes from her bag. She shook a cigarette loose and lit it.

I said, 'You're wearing the white pants suit.'

'That's so you'll be able to recognize me. You sure managed to turn my life inside out, Matt.'

'I guess I did. They're not going to press anything, are they?'

'They couldn't press a pants suit, let alone a charge. Johnny never knew Spinner existed. That should be my biggest headache.'

'You've got other headaches?'

'In a manner of speaking, I just got rid of a headache. It cost me a lot to get rid of him, though.'

'Your husband?'

She nodded. 'He decided without too much trouble that I was a luxury he intended to deny himself. He's getting a divorce. And I am not getting any alimony, because if I give him any trouble he's going to give me ten times as much trouble, and I think he'd probably do it. Not that there wasn't enough shit in the papers already, as far as that goes.'

'I haven't been keeping up with the papers.'

'You've missed some nice stuff.' She drew on her cigarette and blew out a cloud of smoke. 'You really do your drinking in all the class joints, don't you? I tried your hotel but you weren't in, so then I tried Polly's Cage, and they said you came here a lot of the time. I can't imagine why.'

'It suits me.'

She cocked her head, studying me. 'You know something? It does. But me a drink?'

'Sure.'

I got Larry's attention, and she ordered a glass of wine. 'It probably won't be terrific,' she said, 'but at least it's hard for the bartender to fuck it up.' When he brought it she raised her glass to me, and I returned the gesture with my cup. 'Happy days,' she said.

'Happy days.'

'I didn't want him to kill you, Matt.'

'Neither did I.'

'I'm serious. All I wanted was time. I would have handled everything on my own, one way or another. I never called Johnny, you know. How would I have known how to reach him? He called me after he got out of jail. He wanted me to send him some money. He would do that now and then, when he was up against it. I felt guilty about turning state's evidence that time, even though it had been his idea. But when I had him on the phone I couldn't keep myself from telling him I was in trouble, and that was a mistake. He was more trouble than I was ever in.'

'What was the hold he had on you?'

'I don't know. But he always had it.'

'You fingered me for him. That night at Polly's.'

'He wanted to get a look at you.'

'He got it. Then I set up a meeting with you Wednesday. The

cute thing about that was I wanted to tell you you were clear. I thought I already had the killer, and I wanted to let you know the blackmail routine was over and done with. Instead, you put off the meeting for a day and sent him after me.'

'He was going to talk to you. Scare you off, stall for time, something like that.'

'That's not the way he saw it. You must have figured he'd try what he tried.'

She hesitated for a moment, then let her shoulders drop. 'I knew it was possible. He was ... he had a wildness in him.' Her face brightened suddenly, and something danced in her eyes. 'Maybe you did me a favor,' she said. 'Maybe I'm a lot better off with him out of my life.'

'Better off than you know.'

'What do you mean?'

'I mean there was a very good reason why he wanted me dead. I'm just guessing, but I like my guesses. You would have been happy to stall me until you came into some money, which would happen once Kermit came into the principal of his inheritance. But Lundgren couldn't afford to have me around, now or later. Because he had big plans for you.'

'What do you mean?'

'Can't you guess? He probably told you he'd have you divorce Ethridge once he'd come into enough money to make it worthwhile.'

'How did you know?'

'I told you. Just a guess. But I don't think he'd have done it that way. He would have wanted the whole thing. He'd have waited until your husband inherited his money, and then he would have taken his time setting it up right, and all of a sudden you'd turn out to be a very rich widow.

'Oh, God.'

'Then you'd remarry and your name would be Beverly Lundgren. How long do you suppose it would have taken him to put another notch on his knife.'

'God!'

'Of course, it's just a guess.'

'No.' She shivered, and all of a sudden her face lost a lot of its polish and she looked like the girl she had stopped being a long time ago. 'He'd have done it just that way,' she said. 'It's more than a guess. That's just the way he would have done it.'

'Another glass of wine?'

'No.' She put her hand on mine. 'I was all primed to be mad at you for turning my life around. Maybe that's not all you did. Maybe you saved it.'

'We'll never know, will we?'

'No.' She crushed out her cigarette. She said, 'Well, where do I go from here? I was beginning to get used to a life of leisure, Matt. I thought I carried it off with a certain flair.'

'That you did.'

'Now all of a sudden I've got to find a way to make a living.'

'You'll think of something, Beverly.'

Her eyes focused on mine. She said, 'That's the first time you used my name, do you know that?'

'I know.'

We sat there for a while looking at each other. She reached for a cigarette, changed her mind, and pushed it back in the pack. 'Well, what do you know,' she said.

'I didn't say anything.

'I thought I didn't do a thing for you. I was beginning to worry that I was losing my touch. Is there some place we can go? I'm afraid my place isn't my place any more.'

'There's my hotel.'

'You take me to all the class joints,' she said. She got to her feet and picked up her bag. 'Let's go. Right now, huh?'

IN THE MIDST
OF DEATH

For an absent friend

ONE

Octber is about as good as the city gets. The last of the summer heat is gone and the real bite of cold weather hasn't arrived yet. There had been rain in September, quite a bit of it, but that was past now. The air was a little less polluted than usual, and its temperature made it seem even cleaner than it was.

I stopped at a phone booth on Third Avenue in the Fifties. On the corner an old woman scattered bread crumbs for the pigeons and cooed to them as she fed them. I believe there's a city ordinance against feeding pigeons. We used to cite it in the department when explaining to rookies that there were laws you enforced and laws you forgot about.

I went into the booth. It had been mistaken at least once for a public lavatory, which is par for the course. At least the phone worked. Most of them do these days. Five or six years ago most of the phones in outdoor booths didn't work. So not everything in our world is getting worse. Some things are actually getting better.

I called Portia Carr's number. Her answering machine always picked up on the second ring, so when the phone rang a third time, I figured I'd dialed a wrong number. I'd begun to take it for granted that she would never be home when I called.

Then she answered the phone. 'Yes?'

'Miss Carr?'

'Yes, this is she speaking.' The voice was not pitched quite so low as on the tape of the answering machine, and the Mayfair accent was less noticeable.

'My name is Scudder,' I said. 'I'd like to come over and see you. I'm in the neighborhood and –'

'Terribly sorry,' she cut in. ''Fraid I'm not seeing people anymore. Thank you.'

'I wanted to –'

'Do call someone else.' And she broke the connection.

I found another dime and was set to drop it in the slot and call her again when I changed my mind and put the dime back in my pocket. I walked two blocks downtown and one block east to Second Avenue and Fifty-fourth Street, where I scouted up a lunch counter with a pay phone that was in view of the entrance of her building. I dropped my dime in that phone and dialed her number.

As soon as she came on the line I said, 'My name is Scudder, and I want to talk to you about Jerry Broadfield.'

There was a pause. Then she said, 'Who is this?'

'I told you. My name is Matthew Scudder.'

'You called a few moments ago.'

'Right. You hung up on me.'

'I thought –'

'I know what you thought. I want to talk to you.'

'I'm terribly sorry, don't you know, but I'm not giving interviews.'

'I'm not from the press.'

'Then what *is* your interest, Mr Scudder?'

'You'll find out when you see me. I think you'd better see me, Miss Carr.'

'I think not, actually.'

'I'm not sure you have any choice. I'm in your neighborhood. I'll be at your place in five minutes.'

'No, please.' A pause. 'I've just tumbled out of bed, don't you see? You'll have to give me an hour. Can you give me an hour?'

'If I have to.'

'One hour, then, and you'll come round. You have the address, I suppose?'

I told her I did. I rang off and sat at the counter with a cup of coffee and a roll. I faced the window so that I could keep an eye on her building, and I got my first look at her just as the coffee was getting cool enough to drink. She must have been dressed when we spoke because it only took her seven minutes and change to hit the street.

It wasn't much of an accomplishment to recognize her. The description pinned her all by itself – the fiery mane of dark red hair, the height. And she tied it all together with the regal presence of a lioness.

I stood up and moved toward the door, ready to follow her as soon as I knew where she was going. But she kept walking straight toward the coffee shop, and when she came through the door, I turned away from her and went back to my cup of coffee.

She headed straight for the phone booth.

I suppose I shouldn't have been surprised. Enough telephones are tapped so that everyone who is either criminally or politically active knows to regard *all* phones as tapped and to act accordingly. Important or sensitive calls are not to be made from one's own phone. And this was the nearest public telephone to her building. That's why I had chosen it myself, and it was why she was using it now.

I moved a little closer to the booth, just to satisfy myself that it wouldn't do me any good. I couldn't see the number she was dialing, and I couldn't hear a thing. Once I'd established this, I paid for my roll and coffee and left.

I crossed the street and walked over to her building.

I was taking a chance. If she finished her call and hopped into a cab I would lose her, and I didn't want to lose her now. Not after all the time it had taken me to find her. I wanted to know who she was calling now, and if she went someplace I wanted to know where and why.

But I didn't think she was going to grab a taxi. She hadn't even been carrying a purse, and if she wanted to go somewhere, she would probably want to come back for her bag first and throw some clothes in a suitcase. And she had set things up with me to give herself an hour's leeway.

So I went to her building and found a little white-haired guy on the door. He had guileless blue eyes and a rash of broken capillaries on his cheekbones. He looked as though he took a lot of pride in his uniform.

'Carr,' I said.

'Just left a minute ago. You just missed her, couldn't have been more than a minute.'

'I know.' I took out my wallet and flipped it open quickly. There was nothing there for him to see, not even a junior G-man's badge, but it didn't matter. It's the moves that do it, that and looking like a cop in the first place. He got a quick flash of leather and was suitably impressed. It would have been bad form for him to demand a closer look.

'What apartment?'

'I sure hope you don't get me in trouble.'

'Not if you play it by the book. Which apartment is she in?'

'Four G.'

'Give me your passkey, huh?'

'I'm not supposed to do that.'

'Uh-huh. You want to go downtown and talk about it?'

He didn't. What he wanted was for me to go someplace and die, but he didn't say so. He turned over his passkey.

'She'll be back in a couple of minutes. You wouldn't want to tell her I'm upstairs.'

'I don't like this.'

'You don't have to.'

'She's a nice lady, always been nice to me.'

'Generous at Christmastime, huh?'

'She's a very pleasant person,' he said.

'I'm sure you've got a swell relationship. But tip her off and I'll know about it, and I won't be happy. You follow me?'

'I'm not going to say anything.'

'And you'll get your key back. Don't worry about it.'

'That's the least of it,' he said.

I took the elevator to the fourth floor. The G apartment faced the street, and I sat at her window and watched the entrance of the coffee shop. I couldn't tell from that angle whether there was anyone in the phone booth or not, so she could have left already, could have ducked around the corner and into a cab, but I didn't think so. I sat there in a chair and I waited, and after about ten minutes she came out of the coffee shop and stood on the corner, long and tall and striking.

And evidently uncertain. She just stood there for a long moment, and I could read the indecision in her mind. She could have gone in almost any direction. But after a moment she turned decisively and began walking back toward me. I let out a breath I hadn't realized I'd been holding and settled down to wait for her.

When I heard her key in the lock, I moved from the window and flattened out against the wall. She opened the door, closed it behind her, and shot the bolt. She was doing a very efficient job of locking the door but I was already inside it.

She took off a pale blue trenchcoat and hung it in the front closet. Under it she'd been wearing a knee-length plaid skirt and a tailored yellow blouse with a button-down collar. She had very long legs and a powerful, athletic body.

She turned again, and her eyes did not quite reach the spot where I was standing, and I said, 'Hello, Portia.'

The scream didn't get out. She stopped it by clapping her own hand over her mouth. She stood very still for a moment, her body balanced on the tips of her toes, and then she willed her hand to drop from her mouth as she settled back down on her heels. She took a deep breath and made herself hang onto it. Her coloring was very fair to begin with, but now her face looked bleached. She put her hand over her heart. The gesture looked theatrical, insincere. As if she recognized this, she lowered her hand again and breathed deeply several times, in and out, in and out.

'Your name is –'

'Scudder.'

'You called before.'

'Yes.'

'You promised to give me an hour.'

'My watch has been running fast lately.'

'Has it indeed.' She took another very deep breath and let it out slowly. She closed her eyes. I moved out from my post against the wall and stood in the middle of the room within a few steps of her. She didn't look like the sort of person who faints easily, and if she were she probably would have done it already, but she was still very pale and if she was going to flop I wanted a fair shot at catching her on the way down. But the color began to seep back into her face and she opened her eyes.

'I need something to drink,' she announced. 'Will you have something?'

'No, thanks.'

'So I drink alone.' She went to the kitchen. I followed close enough to keep her in sight. She took a fifth of Scotch and a split of club soda from the refrigerator and poured about three ounces of each into a glass. 'No ice,' she said. 'I don't fancy the cubes bumping up against my teeth. But I've got into the habit of taking my drinks chilled. Rooms are kept warmer here, you know, so that room-temperature drinks won't do at all. You're sure you won't join me?'

'Not right now.'

'Cheers, then.' She got rid of the drink in one very long swallow. I watched the muscles work in her throat. A long, lovely neck. She had that perfect English skin and it took a lot of it to cover her. I'm about six feet tall and she was at least my height and maybe a little taller. I pictured her with Jerry Broadfield, who had about four inches on her and could match her with presence of his own. They must have made a striking couple.

She drew another breath, shuddered, and put the empty glass in the sink. I asked her if she was all right.

'Oh, just peachy,' she said. Her eyes were a very pale blue verging on gray, her mouth full but bloodless. I stepped aside and she walked past me into the living room. Her hips just barely brushed me as she passed. That was just about enough. It wouldn't take much more than that, not with her.

She sat on a slate-blue sofa and took a small cigar from a teak box that rested on a clear Plexiglas end table. She lit the cigar with a wooden match, then gestured at the box for me to help myself. I told her I didn't smoke.

'I switched to these because one doesn't inhale them,' she said. 'So I inhale them just the same and of course they are stronger than cigarettes. How did you get in here?'

I held up the key.

'Timmie gave you that?'

'He didn't want to. I didn't give him much choice. He says you've always been nice to him.'

'I tip him enough, the silly little fuck. You gave me a fright, you know. I don't know what you want or why you're here. Or who you are, for that matter. I seem to have forgotten your name already.' I supplied it. 'Matthew,' she said. 'I do not know why you are here, Matthew.'

'Who did you phone from the coffee shop?'

'You were there? I didn't notice you.'

'Who did you call?'

She bought time by puffing on her cigar. Her eyes grew thoughtful. 'I don't think I'm going to tell you,' she said at length.

'Why are you pressing charges against Jerry Broadfield?'

'For extortion.'

'Why, Miss Carr?'

'You called me Portia before. Or was that just for shock value? The peelers always call you by your first name. That's to show their contempt for you, it's supposed to give them some sort of psychological advantage, isn't it?' She pointed at me with her cigar. 'You. You're not a policeman, are you?'

'No.'

'But there's something about you.'

'I used to be a cop.'

'Ah.' She nodded, satisfied. 'And you knew Jerry when you were a policeman?'

'I didn't know him then.'

'But you know him now.'

'That's right.'

'And you're a friend of his? No, that's not possible. Jerry doesn't have friends, does he?'

'Doesn't he?'

'Hardly. You'd know that if you knew him well.'

'I don't know him well.'

'I wonder if anyone does.' Another puff on the cigar, a careful flicking of ash into a sculptured glass ashtray. 'Jerry Broadfield has acquaintances. Any number of acquaintances. But I doubt he has a friend in the world.'

'You're certainly not his friend.'

'I never said I was.'

'Why charge him with extortion?'

'Because the charge is true.' She managed a small smile. 'He insisted I give him money. A hundred dollars a week or he would make trouble for me. Prostitutes are vulnerable creatures, you know. And a hundred dollars a week isn't so terribly much when you consider the enormous sums men are willing to pay to go to bed with one.' She gestured with her hands, indicating her body. 'So I paid him,' she said. 'The money he asked for, and I made myself available to him sexually.'

'For how long?'

'About an hour at a time, generally. Why?'

'For how long had you been paying him?'

'Oh, I don't know. About a year, I suppose.'

'And you've been in this country how long?'

'Just over three years.'

'And you don't want to go back, do you?' I got to my feet, walked over to the couch. 'That's probably how they set the hook,' I said. 'Play the game their way or they'll get you deported as an undesirable alien. Is that how they pitched you?'

'What a phrase. An undesirable alien.'

'Is that what they –'

'Most people consider me a highly desirable alien.' The cold eyes challenged me. 'I don't suppose you have an opinion on the subject?'

She was getting to me, and it bothered the hell out of me. I didn't much like her, so why should she be getting to me? I remembered something Elaine Mardell had said to the effect that a large portion of Portia Carr's client list consisted of masochists.

273

I have never really understood what gets a masochist off, but a few minutes in her presence was enough to make me realize that a masochist would find this particular woman a perfect component for his fantasies. And, in a somewhat different way, she fit nicely into my own.

We went around and around for a while. She kept insisting that Broadfield had really been extorting cash from her, and I kept trying to get past that to the person who had induced her to do the job on him. We weren't getting anywhere – that is, *I* wasn't getting anywhere, and she didn't have anyplace to get to.

So I said, 'Look, when you come right down to it, it doesn't matter at all. It doesn't matter whether he was getting money from you, and it doesn't matter who got you to press charges against him.'

'Then why are you here, angel? Just for love?'

'What matters is what it'll take to get you to drop the charges.'

'What's the hurry?' She smiled. 'Jerry hasn't even been arrested yet, has he?'

'You're not going to take it all the way to the courtroom,' I went on. 'You'd need proof to get an indictment, and if you had any it would have come out by now. So this is just a smear, but it's an awkward smear for him and he'd like to wipe it up. What does it take to get the charges dropped?'

'Jerry must know that.'

'Oh?'

'All he has to do is stop doing what he's been doing.'

'You mean with Prejanian.'

'Do I?' She had finished her cigar, and now she took another from the teak box. But she didn't light it, just played with it. 'Maybe I don't mean anything. But look at the record. That's an Americanism I rather like. Let us look at the record. For all these years Jerry has been doing nicely as a policeman. He has his charming little house in Forest Hills and his charming wife and his charming children. Have you met his wife and children?'

'No.'

'Neither have I, but I've seen their pictures. American men are extraordinary. First they show one pictures of their wives and children, and then they want to go to bed. Are you married?'

'Not anymore.'

'Did you play around when you were?'

'Now and then.'

'But you didn't show pictures around, did you?' I shook my

head. 'Somehow I didn't think so.' She returned the cigar to the box, straightened up, yawned. 'He had all that, at any rate, and then he went to this Special Prosecutor with this long story about police corruption, and he began giving interviews to the newspapers, and he took a leave of absence from the police force, and all of a sudden he's in trouble and accused of shaking down a poor little whore for a hundred dollars a week. It makes you wonder, doesn't it?'

'That's what he has to do? Drop Prejanian and you'll drop the charges?'

'I didn't come right out and say that, did I? And anyway, he must have known that without your digging around. I mean, it's rather obvious, wouldn't you say?'

We went around a little more and didn't accomplish a thing. I don't know what I'd hoped to accomplish or why I had taken five hundred dollars from Broadfield in the first place. Someone had Portia Carr intimidated a lot more seriously than I was likely to manage, for all my cleverness in sneaking into her apartment. In the meantime we were talking pointlessly, and we were both aware of the pointlessness of it.

'This is silly,' she said at one point. 'I am going to have another drink. Will you join me?'

I wanted a drink badly. 'I'll pass.' I said.

She brushed me on the way to the kitchen. I got a strong whiff of a perfume I didn't recognize. I decided I would know it the next time I smelled it. She came back with a drink in her hand and sat on the couch again. 'Silly,' she said again. 'Why don't you come sit next to me and we will talk of something else. Or of nothing at all.'

'You could be in trouble, Portia.'

Her face showed alarm. 'You mustn't say that.'

'You're putting yourself right in the middle. You're a big strong girl, but you might not turn out to be as strong as you think you are.'

'Are you threatening me? No, it's not a threat, is it?'

I shook my head. 'You don't have to worry about me. But you've got enough to worry about without me.'

Her eyes dropped. 'I'm so tired of being strong,' she said. 'I'm good at it, you know.'

'I'm sure you are.'

'But it's tiring.'

'Maybe I could help you.'

'I don't think anyone can.'

'Oh?'

She studied me briefly, then dropped her eyes. She stood and crossed the room to the window. I could have walked along behind her. There was something in her stance that suggested she expected me to. But I stayed where I was.

She said, 'There's something there, isn't there?'

'Yes.'

'But it's just no good at the moment. The timing's all wrong.' She was looking out the window. 'Right now neither of us can do the other any good at all.'

I didn't say anything.

'You'd better go now.'

'All right.'

'It's so beautiful outside. The sun, the freshness of the air.' She turned to look at me. 'Do you like this time of year?'

'Yes. Very much.'

'It's my favorite, I think. October, November, the best time of the year. But also the saddest, wouldn't you say?'

'Sad? Why?'

'Oh, very sad,' she said. 'Because winter is coming.'

TWO

On my way out I left the passkey with the doorman. He didn't seem any happier now, even though he was getting to see me leave this time. I went over to Johnny Joyce's on Second and sat in a booth. Most of the lunch crowd was gone. The ones who remained were one or two martinis over the line now and probably wouldn't make it back to their offices at all. I had a hamburger and a bottle of Harp, then drank a couple shots of bourbon with my coffee.

I tried Broadfield's number. It rang for a while and no one answered it. I went back to my booth and had another bourbon and thought about some things. There were questions I couldn't seem to answer. Why had I passed up Portia Carr's offer of a drink when I wanted a drink so badly? And why (if it wasn't another version of the same question) had I passed up Portia Carr herself?

I did some more thinking on West Forty-ninth Street, in the actors' chapel at St. Malachy's. The chapel is below street level, a large understated room which provides a measure of peace and quiet that is otherwise hard to come by in the heart of the Broadway theater district. I took an aisle seat and let my mind wander.

An actress I used to know a long time ago once told me that she came to St. Malachy's every day when she wasn't working. *'I wonder if it matters that I'm not a Catholic, Matt. I don't think so. I say my little prayer and I light my little candle and I pray for work. I wonder whether or not it helps. Do you suppose it's okay to ask God for a decent part?'*

I must have sat there for close to an hour, running different things through my mind. On the way out I put a couple of bucks in the poor box and lit a few candles. I didn't say any prayers.

I spent most of the evening in Polly's Cage, across the street from my hotel. Chuck was behind the bar and he was in an expansive mood, so much so that the house was buying every other round. I had reached my client late in the afternoon and had given him a brief rundown on my meeting with Carr. He'd asked me where I was going to go from there, and I'd said I would have to work it out and that I'd get in touch when I had something he ought to know. Nothing in that category came up that night, so I didn't have to call him. Nor did I have any reason to call anyone else. I'd picked up a phone message at my hotel: Anita had called and wanted me to call her, but it was not the sort of night on which I wanted to talk to an ex-wife. I stayed at Polly's and emptied my glass every time Chuck filled it up.

Around eleven-thirty a couple of kids came in and started playing nothing but country and western on the jukebox. I can usually stomach that as well as anything else, but for some reason or other it wasn't what I wanted to hear just then. I settled my tab and went around the corner to Armstrong's, where Don had the radio set to WNCN. They were playing Mozart, and the crowd was so thin you could actually hear the music.

'They sold the station,' Don said. 'The new owners are switching to a pop-rock format. Another rock station is just what the city needs.'

'Things always deteriorate.'

'I can't argue the point. There's a protest movement to force them to continue a classical music policy. I don't suppose it'll do any good, do you?'

I shook my head. 'Nothing ever does any good.'

'Well, you're in a beautiful mood tonight. I'm glad you decided to spread sweetness and light here instead of staying cooped up in your room.'

I poured bourbon into my coffee and gave it a stir. I *was* in a foul mood and I couldn't figure out exactly why. It is bad enough when you know what it is that is bothering you. When the demons plaguing you are invisible, it is that much more difficult to contend with them.

It was a strange dream.

I don't dream much. Alcohol has this effect of making you sleep at a deeper level, below the plane on which dreams occur. I am told that d.t.'s represent the psyche's insistence upon having its chance to dream; unable to dream while asleep, one has one's dreams upon awakening. But I haven't had d.t.'s yet and am grateful for my generally dreamless sleep. There was a time when this, in and of itself, was a sufficient argument for drinking.

But that night I dreamed, and the dream struck me as strange. She was in it. Portia, with her size and her striking beauty and her deep voice and her good English accent. And we were sitting and talking, she and I, but not in her apartment. We were in a police station. I don't know what precinct it might have been but remember that I felt at home there, so perhaps it was a place where I had been stationed once. There were uniformed cops walking around, and citizens filing complaints, and all of the extras playing the same roles in my dream that they play in similar scenes in cops-and-robbers movies.

And we were in the midst of all this, Portia and I, and we were naked. We were going to make love, but we had to establish something first through conversation. I don't recall what it was that had to be established, but our conversation went on and on, getting ever more abstract, and we got no closer to the bedroom, and then the telephone rang and Portia reached out and answered it in the voice of her answering machine.

Except that it went on ringing.

My phone, of course. I had incorporated its ring into my dream. If it hadn't awakened me with its ringing I'm sure I would ultimately have forgotten the dream entirely. Instead I shook myself awake while shaking off the vestiges of the dream. I fumbled for the phone and got the receiver to my ear.

'Hello?'

'Matt, I'm sorry as hell if I woke you. I –'

'Who is this?'

'Jerry. Jerry Broadfield.'

I usually put my watch on the bedside table when I turn in. I groped around for it now but couldn't find it. I said, 'Broadfield?'

'I guess you were sleeping. Look, Matt –'

'What time is it?'

'A few minutes after six. I just –'

'Christ!'

'Matt, are you awake?'

'Yeah, damn it, I'm awake. Christ. I said call me, but I didn't say call me in the middle of the night.'

'Look, it's an emergency. Will you just let me talk?' For the first time I was aware of the band of tension in his voice. It must have been there all along, but I hadn't noticed it before. 'I'm sorry I woke you,' he was saying, 'but I finally got a chance to make a phone call and I don't know how long they'll let me stay on. Just let me talk for a minute.'

'Where the hell are you?'

'Men's House of Detention.'

'The Tombs?'

'That's right, the Tombs.' He was talking quickly now, as if to get it all out before I could interrupt again. 'They were waiting for me. At the apartment. Barrow Street, they were waiting for me. I got back there about two-thirty and they were waiting for me and this is the first chance I've had to get to a phone. As soon as I finish with you I'm calling a lawyer. But I'm going to need more than a lawyer, Matt. They got the deck stacked too good for anybody to straighten things out in front of a jury. They got me by the balls.'

'What are you talking about?'

'Portia.'

'What about her?'

'Somebody killed her last night. Strangled her or something, dumped her in my apartment, then tipped the cops. I don't know all the details. They booked me for it. Matt, I didn't do it.'

I didn't say anything.

His voice rose, verging on hysteria. 'I didn't do it. Why would I kill the cunt? And leave her in my apartment? It doesn't make any sense, Matt, but it doesn't have to make any sense because the whole fucking thing is a frame and they can make it stick. Matt, they're gonna make it stick!'

'Easy, Broadfield.'

Silence. I pictured him gritting his teeth, forcing his emotions back under control like an animal trainer cracking his whip at a cageful of lions and tigers. 'Right,' he said, the voice crisp again. 'I'm exhausted and it's starting to get to me. Matt, I'm going to need help on this one. From you, Matt. I can pay you whatever you ask.'

I told him to hang on for a minute. I had been asleep for maybe three hours and I was finally becoming awake enough to realize just how rotten I felt. I put the phone down and went into the bathroom and splashed cold water on my face. I was careful not to look in the mirror because I had a fair idea what the face that glowered back at me might look like. There was about an inch of bourbon left in the quart on my dresser. I took a slug of it straight from the bottle, shuddered, sat down on the bed again and picked up the phone.

I asked him if he'd been booked.

'Just now. For homicide. Once they booked me they couldn't keep me away from a phone any longer. You know what they did? They informed me of my rights when they arrested me. That whole speech, *Miranda-Escobedo*, how many times do you figure I read out that goddam little set piece to some fucking crook? And they had to read it out to me word for word.'

'You've got a lawyer to call?'

'Yeah. Guy who's supposed to be good, but there's no way he can do it all.'

'Well, I don't know what I can do for you.'

'Can you come down here? Not now, I can't see anybody right now. Hang on a minute.' He must have turned away from the phone, but I could hear him asking someone when he could have visitors. 'Ten o'clock,' he told me. 'Could you get here between ten and noon?'

'I suppose so.'

'I got a lot of things to tell you, Matt, but I can't do it over the phone.'

I told him I'd see him sometime after ten. I cradled the phone and tapped the bourbon bottle for another small taste. My head ached dully and I suspected that bourbon was probably not the best thing in the world for it, but I couldn't think of anything better. I got back into bed and pulled the blankets over me. I needed sleep and knew I wasn't going to get any, but at least I could stay horizontal for another hour or two and get a little rest.

Then I remembered the dream I'd been yanked out of by his call. I remembered it, got a clean, vivid flash of it, and started to shake.

THREE

It had started two days earlier, on a crisply cold Tuesday afternoon. I was getting the day started at Armstrong's, doing my usual balancing act with coffee and bourbon, coffee to speed things up and bourbon to slow them down. I was reading the *Post* and I was sufficiently involved in what I was reading so that I didn't even notice when he pulled back the chair opposite mine and dropped into it. Then he cleared his throat and I looked up at him.

He was a little guy with a lot of curly black hair. His cheeks were sunken, his forehead very prominent. He wore a goatee but kept his upper lip clean shaven. His eyes, magnified by thick glasses, were dark brown and highly animated.

He said, 'Busy, Matt?'

'Not really.'

'I wanted to talk to you for a minute.'

'Sure.'

I knew him, but not terribly well. His name was Douglas Fuhrmann and he was a regular at Armstrong's. He didn't drink a hell of a lot, but he was apt to drop in four or five times a week, sometimes with a girl friend, sometimes on his own. He'd generally nurse a beer and talk for a while about sports or politics or whatever conversational topic was on the agenda. He was a writer, as I understood it, although I didn't recall having heard him discuss his work. But he evidently did well enough so that he didn't have to hold a job.

I asked what was on his mind.

'A fellow I know wants to see you, Matt.'

'Oh?'

'I think he'd like to hire you.'

'Bring him around.'

'That's not possible.'

'Oh?'

He started to say something, then stopped because Trina was on her way to find out what he wanted to drink. He ordered a beer and we sat there awkwardly while she went for the beer, brought it, and went away again.

Then he said, 'It's complicated. He can't be seen in public. He's, well, hiding out.'

'Who is he?'

'This is confidential.' I gave him a look. 'Well, all right. If that's today's *Post*, maybe you read about him. You would have read about him anyway, he's been all over the papers the past few weeks.'

'What's his name?'

'Jerry Broadfield.'

'Is that right.'

'He's very hot right now,' Fuhrmann said. 'Ever since the English girl filed charges against him he's been hiding out. But he can't hide forever.'

'Where's he hiding?'

'An apartment he has. He wants you to see him there.'

'Where is it?'

'The Village.'

I picked up my cup of coffee and looked into it as if it was going to tell me something. 'Why me?' I said. 'What does he think I can do for him? I don't get it.'

'He wants me to take you there,' Fuhrmann said. 'There's some money in it for you, Matt. How about it?'

We took a cab down Ninth Avenue and wound up on Barrow Street near Bedford. I let Fuhrmann pay for the cab. We went into the vestibule of a five-storey walk-up. More than half the doorbells lacked identifying labels. Either the building was being vacated prefatory to demolition or Broadfield's fellow tenants shared his desire for anonymity. Fuhrmann rang one of the unlabeled bells, pushed the button three times, waited, pushed it once, then pushed it three times again.

'It's a code,' he said.

'One if by land and two if by sea.'

'Huh?'

'Forget it.'

There was a buzz and he shoved the door open. 'You go on up,' he said. 'The D apartment on the third floor.'

'You're not coming?'

283

'He wants to see you alone.'

I was halfway up one flight before it occurred to me that this was a cute way to set me up for something. Fuhrmann had taken himself out of the picture, and there was no way of knowing what I'd find in apartment 3D. But there was also no one I could think of with a particularly good reason for wanting to do me substantial harm. I stopped halfway up the stairs to think it over, my curiosity fighting a successful battle against my more sensible desire to turn around and go home and stay out of it. I walked on up to the third floor and knocked three-one-three on the appropriate door. It opened almost before I'd finished knocking.

He looked just like his photographs. He'd been all over the papers for the past few weeks, ever since he'd begun cooperating with Abner Prejanian's investigation of corruption in the New York Police Department. But the news photos didn't give you the sense of height. He stood six-four easy and was built to scale, broad in the shoulders, massive in the chest. He was starting to thicken in the gut as well; he was in his early thirties now, and in another ten years he'd add on another forty or fifty pounds and he'd need every inch of his height to carry it well.

If he lived another ten years.

He said, 'Where's Doug?'

'He left me at the door. Said you wanted to see me alone.'

'Yeah, but the knock, I thought it was him.'

'I cracked the code.'

'Huh? Oh.' He grinned suddenly, and it really did light up the room. He had a lot of teeth and he let me look at them, but the grin did more than that. It brightened his whole face. 'So you're Matt Scudder,' he said. 'Come on in, Matt. It's not much but it's better than a jail cell.'

'Can they put you in jail?'

'They can try. They're damn well trying.'

'What have they got on you?'

'They've got a crazy English cunt that somebody's got a hold on. How much do you know about what's going on?'

'Just what I read in the papers.'

And I hadn't paid all that much attention to the papers. So I knew his name was Jerome Broadfield and he was a cop. He'd been on the force a dozen years. Six or seven years ago he made plainclothes, and a couple of years after that he made detective third, which was where he had stayed. Then a matter of weeks ago he threw his shield in a drawer and started helping Prejanian stand the NYPD on its ear.

I stood around while he bolted the door. I was taking the measure of the place. It looked as though the landlord had leased it furnished, and nothing about the apartment held any clues to the nature of its tenant.

'The papers,' he said. 'Well, they're close. They say Portia Carr was a whore. Well, they're right about that. They say I knew her. That's true, too.'

'And they say you were shaking her down.'

'Wrong. They say she *says* I was shaking her down.'

'Were you?'

'No. Here, sit down, Matt. Make yourself comfortable. How about a drink, huh?'

'All right.'

'I got scotch, I got vodka, I got bourbon, and I think there's a little brandy.'

'Bourbon's good.'

'Rocks? Soda?'

'Just straight.'

He made drinks. Neat bourbon for me, a long scotch and soda for himself. I sat on a tufted greenprint couch and he sat on a matching club chair. I sipped bourbon. He got a pack of Winstons out of the breast pocket of his suit jacket and offered me one. I shook my head and he lit it for himself. The lighter he used was a Dunhill, either gold-plated or solid gold. The suit looked custom made, and the shirt was definitely made to measure, with his monogram gracing the breast pocket.

We looked at each other over our drinks. He had a large, square-jawed face, prominent brows over blue eyes, one of the eyebrows bisected by an old scar. His hair was sand-colored and just a shade too short to be aggressively fashionable. The face looked open and honest, but after I'd been looking at it for a while I decided it was just a pose. He knew how to use his face to his advantage.

He watched the smoke rise from his cigarette as if it had something to tell him. He said, 'The newspapers make me look pretty bad, don't they? Smart-ass cop finks on the whole department, and then it turns out he's scoring off some poor little hooker. Hell, you were on the force. How many years was it?'

'Around fifteen.'

'So you know about newspapers. The press doesn't necessarily get everything right. They're in business to sell papers.'

'So?'

'So reading the papers you got to get one of two impressions of me. Either I'm a crook who let the Special Prosecutor's office get some kind of hammerlock on me or else I'm some kind of a nut.'

'Which is right?'

He flashed a grin. 'Neither. Christ, I been on the force going on thirteen years. I didn't just figure out yesterday that a couple of guys are maybe taking a dollar now and then. And nobody had anything on me at all. They been issuing denials out of Prejanian's office left and right. They said all along I was cooperating voluntarily, that I had come to them unasked, the whole number. Look, Matt, they're human. If they managed to set me up and turn me around on their own they'd be bragging about it, not denying it. But they're as much as saying I walked in and handed it all to them on a platter.'

'So?'

'So it's the truth. That's all.'

Did he think I was a priest? I didn't care whether he was a nut or a crook or both or neither. I didn't want to hear his confession. He had had me brought here, presumably for a purpose, and now he was justifying himself to me.

No man has to justify himself to me. I have trouble enough justifying myself to myself.

'Matt, I got a problem.'

'You said they don't have anything on you.'

'This Portia Carr. She's saying I was shaking her down. I demanded a hundred a week or I was going to bust her.'

'But it's not true.'

'No, it's not.'

'So she can't prove it.'

'No. She can't prove shit.'

'Then what's the problem?'

'She also says I was fucking her.'

'Oh.'

'Yeah. I don't know if she can prove that part of it, but hell, it's the truth. It was no big deal, you know. I was never a saint. Now it's all over the papers and there's this extortion bullshit, and all of a sudden I don't know whether I'm coming or going. My marriage is a little shaky to begin with, and all my wife needs is stories for her friends and family to read about how I'm shacking up with this English cunt. You married, Matt?'

'I used to be.'

'Divorced? Any kids?'

'Two boys.'

'I got two girls and a boy.' He sipped his drink, ducked ash from his cigarette. 'I don't know, maybe you like being divorced. I don't want any part of it. And the extortion charge, that's breaking my balls. I'm scared to leave this fucking apartment.'

'Whose place is it? I always thought Fuhrmann lived in my neighborhood.'

'He's in the West Fifties. That your neighborhood?' I nodded. 'Well, this place is mine, Matt. I've had it a little over a year. I got the house out in Forest Hills and I figured it'd be nice to have a place in town in case I needed one.'

'Who knows about this place?'

'Nobody.' He leaned over, stubbed out his cigarette. 'There's a story they tell about these politicians,' he said. 'This one guy, the polls show he's in trouble, his opponent is wiping the floor with him. So his campaign manager says, "Okay, what we'll do, we'll spread a story about him. We'll tell everybody he fucks pigs." So the candidate asks if it's true, and the campaign manager says it's not. "So we'll let him deny it," he says. "We'll let him deny it."'

'I follow you.'

'Throw enough mud and some of it sticks. Some fucking cop is leaning on Portia, that's what's happening. He wants me to stop working with Prejanian and in return she'll drop the charges. That's what it's all about.'

'Do you know who's doing it?'

'No. But I can't break it off with Abner. And I want those charges dropped. They can't do anything to me in court, but that's not the point. Even without going to court they'll have a departmental investigation. Except they won't be investigating a damn thing because they already know what conclusion they want to come up with. They'll suspend me immediately and they'll wind up kicking me out of the department.'

'I thought you resigned.'

He shook his head. 'Why would I resign, for Christ's sake? I got better than twelve years, close to thirteen. Why would I quit now? I took a leave of absence when I first decided to get in touch with Prejanian. You can't be on active duty and play ball with the Special Prosecutor at the same time. The department would have too many openings to shaft you. But I never even thought about resigning. When this is over I expect to be back on the force.'

I looked at him. If he really meant that last sentence, then he was a whole lot stupider than he looked or acted. I didn't know his angle in helping Prejanian, but I knew he was finished for life as far as the police department was concerned. He had turned himself into an untouchable and he would wear the caste mark as long as he lived. It didn't matter whether the investigation shook up the department or not. It didn't matter who was forced to put in for early retirement or who went to slam. None of that mattered. Every cop on the force, clean or dirty, straight or bent, would mark Jerome Broadfield lousy for the rest of his life.

And he had to know it. He'd been carrying a badge for over twelve years.

I said, 'I don't see where I come in.'

'Freshen that drink for you, Matt?'

'No, I'm fine. Where *do* I come in, Broadfield?'

He cocked his head, narrowed his eyes. 'Simple,' he said. 'You used to be a cop so you know the moves. And you're a private detective now so you can operate freely. And –'

'I'm not a private detective.'

'That's what I heard.'

'Detectives take complicated examinations to get their licenses. They charge fees and keep records and file income tax returns. I don't do any of those things. Sometimes I'll do certain things for certain friends. As a favor. They sometimes give me money. As a favor.'

He cocked his head again, then nodded thoughtfully, as if to say that he had known there was a gimmick and that he was happy to know what the gimmick was. Because everybody had an angle and this was mine and he was sharp enough to appreciate it. The boy liked angles.

If he liked angles, what the hell was he doing with Abner Prejanian?

'Well,' he said. 'Detective or not, you could do me a favor. You could see Portia and find out just how tied up in this she wants to be. You could see what kind of a hold they got on her and how we could maybe break the hold. One big thing would be finding out who it is that's got her filing charges. If we knew the bastard's name, we could figure out how to deal with him.'

He went on this way, but I wasn't paying too much attention. When he slowed to take a breath I said, 'They want you to cool it

288

with Prejanian. Get out of town, stop cooperating, something like that.'

'That has to be what they want.'

'So why don't you?'

He stared at me. 'You got to be kidding.'

'Why did you tie up with Prejanian in the first place?'

'That's my business, Matt, don't you think? I'm hiring you to do something for me.' Maybe the words sounded a little sharp to him. He tried softening them with a smile. 'The hell, Matt, it's not like you have to know my date of birth and the amount of change in my pocket in order to help me out. Right?'

'Prejanian didn't have a thing on you. You just walked in on your own and told him you had information that could shake up the whole department.'

'That's right.'

'And it's not as though you spent the last twelve years wearing blinders. You're not a choir-boy.'

'Me?' A big, toothy grin. 'Not hardly, Matt.'

'Then I don't get it. Where's your angle?'

'Do I have to have an angle?'

'You never walked down the street without one.'

He thought about it and decided not to resent the line. Instead he chuckled. 'And do you have to know my angle, Matt?'

'Uh-huh.'

He sipped his drink and thought it over. I was almost hoping he would tell me to fuck off. I wanted to go away and forget about him. He was a man I'd never like involved in something I couldn't understand. I really didn't want to get mixed up in any of his problems.

Then he said, 'You of all people should understand.'

I didn't say anything.

'You were on the force fifteen years, Matt. Right? And you got the promotions, you did pretty good, so you musta known the score. You had to be a guy who played the game. Am I right?'

'Keep talking.'

'So you got fifteen years in and five to go for the meal ticket and you pack it in. Puts you in the same boat as me, doesn't it? You reach a point where you can't hack it anymore. The corruption, the shakedowns, the payoffs. It gets to you. Your case, you just pack it in and get out of it. I can respect that. Believe me, I can respect it. I considered it myself, but then I decided it wasn't enough for me, the approach wasn't right for me, I couldn't just walk away from something I had twelve years in.'

'Going on thirteen.'

'Huh?'

'Nothing. You were saying?'

'I was saying I couldn't just turn my back and walk away. I had to do something to make it better. Not all the way better, but maybe just a little bit better, and that means some heads will have to roll, and I'm sorry about that, but it has to be that way.' A wide grin, sudden and alarming now on this face that has been so preoccupied with the business of being sincere. 'Look, Matt, I'm not some fucking Christer. I'm an angle guy, you called me on that and it's true. I know things that Abner has trouble believing. A guy who's absolutely straight, he's never going to hear these things because the wise guys'll dummy up when he walks into the room. But a guy like me gets a chance to hear everything.' He leaned forward. 'I'll tell you something. Maybe you don't know it, maybe it wasn't quite this bad yet when you were carrying a badge. But this whole fucking city is for sale. You can buy the police force all across the board. Straight on up to Murder One.'

'I never heard that.' Which wasn't quite true. I'd heard it. I'd just never believed it.

'Not every cop, Matt. Not hardly. But I know two cases – that's two I know for a fact – where guys got caught with their cocks on the block for homicide and they bought theirselves out from under. And narcotics, fuck, I don't have to tell you about narcotics. That's an open secret. Every heavy dealer keeps a couple of thou in a special pocket. He won't go out on the street without it. That's called walkaway money – you lay it on the cop who busts you and he lets you walk away.'

Was it always that way? It seemed to me that it wasn't. There were always cops who took, some who took a little and some who took a lot, some who didn't say no when easy money came their way, others who actually went out and hustled for it. But there were also things that nobody ever did. Nobody took murder money, and nobody took narcotics money.

But things do change.

'So you just got sick of it,' I said.

'That's right. And you're the last person I should have to explain it to.'

'I didn't leave the force because of corruption.'

'Oh? My mistake.'

I stood up and walked over to where he'd left the bourbon bottle. I freshened my drink and drank off half of it. Still on my feet I said, 'Corruption never bothered me much. It put a lot of food on my family's table.' I was talking as much to myself as to Broadfield. He didn't really care why I left the force any more than I cared whether he knew the right reason or not. 'I took what came my way. I didn't walk around with my hand out and I never let a man buy his way out of something I considered a serious crime, but there was never a week when we lived on what the city paid me.' I drained my glass. 'You take plenty. The city didn't buy that suit.'

'No question.' The grin again. I didn't like that grin much. 'I took plenty, Matt. No argument. But we all have certain lines we draw, right? Why did you quit, anyway?'

'I didn't like the hours.'

'Seriously.'

'That's serious enough.'

It was as much as I felt like telling him. For all I knew he already had the whole story, or whatever the back-fence version of it sounded like these days.

What happened was simple enough. A few years back I was having a few drinks in a bar in Washington Heights. I was off duty and entitled to drink if I felt like it, and the bar was one where cops could drink on the arm, which may have constituted police corruption but which had never given me a sleepless night.

Then a couple of punks held up the place and shot the bartender dead on their way out. I chased them down the street and emptied my service revolver at them, and I killed one of the bastards and crippled the other, but one bullet didn't go where it was supposed to. It ricocheted off something or other and into the eye of a seven-year-old girl named Estrellita Rivera, and on through the eye and into the brain, and Estrellita Rivera died and so did a large part of me.

There was a departmental investigation which ended with me being completely exonerated and even awarded a commendation, and a little while after that I resigned from the force and separated from Anita and moved to my hotel on Fifty-seventh Street. I don't know how it all fits together, or if it all fits together, but what it seemed to add up to was that I hadn't enjoyed being a cop anymore. But none of this was any of Jerry Broadfield's business, and he wasn't going to hear it from me.

So I said, 'I don't really know what I can do for you.'

291

'You can do more than I can. You're not stuck in this lousy apartment.'

'Who brings you your food?'

'My food? Oh. I been getting out for a bite and like that. But not much and not often. And I'm careful that nobody's watching when I leave the building or come back into it.'

'Sooner or later somebody's going to tag you.'

'Hell, I know that.' He lit another cigarette. The gold Dunhill was just a flat sliver of metal, lost in his large hand. 'I'm just trying to buy myself a couple of days,' he said. 'That's about all. She splashed herself all over the papers yesterday. I been here since then. I figure I can last the week if I get lucky, a quiet neighborhood like this. By then maybe you can pinch her fuse.'

'Or maybe I can't do a thing.'

'Will you try, Matt?'

I didn't really want to. I was running low on money, but that didn't bother me too much. It was the beginning of the month and my rent was paid through the end of the month and I had enough cash on hand to keep me in bourbon and coffee, with a little left over for luxuries like food.

I didn't like the big cocky son of a bitch. But that didn't get in the way. As a matter of fact, I generally prefer to work for men I neither like nor respect. It pains me less to give them poor value.

So it didn't matter that I didn't like Broadfield. Or that I didn't believe that more than 20 percent of what he had told me was the truth. And I wasn't even sure which 20 percent to believe.

That last may have been what made my decision for me. Because I evidently wanted to find out what was true and what was false about Jerome Broadfield. And why he had wound up in bed with Abner Prejanian, and just where Portia Carr fit into the picture, and who was setting him up, and how and why. I don't know why I wanted to know all this, but evidently I did.

'Okay,' I said.

'You'll take a shot at it?'

I nodded.

'You'll want some money.'

I nodded again.

'How much?'

I never know how to set a fee. It didn't sound as though it would take too much time – I'd either find a way to help him or I wouldn't, and either way I'd know soon enough. But I didn't want to price myself cheap. Because I didn't like him. Because he was slick and he wore expensive clothes and he lit his cigarettes with a gold Dunhill.

'Five hundred dollars.'

He thought it seemed pretty steep. I told him he could find somebody else if he wanted. He was quick to assure me he hadn't meant anything of the sort, and he took a wallet from his inside breast pocket and counted out twenties and fifties. There was still a lot left in the wallet after he'd piled five hundred dollars on the table in front of him.

'Hope you don't mind cash,' he said.

I told him cash was fine.

'Not too many people mind,' he said, and he gave me the grin again. I just sat there for a minute or two looking at him. Then I leaned over and picked up the money.

FOUR

Its official name is the Manhattan House of Detention for Men, but I don't think I've ever heard anyone call it that. Everybody calls it the Tombs. I don't know why. But the name somehow fits the washed-out, bottomed-out, burned-out feeling of the structure and its inhabitants.

It's on White Street at Centre, conveniently located near Police Headquarters and the Criminal Courts Building. Every once in a while it gets into the papers and the television news because there's a riot there. Then the citizenry is treated to a report on the appalling conditions, and a lot of good people sign petitions, and someone appoints an investigative commission, and a lot of politicians call press conferences, and the guards ask for a pay increase, and after a few weeks it all blows over.

I don't suppose it's much worse than most urban jails. The suicide rate is high, but that's in part a result of the propensity of Puerto Rican males between the ages of eighteen and twenty-five to hang themselves in their cells for no particular reason – unless you call being Puerto Rican and in a cell adequate reason to kill yourself. Blacks and whites in that age group and those circumstances also kill themselves, but the PRs have a much higher rate, and New York has more of them than most cities.

Another thing that boosts the rate is that the guards at the Tombs wouldn't lose any sleep if every Puerto Rican in America wound up swinging from the light fixtures.

I got to the Tombs around ten-thirty after spending a few hours not getting back to sleep and not coming entirely awake either. I'd grabbed some breakfast and read the *Times* and the *News* without learning anything very exciting about Broadfield or the girl he was supposed to have killed. The *News* at least had the story, and of course they'd given it the headline and a big splash on page three. Portia Carr had not been strangled if I was to believe the newspaper; instead someone had brained her with something heavy and then stuck her in the heart with something sharp.

Broadfield had said on the phone that he thought she'd been strangled. Which meant he might have been being cute, or he might have had the story wrong, or the *News* was full of crap.

That was about all the *News* had, right or wrong. The rest was background. Even so, they were ahead of the *Times* – the late city edition didn't have a line of type on the murder.

They let me see him in his cell. He was wearing a windowpane-check suit, light blue on navy, over another custom shirt. You get to keep your own clothing if you're being held for trial. If you're serving a sentence in the Tombs you wear standard prison issue. In Broadfield's case this wouldn't happen because if he was convicted he would be sent upstate to Sing Sing or Dannemora or Attica. You don't do murder time in the Tombs.

A guard opened his door and locked me in with him. We looked each other over without saying anything until the guard was presumably out of earshot. Then he said, 'Jesus, you came.'

'I said I would.'

'Yeah, but I didn't know whether to believe you or not. When you take a look around and realize you're locked up in a jail cell, that you're a prisoner, that something you never believed could happen to you is actually happening, shit, Matt, you don't know what to believe anymore about anything.' He took a pack of cigarettes from his pocket and offered it to me. I shook my head. He lit himself a cigarette with the gold lighter, then weighed the lighter in his hand. 'They let me hang onto this,' he said. 'That surprised me. I didn't think they let you have a lighter or matches.'

'Maybe they trust you.'

'Oh, sure.' He gestured to the bed. 'I'd say take a chair but they didn't give me one. You're welcome to the bed. Of course there's a good chance there are little creatures living in it.'

'I'm comfortable standing.'

'Yeah, so am I. It's going to be a real picnic, sleeping in that bed tonight. Why couldn't the fuckers at least give me a chair to sit on? You know, they took my tie.'

'I guess that's standard procedure.'

'No question. I had an advantage, you know. The minute I walked in the door I knew I was going to wind up in a cell. At the time I didn't know anything about Portia, that she was there, that she was dead, anything. But as soon as I saw them I knew I was going to be arrested because of the complaint she swore out. Right? So while they're asking me questions I'm taking off my jacket, getting out of my pants, kicking my shoes off. You know why?'

'Why?'

'Because they have to let you get dressed. If you're dressed to begin with they can take you that way, but if you're not they have to let you put something on, they can't haul you downtown in your underwear. So they let me get dressed and I picked out a suit with beltless slacks.' He opened the jacket to show me. 'And a pair of loafers. See?' He hiked a trouser leg to display a navy shoe. The leather looked to be lizard. 'I knew they'd want to take my belt and shoelaces. So I picked out clothes that didn't call for a belt or laces.'

'But you wore a tie.'

He gave me the old grin again. It was the first I'd seen of it this morning. 'Damn right I did. You know why?'

'Why?'

'Because I'm going to get out of here. You're gonna help me, Matt. I didn't do it and you'll find a way to prove it, and as much as they'll hate the idea they're gonna have to let me out. And when they do they'll give me back my watch and my wallet, and I'll put my watch on my wrist and my wallet in my pocket. And they'll give me my tie, and I'll get in front of a mirror and take my time getting the knot just right. I might tie it three or four times to get that knot just the way I like it. And then I'll walk out that front door and down those stone steps looking like a million dollars. And that's why I wore that fucking tie.'

The speech probably did him some good. If nothing else it reminded him that he was a class guy, a guy with style, and that was a useful self-image for him to have in a jail cell. He squared his big shoulders and got the whine of self-pity out of his voice, and I took out my notebook and gave him some questions to answer. The answers weren't all that bad, but they didn't do much to get him off the hook.

He had gone out for a sandwich not long after I'd talked to him, say around six-thirty. He'd bought a sandwich and a few bottles of beer at a delicatessen on Grove Street and brought them back to his apartment. Then he sat around listening to the radio and drinking the beer until the phone rang again a little before midnight.

'I figured it was you,' he said. 'Nobody ever calls me there. The phone's not listed. I figured it was you.'

But it was a voice he didn't recognize. A male voice, and it sounded as though it was being purposely disguised. The caller said he could get Portia Carr to change her mind and drop her charges. Broadfield was to go immediately to a bar on Ovington Avenue in the Bay Ridge section of Brooklyn. He was to sit at the bar and drink beer until somebody got in touch with him.

'To get you away from the apartment,' I said. 'Maybe they were too cute. If you can prove you were at the bar, and if the timing's right —'

'There was no bar, Matt.'

'Huh?'

'I shoulda known better than to go in the first place. But I figured what could I lose, right? If someone wants to arrest me and they already know about my apartment, they don't have to get cute like that, right? So I took a subway out to Bay Ridge and I found Ovington Avenue. You know Brooklyn at all?'

'Not very well.'

'Neither do I. I found Ovington, and this bar's not where it's supposed to be, so I figured I must of fucked up, and I looked in the Brooklyn Yellow Pages and it's not listed, but I keep scouting around, you know, and I finally give up and head back home. At this point I figured I was being set up for something or other, but I still can't spot the angle. Then I walk into my apartment and there's cops and over the place, and then I find out Portia's in the corner with a sheet over her, and that's why some son of a bitch wanted me chasing my tail in Bay Ridge. But there's no bartender could swear I was there because there was no bar called the High Pocket Lounge. There were a couple other bars I hit while I was there, but I couldn't tell you the names. And it wouldn't prove a thing.'

'Maybe one of the bartenders could recognize you.'

'And be positive about the time? And even so, it doesn't prove anything, Matt. I took the subway both ways, and the trains ran slow. Say I took a cab to try and set an alibi. Hell, even with the way the trains ran I could have killed Portia in my apartment around eleven-thirty before I even left for Bay Ridge. Except that she wasn't there when I ·left. Except that I didn't kill her.'

'Who did?'

'It's pretty obvious, isn't it? Somebody who wants to see me locked up for murder where I can't slip the shaft to the good old NYPD. Now who would want to see that happen? Who'd have a reason?'

I looked at him for a minute, then let my eyes slide off to the side. I asked him who knew about the apartment.

'Nobody.'

'That's crap. Doug Fuhrmann knew – he took me there. I knew. I also knew the phone number because you gave it to me. Did Fuhrmann know the number?'

'I think so. Yeah, I'm pretty sure he did.'

'Where did you and Doug get to be such good friends?'

'He interviewed me one time, background for a book he was writing. We got to be good drinking buddies. Why?'

'I just wondered. Who else knew about the apartment? Your wife?'

'Diana? Hell, no. She knew I had to stay over in the city from time to time, but I told her I stayed at hotels. She's the last person I'd tell about the apartment. A man tells his wife he's taking an apartment, it's only gonna mean one thing to her.' He grinned again, as abruptly as always. 'The funny thing is I took the fucking apartment primarily so I'd have a place to catch a little sleep when I wanted. A place to keep a change of clothes and like that. As far as taking broads to the apartment, I hardly ever did that. They'd generally have a place of their own.'

'But you took some women there.'

'Now and then. Meet a married woman in a bar, that sort of thing. Most of the time they'd never know my name.'

'Who else did you take there that might know your name? Portia Carr?'

He hesitated, which was as good as an answer. 'She had a place of her own.'

'But you also took her to the place on Barrow Street.'

'Just once or twice. But she wouldn't get me out of there and then sneak in and knock herself off, would she?'

I let it go. He tried to think of anybody else who might know about the apartment and he didn't come up with anything. And as far as he knew, only Fuhrmann and I knew that he was hiding out in the apartment.

'But anybody who knew about the apartment could have guessed, Matt. All they had to do was pick up the phone and take a shot at it. And anybody could just find out about the apartment talking to some broad in a bar that I might not even remember. 'Oh, I'll bet that bastard's hiding out in that apartment of his' – and then somebody else knows about the place.'

'Did Prejanian's office know about the apartment?'

'Why the hell should they know?'

'Did you speak to them after Carr brought charges against you?'

He shook his head. 'What for? The minute her story hit the papers I ceased to exist for the son of a bitch. No point looking to him for help. All Mr Clean wants is to be the first Armenian elected governor of the state of New York. He's had his eye on Albany all along. He wouldn't be the first guy to make a trip up the Hudson on the strength of a reputation as a crime fighter.'

'I could probably think of one myself.'

'I'm not surprised. No, if I got Portia to change her story, Prejanian would be glad enough to see me. Now she'll never change her story and he'll never try to do me any good. Maybe I'da been better off with Hardesty.'

'Hardesty?'

'Knox Hardesty. US District Attorney. At least he's federal. He's an ambitious son of a bitch himself, but he might do me more good than Prejanian.'

'How does Hardesty come into the picture?'

'He doesn't.' He walked over to the narrow bed, sat down on it. He lit another cigarette and blew out a cloud of smoke. 'They let me bring a carton of cigarettes,' he said. 'I guess if you gotta be in jail it could be worse.'

'Why did you mention Hardesty?'

'I thought about going to him. As a matter of fact I sounded him out but he wasn't interested. He's into municipal corruption but only in a political way. Police corruption doesn't interest him.'

'So he sent you to Prejanian.'

'Are you kidding?' He seemed amazed that I would suggest anything of the sort. 'Prejanian's a Republican,' he said. 'Hardesty's a Democrat. They'd both like to be governor and they might wind up running against each other in a couple of years. You think Hardesty would send anything to Prejaman? Hardesty more or less told me to go home and soak my head. Going to Abner was my idea.'

'And you went because you just couldn't stand the corruption another minute.'

He looked at me. 'That's as good a reason as any,' he said levelly.

'If you say so.'

'I say so.' His nostrils flared. 'What difference does it make why I went to Prejanian? He's done with me now. Whoever framed me got just what he wanted. Unless you can find a way to turn it inside out.' He was on his feet now, gesturing with the cigarettes. 'You have to find out who set me up and how it was done because nothing else really gets me off the hook. I could beat this thing in court, but there would always be a cloud over me. People would just figure I got lucky in court. How many people can you think of who went up on charges for capital crimes that got a lot of heat? And when they got off, you and everybody else takes it for granted they were guilty? They say you don't get away with murder, Matt, but how many names do you know of people you'd swear got away with murder?'

I thought about it. 'I could name a dozen names,' I said. 'And that's off the top of my head.'

'Right. And if you included ones where you think they're *probably* guilty, you could name six dozen. All those guys that Lee Bailey defends and gets off, everybody is always positive the bastards are guilty. More than once I heard cops say So-and-so must be guilty or why would he need Bailey to defend him?'

'I've heard the same line.'

'Of course. My lawyer's supposed to be good, but I need more than a lawyer. Because I want more than acquittal. And I can't get anything out of the cops. The ones who caught this case love it just the way it is. Nothing makes them happier than seeing me with my head on the block. So why should they look any further? All they'll look for is more ways to nail me to the wall. And if they find anything that hurts their case, you can guess what they'll do with it. They'll bury it so deep it'd be easier to reach if you started digging in China.'

We went over a few more things and I wrote down various items in my notebook. I got his home address in Forest Hills, his wife's name, the name of his lawyer, and other bits and pieces. He took a blank sheet of paper from my notebook, borrowed my pen, and wrote out an authorization for his wife to give me twenty-five hundred dollars.

'In cash, Matt. And there's more money if that's not enough.

Spend what you have to. I'll back you all the way. Just fix it so I can put that tie on and get the hell out of here.'

'Where does all the money come from?'

He looked at me. 'Does it matter?'

'I don't know.'

'What the fuck am I supposed to say? That I saved it out of my salary? You know better than that. I already told you I was never a Boy Scout.'

'Uh-huh.'

'Does it matter where the money came from?'

I thought about it. 'No,' I said. 'No, I don't guess it does.'

On our way back through the corridors the guard said, 'You were a cop yourself, right?'

'For a while.'

'And now you're working for him.'

'That's right.'

'Well,' he said judiciously, 'we don't always get to choose who we're gonna work for. And a man's got to make hisself a living.'

'That's the truth.'

He whistled softly. He was in his late fifties, jowly and round-shouldered, with liver spots on the backs of his hands. His voice had been roughened by years of whiskey and tobacco.

'Figure to get him off?'

'I'm no lawyer. If I can turn up some evidence, maybe his lawyer can get him off. Why?'

'Just thinking. If he don't get off, he's apt to wish they still had capital punishment.'

'Why's that?'

'He's a cop, ain't he?'

'So?'

'Well, you just think on it. The present time, we got him in a cell by his lonesome. Awaiting trial and all of that, wearin' his own clothes, keepin' to hisself. But let's just say he's convicted and he's sent up to, say, Attica. And there he is in a prison full to overflowing with criminals who got no use at all for the police, and better'n half of'em coons who was born hating the police. Now there is all kinds of ways to do time, but do you know any harder time than that poor bastard is going to serve?'

'I hadn't thought of that.'

The guard clucked his tongue against the roof of his mouth. 'Why, he'll never have a minute when he won't have to be worryin' about some black bastard comin' at him with a homemade knife. They steal spoons from the mess hall and grind 'em down in the machine shop, you know. I worked Attica some years ago, I know how they do things there. You recall the big riot? When they seized the hostages and all? I was long out of there by that time, but I knew two of the guards who was taken as hostages and killed. That's a hell of a place, that Attica. Your buddy Broadfield gets hisself sent there, I'd say he's lucky if he's alive after two years.'

We walked the rest of the way in silence. As he was about to leave me he said, 'Hardest kind of time in the world is the time a cop serves in a prison. But I got to say the bastard deserves it if anybody does.'

'Maybe he didn't kill the girl.'

'Oh, shoot,' he said. 'Who cares a damn if he killed her? He went and turned on his own kind, didn't he? He's a traitor to his badge, ain't he? I don't care a damn about some filthy prostitute and who killed her or didn't kill her. That bastard in there deserves whatever he gets.'

FIVE

I went there first because of the locations. The Tombs is on White at Centre, and Abner Prejanian and his eager beavers had a suite of offices four blocks away on Worth between Church and Broadway. The building was a narrow yellow brickfront which Prejanian shared with a couple of accountants, a photo-copying service, some import-export people, and, on the ground floor, a shop that repaired shoes and reblocked hats. I climbed steep stairs that squeaked, and too many of them; if he'd been a flight higher I might have given up and turned around. But I got to his floor and a door was open and I walked in.

On Tuesday, after my first meeting with Jerry Broadfield, I had spent almost two dollars' worth of dimes trying to reach Portia Carr. Not all at once, of course, but a dime at a time. She had had an answering machine, and when you reach an answering machine from a public phone you usually lose your dime. If you hang up fast enough, and if you're lucky and your reflexes are good, you get your dime back. As the day wears on, this happens less and less frequently.

When I wasn't wasting dimes that day I tried a few other approaches, and one of them involved a girl named Elaine Mardell. She was in the same line of work as Portia Carr and lived in the same neighborhood. I went over to see Elaine, and she managed to tell me a few things about Portia. Nothing firsthand – she hadn't known her personally – but some gossip she had heard at one time or other. That Portia had specialized in SM fantasy fulfillment, that she was supposedly turning down dates lately, and that she had a 'special friend' who was prominent or notorious or influential or something.

The girl in Prejanian's office looked enough like Elaine to be her sister. She frowned at me and I realized that I was staring at her. A second glance showed me that she didn't really resemble Elaine that closely. The similarity was mostly in the eyes. She had the same dark deep-set Jewish eyes and they dominated her entire face in much the same way.

She asked if she could help me. I said I wanted to see Mr Prejanian and she asked if I had an appointment. I admitted I didn't, and she said he was out to lunch, as was most of his staff. I decided not to assume she was a secretary just because she was a woman, and started to tell her what I wanted.

'I'm just a secretary,' she said. 'Do you want to wait until Mr Prejanian gets back? Or there's Mr Lorbeer. I believe he's in his office.'

'Who's Mr Lorbeer?'

'Staff assistant to Mr Prejanian.'

That still didn't tell me a great deal, but I asked to see him. She invited me to have a seat, pointing to a wooden folding chair that looked about as inviting as the bed in Broadfield's cell. I stayed on my feet.

A few minutes later I was sitting across an old oak veneer desk from Claude Lorbeer. When I was a kid, every schoolroom I was ever in had a desk just like that for the teacher. I'd had only female teachers except for gym and shop, but if I'd had a male classroom teacher he might have looked something like Lorbeer, who certainly looked at home behind that desk. He had short, dark brown hair and a narrow mouth with deeply etched lines like paired parentheses on either side of it. His hands were plump with short, stubby fingers. They were pale and looked soft. He wore a white shirt and a solid maroon tie and he had his shirt-sleeves rolled up. Something about him made me feel as though I must have done something wrong, and that my not knowing what it might be was no excuse at all.

'Mr Scudder,' he said. 'I suppose you're the officer I spoke to over the telephone this morning. I can only repeat what I said earlier. Mr Prejanian has no information to make available to the police. Any criminous action which Mr Broadfield may have performed is beyond the scope of this investigation and surely not in any way known to this office. We have not yet spoken to members of the press but will of course take the same tack with them. We will decline to comment and will stress that Mr Broadfield had volunteered to make certain information available to us but that we had taken no action in respect to information furnished by him nor do we anticipate so doing while Mr Broadfield's legal status is undefined as it is at present.'

He said all of this as though he was reading it from a prepared text. Most people have trouble speaking in sentences. Lorbeer spoke in paragraphs, structurally complicated paragraphs, and he delivered his little speech with his pale eyes fixed on the tip of my left shoulder.

I said, 'I think you've jumped to a conclusion. I'm not a cop.'

'You're from the press? I thought –'

'I used to be a cop. I left the force a couple of years ago.'

His face took on an interesting cast at this news. There was some calculation in it. I got a rush of *déjà vu* looking at him, and it took me a minute to put it in place. He reminded me of Broadfield at our first meeting, head cocked to the side and face screwed up in concentration. Like Broadfield, Lorbeer wanted to know what my angle was. He might be a reformer, he might be working for Mr Clean himself, but in his own way he was as much on the make as a cop looking for a handout.

'I've just been to see Broadfield,' I said. 'I'm working for him. He says he didn't kill the Carr woman.'

'Naturally he'd say that, wouldn't he? I understand her body was found in his apartment.'

I nodded. 'He figures he was deliberately framed for her murder. He wants me to try and find out who framed him.'

'I see.' He was somewhat less interested in me now since I was just trying to solve a murder. He'd been hoping I was going to help him louse up an entire police department. 'Well. I'm not certain how our office would be involved.'

'Maybe you're not. I just want a fuller picture. I don't know Broadfield well, I just met him the first time Tuesday. He's a tricky customer. I can't always tell when he's lying to me.'

A trace of a smile appeared on Claude Lorbeer's lips. It looked out of place there. 'I like the way you put it,' he said. 'He *is* a subtle liar, isn't he?'

'That's what's hard to tell. How subtle is he, and how much does he lie? He says he just came over and volunteered his services to you people. That you didn't have to force him into it.'

'That's quite true.'

'It's hard to believe.'

Lorbeer made a tent of his fingertips. 'No harder for you than for us,' he said. 'Broadfield just walked in off the street. He didn't even call first to tell us he was coming. We'd never heard of him before he barged in offering us the earth and asking nothing in return.'

'That doesn't make sense.'

'I *know* it.' He leaned forward, his expression one of great concentration. I suppose he was about twenty-eight. His manner put extra years on him, but when he grew intense those years dropped away and you realized how young he was underneath it all. 'That's what makes it so difficult to place credence in anything the man says, Mr Scudder. One can see no possible motivation for him. Oh, he asked for immunity from prosecution for anything he might disclose that implicated himself, but we grant that automatically. But he didn't want anything beyond that.'

'Then why did he come here?'

'I have no idea. I'll tell you something. I distrusted him immediately. Not because he's crooked. We deal with crooks all the time. We have to deal with crooks, but at least they are rational crooks, and his behavior was irrational. I told Mr Prejanian that I didn't trust Broadfield. I said I felt he was a kook, an oddball. I didn't want to get involved with him at all.'

'And you said as much to Prejanian.'

'Yes, I did. I would have been happy to believe that Broadfield had had some sort of religious experience and turned into a completely new person. Perhaps that sort of thing happens. Not very often, I don't suppose.'

'Probably not.'

'But he didn't even pretend that was the case. He was the same man he'd been before, cynical and breezy and very much the operator.' He sighed. 'Now Mr Prejanian agrees with me. He's sorry we ever got involved with Broadfield. The man's evidently committed a murder, and, oh, even before that there was the unfortunate publicity which resulted from the charges that woman brought against him. It could all put us in something of a delicate position. We didn't *do* anything, you know, but the publicity can hardly work to our advantage.'

I nodded. 'About Broadfield,' I said. 'Did you see him often?'

'Not very often. He worked directly with Mr Prejanian.'

'Did he ever bring anyone to this office? A woman?'

'No, he was always alone.'

'Did Prejanian or anyone from this office ever meet him elsewhere?'

'No, he always came here.'

'Do you know where his apartment was?'

'Barrow Street, wasn't it?' I perked up at that, but then he said, 'I didn't even know he had an apartment in New York, but there

306

was something about it in the newspaper, wasn't there? I think it was someplace in Greenwich Village.'

'Did Portia Carr's name ever come up?'

'That's the woman he murdered, isn't it?'

'That's the woman who was murdered.'

He managed a smile. 'I stand corrected. I suppose one cannot jump to conclusions, however obvious they seem. No, I'm sure I never heard her name before that item appeared in Monday's newspaper.'

I showed him Portia's photo, torn from the morning's *News*. I added some verbal description. But he had never seen her before.

'Let me see if I have it all straight,' he said. 'He was extorting money from this woman. A hundred dollars a week, I believe it was? And she exposed him Monday, and last night she was murdered in his apartment.'

'She said he was extorting money from her. I met her and she told me the same story. I think she was lying.'

'Why would she lie?'

'To discredit Broadfield.'

He seemed genuinely puzzled. 'But why would she want to do that? She was a prostitute, wasn't she? Why should a prostitute try to impede our crusade against police corruption? And why would someone else murder a prostitute in Broadfield's apartment? It's all very confusing.'

'Well, I won't argue with you on that.'

'Terribly confusing,' he said. 'I can't even understand why Broadfield came to us in the first place.'

I could. At least I had a good idea now. But I decided to keep it to myself.

SIX

I stopped at my hotel long enough to take a quick shower and run an electric razor over my face. There were three messages in my pigeonhole, three callers who wanted to be called back. Anita had called again, and a police lieutenant named Eddie Koehler. And Miss Mardell.

I decided that Anita and Eddie could wait. I called Elaine from the pay phone in the lobby. It wasn't a call I wanted to route through the hotel switchboard. Maybe they don't listen in, but then again maybe they do.

When she answered I said, 'Hello. Do you know who this is?'

'I think so.'

'I'm returning your call.'

'Uh-huh. Thought so. You got phone troubles?'

'I'm in a booth, but how about you?'

'This phone's supposed to be clean. I pay this little Hawaiian cat to come over once a week and check for bugs. So far he hasn't found any, but maybe he doesn't know how to look. How would I know? He's really a very little cat. I think he must be completely transistorized.'

'You're a funny lady.'

'Well, where are we without a sense of humor, huh? But we might as well be reasonably cool on the phone. You can probably guess what I called about.'

'Uh-huh.'

'The questions you were asking the other day, and I'm a girl who reads the paper every morning, and what I was wondering was, can any of this lead back to me? Is that something I should start worrying about?'

'Not a chance.'

'Is that straight?'

'Absolutely. Unless some of the calls you made to find things out can work back toward you. You talked to some people.'

'I already thought of that and sealed it off. If you say I got nothing to worry about, then I don't, and that's the way Mrs Mardell's little girl likes it.'

'I thought you changed your name.'

'Huh? Oh, no, not me. I was born Elaine Mardell, baby. Not saying my father didn't change it a while back, but it was already nice and goyish by the time I came on the scene.'

'I might come over later, Elaine.'

'Business or pleasure? Let me reword that. Your business or mine?'

I found myself smiling into the telephone. 'Maybe a little of both,' I said. 'I have to go out to Queens, but I'll give you a call afterward if I'm coming.'

'Call me either way, baby. If you can't come, call. That's why they put –'

'Dimes in condoms. I know.'

'Awww, you know all my best jokes,' she said. 'You're no fun at all.'

My subway car had been decorated by a lunatic with a can of spray paint. He'd had just one message for the world and he had taken pains to inscribe it wherever the opportunity had presented itself, restating his argument over and over again, working in elaborate curlicues and other embellishments.

WE ARE PEOPLE TWO, he informed us. I couldn't decide whether the last word was a simple spelling error or represented some significant drug-inspired insight.

WE ARE PEOPLE TWO.

I had plenty of time to ponder the meaning of the phrase, all the way out to Queens Boulevard and Continental. I got off the train and walked for several blocks, passing streets named after prep schools. Exeter, Groton, Harrow. I eventually got to Nansen Street, where Broadfield and his family lived. I don't know how they named Nansen Street.

The Broadfield house was a good one, set always back on a nicely landscaped lot. An old maple on the strip of lawn between the sidewalk and the street left no doubt about what time of year it was. It was all on fire with red and gold.

The house itself was two storeys tall and thirty or forty years old. It had aged well, The whole block was composed of similar houses, but they differed sufficiently so that one didn't have the sense of being in a development.

Nor did I have the sense of being within the five boroughs of New York. It is hard to remember, living in Manhattan, just how high a percentage of New Yorkers inhabit one-family houses on tree-lined streets. Even politicians sometimes have trouble keeping this in mind.

I walked up a flagstone path to the front door and rang the bell. I could hear chimes sounding inside the house. Then footsteps approached the door, and it was drawn open by a slender woman with short dark hair. She wore a lime-green sweater and dark green pants. Green was a good color for her, matching her eyes, pointing up the shy wood-nymph quality she projected. She was attractive and would have been prettier still if she hadn't been crying recently. Her eyes were rimmed with red and her face was drawn.

I told her my name and she invited me inside. She said I would have to excuse her, that everything was a mess because it had been a bad day for her.

I followed her into the living room and took the chair she indicated. Despite what she'd said, nothing seemed to be a mess. The room was immaculate and very tastefully furnished. The decor was conservative and traditional without having a museum feel to it. There were photographs here and there in silver frames. A book of music stood open on the upright piano. She picked it up, closed it, put it away in the piano bench.

'The children are upstairs,' she said. 'Sara and Jennifer went to school this morning. They left before I heard the news. When they came home from lunch I kept them home. Eric won't start kindergarten until next year, so he's used to being at home. I don't know what they're thinking and I don't know what to say to them. And the telephone keeps ringing. I'd love to take it off the hook, but what if it's something important? I would have missed your call if I'd taken it off the hook. I just wish I knew what to do.' She winced and wrung her hands. 'I'm sorry,' she said, her voice steadier now. 'I'm in a state of shock. It's made me numb and jittery at the same time. For two days I didn't know where my husband was. Now I know that he's in a prison cell. And charged with murder.' She made herself take a breath. 'Would you like some coffee? I just made a fresh pot. Or I could give you something stronger.'

I said that coffee with whiskey in it would be good. She went to the kitchen and came back with two large mugs of coffee. 'I don't know what kind of whiskey or how much to put in,' she said.

'There's the liquor cabinet. Why don't you pick out what you like?'

The cabinet was well stocked with expensive brands. This did not surprise me. I never knew a cop who didn't get a lot of liquor at Christmas. The people who are a little diffident about giving you cash find it easier to give you a bottle or a case of decent booze. I put a healthy slug of Wild Turkey in my cup. I suppose it was a waste. One bourbon tastes pretty much like another when you pour it in coffee.

'Is it good that way?' She was standing beside me, her own mug held in both hands. 'Maybe I'll try some. I don't normally drink very much. I've never liked the taste of it. Do you think a drink would relax me?'

'It probably wouldn't hurt.'

She held out her mug. 'Please?'

I filled her mug and she stirred it with her spoon and took a tentative sip. 'Oh, that's good,' she said, in what was almost a child's voice. 'It's warming, isn't it? Is it very potent?'

'It's about the same strength as a cocktail. And the coffee tends to counteract some of the effects of the alcohol.'

'You mean you don't get drunk?'

'You still get drunk eventually. But you don't get tired out en route. Do you normally get drunk on one drink?'

'I can usually *feel* one drink. I'm afraid I'm not much of a drinker. But I don't suppose this will hurt me.'

She looked at me, and for a short moment we challenged one another with our eyes. I didn't know then and do not know now precisely what happened, but our eyes met and exchanged wordless messages, and something must have been settled on the spot, although we were not consciously aware of the settlement or even of the messages that preceded it.

I broke the stare. I took the note her husband had written from my wallet and handed it to her. She scanned it once quickly, then read it through more carefully. 'Twenty-five hundred dollars,' she said. 'I suppose you'll want that right now, Mr Scudder.'

'I'll probably be having some expenses.'

'Certainly.' She folded the note in two, then folded it again. 'I don't recall Jerry mentioning your name. Have you known each other for a long time?'

'Not long at all.'

'You're on the force. Did you work together?'

'I used to be on the force, Mrs Broadfield. Now I'm a sort of private detective.'

'Just sort of?'

'The unlicensed sort. After all those years in the department I have an aversion to filling out forms.'

'An aversion.'

'Pardon me?'

'Did I say that aloud?' She smiled suddenly and her whole face brightened. 'I don't think I've ever heard a policeman use that word. Oh, they use large words, but of a certain sort, you know. "Alleged perpetrator" is my favorite phrase of all. And "miscreant" is a wonderful word. Nobody but a policeman or a reporter ever called anybody a miscreant, and reporters just write it, they never say it out loud.' Our eyes locked again and her smile faded out. 'I'm sorry, Mr Scudder. I'm babbling again, aren't I?'

'I like the way you babble.'

For a second I thought she was going to blush, but she didn't. She took a breath and assured me I would have my money in a moment. I said there was no rush but she said it would be just as easy to get it over and done with. I sat down and worked on my coffee and she left the room and climbed a flight of stairs.

She returned a few minutes later with a sheaf of bills which she handed to me. I fanned them. They were all fifties and hundreds. I put them in my jacket pocket.

'Aren't you going to count them?' I shook my head. 'You're very trusting, Mr Scudder. I'm sure you told me your first name but I don't seem to remember it.'

'Matthew.'

'Mine is Diana.' She picked up her coffee mug and drained it quickly, as if downing strong medicine. 'Will it be helpful if I say my husband was with me last night?'

'He was arrested in New York, Mrs Broadfield.'

'I just told you my name. Aren't you going to use it?' Then she remembered what we were talking about and her tone changed. 'What time was he arrested?'

'Around two-thirty.'

'Where?'

'An apartment in the Village. He'd been staying there ever since Miss Carr brought those charges against him. He was decoyed out of there last night, and while he was out somebody brought the Carr woman to his apartment and killed her there and tipped the police. Or brought her there after she was dead.'

'Or Jerry killed her.'

'It doesn't make sense that way.'

She thought about this, then took up another tack. 'Whose apartment was it?'

'I'm not sure.'

'Really? It must have been his apartment. Oh, I've always been sure he has one. There are clothes of his I haven't seen in ages, so I gather he keeps part of his wardrobe somewhere in the city.' She sighed. 'I wonder why he tries to hide things from me. I know so much and he must know that I know, don't you suppose? Does he think I don't know that he has other women? Does he think I care?'

'Don't you?'

She looked long and hard at me. I didn't think she was going to answer the question, but then she did. 'Of course I care,' she said. 'Of course I care.' She looked down at her coffee mug and seemed dismayed to see that it was empty. 'I'm going to have some more coffee,' she said. 'Would you like some, Matthew?'

'Thank you.'

She carried the mugs to the kitchen. On the way back she stopped at the liquor cabinet to doctor them both. She had a generous hand with the Wild Turkey bottle, making my drink at least twice as strong as the one I'd made for myself.

She sat on the couch again, but this time she placed herself closer to my chair. She sipped her coffee and looked at me over the top of her mug. 'What time was that girl killed?'

'According to the last news I heard, they're estimating the time of death at midnight.'

'And he was arrested around two-thirty?'

'Around that time, yes.'

'Well, that makes it simple, doesn't it? I'll say that he came home just after the children went to sleep. He wanted to see me and change his clothing. And he was with me, watching television from eleven o'clock until the Carson show went off, and then he went back to New York and got there just in time to get arrested. What's the matter?'

'It won't do any good, Diana.'

'Why not?'

'Nobody'll buy it. The only kind of alibi that'd do your husband any good would be an ironclad one, and the uncorroborated word of his wife – no, it wouldn't do any good.'

'I suppose I must have known that.'

'Sure.'

'Did he kill her, Matthew?'

'He says he didn't.'

'Do you believe him?'

I nodded. 'I believe someone else killed her. And deliberately framed him for it.'

'Why?'

'To stop the investigation into the police department. Or for private reasons – if someone had cause to kill Portia Carr, your husband certainly made a perfect fall guy.'

'That's not what I meant. What makes *you* believe he's innocent?'

I thought about it. I had some fairly good reasons – among them the fact that he was too bright to commit murder in quite so stupid a fashion. He might kill the woman in his own apartment, but he wouldn't leave her there and spend a couple of hours drifting around without even establishing an alibi. But none of my reasons really mattered all that much and they weren't worth repeating to her.

'I just don't believe he did it. I was a cop for a long time. You develop instincts, intuition. Things have a certain feel to them, and if you're any good you know how to pick up on them.'

'I'll bet you were good.'

'I wasn't bad. I had the moves, I had the instincts. And I was so involved in what I was doing that I wound up using a lot of myself in my work. That makes a difference. It becomes much easier to be good at something that you're really caught up in.'

'And then you left the force?'

'Yes. A few years ago.'

'Voluntarily?' She colored and put a hand to her lips. 'I'm very sorry,' she said. 'That's a stupid question and it's none of my business.'

'It's not stupid. Yes, I left voluntarily.'

'Why? Not that that's any of my business, either.'

'Private reasons.'

'Of course. I'm terribly sorry, I think I *am* feeling this whiskey. Forgive me?'

'Nothing to forgive. The reasons are private, that's all. Maybe I'll like telling you about it someday.'

'Maybe you will, Matthew.'

And our eyes got connected again and stayed locked until she abruptly drew a breath and finished the liquid in her coffee mug.

She said, 'Did you take money? I mean, when you were on the force.'

'Some. I didn't get rich at it, and I didn't go out looking for it, but I took what came my way. We never lived on my salary.'

'You're married?'

'Oh, because I said *we*. I'm divorced.'

'Sometimes I think about divorce. I can't think about it now, of course. Now it is incumbent upon the faithful, long-suffering wife to remain at her husband's side in his hour of need. Why are you smiling?'

'I'll trade you three aversions for one incumbent.'

'It's a trade.' She lowered her eyes. 'Jerry takes a lot of money,' she said.

'So I've gathered.'

'That money I gave you. Twenty-five hundred dollars. Imagine having so much money around the house. All I did, I just went upstairs and counted it out. There's a great deal more left in the strongbox. I don't know how much he has there. I've never counted it.'

I didn't say anything. She was sitting with her legs crossed at the knee and her hands folded neatly in her lap. Dark green pants on her long legs, bright green sweater, cool mint-green eyes. Sensitive hands with long slender fingers and closely trimmed unpolished nails.

'I never even knew about the strongbox until just before he began consulting with that Special Prosecutor. I can never remember that man's name.'

'Abner Prejanian.'

'Yes. Of course I knew Jerry took money. He never said so in so many words, but it was obvious, and he did hint at it. As if he wanted me to know but didn't want to tell me outright. It was obvious to me that we weren't living on what he earned legitimately. And he spends so much money on his clothes, and I suppose he spends money on other women.' Her voice came close to breaking, but she sailed right on as if nothing had happened. 'One day he took me aside and showed me the box. There's a combination lock, and he taught me the combination. He said I could help myself to money anytime I needed it, that there would always be more where that came from.

'I never opened the box until just now. Not to count it or anything. I didn't want to look at it, I didn't want to think about it, I didn't want to know how much money was in there. Do you want to know something interesting? One night last week I was thinking of leaving him and I couldn't imagine how I would be able to afford to do it. Financially, I mean. And I never even gave a thought to the money in the strongbox. It never occurred to me.

'I don't know if I'm a very moral person or not. I don't think I am, really. But there is so very much money there, don't you see, and I don't like to think what a person would have to have done in order to get all that money. Am I making any sense at all to you, Matthew?'

'Yes.'

'Maybe he did kill that woman. If he decided he ought to kill a person, I don't think he'd have any moral compunctions about doing it.'

'Did he ever kill anyone in the line of duty?'

'No. He shot several criminals but none of them died.'

'Was he in the service?'

'He was based in Germany for a couple of years. He was never in combat.'

'Is he violent? Has he ever struck you?'

'No, never. Sometimes I've been afraid of him, but I couldn't explain why. He's never given me real reason for fear. I would leave any man who hit me.' She smiled bitterly. 'At least I think I would. But I once thought I'd leave any man who had other women. Why do we never know ourselves as well as we think we do, Matthew?'

'That's a good question.'

'I have so many good questions. I don't really know that man at all. Isn't that remarkable? I've been married to him for all these years and I don't know him. I have never known him. Did he tell you why he decided to cooperate with the Special Prosecutor?'

'I was hoping he might have told you.'

She shook her head. 'And I have no idea whatsoever. But then I never know why he does things. Why did he marry me? Now there's a good question. There's what I'd call a damn good question, Matthew. What did Jerome Broadfield see in mousy little Diana Cummings?'

'Oh, come on. You must know you're attractive.'

'I know I'm not ugly.'

'You're a lot more than not ugly.' *And your hands perch upon your thigh like a pair of doves. And a man could get altogether lost in your eyes.*

'I'm not very dramatic, Matthew.'

'I don't follow you.'

'How to explain? Let me see. Do you know how some actors can just walk onto a stage and every eye is drawn to them? It doesn't matter if someone else is in the middle of a speech. They just have so much dramatic quality that you have to look at them. I'm not like that, not at all. And of course Jerry is.'

'He's striking, certainly. His height probably has something to do with it.'

'It's more than that. He's tall and good-looking but it's more than that. There's a quality he has. People look at him on the street. They always have as long as I've known him. And don't think he doesn't work at it. Sometimes I've seen him at work on it, Matthew. I'll recognize a deliberately casual gesture that I've caught him using before, and I will know just how calculated it is, and at moments like that I can honestly despise the man.'

A car passed by outside. We sat, our eyes not quite meeting, and we listened to distant street sounds and private thoughts.

'You said you were divorced.'

'Yes.'

'Recently?'

'A few years.'

'Children?'

'Two boys. My wife has custody.'

'I have two girls and a boy. I must have told you that.'

'Sara and Jennifer and Eric.'

'You have a remarkable memory.' She looked at her hands. 'Is it better? Being divorced?'

'I don't know. Sometimes it's better and sometimes it's worse. I don't actually think of it in those terms because there wasn't really any choice involved. It had to be that way.'

'Your wife wanted the divorce.'

'No, I was the one who wanted it. The one who had to live alone. But my wanting wasn't a matter of choice, if that makes any sense to you. I *had* to be by myself.'

'Are you still living alone?'

'Yes.'

'Do you enjoy it?'

'Does anyone?'

She was silent for a long moment. She sat with her hands gripping her knee, her head tilted back, her eyes closed, and her thoughts turned inward. Without opening her eyes she said, 'What's going to happen to Jerry?'

'It's impossible to say. Unless something turns up he'll go to trial. He might get off or he might not. A high-powered lawyer could drag things out for a long time.'

'But it's possible he'll be convicted?'

I hesitated, then nodded.

'And go to prison?'

'It's possible.'

'God.'

She picked up her mug and stared down into it, then raised her eyes to meet mine. 'Should I get us more coffee, Matthew?'

'No more for me.'

'Should I have some more? Should I have another drink?'

'If it's what you need.'

She thought about it. 'It's not what I need,' she decided. 'Do you know what I need?'

I didn't say anything.

'I need you to come over here and sit next to me. I need to be held.'

I sat on the couch beside her and she came into my arms eagerly like a small animal seeking warmth. Her face was very soft against mine, her breath warm and sweet. When my mouth found hers she stiffened for a moment. Then, as if realizing that her decision had long since been reached, she relaxed in my arms and returned the kiss.

At one point she said, 'Let's just make everything go away. Everything.' And then she did not have to say anything after that, and neither did I.

A little later we were sitting as before, she on the couch, I on my chair. She was sipping unspiked coffee, and I had a glass of straight bourbon that I'd finished a little more than half of. We were talking quietly and we stopped our conversation when footsteps sounded on the stairs. A girl about ten years old entered the room. She looked like her mother.

She said, 'Mommy, me and Jennifer want to –'

'Jennifer and I.'

The child sighed theatrically. 'Mommy, *Jennifer* and I want to watch *Fantastic Voyage* and Eric is being a pig and wants to watch *The Flintstones* and me and Jennifer I mean Jennifer and I hate *The Flintstones*.'

'Don't call Eric a pig.'

'I didn't *call* Eric a pig. I just said he was *being* a pig.'

'I suppose there's a difference. You and Jennifer can watch your program in my room. Is that what you wanted?'

'Why doesn't Eric watch in your room? After all, Mommy, he's watching *our* set in *our* room.'

'I don't want Eric alone in my room.'

'Well, me and Jennifer don't want him alone in *our* room, Mommy, and –'

'Sara –'

'Okay. *We'll* watch in *your* room.'

'Sara, this is Mr Scudder.'

'Hello, Mr Scudder. Can I go now, Mommy?'

'Go ahead.'

When the child had disappeared up the staircase, her mother let out a long, low-pitched whistle. 'I don't know what on earth is the matter with me,' she said. 'I've never done anything like that before. I don't mean I've been a saint. I was … last year there was someone I was involved with. But in my own house, God, and with my children at home. Sara could have walked right in on us. I'd never have heard her.' She smiled suddenly. 'I wouldn't have heard World War Three. You're a sweet man, Matthew. I don't know how this happened, but I am not going to make excuses for it. I'm *glad* it happened.'

'So am I.'

'Do you know that you still haven't spoken my name? All you've called me is Mrs Broadfield.'

I'd said her name once aloud and many times silently. But I said it again now. 'Diana.'

'That's much better.'

'Diana, goddess of the moon.'

'And of the hunt.'

'Of the hunt, too? I just knew about the moon.'

'I wonder if it will be out tonight. The moon. It's getting dark already, isn't it? I can't believe it. Where did the summer go? It was just spring the other day and now it's October. In a couple of weeks my three wild Indians will put on costumes and extort candy from the neighbors.' Her face clouded. 'It's a family tradition, after all. Extortion.'

'Diana –'

'And Thanksgiving is just a month away. Doesn't it seem as though we had Thanksgiving three months ago? Or four at the very most?'

'I know what you mean. The days take as long to pass as ever, but the years fly by.'

She nodded. 'I always thought my grandmother was crazy. She would tell me time passed much more quickly when you were older. Either she was crazy or she considered me a very gullible child because how could time possibly alter its pace according to one's age? But there *is* a difference. A year is three percent of my life and ten percent of Sara's, so of course it flies for me and crawls for her. And she's in a hurry for time to rush by, and I wish it would slow itself down a bit. Oh, Matthew, it's not all that much fun getting old.'

'Silly.'

'Me? Why?'

'Talking about being old when you're just a kid yourself.'

'You can't be a kid anymore when you're somebody's mother.'

'The hell you can't.'

'And I'm getting older, Matthew. Look how much older I am today than yesterday.'

'Older? But younger, too, aren't you? In one way?'

'Oh, yes,' she said. 'Yes, you're right. And I hadn't even thought of that.'

When my glass was empty I got to my feet and told her I'd better be going. She said it would be nice if I could stay and I said it was probably a good thing that I couldn't. She thought about that and agreed it was probably true but said it would have been nice all the same.

'You'll be cold,' she said. 'It cools off quickly once the sun is down. I'll drive you to Manhattan. Shall I do that? Sara's old enough to baby-sit for that length of time. I'll run you in, it's faster than the train.'

'Let me take the train, Diana.'

'Then I'll drive you to it.'

'I'd just as soon walk off some of the booze.'

She studied me, then nodded. 'All right.'

'I'll call you as soon as I know anything.'

'Or even if you don't?'

'Or even if I don't.'

I reached out for her, but she backed away. 'I want you to know I'm not going to cling, Matthew.'

'I know that.'

'You don't have to feel you owe me anything.'

'Come here.'

'Oh, my sweet man.'

And at the door she said, 'And you'll go on working for Jerry. Is this going to complicate things?'

'Everything generally does,' I said.

It was cold outside. When I got to the corner and turned north, there was a wind with a lot of bite to it coming right up behind me. I was wearing my suit and it wasn't enough.

Halfway to the subway stop I realized I could have borrowed an overcoat of his. A man with Jerry Broadfield's enthusiasm for clothing was sure to have three or four of them, and Diana would have been happy enough to lend me one. I hadn't thought of it and she hadn't volunteered, and now I decided that it was just as well. So far today I'd sat in his chair and drunk his whiskey and taken his money and made love to his wife. I didn't have to walk around town in his clothes.

The subway platform was elevated and looked like a stop on the Long Island Rail Road. Evidently a train had just gone through, although I hadn't heard it. I was the only person waiting on the westbound platform. Gradually other people joined me and stood around smoking.

It's theoretically illegal to smoke in subway stations whether they're above or below ground. Almost everyone honors this rule below the surface of the earth, and virtually all smokers feel free to smoke on elevated platforms. I've no idea why this is so. Subway stations, above or below ground, are equally fireproof, and the air in both is so foul that smoke won't make it noticeably worse. But the law is obeyed in one type of station and routinely violated (and unenforced) in the other, and no one has ever explained why.

Curious.

The train came eventually. People threw away their cigarettes and boarded it. The car I rode in was festooned with graffiti, but the legends were limited to the now-conventional nicknames and numbers. Nothing as imaginative as WE ARE PEOPLE TWO.

I hadn't planned on fucking his wife.

There was a point where I hadn't even considered it, and another point where I knew for certain that it was going to happen, and the two points had been placed remarkably close together in time.

Hard to say exactly why it happened.

I don't all that frequently meet women I want. It is a less and

321

less frequent occurrence, either because of some facet of the aging process or as a result of my personal metamorphoses. I had met one such woman a day ago, and for a variety of reasons, some known and some unknown, I had done nothing about it. And now she and I would never have a chance to happen to each other.

Perhaps some idiot cells in my brain had managed to convince themselves that, if I did not take Diana Broadfield on her living-room couch, some maniac would come along and slaughter her.

The car was warm but I shivered as if I were still standing on the elevated platform exposed to the sharp edge of the wind. It was the best time of the year but it was also the saddest. Because winter was coming.

SEVEN

There were more messages waiting for me at my hotel. Anita had called again and Eddie Koehler had called twice. I walked over to the elevator, then turned and used the pay phone to call Elaine.

'I said I'd call either way,' I told her. 'I don't think I'm going to drop over tonight. Maybe tomorrow.'

'Sure, Matt. Was it anything important?'

'You remember what we were talking about before. If you could find out some more on that subject I'd make it worth your while.'

'I don't know,' she said. 'I don't want to stick my neck out. I like to keep what they call a low profile. I do my work and I save my pennies for my old age.'

'Real estate, isn't it?'

'Uh-huh. Apartment houses in Queens.'

'Hard to see you as a landlady.'

'The tenants never set eyes on me. This management firm takes care of everything. The guy who handles it for me, I know him professionally.'

'Uh-huh. Getting rich?'

'Doing okay. I'm not going to be one of those old Broadway ladies with a dollar a day to feed themselves on. No way.'

'Well, you could ask a few questions and make a few dollars. If you're interested.'

'I suppose I could try. You'll keep my name out of everything, right? You just want me to come up with something that'll give you an opening.'

'That's right.'

'Well, I could see what happens.'

'Do that, Elaine. I'll drop by tomorrow.'

'Call first.'

I went upstairs, kicked off my shoes, stretched out on the bed. I closed my eyes for a minute or two. I was just on the verge of sleep when I forced myself to sit up. The bourbon bottle on the bedside table was empty. I dropped it into the wastebasket and checked the closet shelf. There was an unopened pint of Jim Beam just waiting for me. I cracked it and took a short pull from it. It wasn't Wild Turkey but it did get the job done.

Eddie Koehler wanted me to call him but I couldn't see any reason why that conversation couldn't wait a day or two. I could guess what he was going to tell me and it wasn't anything I wanted to hear.

It must have been around a quarter after eight when I picked up the phone and called Anita.

We didn't have too much to say to each other. She told me the bills had been heavy lately, she'd had some root-canal work done and the boys seemed to be outgrowing everything at once, and if I could spare a couple of bucks it would be welcome. I said I'd just landed some work and would get a money order off to her in the morning.

'That would be a big help, Matt. But the reason I kept leaving messages for you, the boys wanted to talk to you.'

'Sure.'

I talked to Mickey first. He didn't really say much. School was fine, everything was okay – the usual patter, automatic and mindless. Then he put his older brother on the line.

'Dad? They got this thing in Scouts, like for the Nets' home opener against the Squires? And it's supposed to be a father-son deal, you know? They're getting the tickets through the troop, so everybody'll be sitting together.'

'And you and Mickey would like to go?'

'Well, could we? Me and Mick are both Nets fans, and they ought to be good this year.'

'Jennifer and I.'

'Huh?'

'Nothing.'

'The only thing, it's kind of expensive.'

'How much is it?'

'Well, it's fifteen dollars a person, but that includes the dinner first and the bus ride out to the Coliseum.'

'How much extra do you have to pay if you don't have the dinner?'

'Huh? I don't – *oh.*' He started to giggle. 'Hey, that's really neat,' he said. 'Let me tell Mick. Dad wants to know how much extra you have to pay if you don't have the dinner. Don't you get it, stupid? Dad? How much extra if you don't ride on the bus?'

'That's the idea.'

'I bet the dinner's chicken a la king.'

'It's always chicken a la king. Look, the cost's no problem, and if the seats are halfway decent it doesn't sound like too bad a deal. When is it?'

'Well, it's a week from tomorrow. Friday night.'

'That could be a problem. It's pretty short notice.'

'They just told us at the last meeting. Can't we go?'

'I don't know. I've got a case and I don't know how long it'll run. Or if I can steal a few hours in the middle of it.'

'I guess it's a pretty important case, huh?'

'The guy I'm trying to help is charged with murder.'

'Did he do it?'

'I don't think so, but that's not the same as knowing how to prove it.'

'Can't the police investigate and work it out?'

Not when they don't want to, I thought. I said, 'Well, they think my friend is guilty and they're not bothering to look any further. That's why he has me working for him.' I rubbed my temple where a pulse was starting to throb. 'Look, here's how we'll do it. Why don't you go ahead and make the arrangements, all right? I'm sending your mother some money tomorrow and I'll send an extra forty-five bucks for the tickets. If I can't make it I'll let you know and you can just give one ticket away and tag along with somebody else. How does that sound?'

There was a pause. 'The thing is, Jack said he would take us if you couldn't.'

'Jack?'

'He's Mom's friend.'

'Uh-huh.'

'But you know, it's supposed to be a father-son thing, and he's not our father.'

'Right. Hang on a second, will you?' I didn't actually need a drink, but I couldn't see how it would hurt me. I capped the bottle and said, 'How do you get along with Jack?'

'Oh, he's okay.'

'That's good. Well, see how this sounds. I'll take you if I possibly can. If not, you can use my ticket and take Jack. Okay?'

That's how we left it.

In Armstrong's I nodded to four or five people but didn't find the man I was looking for. I sat down at my table. When Trina came over I asked her if Doug Fuhrmann had been in.

'You're an hour late,' she said. 'He dropped in, drank one beer, cashed a check and split.'

'Do you happen to know where he lives?'

She shook her head. 'In the neighborhood, but I couldn't tell you where. Why?'

'I wanted to get in touch with him.'

'I'll ask Don.'

But Don didn't know either. I had a bowl of pea soup and a hamburger. When Trina brought my coffee she sat down across from me and rested her little pointed chin on the back of her hand. 'You're in a funny mood,' she said.

'I'm always in a funny mood.'

'Funny for you, I mean. Either you're working or you're uptight about something.'

'Maybe both.'

'Are you working?'

'Uh-huh.'

'Is that why you're looking for Doug Fuhrmann? Are you working for him?'

'For a friend of his.'

'Did you try the telephone book?'

I touched my index finger to the tip of her little nose. 'You ought to be a detective,' I said. 'Probably do a lot better at it than me.'

Except that he wasn't in the book.

There were around two dozen Fuhrmanns in the Manhattan directory, twice that number of Furmans, and a handful of Fermans and Fermins. I established all this closeted in my hotel room with a phone book, and then I placed my calls from the booth downstairs, stopping periodically to get more dimes from Vinnie. Calls from my room cost double and it's annoying enough to waste dimes to no purpose. I tried all the Fuhrmanns, however spelled, within a two-mile radius of Armstrong's, and I talked to a lot of people with the same last name as my writer friend and a few with the same first name as well, but I didn't reach anybody who knew him and it took a lot of dimes before I gave up.

I went back to Armstrong's around eleven, maybe a little later. A couple of nurses had my regular table so I took one over on the side. I gave the bar crowd a fast glance just to make sure Fuhrmann wasn't there, and then Trina scurried over and said, 'Don't look or anything, but there's somebody at the bar who's been asking about you.'

'I didn't know you could talk without moving your lips.'

'About three stools from the front. Big guy, he was wearing a hat, but I don't know if he still is.'

'He is.'

'You know him?'

'You could always quit this grind and become a ventriloquist,' I suggested. 'Or you could act in one of those old prison movies. If they still make them. He can't read your lips, kid. You've got your back to him.'

'Do you know who he is?'

'Uh-huh. It's all right.'

'Should I tell him you're here?'

'You don't have to. He's on his way over here. Find out what he's drinking from Don and bring him a refill. And I'll have my usual.'

I watched as Eddie Koehler came over, pulled a chair back, settled himself on it. We looked at each other, careful appraising looks. He took a cigar from his jacket pocket and unwrapped it, then patted his pockets until he found a toothpick to puncture its end. He spent a lot of time lighting the cigar, turning it in the flame to get it burning evenly.

We still hadn't spoken when Trina came back with the drinks. His looked to be scotch and water. She asked if he wanted it mixed and he nodded. She mixed it and put it on the table in front of him, then served me my cup of coffee and my double shot of bourbon. I took a short sip of the bourbon neat and poured the rest of it into my coffee.

Eddie said, 'You're tough to get hold of. I left you a couple of messages. I guess you never got over to your hotel to pick em up.'

'I picked them up.'

'Yeah, that's what the clerk said earlier when I checked. So I guess my line must of been busy when you tried to call me.'

'I didn't call.'

'That so?'

'I had things to do, Eddie.'

'No time to call an old friend, huh?'

'I figured to call you in the morning.'

'Uh-huh.'

'Sometime tomorrow, anyway.'

'Uh-huh. Tonight you were busy.'

'That's right.'

He seemed to notice his drink for the first time. He looked at it as if it was the first one he had ever seen. He switched his cigar to his left hand and lifted the glass with his right. He sniffed it and looked at me. 'Smells like what I been drinking,' he said.

'I told her to bring you another of the same.'

'It's nothing fancy. Seagram's. Same as I been drinking for years.'

'That's right, that's what you always used to have.'

He nodded. "Course, it's rare for me to have more'n two, three in a day. Two, three drinks – I guess that's just about what you have for breakfast, huh, Matt?'

'Oh, it's not quite that bad, Eddie.'

'No? Glad to hear it. You hear things around, you know. Be amazed what you hear around.'

'I can imagine.'

'Sure you can. Well, what do you want to drink to, anyhow? Any special toast?'

'Nothing special.'

'Speaking of special, how about the Special Prosecutor? You got any objection to drinking to Mr Abner L. Prejanian?'

'Whatever you say.'

'Fine.' He raised his glass. 'To Prejanian, may he drop dead and may he rot.'

I touched my cup to his glass and we drank.

'You got no objection to drinking that toast, huh?'

I shrugged. 'Not if it makes you happy. I don't know the man we're drinking to.'

'You never met the son of a bitch?'

'No.'

'I did. Greasy little cocksucker.' He took another sip of his drink, then shook his head with annoyance and put his glass on the table. 'Aw, fuck this, Matt. How long we known each other?'

'It's been a few years, Eddie.'

'I guess it has. What the fuck are you doing with a shithead like Broadfield, will you tell me that? What the fuck are you doing playing games with him?'

'He hired me.'

'To do what?'

'Find evidence that will clear him.'

'Find a way for him to beat a murder charge, that's what he wants you to do. Do you know what a son of a bitch he is? Do you have any fucking idea?'

'I have a pretty good idea.'

'He's gonna try to give the entire department the shaft, that's all he's trying to do. He's gonna help that shitkicker of a rug peddler expose corruption in high places. Christ, I hate that candyass son of a bitch. He was as corrupt a cop as you'd ever want to see. I mean he went out hunting for it, Matt. Not just taking everything they handed him. He hunted it. He would go out and detect like crazy, looking for crap games and smack dealers and everything else. But not to arrest them. Only if they weren't holding money, then they might make the trip to the station house. But he was in business for himself. His badge was a license to steal.'

'I know all that.'

'You know all that and yet you're working for him.'

'What if he didn't kill the girl, Eddie?'

'She was stone dead in his apartment.'

'And you think he's stupid enough to kill her and leave her there?'

'Oh, shit.' He puffed on his cigar and the end glowed red. 'He got out of there and dumped the murder weapons. Whatever he hit her with and whatever he stabbed her with. Say he went down to the river and dumped them. Then he stopped some-where to have a couple of beers because he's a cocky son of a bitch and he's a little bit crazy. Then he came back for the body. He was going to dump her someplace but by then we got men on the scene and they're laying for him.'

'So he walked right into their arms.'

'So?'

I shook my head. 'It doesn't make sense. He may be a little crazy but he's certainly not stupid and you're arguing that he acted like an idiot. How did your boys know to go to that apartment in the first place? The papers said you got a telephone tip. Is that right?'

'It's right.'

'Anonymous?'

'Yeah. So?'

'That's very handy. Who would know to tip you? Did she scream? Anybody else hear her? Where did the tip come from?'

'What's the difference? Maybe somebody looked in a window. Whoever called said there was a woman murdered in such-and-such an apartment, and a couple of the boys went there and found a woman with a bump on her head and a knife wound in her back and she was dead. Who cares how the tipster knew she was there?'

'It might make a difference. If he put her there, for instance.'

'Aw, come on, Matt.'

'You don't have any hard evidence. None. It's all circumstantial.'

'It's enough to nail the lid on. We got motive, we got opportunity, we got the woman dead in his goddam apartment, for Christ's sake. What more do you want? He had every reason to kill her. She was nailing his balls to the wall, and of course he wanted her dead.' He swallowed some more of his drink. He said, 'You know, you used to be a hell of a good cop. Maybe the booze is getting to you these days. Maybe it's more than you can handle.'

'Could be.'

'Oh, hell.' He sighed heavily. 'You can take his money, Matt. A guy has to make a living. I know how it is. Just don't get in the way, huh? Take his money and string him for all he's worth. The hell, he's been on the other end of it often enough. Let him get played for a sucker for a change.'

'I don't think he killed her.'

'Shit.' He took his cigar out of his mouth and stared at it, then clamped his teeth around it and puffed on it. Then, his tone softer, he said, 'You know, Matt, the department's pretty clean these days. Cleaner than it's been in years. Almost all of the old-style pads have been eliminated. There's still some people taking big money, no question about it, but the old system with money delivered by a bagman and distributed through an entire precinct, you don't see that anymore.'

'Even uptown?'

'Well, one of the uptown precincts is probably still a little dirty. It's hard to keep it clean up there. You know how it goes. Aside from that, though, the department stacks up pretty good.'

'So?'

'So we're policing ourselves pretty nicely, and this son of a bitch makes us look like shit all over again, and a lot of good men are going to be up against the wall just because one son of a bitch wants to be an angel and another son of a bitch of a rug peddler wants to be governor.'

'That's why you hate Broadfield but –'

'You're fucking right I hate him.'

'– but why do you want to see him in jail?' I leaned forward. 'He's finished already, Eddie. He's washed up. I talked to one of Prejanian's staff members. They have no use for him. He could get off the hook tomorrow and Prejanian wouldn't dare pick him up. Whoever framed him already did enough of a job on him from your point of view. What's wrong with my going after the killer?'

'We already got the killer. He's in a cell in the Tombs.'

'Let's just suppose you're wrong, Eddie. Then what?'

He stared hard at me. 'All right,' he said. 'Let's suppose I'm wrong. Let's suppose your boy is clean and pure as the snow. Let's say he never did a bad thing in his life. Let's say somebody else killed What's-her-name.'

'Portia Carr.'

'Right. And somebody deliberately framed Broadfield and set him up for a fall.'

'So?'

'And you go after the guy and you get him.'

'So?'

'And he's a cop, because who else would have such a good goddam reason to send Broadfield up?'

'Oh.'

'Yeah, *oh*. That's gonna look terrific, isn't it?' He had his chin jutting at me, and the tendons in his throat were taut. His eyes were furious. 'I don't say that's what happened,' he said. 'Because for my money Broadfield's as guilty as Judas, but if he's not, then somebody did a job on him, and who could it be but a couple of cops who want to give that son of a bitch what he deserves? And that would look beautiful, wouldn't it? A cop kills a girl and pins it on another cop to head off an investigation into police corruption. That would look just beautiful.'

I thought about it. 'And if that's what happened, you'd rather see Broadfield go to jail for something he didn't do than for it to come out in the open. Is that what you're saying?'

'Shit.'

'Is that what you're saying, Eddie?'

'Oh, for Christ's sake. I'd rather see him dead, Matt. Even if I had to blow his fucking head off all by myself.'

*

'Matt? You okay?'

I looked up at Trina. Her apron was off and she had her coat over her arm. 'You leaving?'

'I just finished my shift. You've been putting away a lot of bourbon. I just wondered if you were all right.'

I nodded.

'Who was that man you were talking with?'

'An old friend. He's a cop, a lieutenant working out of the Sixth Precinct. That's down in the Village.' I picked up my glass but put it down again without drinking from it. 'He was about the best friend I had on the force. Not buddy-buddy, but we got along pretty well. Of course, you drift apart over the years.'

'What did he want?'

'He just wanted to talk.'

'You seemed upset after he left.'

I looked up at her. I said, 'The thing is, murder is different. Taking a human life, that's something completely different. Nobody should be allowed to get away with that. Nobody should ever be allowed to get away with that.'

'I don't follow you.'

'He didn't do it, damn it. He didn't, he's innocent, and nobody cares. Eddie Koehler doesn't care. I know Eddie Koehler. He's a good cop.'

'Matt –'

'But he doesn't care. He wants me to coast and not even make an effort because he wants that poor bastard to go to jail for a murder he didn't commit. And he wants the one who really did it to get away with it.'

'I don't think I understand what you're saying, Matt. Look, don't finish that drink, huh? You don't really need it, do you?'

Everything seemed very clear to me. I couldn't fathom why Trina seemed to be having difficulty following me. I was enunciating clearly enough, and my thoughts, at least to me, flowed with crystalline clarity.

'Crystalline clarity,' I said.

'What?'

'I know what he wants. Nobody else can figure it, but it's obvious. You know what he wants, Diana?'

'I'm Trina, Matt. Honey, don't you know who I am?'

'Of course I do. Slip of the tongue. Don't you know what he wants, baby? He wants the glory.'

'Who does, Matt? The man you were talking to?'

'Eddie?' I laughed at the notion. 'Eddie Koehler doesn't give a damn about glory. I'm talking about Jerry. Good old Jerry.'

'Uh-huh.' She uncurled my fingers from around my glass and lifted the glass free. 'I'll be right back,' she said. 'I won't be a minute, Matt.' And then she went away, and shortly after that she was back again. I may have gone on talking to her while she was away from the table. I'm not too certain one way or the other.

'Let's go home, Matt. I'll walk you home, all right? Or would you like to stay at my place tonight?'

I shook my head. 'Can't do that.'

'Of course you can.'

'No. Have to see Doug Fuhrmann. Very important to see old Doug, baby.'

'Did you find him in the book?'

'That's it. The book. He can put us all in a book, baby. That's where he comes in.'

'I don't understand.'

I frowned, irritated. I was making perfect sense and couldn't understand why my meaning was evidently eluding her. She was a bright girl, Trina was. She ought to be able to understand.

'The check,' I said.

'You already settled your check, Matt. And you tipped me, you gave me too much. Come on, please, stand up, that's an angel. Oh, baby, the world did a job on you, didn't it? It's okay. All the times you helped me get it together, I can do it for you once in a while, can't I?'

'The check, Trina.'

'You paid the check, I just told you, and –'

'Fuhrmann's check.' It was easier to talk clearly now, easier to think more clearly, standing on my feet. 'He cashed a check here earlier tonight. That's what you said.'

'So?'

'Check would be in the register, wouldn't it?'

'Sure. So what? Look, Matt, let's get out in the fresh air and you'll feel a lot better.'

I held up a hand. 'I'm all right,' I insisted. 'Fuhrmann's check's in the register. Ask Don if you can have a look at it.' She still didn't follow me. 'His address,' I explained. 'Most people have their address printed on their checks. I should have thought of it before. Go see, will you? Please?'

And the check was in the register and it had his address on it.

333

She came back and read off the address to me. I gave her my notebook and pen and told her to write it down for me.

'But you can't go there now, Matt. It's too late and you're not up to it.'

'It's too late, and I'm too drunk.'

'In the morning –'

'I don't usually get so drunk, Trina. But I'm all right.'

'Of course you are, baby. Let's get out in the air. See? It's better already. That's the baby.'

EIGHT

It was a hard morning. I swallowed some aspirin and went downstairs to the Red Flame for a lot of coffee. It helped a little. My hands were slightly shaky and my stomach kept threatening to turn over.

What I wanted was a drink. But I wanted it badly enough to know not to have it. I had things to do, places to go, people to see. So I stuck with the coffee.

At the Post Office on Sixtieth Street I purchased a money order for a thousand dollars and another for forty-five dollars. I addressed an envelope and mailed them both to Anita. Then I walked around the corner to St Paul's on Ninth Avenue. I must have sat there for fifteen or twenty minutes, not thinking of anything in particular. On the way out I stopped in front of the effigy of St Anthony and lit a couple of candles for some absent friends. One was for Portia Carr, another for Estrellita Rivera, a couple others for a couple of other people. Then I put five fifty-dollar bills in the slot of the poor box and went out into the cold morning air.

I have an odd relationship with churches, and it's one I do not entirely understand myself. It started not long after I moved to my Fifty-seventh Street hotel. I began spending time in churches, and I began lighting candles, and, ultimately, I began tithing. That last is the most curious part of all. I give a tenth of whatever money I make to the first church I happen to stop in after I receive payment. I don't know what they do with the money. They probably spend half of it converting happy pagans and use the rest to buy large cars for the clergy. But I keep giving my money to them and go on wondering why.

The Catholics get most of my money because of the hours they keep. Their churches are more often open. Otherwise I'm as ecumenical as you can get. A tenth of Broadfield's first payment to me had gone to St Bartholomew's, an Episcopal church in

Portia Carr's neighborhood, and now a tenth of his second payment went to St Paul's.

God knows why.

Doug Fuhrmann lived on Ninth Avenue between Fifty-third and Fifty-fourth. To the left of the ground-floor hardware store there was a doorway with a sign over it announcing the availability of furnished rooms by week or month. There were no mailboxes in the vestibule and no individual buzzers. I rang the bell alongside the inner door and waited until a woman with henna-bright hair shuffled to the door and opened it. She wore a plaid robe and had shabby bedroom slippers on her feet. 'Full up,' she said. 'Try three doors down, he's usually got something available.'

I told her I was looking for Douglas Fuhrmann.

'Fourth floor front,' she said. 'He expecting you?'

'Yes.' Although he wasn't.

''Cause he usually sleeps late. You can go on up.'

I climbed three flights of stairs, making my way through the sour smells of a building that had given up along with its tenants. I was surprised that Fuhrmann lived in a place like this. Men who live in broken-down Hell's Kitchen rooming houses don't usually have their addresses printed on their checks. They don't usually have checking accounts.

I stood in front of his door. A radio was playing, and then I heard a burst of very rapid typing, then nothing but the radio. I knocked on the door. I heard the sound of a chair being pushed back, and then Fuhrmann's voice asked who it was.

'Scudder.'

'Matt? Just a second.' I waited and the door opened and Fuhrmann gave me a big smile. 'Come on in,' he said. 'Jesus, you look like hell. You got a cold or something?'

'I had a hard night.'

'Want some coffee? I can give you a cup of instant. How'd you find me, anyway? Or is that a professional secret? I guess detectives have to be good at finding people.'

He scurried around, plugged in an electric tea kettle, measured instant coffee into a pair of white china cups. He kept up a steady stream of conversation, but I wasn't listening to him. I was busy looking over the place where he lived.

I hadn't been prepared for it. It was just one room, but it was a large one, measuring perhaps eighteen by twenty-five feet, with two windows overlooking Ninth Avenue. What made it remarkable was the dramatic contrast between it and the building it was situated in. All of the drabness and decay stopped at Fuhrmann's threshold.

He had a rug on the floor, either an authentic Persian or a convincing imitation. His walls were lined with floor-to-ceiling, built-in bookshelves. A desk a full twelve feet in length extended in front of the windows. It too had been built in. Even the paint on the walls was distinctive, the walls themselves – where they were not covered with bookshelves – painted in a dark ivory, the trim set off in a glossy white enamel.

He saw me taking it all in, and his eyes danced behind his thick glasses. 'That's how everybody reacts,' he said. 'You climb those stairs and it's depressing, right? And then you walk into my little retreat and it's almost shocking.' The kettle whistled and he made our coffee. 'It's not as though I planned it this way,' he said. 'I took this place a dozen years ago because I could afford it and there wasn't much else I could afford. I was paying fourteen dollars a week. And I'll tell you something, there were weeks when it was a struggle to come up with the fourteen bucks.'

He stirred the coffee, passed my cup to me. 'Then I got so I was making a living, but even so, I was a little hesitant about moving. I like the location, the sense of neighborhood. I even like the *name* of the neighborhood. *Hell's Kitchen.* If you're going to be a writer, where better to live than a place called Hell's Kitchen? Besides, I didn't want to commit myself to a big rent. I was getting ghostwriting assignments, I was building up a list of magazine editors who knew my work, but even so, it's not a steady business and I didn't want to have a big monthly nut to crack. So what I did, I started fixing this place up and making it bearable. I'd do a little at a time. First thing I did was put in a full burglar alarm system because I got really paranoid about the idea of some junkie kicking the door in and ripping off my typewriter. Then the bookshelves because I was tired of having all my books piled up in cartons. And then the desk, and then I got rid of the original bed, which I think George Washington must have slept in, and I bought that platform bed which sleeps eight in a pinch, and little by little the whole place came together. I kind of like it. I don't think I'm ever going to move.

'It suits you, Doug.'

He nodded eagerly. 'Yeah, I think it does. A couple of years ago I started to twitch because it occurred to me that they could boot me out. Here I got a ton invested in the place and what do I do if they raise my rent? I mean I was still paying by the week, for Christ's sake. The rent was up, it was maybe twenty bucks, but suppose they raise it to a hundred a week? Who knows what they're gonna do, you know? So what I did, I told'em I'd pay a hundred and twenty-five a month, and on top of that I'd give them five hundred in cash under the table. For that I wanted a thirty-year lease.'

'And they gave it to you?'

'You ever heard of anybody with a thirty-year lease on a room on Ninth Avenue? They thought they had a real idiot on their hands.' He chuckled. 'On top of which they never rented a room for more than twenty a week, and I was offering thirty plus cash under the table. They drew up a lease and I signed it. You know what people pay for a studio apartment this size and this location?'

'Now? Two-fifty, three hundred.'

'Three hundred easy. I still pay one and a quarter. In another two or three years this place'll be worth five hundred a month, maybe a thousand if the inflation keeps up. And I'll *still* pay one and a quarter. There's a guy buying up property all up and down Ninth Avenue. Someday they're going to start knocking down these buildings like tenpins. But they'll have to either buy up my lease from me or wait until 1998 to knock the building down because that's how much time I got left on my lease. Beautiful?'

'You got a good deal, Doug.'

'Only clever thing I ever did in my life, Matt. And I wasn't looking to be clever. It's just I'm comfortable here and I hate moving.'

I took a sip of my coffee. It wasn't much worse than what I'd had for breakfast. I said, 'How did you and Broadfield get to be such buddies?'

'Yeah, I figured that's why you were here. Is he crazy or something? Why did he go and kill her? There's no point to it at all.'

'I know it.'

'He always struck me as an even-tempered guy. Men that size have to be steady or they do too much damage. A guy like me could have a short fuse and it wouldn't matter because I'd need a cannon to do any damage, but Broadfield – I guess he blew up and killed her, huh?'

I shook my head. 'Somebody knocked her over the head and then stuck a knife into her. You don't do that on an impulse.'

'The way you said it, you sound as though you don't think he did it.'

'I'm sure he didn't.'

'Jesus, I hope you're right.'

I looked at him. The large forehead and the thick glasses gave him the look of an extremely intelligent insect. I said, 'Doug, how do you know him?'

'An article I was doing once. I had to talk to some cops for research, and he was one of the ones I talked to. We hit it off pretty well.'

'When was that?'

'Maybe four, five years ago. Why?'

'And you're just friends? And that's why he decided to turn to you when he was on the spot?'

'Well, I don't think he *has* too many friends, Matt. And he couldn't turn to any cop friends of his. He told me once that cops don't usually have many friends off the force.'

That was true enough. But Broadfield didn't seem to have many friends *on* the force, either.

'Why did he go to Prejanian in the first place, Doug?'

'Hell, don't ask me. Ask Broadfield.'

'But you know the answer, don't you?'

'Matt –'

'He wants to write a book. That's it, isn't it? He wants to make a big enough splash to be a celebrity, and he wants you to write his book for him. And then he can do all the television talk shows and grin that cute grin of his and call a lot of important people by their first names. That's where you come into it. That's the only way you can come into it, and it's the only reason that would have sent him to Abner Prejanian's office.'

He wouldn't look at me. 'He wanted it a secret, Matt.'

'Sure. And afterward he would just happen to write a book. In response to popular demand.'

'It could be dynamite. Not just his role with the investigation but his whole life. He's told me the most fascinating stuff I've ever heard. I wish he'd let me tape some of it, but so far everything's off the record. When I heard he killed her I saw the chance of my life going down the drain. But if he's really innocent –'

'Where did he get the idea of doing the book?'

He hesitated, then shrugged. 'You might as well know it all. It's a natural idea, cop books are big these days, but he might not have thought of it by himself.'

'Portia Carr.'

'That's right, Matt.'

'She suggested it? No, that doesn't make sense.'

'She was talking about doing a book herself.'

I put my cup down and went over to the window. 'What kind of a book?'

'I don't know. Something like *The Happy Hooker*, I suppose. What's the difference?'

'Hardesty.'

'Huh?'

'I'll bet that's why he went to Hardesty.'

He looked at me.

'Knox Hardesty,' I said. 'The U.S. District Attorney. Broadfield went to him before he went to Prejanian, and when I asked him why he didn't make much sense. Because Prejanian was the logical man to go to. Police corruption is his special area of interest, and it wouldn't carry much weight with a federal D.A.'

'So?'

'So Broadfield would have known that. He only would have picked Hardesty if he thought he had some kind of an in there. He probably got the idea of writing a book from Portia Carr. Maybe he got the idea of Hardesty from the same place.'

'What does Portia Carr have to do with Knox Hardesty?'

I told him it was a good question.

NINE

Hardesty's offices were at 26 Federal Plaza with the rest of the Justice Department's New York operations. That put him just a couple of blocks from Abner Prejanian; I wondered if Broadfield had dropped in on both of them the same day.

I called first, to make sure Hardesty wasn't in court or out of town. He was neither, but I saved myself a trip downtown because his secretary told me he hadn't come in, that he was home with stomach flu. I asked for his home address and telephone number, but she wasn't allowed to give them to me.

The telephone company wasn't similarly restricted. He was listed. *Hardesty, Knox, 114 East End Avenue*, and a phone number with a Regent 4 exchange. I called the number and got through to Hardesty. He sounded as though stomach flu had been a polite term for hangover. I told him my name and that I wanted to see him. He said he didn't feel well and started to hedge, and the only decent card I had was Portia Carr's name, so I played it.

I'm not sure exactly what reaction I expected, but it certainly wasn't the one I got. 'Poor Portia. That was a tragic thing, wasn't it? You were a friend of hers, Scudder? Be very anxious to get together with you. Wouldn't happen to be free right now, I don't suppose. You would? Good, very good. You know the address here?'

I figured it out in the cab on the way over there. I'd somehow managed to take it for granted that Hardesty had been one of Portia's clients, and I'd envisioned him hopping around in a tutu while she flailed at him with a whip. And men in public office with political ambitions don't usually welcome inquiries on their unorthodox sexual practices from total strangers. I'd expected outright denial that he knew Portia Carr ever existed, or some hedging at the very least. Instead I got a very eager welcome.

So I'd obviously added things wrong. The list of Portia's prominent clients didn't include Knox Hardesty. Theirs was a

341

professional relationship, no doubt, but it was his profession that was involved, not hers.

And that way it made plenty of sense. And it fit in with Portia's literary aspirations and connected neatly to Broadfield's ambitions in that direction.

Hardesty's building was a prewar stonefront fourteen stories tall. It had an Art Deco Lobby with high ceilings and a lot of black marble. The doorman had auburn hair and a guardsman's moustache. He established that I was expected and passed me on to the elevator operator, a diminutive black who was barely tall enough to reach the top button. And he had to reach it because Hardesty had the penthouse.

And the penthouse was impressive. High ceilings, rich, high-pile carpet, fireplaces, oriental antiques. A Jamaican maid led me into the study where Hardesty was waiting for me. He stood up and came out from behind his desk, his hand extended. We shook hands and he waved me to a chair.

'A drink? A cup of coffee? I'm drinking milk myself because of this damned ulcer. I picked up a touch of stomach flu and it always aggravates the ulcer. But what will you have, Scudder?'

'Coffee, if it's no trouble. Black.'

Hardesty repeated the order to the maid as if she couldn't have been expected to follow our conversation. She returned almost immediately with a mirrored tray holding a silver pot of coffee, a bone-china cup and saucer, a silver cream and sugar set, and a spoon. I poured out a cup of coffee and took a sip.

'So you knew Portia,' Hardesty said. He drank some milk, put the glass down. He was tall and thin, his hair graying magnificently at his temples, his summertime tan not entirely faded yet. I'd been able to picture what a striking couple Broadfield and Portia must have made. She would have looked good on Knox Hardesty's arm, too.

'I didn't know her terribly well,' I said. 'But I knew her, yes.'

'Yes. Hmmm. I don't believe I asked you your profession, Scudder.'

'I'm a private detective.'

'Oh, very interesting. Very interesting. Is that coffee all right, incidentally?'

'It's the best I've ever tasted.'

He allowed himself a smile. 'My wife's the coffee fanatic. I was never that much of an enthusiast, and with the ulcer I tend to stick to milk.

I could find out the brand for you if you're interested.'

'I live in a hotel, Mr Hardesty. When I want coffee I go around the corner for it. But thank you.'

'Well, you can always drop in here for a decent cup of the stuff, can't you?' He gave me a nice rich smile. Knox Hardesty didn't live on his salary as United States Attorney for the Southern District of New York. That wouldn't cover his rent. But that didn't mean he walked around with his hand out. Grandfather Hardesty had owned Hardesty Iron and Steel before U.S. Steel bought him up, and Grandfather Knox had followed a long line of New England Knoxes in shipping. Knox Hardesty could spend money with both hands and still never have to worry where his next glass of milk was coming from.

He said, 'A private detective, and you were acquainted with Portia. You could be very useful to me, Mr Scudder.'

'I was hoping things might work the other way around.'

'I beg your pardon?' His face changed and his back stiffened and he looked as though he had just smelled something extremely unpleasant. I guess my line had sounded like the overture of a blackmail pitch.

'I already have a client,' I said. 'I came to you to find something out, not to give information away. Or even to sell it, as far as that goes. And I'm not a blackmailer, sir. I wouldn't want to give that impression.'

'You have a client?'

I nodded. I was just as glad I'd given the impression I did, although it had been unintentional on my part. His reaction had been unequivocal enough. If I was a blackmailer he wanted no part of me. And that generally means the person in question doesn't have reason to fear being blackmailed. Whatever his relationship with Portia, it wasn't something he would have trouble living down.

'I'm representing Jerome Broadfield.'

'The man who killed her.'

'The police think so, Mr Hardesty. Then again, you'd expect them to think so, wouldn't you?'

'Good point. I'd been given to understand he was virtually caught in the act. That's not the case?' I shook my head. 'Interesting. And you'd like to find out –'

'I'd like to find out who killed Miss Carr and framed my client.'

He nodded. 'But I don't see how I can help you toward that end, Mr Scudder.'

I'd been promoted – from Scudder to Mr Scudder. I said, 'How did you happen to know Portia Carr?'

'One has to know a wide variety of people in my line of work. The most fruitful contacts are not necessarily those persons with whom one would prefer to associate. I'm sure that has been your own experience as well, hasn't it? One sort of investigative work is rather like another, I suspect.' He smiled graciously; I was supposed to be complimented that he saw his work as being similar to mine.

'I heard of Miss Carr before I met her,' he went on. 'The better sort of prostitutes can be very useful to our office. I was informed that Miss Carr was quite expensive and that her client list was primarily interested in, oh, less orthodox forms of sex.'

'I understand she specialized in masochists.'

'Quite.' He made a face; he'd have preferred it if I'd been less specific. 'English, you know. That's the English vice, so-called, and an American masochist would find an English mistress especially desirable. Or so Miss Carr informed me. Did you know that native-born prostitutes oftimes affect English or German accents for the benefit of their masochistic clients? Miss Carr assured me it's common practice. German accents for the Jewish clients in particular, which I find fascinating.'

I freshened my cup of coffee.

'The fact that Miss Carr's accent was quite authentic increased my interest in her. She was vulnerable, you see.'

'Because she could be deported.'

He nodded. 'We have a good enough working relationship with the fellows in Immigration and Naturalization. Not that it's often necessary to follow through on one's threats. The prostitute's traditional tight-lipped loyalty to her clientele is as much a romantic conceit as her heart of gold. The merest threat of deportation is enough to bring immediate offers of full cooperation.'

'And that was the case with Portia Carr?'

'Absolutely. In fact she became quite eager. I think she relished the Mata Hari role, garnering information in bed and passing it on to me. Not that she managed to supply me with too terribly much, but she was shaping up as a promising source for my investigations.'

'Any investigation in particular?'

There was just a little hesitation. 'Nothing specific,' he said. 'I could just see that she would be useful.'

I drank some more coffee. If nothing else, Hardesty was enabling me to find out just how much my own client knew. Since Broadfield had chosen to play coy with me, I had to get this information in an indirect fashion. But Hardesty didn't know that Broadfield hadn't been completely straight with me, so he couldn't deny anything that I might have presumably learned from him.

'So she cooperated enthusiastically,' I said.

'Oh, very much so.' He smiled in reminiscence. 'She was quite charming, you know. And she had the notion of writing a book about her life as a prostitute and her work for me. I think that Dutch girl was an inspiration to her. Of course the Dutch girl can't set foot in the country because of the role she played, but I don't really think Portia Carr would have ever gotten round to writing that book, do you?'

'I don't know. She won't now.'

'No, of course not.'

'Jerry Broadfield might, though. Was he terribly disappointed when you told him you weren't interested in police corruption?'

'I'm not sure I put it quite that way.' He frowned abruptly. 'Is that why he came to me? For heaven's sake. He wanted to write a book?' He shook his head in disbelief. 'I'll never understand people,' he said. 'I knew that selfrighteousness was a pose, and that made me resolve not to have anything to do with him, that more than the sort of information he had to offer. I simply couldn't trust him and felt he'd do my investigations more harm than good. So then he popped over to see that Special Prosecutor chap.'

That Special Prosecutor chap. It wasn't hard to tell what Knox Hardesty thought of Abner L. Prejanian.

I said, 'Did it bother you that he went to Prejanian?'

'Why on earth should it bother me?'

I shrugged. 'Prejanian started to get a lot of ink. The papers gave him a nice play.'

'More power to him if publicity is what he wants. It seems rather to have backfired on him now, though. Wouldn't you say?'

'And that must please you.'

'It confirms my judgment, but aside from that why should it please me?'

'Well, you and Prejanian are rivals, aren't you?'

'Oh, I'd hardly put it that way.'

'No? I thought you were. I figured that's why you got her to accuse Broadfield of extortion.'

'What!'

'Why else would you do it?' I made my tone deliberately offhand, not accusing him but taking it for granted that it was something we both knew and acknowledged. 'Once she was pressing charges against him he was defused and Prejanian didn't even hear his name mentioned. And it made Prejanian look gullible for having used Broadfield in the first place.'

His grandfather or great-grandfather might have lost control. But Hardesty had enough generations of good breeding behind him so that he was able to keep almost all of his cool. He straightened in his chair, but that was about the extent of it. 'You've been misinformed,' he told me.

'The charge wasn't Portia's idea.'

'Nor was it mine.'

'Then why did she call you around noon the day before yesterday? She wanted your advice, and you told her to go on acting as if the charge was true. Why did she call you? And why did you tell her that?'

No indignation this time. A little stalling – picking up the glass of milk, putting it down untasted, fussing with a paperweight and a letter opener. Then he looked at me and asked how I knew she'd called him.

'I was there.'

'You were –' His eyes widened. 'You were the man who wanted to talk with her. But I thought – then you were working for Broadfield *before* the murder.'

'Yes.'

'For heaven's sake. I thought – well, obviously I thought you'd been engaged after he was arrested for homicide. Hmmm. So you were the man she was so nervous about. But I spoke to her before she had met you. She didn't even know your name when we talked. How did you know – she didn't tell you, that's the last thing she would have done. Oh, for heaven's sake. That was a bluff, wasn't it?'

'You could call it an educated guess.'

'I'd just as soon call it a bluff. I'm not sure I'd care to play poker with you, Mr Scudder. Yes, she called me – I might as well admit it since it's fairly obvious. And I told her to insist that the charge was true, although I knew it wasn't. But I didn't put her up to making the charge in the first place.'

'Then who did?'

'Some policemen. I don't know their names, and I'm not inclined to think Miss Carr did. She said she didn't, and it's likely she'd have been open with me on that subject. You see, she hadn't wanted to press those charges. If there was a chance I could have gotten her off that hook, she'd have done what she could.' He smiled. 'You may think I had reason to cast a pall on Mr Prejanian's investigation. While I'm not saddened by the spectacle of that man with egg on his face, I'd never have taken the trouble to put it there. Certain policemen, however, had a much stronger motive for sabotaging that inquiry.'

'What did they have on Carr?'

'I don't know. Prostitutes are always vulnerable, of course, but –'

'Yes?'

'Oh, this is just intuitive on my part. I had the impression that they were threatening her not with the law but with some extralegal punishment. I believe she was physically afraid of them.'

I nodded. That checked out with the vibrations I'd picked up at my own meeting with Portia Carr. She hadn't acted like someone afraid of deportation or arrest, but like someone worried about being beaten up or killed. Someone worried because it was October and she was waiting for winter.

TEN

Elaine lived just three blocks from where Portia Carr had lived. Her building was on Fifty-first between First and Second. The doorman checked me on the intercom and motioned me on through. By the time the elevator got me to the ninth floor, Elaine was waiting in her open doorway.

I decided she looked a lot better than Prejanian's secretary. I suppose she's around thirty by now. She has always looked younger than her years and she has a face full of good bones that will age well. Her softness contrasted dramatically with the stark, modern feel of her apartment. She had the place carpeted in white shag, and the furniture was all angles and geometric planes and primary colors. I don't ordinarily like rooms done that way, but somehow her place worked for me. She'd told me once that she had done her own decorating.

We kissed each other like the old friends we were. Then she gripped my elbows and leaned backward. 'Secret Agent Mardell reporting,' she said. 'I'm not to be taken lightly, man. This camera of mine just looks like a camera. It's actually a tie clip.'

'I think that's backward.'

'Well, I certainly hope so.' She turned, flounced away. 'Actually I haven't found out a hell of a lot. You want to know what prominent people were in her book, is that right?'

'Especially if they're politically prominent.'

'That's what I meant. Everybody I asked kept coming up with the same three or four names. Actors, a couple of musicians. Honestly, some call girls are as bad as groupies. Boasting like any other celebrity-fuckers.'

'You're the second person today to tell me call girls don't keep everything confidential.'

'Ha! Your average hooker isn't exactly Stella Stable, Matt. Of course I'm the winner of the Miss Mental Health contest.'

'Absolutely.'

'If she didn't mention what politicians were in her book, it's probably because she wasn't that proud of them. If she'd been fucking the governor or a U. S. senator, people would have heard about it, but if it's somebody local, who cares? What's the matter?'

'Politicians would probably be sad to learn that they're not so important.'

'They'd positively shit, wouldn't they?' She lit a cigarette. 'What you ought to have is her john book. Even if she had the brains to code it, you'd have the phone numbers and you can work backward from there.'

'Is yours in code?'

'The names *and* the numbers, sugar.' She smiled triumphantly. 'Anybody who steals my book steals trash, just like Othello's purse. But that's because I'm Brenda Brilliant. Could you get your hands on Portia's book?'

I shook my head. 'I'm sure the cops have tossed her place. And if she had a book, they found it – and tossed it. In the river. They don't want any loose ends that might give Broadfield's lawyer an opening. They want him drawn and quartered, and the only way they'd leave her book around is if Broadfield's name was the only one in it.'

'Who do you figure killed her, Matt? Some cops?'

'People keep suggesting it. Mabye I've been off the force too long. I have trouble believing that police officers would actually murder some innocent hooker just to frame someone else.'

She opened her mouth, then closed it.

'Something?'

'Well, maybe you've been off the force too long.' She looked about to say something else, then gave her head a quick shake. 'I think I'll make myself a cup of tea. I'm a rotten hostess. A drink? I'm out of bourbon, but there's Scotch.'

It was time. 'A small one, straight.'

'Coming right up.'

While she was in the kitchen I thought about the relationship of cops and whores, and the relationship of Elaine and myself. I had gotten to know her a couple of years before I left the police department. Our first meeting was social, though I do not remember the precise circumstances. I believe we were introduced by a mutual friend at some restaurant or other, but we may have met at a party. I don't remember.

It's useful for a hooker to have a cop with whom she's on

particularly good terms. He can smooth things out if a brother officer is giving her a hard time. He can furnish her with a brand of reality-oriented legal advice that is often more useful then the advice she would get from a lawyer. And she reciprocates for all of this, of course, as women have always reciprocated for the favors men do for them.

So I spent a couple of years on Elaine Mardell's free list, and I was the person she called when the walls started coming together around her. Neither of us abused the privilege. I would see her once in a while if I happened to be in the neighborhood, and she called me perhaps half a dozen times all told.

Then I left the force, and for a period of several months I wasn't interested in any human contact, least of all sexual contact. Then one day I was, and I called Elaine and went over to see her. She never mentioned that I wasn't a cop anymore and that our relationship was thus due to change. If she had, I probably wouldn't have wanted to see her again. But on the way out I put some money on the coffee table, and she said she hoped she'd see me again soon, and every now and then she does.

I suppose our original relationship had constituted a form of police corruption. I hadn't been acting as Elaine's protector, nor had it been my job to arrest her. But I had seen her on the city's time, and it had been my official position that earned me the right to share her bed. Corruption, I suppose.

She brought me my drink, a juice glass with around three ounces of Scotch in it, and sat down on the couch with a cup of tea with milk. She curled her legs under her compact little behind and stirred her tea with a demitasse spoon.

'Beautiful weather,' she said.

'Uh-huh.'

'I wish I was closer to the park. I take long walks every morning. Days like this I'd like to take my walks in the park.'

'You take long walks every morning?'

'Sure. It's good for you. Why?'

'I figured you'd sleep until noon.'

'Oh, no. I'm an early riser. And I'll get visitors from noon on, of course. And I can get to sleep early because it's rare I have anyone here after ten o'clock at night.'

'That's funny. You think of it as a business for night people.'

'Except it's not. The guys, you know, they have to get home to their families. I'd say from noon to six-thirty is maybe ninety percent of the people I see.'

'Makes sense.'

'I got somebody coming in a while, Matt, but we got time if you feel like it.'

'I'd better take a raincheck.'

'Well, that's cool.'

I drank some of my drink. 'Back to Portia Carr,' I said. 'You didn't come up with anybody who might have had some kind of a government connection?'

'Well, I might have.' My face must have changed expression because she said, 'No, I'm not hustling you, for God's sake. I learned a name, but I don't know if I got it right and I don't know who it is.'

'What's the name?'

'Something like Mantz or Manch or Manns. I don't know it exactly. I know he's somebody connected to the mayor, but I don't know what. At least that's the story I got. Don't ask me the guy's first name because nobody knows. Does that give you anything? Manns or Mantz or Manch or something like that?'

'It doesn't ring a bell. He's connected to the mayor?'

'Well, that's what I heard. I know what he likes to do if that helps. He's a toilet slave.'

'What the hell is a toilet slave?'

'I wish you knew because it doesn't especially thrill me to discuss it.' She put her teacup down. 'A toilet slave is, well, they'll have different kinds of kinks, but an example would be that he wants to be ordered to drink piss or eat shit, or to clean out your ass with his tongue, or clean out the toilet, or other things. What you have to tell him to do can be really disgusting or it can just be sort of symbolic, like if you made him mop the bathroom floor.'

'Why would anybody – never mind, don't tell me.'

'It's getting to be a very strange world, Matt.'

'Uh-huh.'

'Like nobody seems to fuck anymore. You can make a ton doing masochist tricks. They'll pay a fortune if you can fill up their fantasy for them. But I don't think it's worth it. I'd rather not have to contend with all that weirdness.'

'You're just an old-fashioned girl. Elaine.'

'That's me. Crinolines and lavender sachets and all those good things. 'Nother drink?'

'Just a touch.'

When she brought it I said, 'Manns or Manch or something like that. I'll see if that goes anywhere. I think it's a dead-end street anyway. I'm getting more and more interested in cops.'

'Because of what I said?'

'That, and also something some other people have said. Did she have somebody on the force that sort of looked out for her?'

'You mean the way you used to for me? Sure she did, but where does that get you? It was your friend.'

'Broadfield?'

'Sure. That extortion number was pure bullshit, but I guess you knew that.'

I nodded. 'She have anybody else?'

'Could be, but I never heard about it. And no pimp and no boyfriends, unless you count Broadfield as a boyfriend.'

'Any other cops in her life? Giving her a hard time, anything like that?'

'Not that I heard about.'

I took a sip of scotch. 'This is off the subject a little, Elaine, but do cops ever give you a hard time?'

'Do you mean do they or have they ever? It's happened in the past. But then I learned a little. You have somebody regular, and the rest of the guys let you be.'

'Sure.'

'And if I get a hard time from somebody else, I mention some names or I make a phone call and everything cools down. You know what's worse? Not cops. Guys pretending to be cops.'

'Impersonating an officer? That's a criminal offense, you know.'

'Well, shit, Matt, am I gonna press charges? Like I've had cats flash badges at me, the whole number. You take a green kid who just got to town and all she's got to see is a silver shield and she'll curl up in a corner and have kittens. I'm supercool myself. I take a good look at the badge and it turns out to be a toy thing that a little kid'll get to go with his cap pistol. Don't laugh, I mean it. I've had that happen.'

'And what do they want from you? Money?'

'Oh, they pretend it's a gag after I pick up on them. But it's no gag. I've had them want money, but mostly all they want is to get fucked for free.'

'And they flash a toy badge.'

'I've seen badges you'd swear came out of crackerjack boxes.'

'Men are weird animals.'

'Oh, men and women both, honey. I'll tell you something.

Everybody's weird, fundamentally everybody is a snap. Sometimes it's a sexual thing and sometimes it's a different kind of weirdness, but one way or another everybody's nuts. You, me, the whole world.'

It wasn't particularly difficult to discover that Leon J. Manch had been appointed assistant deputy mayor a year and a half ago. All it took was a short session in the Forty-second Street library. There were a variety of Mannses and Mantzes in the volume of the *Times Index* I consulted, but none of them seemed to have anything significant to do with the current administration. Manch was mentioned only once in the *Times Indexes* for the past five years. The story dealt with his appointment, and I went to the trouble of reading the article in the microfilm room. It was a brief article, and Manch was one of half a dozen people treated in it; about all it did was announce that he'd been appointed and identify him as a member of the bar. I learned nothing about his age, residence, marital status, or much of anything else. It didn't say he was a toilet slave, but I already knew that.

I couldn't find him in the Manhattan telephone book. Maybe he lived in another borough, or outside of the city limits altogether. Maybe he had an unlisted phone or listed it in his wife's name. I called City Hall and was told that he'd left for the day. I didn't even try for his home number.

I called her from a bar on Madison and Fifty-first called O'Brien's. The bartender's name was Nick, and I knew him because he had worked at Armstrong's a year or so ago. We assured each other that it was a small world, bought each other a few drinks, and then I went to the phone booth in the back and dialed her number. I had to look it up in my notebook.

When she answered I said, 'It's Matthew. Can you talk?'

'Hello. Yes, I can talk. I'm all alone here. My sister and her husband drove in from Bayport and picked up the children this morning. They'll be staying out there for, oh, for a while, anyway. They thought it would be better for the children and easier for me. I didn't really want them to take the kids, but I didn't have the strength to argue, and maybe they're right, maybe it's better this way.'

'You sound a little shaky.'

'Not shaky. Just very drawn, very worn out. Are you all right?'

'I'm fine.'

'I wish you were here.'

'So do I.'

'Oh, dear. I wish I knew how I felt about all of this. It frightens me. Do you know what I mean?'

'Yes.'

'His lawyer called earlier. Have you spoken to him?'

'No. Was he trying to get in touch with me?'

'He didn't seem very interested in you, as a matter of fact. He was very confident about winning in court, and when I said that you were trying to find out who really killed that woman, he seemed – how shall I put it? I got the impression that he believed Jerry was guilty. He intends to get him acquitted, but he doesn't really believe for a minute that he's really innocent.'

'A lot of lawyers are like that, Diana.'

'Like a surgeon who decides it's his job to remove an appendix. Whether there's anything wrong with the appendix or not.'

'I'm not sure it's exactly the same thing, but I know what you mean. I wonder if there's any point in my contacting that lawyer.'

'I don't know. What I was starting to say … Oh, it's silly, and it's hard to say. Matthew? I was disappointed when I picked up the phone and it was the lawyer. Because I was hoping, oh, that it would be you.' Pause. 'Matthew?'

'I'm here.'

'Should I not have said that?'

'No, don't be silly.' I caught my breath. The telephone booth had gotten unbearably warm. I opened the door a little. 'I wanted to call you earlier. I shouldn't be calling now, really. I can't say I've made very much progress.'

'I'm glad you called, anyway. Are you getting anywhere at all?'

'Maybe. Did your husband ever say anything to you about writing a book?'

'Me write a book? I wouldn't know where to start. I used to write poetry. Not very good poetry, I'm afraid.'

'I meant did he say anything about the possibility of him writing a book.'

'Jerry? He doesn't *read* books, let alone *write* them. Why?'

'I'll tell you when I see you. I'm learning things. The question is whether or not they'll fit together into something significant. He didn't do it. I know that much.'

'You're more certain of it than you were yesterday.'

'Yes.' Pause. 'I've been thinking about you.'

'That's good. I think it's good. What sort of thoughts?'
'Curious ones.'
'Good curious or bad curious?'
'Oh, good, I guess.'
'I've been thinking, too.'

ELEVEN

I wound up spending the evening in the Village. I was oddly restless, possessed of an undirected energy that enervated me and kept me moving. It was a Friday night, and the better downtown bars were crowded and noisy as they always are on Fridays. I hit the Kettle and Minetta's and Whitey's and McBell's and the San Giorgio and the Lion's Head and the Riviera and other places the names of which I don't remember. But because I couldn't settle in anywhere I wound up having only one drink to a bar and walking off most of the effect of the alcohol between drinks. I kept moving and I kept drifting west, away from the tourist area and closer to where the Village rubs up against the Hudson River.

It must have been around midnight when I hit Sinthia's. It was fairly far west on Christopher Street, the last stop for gay cruisers on their way to meet the longshoremen and truckers in the shadow of the docks. Gay bars do not threaten me, but neither are they places I habitually seek out. I sometimes dropped in to Sinthias's when I was in the neighborhood because I know the owner fairly well. Fifteen years back I'd had to arrest him for contributing to the delinquency of a minor. The minor in question had been seventeen and jaded, and I'd only made the collar because I'd had no choice – the boy's father had lodged a formal complaint. Kenny's lawyer had a quiet talk with the boy's father and gave him an idea what he would bring out in open court, and that was the end of that.

Over the years Kenny and I had developed a relationship somewhere in the uncertain ground between acquaintance and friendship. He was behind the bar when I walked in, and as always he looked a young twenty-eight years old. His real age must be just about double that, and you have to stand very close to him to spot the face-lift scars. And the carefully combed hair is all Kenny's own, even if the blond color is a gift from a lady named Clairol.

He had around fifteen customers. Seeing them one at a time you'd have no cause to suspect they were gay, but collectively their homosexuality became unmistakable, almost a presence in the long narrow room. Perhaps it was their reaction to my intrusion that was palpable. People who spend their lives in any sort of half-world can always recognize a cop, and I still haven't learned how to avoid looking like one.

'Sir Matthew of Scudder,' Kenny sang out. 'Welcome, welcome as always. The trade around here is rarely quite so rough as your estimable self. Still bourbon, darling? Still heat?'

'Fine, Kenny.'

'I'm glad to see nothing changes. You are a constant in a madcap world.'

I took a seat at the bar. The other drinkers had relaxed when Kenny hailed me, which may well be what he'd had in mind in making such a production out of it. He poured quite a lot of bourbon into a glass and set it on the bar in front of me. I drank some of it. Kenny leaned toward me, propping himself up on his elbows. His face was deeply tanned. He spends his summers on Fire Island and uses a sunlamp the rest of the year.

'Working, sweets?'

'Yes, as a matter of fact.'

He sighed. 'It happens to the best of us. I've been back in harness since Labor Day and I'm still not used to it. Such a joy lying in the sun all summer and leaving this place for Alfred to mismanage. You know Alfred?'

'No.'

'I'm certain he stole me blind and I don't even care. I only kept the place open to accommodate my trade. Not out of the goodness of my heart, but because I don't want these girls to find out there are other establishments in the city that sell liquor. So as long as I covered my overhead I was blissfully happy. And then I wound up showing a slight profit, which was nothing but gravy.' He winked, then scuttled the length of the bar to replenish some drinks and collect some money. Then he returned and posed once again with his chin cupped in his two hands.

He said, 'Bet I know what you're up to.'

'Bet you don't.'

'For a drink? You're on. Let me see now – its initials wouldn't just happen to be J. B. by any chance, would it? And I don't mean

357

the Jim Beam you're drinking. J. B. and his good friend P.C.?'
His eyebrows ascended dramatically. 'Heavens, why is your poor
jaw plummeting halfway to the dusty floor, Matthew? Isn't that
what drew you to this den of ubiquity in the first place?'

I shook my head.

'Really?'

'I just happened to be in the neighborhood.'

'That's quite remarkable.'

'I know he was living just a few blocks from here, but why does
that tie him to this place, Kenny? There are dozens of bars as
close to his apartment on Barrow. Were you just guessing that I
was on his case, or did you hear something?'

'I don't know if you'd call it a guess. More an assumption. He
used to drink here.'

'Broadfield?'

'The very same. Not all that often, but every once in a while.
No, he's not gay, Matthew. Or if he is, *I* don't know it, and I don't
think he does, either. He's certainly given no evidence of it here,
and God knows he wouldn't have had any trouble finding
someone who would have been thrilled to take him home. He's
absolutely gorgeous.'

'Not your type though, is he?'

'Not *my* type at all. I like dirty little boys myself. As you well
know.'

'As I well know.'

'As everybody well knows, sweetheart.' Someone tapped a
glass on the bar for service. 'Oh, keep it in your pants, Mary,'
Kenny told him, in a mock British accent. 'I'm just having a spot
of chat with a gent from the Yard.' To me he said, 'Speaking of
Limey accents, he brought *her* here, you know. Or didn't you
know? Well, you do now. Another drink? You already owe me for
two doubles – the one you drank and the one you lost in the bet.
Let's make it three.' He poured a generous double, set the bottle
down. 'So naturally I guessed why you were here. This is not,
after all, your normal watering hole. And they had been here both
separately and together, and now she's dead and he's in the hotel
with the bars on the windows, and the conclusion seemed
inescapable. M. S. wants to know about J. B. and P. C.'

'The last part is certainly true.'

'Then ask questions of me.'

'He came here first by himself?'

'For the longest time he came here *only* by himself. I'd say he first showed up perhaps a year and a half ago. I would see him a couple of times a month, and always alone. Of course I didn't know anything about him at the time. He looked like law, but at the same time he didn't. Do you know what I mean? Maybe it was his clothes. No offense, but he dressed terribly well.'

'Why should I be offended?' He shrugged and moved off to tend to business. While he was gone I tried to figure out why Broadfield would patronize Sinthia's. The only way it made much sense was that there had been times when he wanted to get out of his apartment but didn't want to run into anybody he knew. A gay bar would have suited his needs perfectly.

When Kenny came back I said, 'You mentioned he showed up here with Portia Carr. When?'

'I can't be positive. He could have brought her here during the summer and I wouldn't have known about it. The first time I saw them together was – three weeks ago? It's hard for me to fix events temporally when I had no idea at the time that they would turn out to be important.'

'Was it before or after you knew who he was?'

'Ah, clever, clever! It was *after* I knew who he was, so three weeks is probably about right because I became familiar with his name when he first made contact with that investigator, and then I saw his photo in the newspaper, and then he turned up with the Amazon.'

'How many times were they here together?'

'At least twice. Maybe three times. That was all within the space of a week. May I replenish that drink for you?' I shook my head. 'Then I didn't see the two of them again, but I did see her.'

'Alone?'

'Briefly. She came in, sat at a table, ordered a drink.'

'When was this?'

'What's today, Friday? This would have been Tuesday night.'

'And she was killed Wednesday night.'

'Well, don't look at *me*, lover. *I* didn't do it.'

'I'll take your word for it.' I remembered the dimes I had dropped into various phones Tuesday night, calling Portia Carr's number and getting her answering machine. And she had been here then.

'Why did she come here, Kenny?'

'To meet someone.'

'Broadfield?'

'That's what I assumed, but the man who ultimately met her

was a far cry indeed from Broadfield. It was hard to believe they were both members of the same species.'

'And he was the one she was waiting for?'

'Oh, absolutely. He walked in looking for her, and she had been looking up every time the door opened.' He scratched his head for a moment. 'I don't know if she knew him or not. By sight, I mean. I have a vague feeling that she didn't, but I'm just guessing. This wasn't long ago, Matt, but I didn't really pay too much attention.'

'How long were they together?'

'They were together here for perhaps half an hour. Maybe a little longer than that. Then they left together, so they may have spent hours on end in one another's company. They didn't see fit to take me into their confidence.'

'And you don't know who the guy was.'

'Never saw him before or since.'

'What did he look like, Kenny?'

'Well, he didn't look like much, I'll tell you that. But you want a description rather than a critique, I would suppose. Let me just think.' He closed his eyes, drummed his fingers on the bartop. Without opening his eyes he said, 'A small person, Matt. Short, slender. Hollow cheeks. A great deal of forehead and an appalling absence of chin. Wore a rather tentative beard to conceal the lack of chin. No mustache. Heavy horn-rimmed glasses, so I didn't see his eyes and couldn't really swear that he had any, although I would guess that he did, as most people generally do. A left one and a right one, conventionally, although now and then – is something wrong?'

'Nothing's wrong, Ken.'

'Do you know him?'

'Yeah. I know him.'

I left Kenny's shortly after that. Then there's a stretch of time I don't remember clearly. I probably hit a bar or two. Eventually I found myself in the vestibule of Jerry Broadfield's building on Barrow Street.

I don't know what led me there or why I thought I ought to be there. But it must have made some sort of sense to me at the time.

A strip of celluloid popped the inner lock, and did the same job on the door to his apartment. Once inside his apartment, I locked the door and went around turning on lights, making myself at home. I found the bottle of bourbon and poured myself a drink, got a beer from the refrigerator for a chaser. I sat sipping bourbon and chasing it with beer. After a little while I turned on the radio and found a station that played unobtrusive music.

After some more bourbon and some more beer I took off my suit and hung it neatly in his closet. I got out of the rest of my clothes and found a pair of his pajamas in the bureau drawer. I put them on. I had to turn up the trouser bottoms because they were a little long on me. Aside from that they weren't a bad fit. A little loose, but not a bad fit.

Sometime just before I went to bed I picked up the telephone and dialed a number. I hadn't dialed it in a few days, but I still remembered it.

A deep voice with an English accent. 'Seven-two-five-five. I am sorry, but no one is at home at the moment. If you will leave your name and number at the sound of the tone, your call will be returned as soon as possible. Thank you.'

A gradual process, death. Someone had stabbed her to death forty-eight hours ago in this very apartment, but her voice still answered her telephone.

I called two more times just to hear her voice. I didn't leave any messages. Then I had another can of beer and the rest of the bourbon and crawled into his bed and slept.

TWELVE

I woke up confused and disoriented, chasing the traces of a formless dream. For a moment I stood beside his bed in his pajamas and did not know where I was. Then memory flooded back, fully and completely. I took a quick shower, dried off, put my own clothes back on again. I had a can of beer for breakfast and got out of there, walking out into bright sunlight and feeling like a thief in the night.

I wanted to get moving right away. But I made myself have a big breakfast of eggs and bacon and toast and coffee at Jimmy Day's on Sheridan Square and drank a lot of coffee with it and then took the subway uptown.

There was a message waiting for me at my hotel, along with a lot of junk mail that went straight into the wastebasket. The message was from Seldon Wolk, who wanted me to call him at my convenience. I decided it was as convenient as it would ever be, and I called him from the hotel lobby.

His secretary put me through right away. He said, 'I saw my client this morning, Mr Scudder. He wrote out something for me to read to you. May I?'

'Go ahead.'

'"Matt – Don't know anything about Manch in connection with Portia. Is he a mayoral assistant? She had a few politicians in her book but wouldn't tell me who. I am not holding out on you anymore. I held out about Fuhrmann and our plans because I didn't see how it mattered and I like to keep things to myself. Forget all that. Thing to concentrate on is two cops who arrested me. How did they know to come to my apartment? Who tipped them? Work that angle."'

'That's all?'

'That's it, Mr Scudder. I feel like a messenger service, relaying questions and answers without understanding them. They might as well be in code. I trust the message makes some sense to you?'

'Some. How did Broadfield seem to you? Is he in good spirits?'

'Oh, very much so. Quite confident he'll be acquitted. I think his optimism is justified.' And he had a lot to say about various legal maneuvers that would keep Broadfield out of jail, or get his conviction reversed on appeal. I didn't bother listening, and when he slowed down a little I thanked him and said good-bye.

I stopped at the Red Flame for coffee and thought about Broadfield's message. His suggestion was all wrong, and after thinking about it for a while I realized why.

He was thinking like a cop. That was understandable – he had spent years learning to think like a cop, and it was hard to reorient yourself immediately. I still thought like a cop a lot of the time myself, and I'd had a few years to unlearn old habits. From a cop's point of view, it made very good sense to tackle the problem the way Broadfield wanted to. You stayed with hard data and you worked backward, tracking down every possible avenue of approach until you found out who had called in the homicide report. The odds were that the caller was also the murderer. If not, he'd probably seen something.

And if he hadn't, somebody else had. Someone may have seen Portia Carr enter the Barrow Street building on the night of her death. She hadn't entered it alone. Someone had seen her walk in arm in arm with the person who subsequently killed her.

And that was the kind of thing a cop could have run down. The police department had two things that made that sort of investigation work for them – the manpower and the authority. And you needed both to bring it off. One man working alone was not going to get anywhere. One man, with not even a junior G-man badge to convince people they ought to talk to him, would not even begin to accomplish anything that way.

Especially when the police would not even cooperate with him in the first place. Especially when they were opposed to any investigation that might get Broadfield out of the hot seat.

So my approach had to be a very different one, and one that no policeman could be expected to approve. I had to find out who had killed her, and then I had to find the facts that might back up what I'd already doped out.

But first I had to find somebody.

A small person, Kenny had said. Short, slender. Hollow cheeks. A great deal of forehead and an appalling absence of chin. A tentative beard. No mustache. Heavy horn-rimmed glasses ...

I dropped by Armstrong's first to check. He wasn't there and hadn't been in yet that morning. I thought about having a drink but decided I could tackle Douglas Fuhrmann without one.

Except that I didn't get the chance. I went to his rooming house and rang the bell, and the same slatternly woman answered it. She may have been wearing the same robe and slippers. Once again she told me she was full up and suggested I try three doors down the street.

'Doug Fuhrmann,' I said.

Her eyes took the trouble to focus on my face. 'Fourth floor front,' she said. She frowned a little. 'You were here before. Looking for him.'

'That's right.'

'Yeah, I thought I seen you before.' She rubbed her forefinger across her nose, wiped it on her robe. 'I don't know if he's in or not. You want to knock on his door, go ahead.'

'All right.'

'Don't mess with his door, though. He's got this burglar alarm set up, makes all kinds of noise. I can't even go in there to clean for him. He does his own cleaning, imagine that.'

'He's probably been with you longer than most.'

'Listen, he's been here longer than me. I been working here what? A year? Two years?' If she didn't know, I couldn't help her out. 'He's been here years and years.'

'I guess you know him pretty well.'

'Don't know him at all. Don't know any of 'em. I got no time to get to know people, mister. I got problems of my own, you can believe it.'

I believed it, but that didn't make me want to know what they were. She evidently wasn't going to be able to tell me anything about Fuhrmann, and I wasn't interested in whatever else she might tell me. I moved past her and climbed the stairs.

He wasn't in. I tried the knob, and the door was locked. It probably would have been easy enough to slip the bolt, but I didn't want to set the alarm off. I wonder if I would have remembered it if the old woman hadn't reminded me.

I wrote a note to the effect that it was important he get in touch with me immediately. I signed my name, added my telephone number, slipped the piece of paper under his door. Then I went downstairs and let myself out.

There was a Leon Manch listed in the Brooklyn book. The

address was on Pierrepont Street, which would put him in Brooklyn Heights. I decided that was as good a place as any for a toilet slave to live. I dialed his number, and the phone rang a dozen times before I gave up.

I tried Prejanian's office. No one answered. Even crusaders only work a five-day week. I tried City Hall, wondering if Manch might have gone to the office. At least there was someone around there to answer the phone, even if there wasn't anyone present named Leon Manch.

The phone book had Abner Prejanian listed at 444 Central Park West. I had his number halfdialed when it struck me as pointless. He didn't know me from Adam and would hardly be inclined to cooperate with a total stranger over the telephone. I broke the connection, retrieved my dime, and looked up Claude Lorbeer. There was only one Lorbeer in Manhattan, a J. Lorbeer on West End Avenue. I tried the number, and when a woman answered I asked for Claude. When he came to the phone I asked him if he had had any contact with a man named Douglas Fuhrmann.

'I don't believe I've heard the name. In what context?'

'He's an associate of Broadfield's.'

'A policeman? I don't believe I've heard the name.'

'Maybe your boss did. I was going to call him, but he doesn't know me.'

'Oh, I'm glad you called me instead. I could call Mr Prejanian and ask him for you, and then I could get back to you. Anything else you'd want me to ask him?'

'Find out if the name Leon Manch rings any kind of a bell with him. In connection with Broadfield, that is.'

'Certainly. And I'll get right back to you, Mr Scudder.'

He rang back within five minutes. 'I just spoke to Mr Prejanian. Neither of the names you mentioned were familiar to him. Uh, Mr Scudder? I'd avoid any direct confrontation with Mr Prejanian if I were you.'

'Oh?'

'He wasn't precisely thrilled that I was co-operating with you. He didn't say so right out, but I think you understand what I'm getting at. He'd prefer that his staff pursue a policy of benign neglect, if I can revive that phrase. Of course you'll keep it between us that I said as much, won't you?'

'Of course.'

'You still remain convinced that Broadfield is innocent?'

'More now than ever.'

'And this man Fuhrmann holds the key?'

'He might. Things are starting to come together.'

'It sounds fascinating,' he said. 'Well, I won't keep you. If there's anything I can do, just give me a ring, but do let's keep it confidential, shall we?'

A little later I called Diana. We arranged to meet at eight-thirty at a French restaurant on Ninth Avenue, the Brittany du Soir. It is a quiet and private place where we would have a chance to be quiet and private people.

'I'll see you at eight-thirty then,' she said. 'Have you been making any headway? Oh, you can tell me when you see me.'

'Right.'

'I've done so much thinking, Matthew. I wonder if you know what it's like. I've spent so much time *not* thinking, almost willing myself not to think, and it's as though something has been unleashed. I shouldn't say all this. I'll just frighten you.'

'Don't worry about it.'

'That's what's strange. I'm not worried. Wouldn't you say that was strange?'

On my way back to the hotel I stopped at Fuhrmann's building. The manager didn't answer my ring. I guess she was busy with some of the problems she'd alluded to. I let myself in and climbed the stairs. He wasn't in and evidently hadn't been in – I could see the note I'd left him under his door.

I wished I'd taken down his phone number. Assuming he had a phone – I hadn't seen one on my visit, but his desk had been cluttered. He could have had a phone under one of those piles of paper.

I went home again, showered, shaved, straightened up the room. The maid had given it a cursory cleaning, and there wasn't much more I could do. It would always look like what it was, a small room in an unprepossessing hotel. Fuhrmann had chosen to transform his furnished room into an extension of himself. I had left mine as I found it. Initially I had found its stark simplicity somehow fitting. Now I had long since ceased to notice it, and only the prospect of entertaining a guest within it made me aware of its appearance.

I checked the liquor supply. There looked to be enough for me, and I didn't know what she preferred to drink. The store across the street would deliver until eleven.

Put on my best suit. Dabbed on a little cologne. The boys had given it to me for a Christmas present. I wasn't even sure which Christmas and couldn't remember when I'd used it last. Dabbed some on and felt ridiculous, but in a way that was not unpleasant.

Stopped at Armstrong's. Fuhrmann had been in and out an hour or so earlier. I left him a note. Called Manch, and this time he answered the phone.

I said, 'Mr Manch, my name is Matthew Scudder. I'm a friend of Portia Carr's.'

There was a pause, a long enough one to make his reply unconvincing. 'I'm afraid I don't know anyone by that name.'

'I'm sure you do. You don't want to try that stance, Mr Manch. It's not going to work.'

'What do you want?'

'I want to see you. Sometime tomorrow.'

'What about?'

'I'll tell you when I see you.'

'I don't understand. What did you say your name was?'

I told him.

'Well, I don't understand, Mr Scudder. I don't know what you want from me.'

'I'll be at your place tomorrow afternoon.'

'I don't –'

'Tomorrow afternoon,' I said. 'Around three. It would be a very good idea for you to be there.'

He started to say something, but I didn't stay on the line long enough to hear it. It was a few minutes past eight. I went outside and walked down Ninth toward the restaurant.

THIRTEEN

We sat in a booth. She wore a simple black sheath and no jewelry. Her perfume was a floral scent with an undertone of spice. I ordered dry vermouth on the rocks for her and bourbon for myself. The conversation stayed light and airy through the first round of drinks. When we ordered a second round we also gave the waitress the dinner order – sweetbreads for her, a steak for me. The drinks came, and we touched glasses again, and our eyes met and led us into a silence that was just the slightest bit awkward.

She broke it. She extended her hand and I took it, and she lowered her eyes and said, 'I'm not terribly good at this. Out of practice, I guess.'

'So am I.'

'You've had a few years to get used to being a bachelor. I've had one little affair, and it wasn't really very much of anything. He was married.'

'You don't have to talk about it.'

'Oh, I know that. He was married, it was very casual and purely physical, and to be honest it wasn't even that wonderful physically. And it didn't last very long.' She hesitated. She may have been waiting for me to say something, but I remained silent. Then she said, 'You may want this to be, oh, casual, and that's all right, Matthew.'

'I don't think we can be casual with each other.'

'No, I don't suppose we can. I wish – I don't know what I wish.' She lifted her glass and sipped. 'I'm probably going to get a little bit drunk tonight. Is that a bad idea?'

'It might be a good idea. Shall we have wine with the meal?'

'I'd like that. I suppose it's a bad sign, having to get a little drunk.'

'Well, I'm the last person to tell you it's a bad idea. I get a little bit drunk every day of my life.'

'Is that something I should be worried about?'

'I don't know. It's damned well something you should be aware of, Diana. You ought to know who you're getting involved with.'

'Are you an alcoholic?'

'Well, what's an alcoholic? I suppose I drink enough alcohol to qualify. It doesn't keep me from functioning. Yet. I suppose it will eventually.'

'Could you stop drinking? Or cut down?'

'Probably. If I had a reason.'

The waitress brought our appetizers. I ordered a carafe of red wine. Diana impaled a mussel with a little fork, paused with it halfway to her mouth. 'Maybe we shouldn't talk about this yet.'

'Maybe not.'

'I think we feel the same about most things. I think what we want is the same, and I think our fears are the same.'

'Or pretty close, at least.'

'Yes. Maybe you're no bargain, Matthew. I think that's what you've been trying to tell me. I'm no bargain myself. I don't drink, but I might as well. I just found a different way to retire from the human race. I gave up being me. I feel –'

'Yes?'

'As if I've got a second chance. As if I had that chance all along, but you only have it when you know you have it. And I don't know if you're a part of that chance or if you just made me aware of it.' She put her fork on her plate, the mussel still gripped by the tines. 'Oh, I'm enormously confused. All the magazines tell me I'm just the right age for an identity crisis. Is that what this is or am I falling in love and how do you tell the difference? Do you have a cigarette?'

'I'll get some. What brand do you smoke?'

'I don't smoke. Oh, any brand. Winstons, I guess.'

I got a pack from the machine. I opened it, gave her a cigarette, took one for myself. I struck a match and her fingers fastened around my wrist as she got her cigarette going. The tips of her fingers were very cool.

She said, 'I have three young children. I have a husband in jail.'

'And you're taking up drinking and smoking. You're a mess, all right.'

'And you're a sweet man. Have I told you that before? It's still true.'

I saw to it that she had most of the wine with dinner. Afterward she had a pot of espresso and a little snifter of brandy. I went back to coffee and bourbon. We did a lot of talking and shared a lot of long silences. These last were as communicative in their own way as our conversations.

It was close to midnight when I settled the tab. They were anxious to close, but our waitress had been very decent about letting us alone. I showed my appreciation of her forbearance with a tip that was probably excessive. I didn't care. I loved the whole world.

We went out and stood on Ninth Avenue drinking the cold air. She discovered the moon and shared it with me. 'It's almost full. Isn't it beautiful?'

'Yes.'

'Sometimes I think I can almost feel the pull of the moon. Silly, isn't it?'

'I don't know. The sea feels it. That's why there are tides. And there's no denying that the moon influences human behavior. All cops know that. The crime rate changes with the moon.'

'Honest?'

'Uh-huh. Especially the weird crimes. The full moon makes people do odd things.'

'Like what?'

'Like kissing in public.'

A little later she said, 'Well, I don't know that that's odd. I think it's nice, actually.'

At Armstrong's I ordered coffee and bourbon for both of us. 'Because I like the feeling I'm getting Matthew, but I don't want to get sleepy. And I liked the way it tasted the other day.'

When she brought the drinks, Trina handed me a slip of paper. 'He was in about an hour ago,' she said. 'Before then he called a couple of times. He's very anxious for you to get in touch with him.'

'I unfolded the slip of paper. Doug Fuhrmann's name and a telephone number.

I said, 'Thanks. It's nothing that can't wait until morning.'

'He said it was urgent.'

'Well, that's one man's opinion.' Diana and I poured our bourbon into our coffee, and she asked me what it was about. 'A guy who's been close to your husband,' I said. 'He was also getting close to the girl who was murdered. I think I know why, but I want to talk to him about it.'

'Do you want to call him? Or see him for a while? Don't pass him up on my account, Matthew.'

'He can wait.'

'If you think it's important –'

'It's not. He can wait until tomorrow.'

Evidently Fuhrmann didn't think so. A little later the phone rang. Trina answered it and made her way to our table. 'Same caller,' she said. 'Do you want to talk to him?'

I shook my head. 'I was in,' I said. 'I got his message and said something about calling him in the morning. And then I had a drink and left.'

'Gotcha.'

Ten or twenty minutes later we did leave. Esteban was swinging the midnight-to-eight shift at the desk of my hotel. He gave me three messages, all of them from Fuhrmann.

'No calls,' I told him. 'No matter who. I'm not in.'

'Right.'

'If the phone rings I'll figure the building's on fire because otherwise I don't want any calls.'

'I understand.'

We rode up in the elevator, walked down the hallway to my door. I opened it and stood aside to let her in. With her at my side the little room looked starker and more barren than ever.

'I thought of other places we could go,' I told her. 'A better hotel or a friend's apartment, but I decided that I wanted you to see where I live.'

'I'm glad, Matthew.'

'Is it all right?'

'Of course it's all right.'

We kissed. We held each other for a long time. I smelled her perfume and tasted the sweetness of her mouth. After a time I released her. She moved slowly and deliberately around my room, examining things, getting a sense of the place. Then she turned to me and smiled a very gentle smile, and we began undressing.

FOURTEEN

All through the night one of us would wake and awaken the other. Then I woke up for the last time and found I was alone. Pale sunlight filtered by bad air gave the room a golden cast. I got out of bed and picked my watch up from the bedside table. It was almost noon.

I had almost finished dressing when I found her note. It was wedged between the glass and the frame of the mirror over my dresser. Her handwriting was very neat and quite small.

I read:

Darling –
What is it that the children say? Last night was the first night of the rest of my life. I have so much to say, but I am in no condition to express my thoughts well.
Please call me. And call me, please,

Your Lady

I read it through a couple of times. Then I folded it carefully and tucked it into my wallet.

There was a single message in my box. Fuhrmann had called a final time around one-thirty. Then he had evidently given up and gone to sleep. I called him from the lobby and got a busy signal. I went out and had some breakfast. The air, which had looked to be polluted from my window, tasted clean enough on the street. Maybe it was my mood. I hadn't felt this well in a long time.

I got up from the table again and called Fuhrmann again after my second cup of coffee. The line was still busy. I went back and had a third cup and smoked one of the cigarettes I had bought for Diana. She had had three or four the previous night, and I had smoked one each time she did. I burned up about half of this one, left the pack on the table, tried Fuhrmann a third time, paid my check, and walked over to Armstrong's just to check if he was there or had been in yet. He wasn't and hadn't.

Something hovered on the edge of consciousness, whining plaintively at me. I used the pay phone at Armstrong's to call him again. The same busy signal, and it sounded different to me from the usual sort of busy signal. I called the operator and told her I wanted to know if a certain number was engaged or if the telephone was simply off the hook. I got a girl who evidently didn't speak much English and wasn't sure how to perform the task I'd asked of her. She offered to put me in touch with her supervisor, but I was only half a dozen blocks from Fuhrmann's place, so I told her not to bother.

I was quite calm when I set out for his place and extremely anxious by the time I got there. Maybe I was picking up signals and they were coming in stronger as the distance decreased. But for one reason or another I didn't ring the bell in his vestibule. I looked inside and saw no one around, and then I used my piece of celluloid to slip the lock.

I climbed the stairs to the top floor without running into anyone. The building was absolutely silent. I went to Fuhrmann's door and knocked on it, called his name, knocked again.

Nothing.

I took out my strip of celluloid and looked at it and at the door. I thought about the burglar alarm. If it was going to go off I wanted to have the door open by the time it began to make noises so I could get the hell out of there. Which ruled out slipping the bolt back. Subtlety has its uses, but sometimes brute force is called for.

I kicked the door in. It only took one kick because the dead bolt had not been set. You need the key to set the dead bolt, just as you need a key to set the alarm, and the person who had last left Fuhrmann's apartment had not had those keys or had not troubled to use them. So the alarm did not go off, which was all to the good, but that was all the good news I was going to get.

The bad news was waiting for me inside, but I'd known what it would be from the instant the alarm had failed to sound. In a sense I'd known before I even reached the building but that was instinctive knowledge, and when the alarm stayed quiet it became deductive knowledge, and now that I could see him it was just cold, hard fact.

He was dead. He was lying on the floor in front of his desk, and it looked as though he had been leaning over his desk when his killer took him. I didn't have to touch him to know he was dead. The left rear portion of his skull was pulped, and the room itself reeked of death. Dead colons and bladders divest themselves of their contents. Corpses, before the working of the undertaker's art, smell as foul as the death that grips them.

I touched him anyway to guess how long he'd been dead. But his flesh was cold, so I could only know that he'd been dead a minimum of five or six hours. I'd never bothered to pick up much knowledge of forensic medicine. The lab boys handle that area, and they're reasonably good at it, if not half so good as they like to pretend.

I went over to the door and closed it. The lock was useless, but there was a plate for a police lock on the floor, and I found the steel bar and set it in place. I didn't intend to stay long but wanted no interruptions while I was there.

The phone was off the hook. There were no other signs of a struggle, so I assumed the killer had taken the phone off the hook to retard discovery of the body. If he was that cute, there weren't going to be any prints around, but I still took the trouble not to add any of my own or smear any that he might inadvertently have made.

When had he been killed? The bed was unmade, but perhaps he didn't make it every day. Men who live alone often don't. Had it been made up when I'd visited him? I thought about it and decided I couldn't be certain one way or the other. I recalled an impression of neatness and precision, which suggested it had indeed been made up, but there was also an impression of comfort, which would mesh well enough with an unmade bed. The more I thought about it, the more I decided it didn't make any difference one way or the other. The medical examiner would fix the time of death, and I was in no rush to know what I would learn from him soon enough.

So I sat on the edge of the bed and looked at Doug Fuhrmann and tried to remember the precise sound of his voice and the way his face had looked.

He had tried to reach me. Over and over again, and I wouldn't take his calls. Because I was a little peeved with him for holding out on me. Because I was with a woman who was using up all my attention, and that was such a novel experience for me that I hadn't wanted it diluted even for a moment.

And if I'd taken his call? Well, he might have told me something that he would never tell me now. But it was more likely that he would only confirm what I had already guessed about his relationship with Portia Carr.

If I'd taken his call, would he be alive now?

I could have wasted the whole day sitting on his bed and asking myself that sort of question. And whatever its answer, I had already wasted enough time.

I unlocked the police lock, opened the door a crack. The hallway was empty. I let myself out of Fuhrmann's room and went down the stairs and out of the building without encountering anyone at all.

Midtown North – it used to be the Eighteenth Precinct – is on West Fifty-fourth just a few blocks from where I was. I rang them from a booth in a saloon called the Second Chance. There were two wine drinkers at the bar and what looked to be a third wino behind it. When the phone was answered I gave Fuhrmann's address and said that a man had been murdered there. I replaced the receiver while the duty officer was patiently asking me my name.

I was in too much of a hurry to take a cab. The subway was faster. I rode it to the Clark Street station just over the bridge in Brooklyn. I had to ask directions to get to Pierrepont Street.

The block was mostly brownstones. The building where Leon Manch lived was fourteen stories tall, a giant among its fellows. The doorman was a stocky black with three deep horizontal lines running across his forehead.

'Leon Manch,' I said.

He shook his head. I reached for my notebook, checked his address, looked up at the doorman.

'You have the right address,' he said. His accent was West Indian, and the *a*'s came out very broad. 'You come the wrong day is all the problem.'

'I'm expected.'

'Mr Manch, he is not here no more.'

'He moved out?' It seemed impossible.

'He doan' want to wait for the elevator,' he said. 'So he take a shortcut.'

'What are you talking about?'

The jive, I decided later, was not flippancy; it was an attempt to speak around the edges of the unspeakable. Now, abandoning that tack, he said, 'He jump out the window. Land right there.'

He pointed to a portion of the sidewalk that looked no different from the rest. 'He land there,' he repeated.

'When?'

'Las' night.' He touched his forehead, then made a sign similar to genuflection. I don't know whether it was a personal ritual or part of a religion with which I was unfamiliar. 'Armand was working then. If I am working and man jump out window, I doan' know what I do.'

'Was he killed?'

He looked at me. 'What you think, man? Mr Manch, he lives on fourteen. What you think?'

The nearest precinct house, and the one that figured to have the case, was on Joralemon near Borough Hall. I got lucky there – I recognized a cop named Kinsella whom I'd worked with some years back. And I was lucky a second time because he evidently hadn't heard I'd gone to work for Jerry Broadfield, so he had no reason not to cooperate with me.

'Happened last night,' he said. 'I wasn't on when it happened, but it looks to be pretty clear cut, Matt.' He shuffled some papers, set them down on the desk. 'Manch lived alone. I suppose he was a fruit. A guy living alone in that neighborhood, you can draw your own conclusions. Nine out of ten he's gay.'

And one out of ten he's a toilet slave.

'Let's see now. Went out the window, did a header, dead on arrival at Adelphi Hospital. Identification based on contents of pockets and clothing labels plus which window was open.'

'No identification by next of kin?'

'Not that I know of. Nothing listed here. Any question that it's him? If you want to go take a look at him it's your business, but he landed headfirst, so –'

'I never saw him, anyway. He was alone when he went out the window?' Kinsella nodded. 'Any eyewitnesses?'

'No. But he left a note. It was in a typewriter on his desk.'

'Was the note typewritten?'

'It doesn't say.'

'I don't suppose I could have a look at the note?'

'Not a chance, Matt. I don't have access to it myself. You want to talk to the officer in charge, that's Lew Marko, he'll be coming on duty sometime tonight. Maybe he can help you out.'

'I don't suppose it matters.'

'Wait a minute, the wording's copied down here. This help you at all?'

I read:

Forgive me. I cannot go on this way. I have lived a bad life.

Nothing about murder.

Could he have done it? A lot depended on when Fuhrmann was killed, and I wouldn't know that until I found out what the medical examiner learned. Say Manch killed Fuhrmann, came home, was overtaken by remorse, opened his window –

I didn't like it much.

I said, 'What time did he do it, Jim? I don't see it listed.'

He looked through the records, frowning. 'There ought to be a time here. I don't see it. He was DOA at Adelphi at eleven thirty-five last night, but that don't tell us what time he went out the window.'

But then again it didn't really have to. Doug Fuhrmann made his final call to me at one-thirty, an hour and fifty-five minutes after a physician pronounced Leon Manch dead.

I liked it better that way the more I thought about it. Because everything was starting to fall into place for me, and the way it was breaking Manch wasn't Fuhrmann's killer or Portia Carr's killer, either. Maybe Manch was Manch's killer, maybe he'd typed a suicide note because he couldn't find a pen, maybe his remorse was compounded of disgust with the life of a toilet slave. *I have lived a bad life* – well, who the hell has not?

For the time being, it didn't matter whether Manch had killed himself or not. Maybe he'd had help, but that was something I couldn't know yet and didn't have to know how to prove.

I knew who had killed the other two, Portia and Doug. I knew it in much the same way that I had known before reaching his building that Doug Fuhrmann would be dead. We call such knowledge the product of intuition because we cannot precisely chart the working of the mind. It goes on playing computer while our consciousness is directed elsewhere.

I knew the killer's name. I had some strong ideas about his motive. I had more ground to cover before it would all be wrapped up, but the hard part was over. Once you know what you're looking for, the rest comes easy.

FIFTEEN

It was another three or four hours before I got out of a cab in the West Seventies and gave my name to a doorman. It was not the first taxi I'd taken since I got back from Brooklyn. I had had to see several people. I'd been offered drinks but hadn't accepted any. I had had some coffee, including a couple of cups of the best coffee I'd ever had.

The doorman announced me, then steered me to the elevator. I rode upstairs to the sixth floor, found the appropriate door, knocked. The door was opened by a small, birdlike woman with blue-gray hair. I introduced myself and she gave me her hand. 'My son's watching the football game,' she said. 'Do you care for football? I don't find it of any real interest myself. Now you just have a seat and I'll tell Claude you're here.'

But it wasn't necessary to tell him. He was standing in an archway at the rear of the living room. He wore a sleeveless brown cardigan over a white shirt. He had bedroom slippers on his feet. The thumbs of his pudgy hands were hooked into his belt. He said, 'Good afternoon, Mr Scudder. Won't you come this way? Mom, Mr Scudder and I will be in the den.'

I followed him into a small room in which several overstuffed chairs were grouped around a color television set. On the large screen an oriental girl was bowing before a bottle of men's cologne.

'Cable,' Lorbeer said. 'Makes for absolutely perfect reception. And it only costs a couple of dollars a month. Before we signed up for it we just never got really satisfactory reception.'

'You've lived here a long time?'

'All my life. Well, not quite. We moved here when I was about two and a half years old. Of course my father was alive then. This was his room, his study.'

I looked around. There were English hunting prints on the walls, several racks of pipes, a few framed photographs. I walked over to the door and closed it. Lorbeer noted this without commenting.

I said, 'I spoke to your employer.'

'Mr Prejanian?'

'Yes. He was very pleased to hear that Jerry Broadfield will be released soon. He said he's not sure how much use he'll get out of Broadfield's testimony but that he's glad to see the man won't be convicted of a crime he didn't commit.'

'Mr Prejanian's a very generous man.'

'Is he?' I shrugged. 'I didn't get that impression myself, but I'm sure you know him better than I do. What I sensed was that he's glad to see Broadfield proved innocent because his own organization doesn't look so bad now. So he was hoping all along that Broadfield would turn out to be innocent.' I watched him carefully. 'He says he'd have been glad to know earlier that I was working for Broadfield.'

'Really.'

'Uh-huh. That's what he said.'

Lorbeer moved closer to the television set. He rested a hand on top of it and looked down at the back of his hand. 'I've been having hot chocolate,' he said. 'Sundays are days of complete regression for me. I sit around in comfy old clothes and watch sports on television and sip hot chocolate. I don't suppose you'd care for a cup?

'No, thank you.'

'A drink? Something stronger?'

'No.'

He turned to look at me. The pairs of parenthetical lines on either side of his little mouth seemed to be more deeply etched now. 'Of course I can't be expected to bother Mr Prejanian with every little thing that comes up. That's one of my functions, screening him from trivia. His time is very valuable, and there are already far too many demands on it.'

'That's why you didn't bother to call him yesterday. You told me you'd spoken with him, but you hadn't. And you warned me to route inquiries through you so as to avoid antagonizing Prejanian.'

'Just doing my job, Mr Scudder. It's possible I committed a judgmental error. No one is perfect, nor have I ever claimed perfection.'

I leaned over, turned off the television set. 'It's-a distraction,' I explained. 'We should both pay attention to this. You're a murderer, Claude, and I'm afraid you're not going to get away with it. Why don't you sit down?'

'That's a ridiculous accusation.'

'Have a seat.'

'I'm quite comfortable standing. You've just made a completely absurd charge. I don't understand it.'

I said, 'I suppose I should have thought about you right at the beginning. But there was a problem. Whoever killed Portia Carr had to connect up with Broadfield in one way or another. She was killed in his apartment, so she had to be killed by someone who knew where his apartment was, somebody who took the trouble to decoy him out of it first and send him off to Bay Ridge on a wild-goose chase.'

'You're assuming Broadfield is innocent. I still don't see any reason to be sure of that.'

'Oh, I knew he was innocent for a dozen reasons.'

'Even so, didn't the Carr woman know about Broadfield's apartment?'

I nodded. 'As a matter of fact, she did. But she couldn't have led her killer there because she was unconscious when she made the trip. She was hit on the head first and then stabbed. It stood to reason that she'd been hit elsewhere. Otherwise the killer would have just gone on hitting her until she was dead. He wouldn't have stopped to pick up a knife. But what you did, Claude, was knock her out somewhere else and then get her to Broadfield's apartment. By then you'd disposed of whatever you'd hit her with, so you finished the job with a knife.'

'I think I'll have a cup of chocolate. You're sure you wouldn't care for some?'

'Positive. I didn't want to believe a cop would kill Portia Carr in order to frame Broadfield. Everything pointed that way, but I didn't like the feel of it. I preferred the idea that framing Broadfield was a handy way to get away with murder, that the killer's main object was to get rid of Portia. But then how would he know about Broadfield's apartment and phone number? What I needed was somebody who was connected to both of them. And I found somebody, but there was no motive apparent.'

'You must mean me,' he said calmly. 'Since I certainly had no motive. But then I didn't know the Carr person either, and barely knew Broadfield, so your reasoning breaks down, doesn't it?'

'Not you. Douglas Fuhrmann. He was going to ghostwrite Broadfield's book. That's why Broadfield had turned informer –

380

he wanted to be somebody important and write a best-seller. He got the idea from Carr because she was going to go the Happy Hooker one better. Fuhrmann got the idea of playing both ends and got in touch with Carr to see if he could write her book, too. That's what tied the two of them together – it has to be – but it's not a murder motive.'

'Then why am I elected? Because you don't know of anyone else?'

I shook my head. 'I knew it was you before I really knew why. I asked you yesterday afternoon if you knew anything about Doug Fuhrmann. You knew enough about him to go over to his house last night and kill him.'

'This is remarkable. Now I'm being accused of the murder of a man I never heard of.'

'It won't work, Claude. Fuhrmann was a threat to you because he'd been talking with both of them, with Carr and with Broadfield. He was trying to reach me last night. If I'd had time to see him, maybe you wouldn't have been able to kill him. And maybe you would have, because maybe he didn't know what he knew. You were one of Portia Carr's clients.'

'That's a filthy lie.'

'Maybe it's filthy. I wouldn't know. I don't know what you did with her or what she did with you. I could make some educated guesses.'

'Damn you, you're an animal.' He didn't raise his voice, but the loathing in it was fierce. 'I will thank you not to talk like that in the same house with my mother.'

I just looked at him. He met my eyes with confidence at first, and then his face seemed to melt. All the resolve went out of it. His shoulders sagged, and he looked at once much older and much younger. Just a middle-aged little boy.

'Knox Hardesty knew,' I went on. 'So you killed Portia for nothing. I can pretty much figure out what happened, Claude. When Broadfield turned up at Prejanian's office, you learned about more than police corruption. You learned through Broadfield that Portia was in Knox Hardesty's pocket, feeding him her client list in order to escape deportation. You were on that list and you figured it was just a question of time before she handed you over to him.

'So you got Portia to press charges against Broadfield, accusing him of extortion. You wanted to give him a motive for killing her, and that was an easy one to arrange. She thought you were a cop when you called her, and it was easy enough for her to go along with it. One way or another, you managed to scare her pretty well. Whores are easy to scare.

'At this point you had Broadfield set up beautifully. You didn't even have to be particularly brilliant about the murder itself because the cops would be so anxious to tie it to Broadfield. You decoyed Portia to the Village at the same time that you sent Broadfield off to Brooklyn. Then you knocked her out, dragged her into his apartment, killed her, and got out of there. You dropped the knife in a sewer, washed your hands, and came on home to Mama.'

'Leave my mother out of this.'

'That bothers you, doesn't it? My mentioning your mother?'

'Yes, it does.' He was squeezing his hands together as if to control them. 'It bothers me a great deal. That's why you're doing it, I suppose.'

'Not entirely, Claude.' I drew a breath. 'You shouldn't have killed her. There was no point to it. Hardesty already knew about you. If he'd thrown your name into the open at the beginning, a lot of time would have been saved and Fuhrmann and Manch would still be alive. But –'

'Manch?'

'Leon Manch. It looked as though he might have killed Fuhrmann, but the timing was wrong. And then it looked as though you might have set it up, but you would have done it better. You would have killed them in the right order, wouldn't you? First Fuhrmann and then Manch, and not the other way around.'

'I don't know what you're talking about.'

And this time he evidently didn't, and the difference in is tone was obvious. 'Leon Manch was another name on Portia's client list. He was also Knox Hardesty's pipeline into the mayor's office. I called him yesterday afternoon and arranged to see him, and I guess he couldn't handle it. He jumped out a window last night.'

'He actually killed himself.'

'It looks that way.'

'He could have killed Portia Carr.' He said it not argumentatively but thoughtfully.

I nodded. 'He could have killed her, yes. But he couldn't have killed Fuhrmann because Fuhrmann made a couple of telephone calls after Manch had been officially pronounced dead. You see what that means, Claude?'

'What?'

'All you had to do was leave that little writer alone. You couldn't know it, but that was all you had to do. Manch left a note. He didn't confess to murder, but it could have been interpreted that way. I would certainly have interpreted it that way and I would have done everything possible to pin the Carr murder on Manch's dead body. If I managed it, Broadfield was clear. If not, he would stand trial himself. Either way, you would have been home free because I would have settled on Manch as the killer and the cops had already settled on Broadfield and that left nobody in the world hunting for you.'

He said nothing for a long time. Then he narrowed his eyes and said, 'You're trying to trap me.'

'You're already trapped.'

'She was an evil, filthy woman.'

'And you were the Lord's avenging angel.'

'No. Nothing of the sort. You are trying to trap me, and it won't work. You can't prove a thing.'

'I don't have to.'

'Oh?'

'I want you to come over to the police station with me, Claude. I want you to confess to the murders of Portia Carr and Douglas Fuhrmann.'

'You must be insane.'

'No.'

'Then you must think I'm insane. Why on earth would I do something like that? Even if I did commit murder –'

'To spare yourself, Claude.'

'I don't understand.'

I looked at my watch. It was still early, and I felt as though I'd been awake for months.

'You said I can't prove anything,' I told him. 'And I said you were right. But the police can prove it. Not now, but after they've spent some time digging. Knox Hardesty can establish that you were a client of Portia Carr's. He gave me the information once I was able to show him how it was bound up in murder, and he'll hardly hold it back in court. And you can bet that somebody saw you with Portia in the Village and somebody saw you on Ninth Avenue when you killed Fuhrmann. There's always a witness, and when the police and the district attorney's office are both putting in time, the witnesses tend to turn up.'

'Then let them turn up these people if they exist. Why should I confess to make things easier for them?'

'Because you'd be making things easier for yourself, Claude. So much easier.'

'That doesn't make sense.'

'If the police dig, they'll get everything, Claude. They'll find out why you were seeing Portia Carr. Right now nobody knows. Hardesty doesn't know, I don't know, no one does. But if they dig, they'll find out. And there will be insinuations in the newspapers, and people will suspect things, perhaps they'll suspect worse than the truth –'

'Stop it.'

'Everyone will know about it, Claude.' I inclined my head toward the closed door. 'Everyone,' I said.

'Damn you.'

'You could spare her that knowledge, Claude. Of course a confession might also get you a lighter sentence. It theoretically can't happen in Murder One, but you know how the game is played. It certainly wouldn't hurt your chances. But I think that's a secondary consideration as far as you're concerned, Claude. Isn't it? I think you'd like to save yourself some scandal. Am I right?'

He opened his mouth but closed it without speaking.

'You could keep your motive a secret, Claude. You could invent something. Or just refuse to explain. No one would pressure you, not if you'd already confessed to homicide. People close to you would know you had committed murder, but they wouldn't have to know other things about your life.'

He lifted his cup of chocolate to his lips. He sipped it, returned it to its saucer.

'Claude –'

'Just let me think for a moment, will you?'

'All right.'

I don't know how long we remained like that, me standing, him seated before the silent television set. Say five minutes. Then he sighed, scuffed off his slippers, reached to put on a pair of shoes. He tied them and got to his feet. I walked to the door and opened it and stood aside so he could precede me through it into the living room.

He said, 'Mother, I'll be going out for a little while. Mr Scudder needs my help. Something important has come up.'

'Oh, but your dinner, Claude. It's almost ready. Perhaps your friend would care to join us?'

I said, 'I'm afraid not, Mrs Lorbeer.'

'There's just no time, Mother,' Claude agreed. 'I'll have to have dinner out.'

'Well, if it can't be helped.'

He squared his shoulders, went to the front closet for a coat. 'Now wear your heavy overcoat,' she told him. 'It's turned quite cold outside. It is cold out, isn't it, Mr Scudder?'

'Yes,' I said. 'It's very cold out.'

SIXTEEN

My second trip to the Tombs was very different from my first. It was about the same hour of the day, around eleven in the morning, but this time I'd had a good, full night's sleep and very little to drink the night before. I'd seen him in a cell the first time. Now I was meeting him and his lawyer at the front desk. He had left all that tension and depression in his cell and he looked like the conquering hero.

He and Seldon Wolk were already on hand when I walked in. Broadfield's face lit up at the sight of me. 'There's my man,' he called out. 'Matt, baby, you're the greatest. Absolutely the greatest. If I did one intelligent thing in my life, it was getting hooked up with you.' And he was pumping my hand and beaming down at me. 'Didn't I tell you I was getting out of this toilet? And didn't you turn out to be the guy to spring me?' He inclined his head conspiratorially, lowered his voice to a near-whisper. 'And I'm a guy knows how to say thank you so you know I mean it. You got a bonus coming, buddy.'

'You paid me enough.'

'The hell I did. What's a man's life worth?'

I had asked myself the same question often enough, but not in quite the same way. I said, 'I made something like five hundred dollars a day. That'll do me, Broadfield.'

'Jerry.'

'Sure.'

'And I say you got a bonus coming. You met my lawyer? Seldon Wolk?'

'We've spoken,' I said. Wolk and I shook hands and made polite sounds at each other.

'Well, it's about that time,' Broadfield said. 'I guess any reporters who're gonna show up are already waiting out there, don't you think? If any of 'em miss out, it'll teach 'em to be on time next shot. Is Diana out there with the car?'

'She's waiting where you wanted her to wait,' the lawyer told him.

'Perfect. You met my wife, didn't you, Matt? Of course you did, I gave you that note to take out there. What we gotta do, you get a woman, and the four of us'll have dinner one of these nights. We ought to get to know each other better, all of us.'

'We'll have to do that,' I agreed.

'Well,' he said. He tore open a manila envelope and shook out its contents on the top of the desk. He put his wallet into his pocket, slipped his watch onto his wrist, scooped up and pocketed a handful of coins. Then he put his tie around his neck and under his shirt collar and made an elaborate performance of tying it. 'Did I tell you, Matt? Thought I might have to tie it twice. But I think the knot looks just about right, don't you?'

'It looks fine.'

He nodded. 'Yeah,' he said. 'I think it looks pretty good, all right. I'll tell you something. Matt, I *feel* good. How do I look, Seldon?'

'You look fine.'

'I feel like a million dollars,' he said.

He handled the reporters pretty nicely. He answered questions, striking a nice balance between sincere and cocky, and while they still had questions to ask him he flashed the number-one grin, gave a victorious wave, and pushed through them and got into his car. Diana stepped on the gas, and they drove down to the end of the block and turned the corner. I stood there watching until they were out of sight.

Of course she'd had to come to pick him up. And she would take it easy for a day or two, and then she'd let him know how things stood. She'd said she didn't expect much trouble from him. She was certain he didn't love her and that she had long since ceased to be important in his life. But I was to give her a couple of days, and then she would call.

'Well, that was pretty exciting,' a voice behind me said. 'I figured maybe we were supposed to throw rice at the happy couple, something like that.'

Without turning I said, 'Hello, Eddie.'

'Hello, Matt. Beautiful morning, isn't it?'

'Not bad.'

'I suppose you're feeling pretty good.'

'Not too bad.'

'Cigar?' Lieutenant Eddie Koehler didn't wait for an answer, put the cigar in his own mouth and lit it. It took him three matches because the wind blew out the first two. 'I oughta get a lighter,' he said. 'You check out that lighter Broadfield was using before? Looked expensive.'

'I think it probably is.'

'Looked like gold to me.'

'Probably. Though gold and gold plate look pretty much the same.'

'They don't cost the same, though. Do they?'

'Not as a general rule.'

He smiled, swung out a hand, and gripped my upper arm. 'Aw, you son of a bitch,' he said. 'Lemme buy you a drink, you old son of a bitch.'

'It's a little early for me, Eddie. Maybe a cup of coffee.'

'Even better. Since when is it ever too early to buy you a drink?'

'Oh, I don't know. Maybe I'll take it a little easier on the booze, see if it makes a difference.'

'Yeah?'

'Well, for a while, anyway.'

He eyed me appraisingly. 'You sound like your old self a little, you know that? I can't remember the last time you sounded like this.'

'Don't make too much out of it, Eddie. All I'm doing is passing up a drink.'

'No, there's something else. I can't put my finger on it, but something's different.'

We went over to a little place on Reade Street and ordered coffee and Danish. He said, 'Well, you sprung the bastard. I hate to see him off the hook, but I can't hardly hold it against you. You got him off.'

'He shouldn't have been on in the first place.'

'Yeah, well, that's something else, isn't it?'

'Uh-huh. You ought to be glad the way things worked out. He's not going to be a tremendous amount of use to Abner Prejanian because Prejanian's going to have to keep a low profile for the next little while. He doesn't look too good himself now. His assistant just got nailed for killing two people and framing Abner's star witness. You were complaining that he loved to see his name in the papers. I think he's going to try to keep his name out of the papers for a couple of months, don't you?'

'Could be.'

'And Knox Hardesty doesn't look too good, either. He's all right as far as the public is concerned, but the word's going to get around that he's not very good at protecting his witnesses. He had Carr, and Carr gave him Manch, and they're both dead, and that's not a good track record to have when you're trying to get people to cooperate with you.'

'Of course he hasn't been bothering the department, anyway, Matt.'

'Not yet. But with Prejanian quiet he might have wanted to come on in. You know how it goes, Eddie. Whenever they want headlines they take a shot at the cops.'

'Yeah, that's the fucking truth.'

'So I didn't do so badly by you, did I? The department doesn't wind up looking bad.'

'No, you did all right, Matt.'

'Yeah.'

He picked up his cigar, puffed on it. It had gone out. He lit it again with a match and watched the match burn almost to his fingertips before shaking it out and dropping it into the ashtray. I chewed a bite of Danish and chased it with a gulp of coffee.

I could cut down on the drinking. There would be times when it got difficult. When I thought about Fuhrmann and how I could have taken that call from him. Or when I thought about Manch and his plunge to the ground. My phone call couldn't have done it all by itself. Hardesty had been pressuring him all along, and he'd been carrying a load of guilt for years. But I hadn't helped him, and maybe if I hadn't called –

Except you can't let yourself think that way. What you have to do is remind yourself that you caught one murderer and kept one innocent man out of prison. You never win them all, and you can't blame yourself whenever you drop one.

'Matt?' I looked at him. 'That conversation we had the other night. At that bar where you hang out?'

'Armstrong's.'

'Right, Armstrong's. I said some things I didn't have to say.'

'Oh, the hell with that, Eddie.'

'No hard feelings?'

'Of course not.'

Pause. 'Well, a few guys who knew I was gonna drop down today, which I was doing, figuring you'd be here, they asked me to let you know there's no hard feelings toward you. Not that

389

there ever was in a general sense, just that they wished you weren't hooked up with Broadfield at the time, if you get my meaning.'

'I think I do.'

'And they hope you got no bad feelings toward the department, is all.'

'None.'

'Well, that's what I figured, but I thought I'd get it out in the open and be sure.' He ran a hand over his forehead, ruffled his hair. 'You're really figuring to take it easier on the booze?'

'Might as well give it a try. Why?'

'I don't know. You think maybe you're ready to rejoin the human race?'

'I never resigned, did I?'

'You know what I'm talking about.'

I didn't say anything.

'You proved something, you know. You're still a good cop, Matt. It's what you're really good at.'

'So?'

'It's easier to be a good cop when you're carrying a badge.'

'Sometimes it's harder. If I'd had a badge this past week, I would have been told to lay off.'

'Yeah, and you were told that, anyway, and you didn't listen, and you wouldn't have listened, badge or no badge. Am I right?'

'Maybe. I don't know.'

'The best way to get a good police department is to keep good policemen in it. I'd like it a hell of a lot to see you back on the force.'

'I don't think so, Eddie.'

'I wasn't asking you to make a decision. I was saying you could think about it. And you can think it over for the next little while, can't you? Maybe it'll be something that starts to make sense when you don't have a skinful of booze in you twenty-four hours a day.'

'It's possible.'

'You'll think about it?'

'I'll think about it.'

'Uh-huh.' He stirred his coffee. 'You hear from your kids lately?'

'They're fine.'

'Well, that's good.'

'I'm taking them this Saturday. There's some kind of father-son thing with their Scout troop, a rubber-chicken dinner and then seats for the Nets game.'

'I could never get interested in the Nets.'

'They're supposed to have a good team.'

'Yeah, that's what they tell me. Well, it's great that you're seeing them.'

'Uh-huh.'

'Maybe you and Anita –'

'Drop it, Eddie.'

'Yeah, I talk too much.'

'She's got somebody else, anyway.'

'You can't expect her to sit around.'

'I don't, and I don't care. I've got somebody else myself.'

'Oh. For serious?'

'I don't know.'

'Something to take it slow and see what happens, I guess.'

'Something like that.'

That was Monday. For the next couple of days I took a lot of long walks and spent time at a lot of churches. I would have a couple of drinks in the evening to make it easier to get to sleep, but to all intents and purposes I wasn't doing any serious drinking at all. I walked around, I enjoyed the weather, I kept checking my telephone messages, I read the *Times* in the morning and the *Post* at night. I began wondering after a while why I wasn't getting the phone message I was waiting for, but I wasn't upset enough to pick up the phone and place a call myself.

Then Thursday around two in the afternoon I was walking along, not going anywhere in particular, and as I passed a newsstand at the corner of Fifty-seventh and Eighth, I happened to glance at the headline of the *Post*. I normally waited and bought the late edition, but the headline caught me and I bought the paper.

Jerry Broadfield was dead.

SEVENTEEN

When he sat down across from me, I knew who it was without raising my eyes. I said, 'Hi, Eddie.'

'Figured I'd find you here.'

'Not hard to guess, was it?' I waved a hand to signal Trina. 'What is it, Seagram's? Bring my friend here a Seagram's and water. I'll have another of these.' To him I said, 'It didn't take you long. I've only been here about an hour myself. Of course the news must have hit the street with the noon edition. I just didn't happen to see a paper until an hour ago. It says here that he got it around eight this morning. Is that right?'

'That's right, Matt. According to the report I saw.'

'He walked out the door and a late-model car pulled up at the curb and somebody gave him both barrels of a sawed-off shotgun. A school kid said the man with the gun was white but didn't know about the man in the car, the driver.'

'That's right.'

'One man's white and the car's described as blue and the gun was left at the scene. No prints, I don't suppose.'

'Probably not.'

'No way to trace the sawed-off, I don't guess.'

'I haven't heard, but –'

'But there won't be any way to trace it.'

'Doesn't figure to be.'

Trina brought the drinks. I picked mine up and said, 'Absent friends, Eddie.'

'Sure thing.'

'He wasn't your friend, and though you may not believe it, he was less my friend than yours, but that's how we'll drink the toast, to absent friends. I drank your toast the way you wanted it, so you can drink mine.'

'Whatever you say.'

'Absent friends,' I said.

We drank. The booze seemed to have more of a punch after a few days of taking it easy. I certainly hadn't lost my taste for it, though. It went down nice and easy and made me vitally aware of just who I was.

I said, 'You figure they'll ever find out who did it?'

'Want a straight answer?'

'Do you think I want you to lie to me?'

'No, I don't figure that.'

'So?'

'I don't suppose they'll ever find out who did it, Matt.'

'Will they try?'

'I don't think so.'

'Would you, if it were your case?'

He looked at me. 'Well, I'll be perfectly honest with you,' he said after a moment's thought. 'I don't know. I'd like to think I'd try. I think some – I think, *fuck* it, I think a couple of our own must of done it. What the hell else can you think, right?'

'Right.'

'Whoever did it was a fucking idiot. An absolute fucking idiot who just did the department more harm than Broadfield could ever hope to do. Whoever did it ought to hang by the neck, and I like to think I'd go after the bastards with everything I had if it was my case.' He lowered his eyes. 'But to be honest, I don't know if I would. I think I'd go through the motions and sweep it under the rug.'

'And that's what they'll do out in Queens.'

'I didn't talk to them. I don't know for a fact that's what they'll do. But I'd be surprised if they did anything else, and so would you.'

'Uh-huh.'

'What are you going to do, Matt.'

'Me?' I stared at him. 'Me? What *should* I do?'

'I mean, are you going to try and go after them? Because I don't know if it's a good idea.'

'Why should I do that, Eddie?' I spread my hands palms up. 'He's not my cousin. And nobody's hiring me to find out who killed him.'

'Is that straight?'

'It's straight.'

'You're hard to figure. I think I got you pegged, and then I don't.' He stood up and put some money on the table. 'Let me buy that round,' he said.

'Stick around, Eddie. Have another drink.'

He hadn't done more than touch the one he'd had. 'No time,' he said. 'Matt, you don't have to crawl into the bottle just because of this. It doesn't change anything.'

'It doesn't?'

'Hell, no. You still got a life of your own. You got this woman you're seeing, you got—'

'No.'

'Huh?'

'Maybe I'll see her again. I don't know. Probably not. She could have called by this time. And after it happened, you would think she'd have called if it was real.'

'I don't follow you.'

But I wasn't talking to him. 'We were in the right place at the right time,' I went on. 'So it looked as though we might turn out to be important for each other. If it ever had a chance, I'd say the chance died this morning when the gun went off.'

'Matt, you're not making sense.'

'It makes sense to me. Maybe that's my fault. We might see each other again, I don't know. But whether we do or don't, it's not going to change anything. People don't get to change things. Things change people once in a while, but people don't change things.'

'I gotta go, Matt. Take it a little easy on the booze, huh?'

'Sure, Eddie.'

Sometime that night I dialed her number in Forest Hills. The phone rang a dozen times before I gave up and got my dime back.

I called another number. A leftover voice recited, 'Seven-two-five-five. I am sorry, but no one is at home at the moment. If you will leave your name and number at the sound of the tone, your call will be returned as soon as possible. Thank you.'

The tone sounded, and it was my turn. But I couldn't seem to think of anything to say.